INFERNO!

VOLUME 4

WARHAMMER 40,000

WARHAMMER AGE of SIGMAR

INFERNO!

Also available

NECROMUNDA®

INFERNO!

TALES FROM THE WORLDS OF WARHAMMER

VOLUME 4

INCLUDES STORIES BY GEORGE MANN, DENNY FLOWERS, FILIP WILTGREN,
GUY HALEY, JONATHAN GREEN, JAMIE CRISALLI, THOMAS PARROTT, EDOARDO ALBERT,
ERIC GREGORY, MIKE BROOKS, NICK HORTH AND J C STEARNS

BLACK LIBRARY

A BLACK LIBRARY PUBLICATION

This edition published in Great Britain in 2019 by
Black Library,
Games Workshop Ltd.,
Willow Road,
Nottingham, NG7 2WS, UK.

10 9 8 7 6 5 4 3 2 1

Produced by Games Workshop in Nottingham.
Cover illustration by Mauro Belfiore.

A CIP record for this book is available from the British Library.

ISBN 13: 978-1-78193-960-4

See Black Library on the internet at

blacklibrary.com

Find out more about Games Workshop
and the worlds of Warhammer at

games-workshop.com

Printed and bound by CPI Group (UK) Ltd, Croydon, CR0 4YY

CONTENTS

INTRODUCTION

Greetings, faithful reader.

You have been entrusted with a document of the utmost importance, for the tome you hold in your hands is a repository of arcane knowledge, strange tales and deadly secrets. The dark truths held within this volume have broken many a fragile mind. It is paramount that you tread carefully if you are to retain your sanity...

The new incarnation of *Inferno!* has been here for over a year already, and has brought us dozens of original and thrilling stories from the worlds of Warhammer. Authors both familiar and new have expanded the archives of the Black Library, bringing us tales of heroism and villainy in the Mortal Realms, of suffering and triumph in the 41st millennium.

This is the biggest *Inferno!* yet, containing no less than twelve fantastic new stories. Long-time fans of Black Library will recognise veteran authors such as George Mann and Nick Horth, who add their distinctive voices to this anthology for the first time, as well as Guy Haley, who brings us the fourth instalment of his serialised story-within-a-story narrative, 'At the Sign of the Brazen Claw'. We are also pleased to welcome back authors such as Mike Brooks, Thomas Parrott and Jamie Crisalli to the pages of *Inferno!* all having made their debuts in previous volumes. Speaking of debuts, Denny Flowers and Eric Gregory, both of whom came to Black Library via Open Submissions, are making their first forays into *Inferno!*, and we are thrilled to be showcasing their work, along with that of many other brilliant authors.

You may wish to dive straight in and explore these undiscovered worlds, but beware – danger lurks on every page. You will find tales of sorcery and heresy, of greed and pride, and many other sins besides. Stories of greenskin hordes, underhive ne'er-do-wells and those who worship strange and terrible gods will challenge your resolve and perhaps even test your faith.

If you feel you are ready, you may begin your investigation within these hallowed pages. But keep your wits about you, and remember that the information with which you have been entrusted should be guarded with the utmost secrecy.

Knowledge is power. Use it well. And trust no one.

Richard Garton
Submissions Editor, February 2019

END TRANSMISSION

THE KARSHARAT ABOMINATION

George Mann

In George Mann's Inferno! *debut we meet Inquisitor Sabbathiel and her retinue of agents, brought to life here in fiction for the first time as they transition from the glorious technicolour of the comic book page! In a dark and twisted tale, and one that exploits George's penchant for telling gripping mystery stories, Sabbathiel leads her warband in the investigation of the abandoned Ecclesiarchy outpost on Karsharat and a strange Mechanicus cult.*

The sky was bleeding.

The rent in the atmosphere was a thick, purple scar, an angry ribbon across the heavens, casting everything below in its vague, unreal light. Shadows danced in twisting interplay, describing shifting patterns of movement. Figures seemed to emerge threateningly from behind every broken lintel, every stub of tumbledown wall, before dissipating again within moments, nothing more than an unwelcome trick of the eye.

From the heart of the rent, fat droplets tumbled in a drizzly veil, pattering against Bledheim's cloak, so that his hood and shoulders had become sodden, cumbersome. The red fluid streaked his upturned cheeks, oily and gritty against his skin. The air was filled with its rich, iron tang. It sloshed around his boots with every ponderous step.

Bledheim turned to regard the others, who were trudging along beside him in the slick loam. 'Anyone would think we weren't welcome here,' he said, wiping more of the foul liquid from his mouth with the back of his hand.

Inquisitor Sabbathiel turned to meet his gaze, her features set in a grim smile. Despite the torrent, she looked resplendent in her white and red armour, although her hair, loose and tumbling across her gorget, was now streaked with the greasy fluid. It ran in rivulets down the front of her chestplate, pooling in the graven Inquisition symbol that adorned her lower torso, turning the ceramite pink. 'Your insights never cease to astound me, Bledheim,' she said. Next to Sabbathiel, the woman, Mercy, emitted a wet chuckle, regarding him with a half-cocked eyebrow. He'd never liked her, and the wicked smile on her lips did little to alter his opinion.

Bledheim sighed. While he understood the necessity of their visit to this Emperor-forsaken backwater, he longed for it to be over. He didn't even know why Sabbathiel had brought him here, to Karsharat. Mercy and Brondel – well, they were muscle, pure and simple – but it wasn't as if Bledheim could do much to help in a fight. He supposed she might be anticipating the need for interrogation – his own particular speciality – but that wasn't what she'd said back on the ship. To all intents and purposes, it was a straightforward mission: storm the ruins, kill the heretics and put a stop to whatever abominable weapon they were devising in there. He'd heard the same story a dozen times before; more, maybe. This was what they did – what *Sabbathiel* did – and yet, somehow, this time it felt different.

He supposed he'd find out soon enough. He should have paid more attention during the briefing.

The ruins here had once been an Ecclesiarchy outpost but, from what he'd been able to ascertain, had been abandoned some time during the last century. He hadn't managed to establish why, and he didn't suppose it mattered all that much, except that the moon had been left unguarded, and now something else had moved in. A renegade Martian, was the working hypothesis, one that Metik – who, Bledheim noted, had somehow managed to remain behind on the ship – had been tracking for some time. A renegade with a particular interest in *experimentation*. A renegade that Sabbathiel had decided she wanted destroyed.

Still, that didn't explain the constant shower of blood or the rent in the sky, which raised the dismaying prospect that there might be other forces at play here, too. Forces that Bledheim didn't want to begin to consider.

And they still had to find a way into the ruins.

Bledheim peered into the hazy curtain of rain, cupping his hand around his eyes. Ahead of them, the remains of the citadel were a towering silhouette, jagged and half-collapsed. Why would anyone choose to come to this place? As a base of operations, it lacked subtlety – and a roof – but he supposed it might very well be the last place people would look for a wanted outcast. Unless those people were Metik and Sabbathiel, of course.

He saw a shape emerging from the rain, and slipped his other hand inside his cloak, his fingers curling around the grip of his pistol. Then he caught sight of the flickering blue light, drifting lazily over the figure's head, and he relaxed, coming to a stop to await the arrival of the newcomer.

Moments later, a filthy, mud-encrusted squat emerged from the rainstorm, flanked by a servo-skull that seemed to be guiding his way with its winking diodes.

'Frecking Krull, but it's a beautiful day,' said Brondel, his voice a low, throaty growl. He shook his head, shaking loose a cascade of blood from his matted beard.

'Brondel,' said Sabbathiel, her voice level. 'You've found a way in?'

'Aye,' said Brondel. 'There's a door on the west side. It looks as if the structure there has been partially rebuilt, although you wouldn't know it until you're on top of it. Whatever's holed up in there isn't going to look kindly on visitors.' He spat, and then ground the phlegm into the mud with the heel of his boot.

'All the more reason to get on with it and crack some skulls,' said Mercy. She, of all of them, looked truly menacing, her exposed face and arms spattered in blood, towering over the diminutive squat. The whirring instruments in her chest – an artificial set of heart and lungs, installed by Metik some years earlier after he found her wounded in the lower levels of a hive city – seemed to grind and sputter noisily in the damp. She was clutching a lasrifle in both hands, and the immense two-handed power sword that she usually wielded was slung in a harness across her back. Bledheim knew that, no matter what she said, she had deeper motives than simply cracking skulls – she'd never truly forgiven Metik for what he'd done to her, bringing her back from the brink of death by riddling her body with machine parts, and perhaps taking down a rogue Martian with a penchant for experimenting on people might go some way to at least temporarily quelling her need for vengeance.

Sabbathiel glanced up at the servo-skull. 'Fitch?'

'There are life signs within the structure, ma'am,' said the servo-skull, its voice mimicking the speech patterns of its erstwhile owner, but laced with a sluggish, technological burr. Bledheim shuddered.

'How many?'

The servo-skull hesitated, as if pondering the answer. 'Difficult to ascertain. No fewer than five, no greater than twelve.'

'That's quite a range,' said Bledheim.

'The readings are in flux,' said the servo-skull.

'You can say that again,' murmured Brondel.

Sabbathiel swung her force stave up and around, indicating the ruined citadel with its tip. 'Fan out and approach the building slowly. We'll converge again by the door. They might be watching us from the ruins, waiting for us to get close.'

Bledheim nodded, and then slipped away into the rain, edging ever on towards the melancholy ruins. At least, he decided, they might finally get out of the bloody rain.

The jagged remnants of a toppled stone balustrade served as a perfect vantage point from which Bledheim could safely observe the goings-on at the door. It was huge, an ornate archway that had once clearly served as an entrance to a courtyard but had now been barricaded by heavy plasteel panelling. Strange mechanical contrivances – segmented tubular structures – had been arranged around the frame, and they glistened in the red rain. For the life of him, Bledheim could not fathom their purpose.

The others were gathered before the opening, the servo-skull – he refused to call it 'Fitch', despite its apparent history – buzzing over Sabbathiel's shoulder like some skittish familiar.

'Stand aside,' he heard Sabbathiel say, and watched as the others retreated a few steps to give her room. She stepped forwards, the servos in her massive armour grinding as she transferred her weight to her front foot. The armour had been modelled on the Terminator patterns of the Adeptus Astartes, constructed by artificers on the forge world of Pholon, designed to Sabbathiel's precise size and specification. In truth, it seemed to Bledheim to utterly dwarf her, entombing her in its cavernous depths, but time and again it had saved her life – and his, if he was honest – and, wearing it, she became even more the fearsome figure she was without it.

'What are you going to do?' asked Mercy. She'd already raised her lasrifle to her shoulder, sighting along its length in anticipation of what the door might open to reveal.

'I'm going to knock,' said Sabbathiel. She lurched forwards, curling her gauntleted hand into a fist as she extended her arm. She struck the door with a thunderous report, the plasteel flexing beneath the force of the blow, dislodging a shower of broken masonry from above. It had, however, refused to give.

Sabbathiel stepped back, regarding the pitted door before her. The sound of the blow was still ringing out into the ruins around them, the lament of a discordant bell.

Bledheim turned to see a crow, lifting away from its perch atop the broken wing of a monumental aquila that was half-buried in the mud close by. The bird circled overhead for a moment, ignoring the thrumming rain, before dipping low and disappearing into the depths of the ruins.

'They know we're here,' said Bledheim, dropping down from his perch. 'And before you say it,' he added, turning to Mercy, 'I don't mean because we knocked. That crow – it was watching us.'

Brondel spat again, frowning in disgust.

'We're going to have to blo–' Sabbathiel stopped suddenly, her sentence giving way to a grunt of surprise. Bledheim turned, pulling his laspistol from his robes, half expecting to see the door had opened and guards were spilling out. Instead, he was greeted with a view of seven snaking mecha-dendrites, which had erupted from the frame around the door, writhing and thrashing in Sabbathiel's direction. Two of the appendages had already snared her right arm and leg and were dragging her closer – despite the bulk of her armour – while the others quested for her exposed head. At least, Bledheim supposed, he now understood what the mechanical structures around the door were for.

He raised his pistol and tried to draw a bead on one of the twisting appendages, but they were moving too quickly, and in the driving rain he risked hitting Sabbathiel in the process. Grunting in frustration, he lowered the weapon.

Nearby, Mercy had come to a similar conclusion. Discarding her lasrifle, she dragged the massive sword from its harness, swinging it up and over her shoulders, and ran headlong into the morass of tentacles, screaming like some maniacal primitive. Three swift chopping motions later, and Sabbathiel was free, sparks spitting in the rain as the remnants of the two appendages continued to writhe and fizz amongst the nest of their strange kin.

Brondel glanced over at Bledheim and shrugged.

'Stand aside, Mercy,' said Sabbathiel, her voice level. She righted herself, paced back from the door and raised her left arm, so that the nose of her wrist-mounted storm bolter was pointed in the direction of the morass of mechanical limbs.

Mercy, who was attempting to wrestle another mechadendrite into submission, gave a short, dutiful nod, and then released the appendage, stepping slowly away. From her sullen expression, Bledheim could see that she was more than a little disappointed.

There was a sudden eruption of noise and light, originating from Sabbathiel's outstretched arm, and then the door was buckling inwards, as if folding around the detonating shells, trying to contain their destruction. The mass of tentacles exploded, filling the air with glittering shards that twinkled in the rain as they fell, thudding into the wet ground. A stray shard caught Mercy in the upper arm and she winced, but then, as casually as if plucking an errant hair, she spiked her sword in the ground, dug her fingers into the wound and pulled the bloody fragment free. She examined it for a moment, and then tossed it away, lost in the deluge.

Brondel sighed, and then marched in the direction of the open door.

Brondel had been right, for, on the other side of the archway, they found themselves in a poorly lit tunnel, which seemed to have been constructed – somewhat hastily – from a mix of plasteel and broken fragments of the old building. Here, the new sat alongside the old in glaring juxtaposition, the smooth, industrial plating melding unconvincingly with the ornate stonework of ages past. Every few feet, Bledheim could make out fragments of ancient frescoes, faded now from exposure to the elements, but still vibrant and clear. They seemed to be telling the tale of the Wretch of Menarchus – he had long ago studied such tales during a prolonged stay on the island of Relomas – but in truth it was difficult to be sure as so much of the original painting had been lost, and what survived here had been repositioned in haphazard order.

'Finally, a reprieve from that frecking awful rain,' said Brondel, his low voice echoing along the otherwise empty tunnel.

Bledheim nodded, throwing back his hood to reveal his bald pate. Bizarrely, the fabric felt light and dry to the touch. Frowning, he glanced down at his hands, to see that all trace of the bloody precipitation had gone. A quick look at the others established that they, too, were now free from any trace of the dreadful fluid.

Sabbathiel had noticed it too. 'It seems we can no longer be sure of our own senses,' she said, a note of caution in her voice.

'The work of the Ruinous Powers?' ventured Bledheim.

'Perhaps... or perhaps not.' Sabbathiel waved them on. Bledheim had the sense that there was more to her response than he could yet understand, but he'd long ago learned when and how to question her, and now was not the time. 'Come,' she said. 'No doubt the guardians of this place are stirring. We will see battle before the day is out. Be vigilant.'

They moved on, deeper into the network of tunnels. For once, Bledheim was glad to have Mercy looming over his shoulder.

Ahead, the tunnel branched out, splitting off in three different directions. Sabbathiel hesitated at the junction, as if deciding which of them to send each way, but then indicated the central tunnel with a wave of her hand.

'We stay together,' she said, anticipating their questions. 'There's something... unreliable about the atmosphere in this place.' She didn't need to add the remainder of the thought – *if I send you off, I'll probably never see you again.*

She was right, though – the deeper they'd come, the more Bledheim had sensed a growing sensation somewhere in the back of his skull: something akin to an itch, but far more invasive, persistent. He could feel it there now, as if some terrible, multi-legged creature had somehow wormed its way inside his head and was even now scuttling about, its tiny feet pricking the undulating surface of his brain. He shuddered at the sudden thought, his hand unconsciously rubbing at the back of his neck.

Everything about the place seemed *wrong*. The tunnels

seemed to stretch on interminably, terminating in nothing but further tunnels. They all looked the same, and all were cloaked in some cloying atmosphere, as if the walls were threatening to close in at any moment. He felt trapped, claustrophobic, fearful that he might never see the sky again. He'd only been in here for – what? – a few minutes, but already it felt excruciating, as if he'd been tramping along these passages forever.

He glanced at Brondel, but it was difficult to tell what the squat was thinking. His expression seemed forever fixed as either thunderously perturbed, or gleefully amused. Presently, he looked as gloomy as he ever did, his heavy brow wrinkled in a frown.

Above them, the servo-skull slid quietly through the air, its blue search lamp rebounding off the plasteel walls to generate an eerie, midnight quality to the light.

Bledheim had slid his pistol back inside his robes, and, as he walked, had begun, almost unconsciously, to massage the palm of his right hand. This was the real tool of his trade – the hand with which he encouraged compliance within those he was brought in to question. Each of the fingers had been replaced by thin, mechanical talons that each terminated in a tiny, retractable needle. These needles were fed from small canisters mounted in a brace upon the back of his hand, containing a variety of colourful fluids designed to incite raw emotions in his subjects. One might sedate, while another excited. A third might inspire fear, a fourth uncertainty and anguish. Choosing which of the poisons to administer, in which order and in what quantity, was the colour with which he painted his masterpieces. He *always* got his charges to talk.

Now, though, something deep within his palm had begun

to ache, and the more he rubbed at it, the more insistent it became. Had he done something to it during the journey here? Was it somehow malfunctioning? He shoved it inside his robes and tried to put it out of mind.

Up ahead, the tunnel disgorged into a vast chamber that was flooded with shimmering light. Sabbathiel motioned for them to fan out, their backs to the walls, as they slowly entered the room.

Bledheim saw immediately that this had once been the refectory of an Ecclesiarchy temple – the towering pillars, the stone arches that had once held panels of coloured glass, the vast, vaulted ceiling. As he watched, the ceiling rippled and began to peel back, exposing a bright and glorious vista of the heavens. Bledheim stood, enraptured, as strange and wonderful shapes – geometric constellations that could never exist – tumbled across a golden sky, and beyond that, twinkling in the distance, the stars, shifting and altering their patterns, dancing into new alignments.

He felt the throbbing in his palm intensify, and tore his eyes away from the view, glancing down. His hand had grown rigid, clawlike, and to his horror, he saw that the poisons in the row of chambers had all discharged, flowing not through the needle tips of his fingers, but back into his arm. The veins beneath the skin were black and pulsating, and he could feel the poison coursing through him, a burning fire spreading up his arm and into his shoulder.

Suddenly, the world shifted. He was surrounded by dancing flames that licked hungrily at his boots, at his robes, at his flesh. He looked around, frantic, searching for Brondel, Mercy, Sabbathiel – but he was already too late. There was nothing any of them could do to help him now. They, too, had been consumed by the unnatural conflagration, their eyes melting to blackened pits, skin peeling from hot, white bones.

Was it the poison? Was that what he was seeing?

Bledheim dropped to his knees, screaming. With his left arm, he searched frantically for his knife. He had to remove the hand, the arm. It was the only way he could stop more of the poison flooding his system. But the knife had gone.

He slumped to the ground, feeling the flames lapping at his face. It was too late. Too late…

A slap brought him around, his cheek hot and stinging. He looked up, confused, to see Mercy standing over him, a crooked grin on her lips.

'Fine time to wake up, interrogator, now that the battle's over.'

Bledheim groaned, and then, as it all came back to him in a sudden rush – the flames, the poison – he sat up, tearing frantically at his robes to reveal his right hand. The skin there was pink and smooth, the cylinders in the brace still filled with the same colourful fluids he'd filled them with back on the ship.

He looked up at Mercy, incomprehension in his eyes. She laughed again, and strode away, her boot steps echoing in the cavernous space.

'Bledheim.'

It was Sabbathiel's voice. He turned to see her standing over the mangled corpse of… *something*. It looked as if it had once been human, but it had a brace of what appeared to be electrical filaments erupting from its shoulders and was covered in an array of fine cables and wires. Sparks were still discharging from two metal bracelets encircling its wrists. Sabbathiel's armoured foot was resting on the side of its head. He could see another three or four of the things scattered amongst the dust and detritus that lined the floor. One of them was missing its head.

'Ma'am.'

'*Fear*. It is a weapon.'

'Ma'am?'

'On you, it was ably deployed.'

Bledheim nodded. Psychic attack. He understood now, all too well. The blood rain, the claustrophobia, the poison… It had been deployed ably indeed. 'So, this is the weapon we seek? The one being crafted here by the renegade?'

Sabbathiel gave a curt nod, then turned away. 'We must *all* face our fears, in this place, Bledheim. We must all be strong. We are close now. Our enemy seeks to unsettle us. We shall not be so easily dissuaded.'

Bledheim felt a hand on his shoulder. It was Brondel. He was wearing a fresh scar on his left cheek, and his beard was standing proud where he'd evidently been subject to an electrical attack. He clasped Bledheim by the wrist – being careful to select the left one – and hauled the interrogator to his feet.

'My thanks.'

By way of response, Brondel simply spat on the ground and wiped his mouth on the corner of Bledheim's robe.

The itching sensation at the back of Bledheim's skull was a constant distraction, growing in intensity with every step as they hurried towards the heart of the old citadel, but at least now, he mused, he understood what it was. In its way, it was a kind of poison, too, just like those he might administer – an evil thought that had wormed its way into his head and sought to destabilise him, to throw him off, to dissuade him from completing his mission. But, just like a poison, there was an antidote, and Bledheim was adept at those, too.

In his years of training he had been subjected to all manner of mind-altering substances, testing them upon himself to better understand their effects. In doing so, he had discovered ways to throw up barriers, to parcel off small parts of his mind and keep them free from alteration, from outside influence. This, he had never discussed with any other, as he knew that to harbour such abilities might be seen as heretical, but this was not, he knew, a form of witchcraft, but merely a deep understanding of discipline. He had trained himself to step outside of the effects of the poison coursing through his blood, to reserve a tiny fraction of his mind, so that he might remain, to a degree, in control of his own faculties.

Now that he better understood the threat, now that he had experienced the horror of it, he knew better how to shield himself from its effects.

The others, bar Sabbathiel, seemed not to be faring as well. Mercy had grown increasingly agitated during the last few minutes, twitching at every shadow, her hand constantly playing across the hilt of her sword. He knew it wouldn't take much to make her snap, and in the confined space of the tunnels, she posed a very real and present threat. If she mistook one of their party for an enemy combatant… well, he'd seen what she could do when her ire was up.

Likewise, Brondel had begun muttering to himself. The words themselves were unintelligible – Bledheim half believed them to be spoken in a different language – but he appeared to be growing increasingly angry and resentful, threatening to boil over at any moment.

Only Sabbathiel herself remained impassive, her expression

benign. Bledheim wondered what sort of war she might be fighting behind that implacable facade.

She raised her hand to halt their progress. Peering around the bulk of her armour, Bledheim saw that, ahead of them, the tunnel ended in a T-junction. To the left, the passage looked ill-lit and foreboding, draped in a filthy smear of spider's webs. To the right, the tunnel was punctuated by hovering lume globes, and had clearly seen more recent use.

'That way,' said Sabbathiel, indicating they should follow her to the left.

'But…' started Bledheim, his stomach turning at the very thought – but he stopped himself short, recognising the truth in Sabbathiel's earlier words. *We must face our fears.* Once again, he'd allowed the tendrils of that psychic presence to burrow insidiously into his mind. Fear was their weapon, but it was also their defence. The images in their minds – the sense of foreboding – they were trying to push Sabbathiel and her party along the opposite route.

'Ready your weapons,' said Sabbathiel. Her voice seemed to carry along the entire corridor. Then, with a deep breath, she strode forwards into the darkness, allowing the spectral cobwebs to brush over her face.

Bledheim and the others hurried along behind her.

The tunnel emerged into what had once been a dormitory, during the days of the Ecclesiarchy occupation, but had now been refashioned into a makeshift laboratory. Nests of mechanical arms hung from the ceiling, and upright glass chambers lined the walls, many of them occupied by what looked to be human corpses – although Bledheim could see a man trapped in one of them, his face a visage of utter terror, clawing at the door to his chamber so violently that he had broken all of his fingers.

The place was filthy, rank with spilt blood and discarded, rotting tissue. Trays of surgical tools lay upon stained work surfaces, and tiny mechanical spiders scuttled over the walls and ceiling, red diodes winking.

Strapped to a gurney against one wall was a painfully thin, naked man, his skin so pale that Bledheim initially took him for another corpse, until he noticed the ragged shudder of the man's breathing, the rattle of the mechanised box strapped to his chest, filtering his air. He was bald, his cheeks sallow, his eyes now fitted with lenses and bionics where once the biological organs had sat. He was peering at them, his mouth hanging limp and open, drool pooling on his chest.

Bledheim heard a clicking sound, and looked round to see a tall, ungainly figure emerging from the shadows at the other end of the room, where an open door appeared to lead off into another area of the complex. As the figure shuffled forwards into the light, Bledheim sensed Mercy recoil at the sight of it.

It was huge, a four-legged monstrosity, now more machine than man. Its body was fat and segmented like that of an insect, formed from interlocking plates that clacked and shifted as it moved, rasping and grating like an ancient machine. Four arms projected from its upper torso, and in one of them it carried a staff, which it used to steady itself as it moved. Its head was hidden beneath a ragged cowl, and jutted forwards inquisitively, pipes and tubes erupting from the place where its face should have been. It issued a hideous noise that might have resembled a laugh, if it hadn't sounded more like the misfiring of broken pistons. A vent opened in the side of its chest, and a gout of tubercular steam hissed out.

Behind it, two shambling metal constructs loomed, as

large as Sabbathiel in her armour, with buzzing saw blades as hands, and heads that resembled those of insects more than men.

'Restak.' Sabbathiel stepped forwards, swinging her force stave around before her.

'Inquisitor Sabbathiel,' replied the renegade. 'I *am* honoured.'

'It is no honour,' said Sabbathiel. 'I have merely come to put an end to your little experiments.' She glanced back at the others, and Mercy and Brondel moved around to flank her. Bledheim slid his pistol from his robes but held back in the mouth of the tunnel. From here, he might be able to pick off a few choice shots.

Restak gestured to the lumbering constructs behind him, and they lurched forwards slavishly, heads swaying, arms raised and buzz saws screaming.

Sabbathiel's storm bolter barked, and explosive shells thundered into the construct on the right, chewing two great holes into its heavily plated chest. The construct seemed hardly to notice the impact, however, other than to momentarily correct its shambling gait, before continuing its lumbering, deadly approach.

Mercy went wide, swinging her power sword back and forth before her, flexing her shoulders. Brondel seemed to have momentarily disappeared, but Bledheim knew from experience that he was simply seeking a vantage point from which to unleash his own particular brand of devastation.

With a roar, Sabbathiel charged, her footsteps causing the entire room to tremble as she rushed in to close on the construct on the left, her force stave cutting a wide arc, slicing through thick plasteel until it wedged, with a clang, against the construct's raised arm. She tugged on the shaft but it was stuck fast, and the construct twisted, wrenching it from her grasp.

With a grunt of frustration, Sabbathiel stepped back, raising her arm just in time to block the downward arc of the buzz saw coming for her face. It bit into her vambrace, chewing into the plasteel with a grinding scream. Grimacing, Sabbathiel raised her other arm, jammed the nose of her storm bolter into the construct's face – or what passed for it – and fired.

The detonation sent Sabbathiel reeling backwards, but the construct had fared worse, its entire head and shoulders caving inwards under the intense force of the blast. It toppled over with a metallic thud, the force stave still wedged in its arm. Sabbathiel, shaking her head as if to clear the ringing, lurched forwards and set to work freeing her stave. She wrenched it loose a moment later.

On the other side of the laboratory, Mercy had locked the other construct into a spiralling dance, weaving circles around it as it tried to get a fix on her with its saw. Her movements were graceful, fluid, punctuated only by the regular downward thrust of her blade, as she cut furrow after furrow into the construct's armour. It seemed untroubled by the damage, but Bledheim knew what game she was playing – she was keeping it busy.

A moment later, from the shadows behind one of the glass chambers, Brondel bellowed for her to get down. She hit the floor just as a lobbed grenade clanged against the construct's head, tumbling down into the hole punched in its chest by Sabbathiel's earlier shot.

The construct glanced down at Mercy, raised its arm as if to strike her, and then exploded, rupturing out in a bloom of heat and light, shattering several glass chambers and causing thick, viscous fluid to gush out across the floor.

Bledheim, however, had been watching Restak at the time,

as he clacked slowly over towards the thin man strapped to the gurney by the far wall. As Sabbathiel righted herself, having finally freed her weapon, Restak gripped the man by the shoulder, and he screamed.

The sound was like fire ripping through Bledheim's mind, like the entire world had suddenly begun to boil. Blinding light flared in his vision. He could feel himself babbling, could feel warm blood trickling from his nose. And yet, there was a part of him that watched all of this with cool impartiality. That knew precisely what was occurring, that understood that his mind could no longer be trusted, and that the man on the gurney was behind everything that was happening to him.

Bledheim blinked, fighting against the wave of terror and pain that threatened to completely engulf him. Mercy was on the ground, writhing in agony, and Brondel had dropped to his knees, banging the heels of his hands against his head.

Only Sabbathiel had managed to stand her ground, and although clearly in abject pain, she was moving towards Restak, her stave raised.

She lurched at Restak, thrusting with her weapon. He tried to scuttle out of the way, but she caught his lower left arm with a glancing blow and it tore free in a shower of oil and wires, clattering to the floor.

Restak, furious, swept forwards, grabbing for Sabbathiel, battering her stave out of the way and pinning both of her arms, raising his staff in readiness to strike.

As Bledheim watched, his own vision foggy with blood and pain, Sabbathiel slumped, staring down in horror at her own body, as if reliving some distant nightmare. She screamed, and the sound of it was enough to stir Bledheim to action.

Restak was distracted. He had to act now.

Gasping for breath, fighting waves of nausea, Bledheim moved. One foot after the other, wobbling, unstable, he lurched across the room towards the man on the gurney. The man was spasming, frothing at the mouth, his eyes rolled back in their sockets, as whatever power was coursing through him ravaged his own body as much as it was ravaging Bledheim's mind.

From the corner of his eye he saw Restak turn, call out for him to stop, but it was too late – Bledheim's fingers had found their mark in the psyker's chest, and the sedatives were discharging from their capsules.

He fell back, dropping to his knees, before sliding fully to the floor, slick with the spilled fluid from the glass chambers. The fire in his head had dulled, petering out, but the pain was still ferocious, his mind reeling. He watched, only half-aware, as Sabbathiel, still caught in the grip of the renegade tech-priest, wrenched herself loose, grasped the monster's head in both hands, and pulled it free with a disgusting sucking sound.

Restak's body twitched nervously, its servos whining, before it skittered back into the wall and sunk to the ground, blood oozing from the stump of its neck.

Bledheim blinked, and the lights went out.

'That's twice today I've had to slap you awake,' said Mercy, as Bledheim shifted, dragging himself up into a sitting position. 'I think I might make a habit of it.'

He looked up at her blearily, then sighed.

Sabbathiel was standing nearby, in the process of strapping the psyker's body to a stretcher.

'Brondel, you know what to do. I don't want to leave any of this standing.'

'Ma'am,' said Brondel, not even bothering to conceal his gleeful smile.

Bledheim got unsteadily to his feet. 'We're taking the body?' he said, with a nod towards the remains of the psyker. As soon as he'd done it, he wished he hadn't, as stars bloomed in his vision. He drew a deep breath.

'Body?' said Sabbathiel. She looked at him quizzically. Then something seemed to dawn on her. 'Oh, he's still alive. Your sedation should last long enough to get him back to the ship.'

'Alive? I thought we were here to destroy the weapon?'

Sabbathiel offered him a crooked smile. 'No, Bledheim. We were here to claim it.' She met his gaze, and then, with a sigh, she turned and walked from the room. 'Come along, Brondel is anxious to put this place to the torch, and I can't say I blame him. Bring the weapon, too. You should be able to manage that, shouldn't you?'

Bledheim watched her go. He felt nauseous. 'Yes, ma'am,' he said. 'I should be able to manage that.'

THE HAND OF HARROW

Denny Flowers

*Caleb Cursebound is the underhive's ninth most dangerous
man. Probably. The ambitious cat burglar's hunt for the
legendary Hand of Harrow leads him to conduct a daring heist
at an exclusive ball, and he and his ratskin accomplice, Iktomi,
must use all of their resources to escape with their lives –
and their prize.*

*In Denny Flowers' witty, fast-paced Black Library debut, we
follow Caleb and Iktomi as they venture into the spires of
Necromunda's upper hive in search of a mysterious treasure.*

Lord Harrow raised his hand.

The theatre fell silent, all eyes rising to the royal box. There was a tremble to his movement, his gaunt fingers twitching as they curled about the throne's gilded armrest. But his eyes were clear and, though his voice lacked power, his words still carried weight.

'My friends,' he said, addressing the auditorium. 'Once again, we stand together in celebration of our house, our family and, most of all, our future. On this night we bid farewell to our children, for the next time we see them they will be fully fledged members of our house. This is a path paved with trial and trepidation, but I know that every single one of them will exceed my expectations.'

Caleb didn't think it was a bad speech, but he held only half an ear to it, his focus on the ruby signet ring adorning Harrow's left hand. He remembered the dingy office in the depths of Slag Row, where Mr Kreep had first outlined the plan. Everything hinged on that ring.

'The museum can only be accessed by the ring's wearer,' Kreep told him, his voice but a whisper. 'Cameras, alarms, security measures – the ring bypasses everything. Once you have it, you merely stride down this passageway and open this door.'

'And without it?'

'You're either incinerated or decapitated at about the half-way mark.'

Caleb leant closer, pretending to scrutinise the schematics splashed across the far wall. Kreep certainly made the job sound compelling: a priceless artefact languishing in a dis-used museum with sophisticated, but easily circumvented security. It was the perfect target – low risk, high reward.

Why was he nervous?

'Care to share your thoughts?' Kreep said. 'Surely the underhive's ninth most dangerous man isn't intimidated by a simple burglary?'

He grinned expectantly, his artificial eyes gleaming. Since his ejection from House Delaque, Kreep had replaced his bulky ocular implants with lifelike replicas of crystal blue. The effect would have been less disconcerting if he still remembered how to blink.

'What's our exit strategy?' Caleb asked, playing for time.

'You leave via the window,' Kreep replied, tracing with his finger. 'Security protocols are deactivated providing the ring-wearer remains in the museum. That way he or she can take their time with the exhibits. But there's a flaw in the sys-tem. Not only does the internal security go down, but so does the shielding on the outer hive. I have access to a drainage valve a few levels below the museum. Your partner makes a short climb, cuts a hole through this access port, and the two of you grav-chute to safety.'

A short climb. Kreep had a gift for speaking from both sides of his mouth. In a sense it was a short climb; the hive was both mountain and pit, the spires of the upper houses stretching to the mesosphere, the tendrils of the underhive infesting the planet's crust. Set against this vast scale the path outlined on the schematics was nothing, little more than half a mile. But it was a vertical climb, through acid rain and choking ash clouds, across the twisted frame of the outer hive.

He glanced at Iktomi. The ratskin stood a little behind him, keeping the office's doorway in her line of vision. She studied the proposed ascent, her eyes framed by the crimson scars worn by her tribe. She nodded.

Lord Harrow was still addressing the crowd.

Caleb blinked, trying to focus on the moment. Whatever his reservations it was too late to back out now. Iktomi would be scaling the hive's exterior. Until he deactivated the museum's security system she would be stranded out there. The ratskin was as tough as anyone he'd ever met, but even she had limits. No one could survive long in those conditions. He needed the ring.

He made his move, picking a path through the throng towards a stairway that led to the upper balcony. Most of the revellers ignored him, intent on Lord Harrow, but more than one glanced as he passed. He looked nervous, but why shouldn't he? He was dressed as a valet, but clearly a flustered one, cringing and bowing as he earnestly made his way through the crowd, a shining pocket watch clearly visible in his hand. A few of the nobles, resplendent in their finery, eyed his drab attire with contempt or sympathy; most paid him no attention at all. He was a servant, and from all appearances a bad one at that. Why would anyone waste time on him?

The stairway was not unguarded. The two men were not especially imposing, at least not physically. But Caleb knew them from their stance: proud, even arrogant, but always in perfect balance. Always alert. They were most likely enforcers, or the nobles' equivalent.

Caleb lowered his head as he approached, stumbling through a carefully crafted speech. He had forgotten his master's prize heirloom and had been sent to retrieve it. If he was delayed, if his master was left waiting but a moment more, the consequences would be dire. Neither seemed particularly convinced by his story, but it was their job to be suspicious. A brief retinal scan seemingly confirmed his credentials, and neither guard wished to waylay him and risk offending one of the nobles.

'Our opening will be the debutantes' ball,' Kreep had told him. 'There are so many protocols and sacraments to observe that the whole process is virtually automated. Once your biometrics are added to the data logs you will become just another cog in the machine. They won't even notice you.'

That part still didn't sit well with Caleb. Kreep was a skilled info-broker and still maintained contacts from his time in House Delaque, but it was difficult to believe even his influence extended this far uphive. Something didn't sit right. It was the second most troubling part of the job.

On the far side of the auditorium Lord Harrow's speech had almost concluded. It was clear the old man was tiring, but there was still iron in his closing words.

'I now bid farewell to all of our debutantes,' he said. 'But most of all I bid farewell to my daughter Elissa. It saddens me that the girl I love so much will soon be gone, even though I could not be prouder of the young woman who will one day take my place. But the time for words is over. My family and friends, please let me present our future!'

With this the theatre went dark, all except the main stage, which was now bathed in an amber haze. Music rose from the orchestra, the symphony soft and soothing, like honeyed wine. The curtain rose to reveal a spiral staircase of burnished bronze. Arm in arm, the debutantes descended, mirrorglass robes flowing from their shoulders, the mesh so fine that it rippled in the sudden breeze. Caleb sniffed, his eyes drawn to the main intake fan. He'd never smelt air like it: fresh and so sweet that it was almost sickly.

He risked a glance to the royal box, where Lord Harrow slumped in his throne. His arm hung limp by his side, the signet ring loose on his gaunt fingers. But his eyes were clear and fixed upon the performance. The debutantes had silently reached the main stage, their footsteps stifled by micro-stummers embedded in the heels of their ripperskin boots. With practised grace they fanned out into a semi-circle, their robes falling from their shoulders. Each wore a corset or waistcoat of sombre black emblazoned with the Harrow family crest: a golden blade on a scarlet field. Most were also bedecked in shimmering headdresses forged in the forms of beasts and birds. Some wore wings upon their backs crafted from gold-leaf. A single feather was worth more than he saw in a cycle.

He crept along the balcony, his gaze flitting from the performance to the royal box. With the audience intent on the stage the old man seemed to have shrunk further into his throne. He motioned to his attendant, who lifted a gilded respirator to his lips, and he drank deep, emerald fumes wafting about his face. As Caleb watched, his posture shifted, straightening, his hands twitching involuntarily, the ruby ring sliding a fraction down his finger.

'The dance is your opening,' Kreep had explained. 'The audience will be too busy cooing over the performance to pay you much attention. Harrow's own daughter is one of the debutantes this year, so the old man will be particularly distracted. Just slip the ring from his finger and replace it with this replica. It's simple sleight of hand.'

Caleb took the ring, pocketing it. Kreep had worn a broad smile, though the expression didn't extend to his artificial eyes.

'I thought pickpocketing was One-eyed Tippet's forte?'

'I no longer work with him,' Kreep replied, his expression barely flickering.

On the main stage the dancers lined up for the minuet, the debutantes taking centre stage. Behind and beneath them the rest of the ensemble shuffled from the shadows with faux awkwardness. Their costumes were neither elaborate nor finely wrought: stained leather and tarnished iron cobbled together with wire and chain. Some wore extravagant wigs in neon pink, styled into crests and spikes the length of a sword's blade. Others were clad in vivid survival-suits bedecked with hazard markings. Their faces were dour as they assembled on the left of the stage, loose wires trailing in their wake.

On the right a trio of performers bumbled into place. Their movements were clumsy, restricted by bodysuits so padded that the performers were almost as wide as they were tall. As one they flexed their swollen frames, eyes crossed as they stared blindly into the crowd. There was laughter.

Then came a commotion in the orchestra pit, the musicians

stuttering their way through a carefully crafted cacophony as dancers scuttered between them, rummaging through sheet music and stealing drumsticks. As they crept onto the stage the nearest turned and bowed to the crowd, wax dripping from the candles flanking his helmet. He gave a slack-jawed grin, exposing blacked-out teeth. Despite himself, Caleb found his gaze lingering on the stage as he approached the enclosed entrance to the royal box. Perhaps it was satire. Perhaps this was honestly how the nobles saw them. For it was clear even to him that the dancers were dressed as a crude parody of the underhivers.

The orchestra surged to life as the debutantes extended their hands. The faux-underhivers took them with graceless bows, pirouetting about the stage. As the pace quickened the underhivers stumbled and dithered, the debutantes remaining perfectly poised, heads held high, each with one hand clasped behind their back, the other directing their partner like a puppet on a string. On the next pass the underhivers staggered, almost falling as they seamlessly switched partners. The debutantes turned, feet wide, arms spread like wings, their fingers curled into talons. The music had risen to a crescendo now, the string section sawing at their instruments, the beat pounding like a hammering heart.

His own heart was pounding too. He was close now, close to the biggest score of his career. He'd heard the stories, that the Harrow family held an artefact from another age, a treasure known only as the Hand of Harrow. Some said it was a weapon so powerful that it could topple a hive, others that the ancient technology could cure any illness, or even stave off death itself. He didn't know for sure, but that wasn't what worried him. What worried him was that, from what he could tell, Kreep didn't know what it was either.

* * *

'The Hand?' Kreep had said, a frown briefly passing across his ashen face. 'I already told you, it's an artefact, an old family heirloom. Priceless to the right buyer, worthless to the general populous. You procure it, we split the profit fifty-fifty.'

'What sort of artefact?' Caleb persisted. 'A gemstone? A sceptre? A historic battle cannon?'

'It's small, easily transported.'

'But what is it?'

'I don't have a detailed description. You will know it when you see it. The entire museum is built around it.'

'How am I supposed to steal something when I don't know what it is?'

'It's a museum!' Kreep snapped, his mask slipping for just a second. 'There will be a label or description on the cabinet. I assume you at least can read?'

This last remark seemed to be directed at Iktomi. If she registered the insult she did not acknowledge it.

'You're not telling me something,' Caleb said as Kreep sighed, turning to his desk and retrieving a bottle of Wildsnake from the bottom drawer.

'Obviously,' Kreep replied, popping the cork and pouring three glasses. 'There are lots of things I'm not telling you – my contact in Harrow's family, the name of the buyer. I'm an info-broker, it's my job to keep everyone informed without letting anyone know too much about anyone else. This is a theft from the upper hive, we need to be discreet.'

He handed Caleb a glass before turning his gaze to Iktomi. She shook her head.

'I'd feel better if I knew exactly what I was taking.'

'I appreciate that, I really do,' Kreep replied, leaning against his desk and taking a sip. 'But I've told you all I can. You will have to trust me.'

'Isn't there an expression about trusting a Delaque? Something about it being wiser to kiss a sumpkroc?'

'Now that is hardly fair. You know I am estranged from the House of Secrets.'

That was certainly the rumour. Kreep had apparently been ejected for some slight against House Delaque. The precise details of his crime were unclear, as was the reason the house had not sought restitution by removing some of his organs. The two prevailing theories were that he either held information that was of such value that his former house was reluctant to move against him, or that he had never actually been ejected at all and his apparent fall from grace was part of an elaborate scheme.

Still, thus far his relationship with Caleb had been mutually beneficial.

'I fear your paranoia is getting the better of you,' Kreep sighed, setting down his glass. 'This is a simple job with a tidy payoff. Surely it is not beyond the skills of Caleb Cursebound? Are you not the ninth most dangerous man in the underhive?'

'So they tell me.'

'The man who single-handedly brought down Bonesnapper's Badrock Boys?'

'I had to use two hands, but sure.'

'The man who slew the Unseen Beast of Sumptown?'

'Well, it was hard to tell for sure without actually being able to see the body, but–'

'The man who survived the Blood River Massacre, saving a poor ratskin brave in the process?'

He nodded to the spot where Iktomi had formerly stood.

She was no longer there.

Instead she was now behind Kreep, her arm hooked around his throat, a blade poised above his left eye.

Caleb rose slowly, reaching out and lowering her arm with practised calm.

'We don't talk about it.'

Harrow was still intent on the stage. The faux underhivers had been herded into centre stage, the debutantes encircling them. They still moved with the same polished grace, but this was no longer a dance. There was no pretence of harmony or partnership. One by one they struck and the underhivers gasped and fell, collapsing from the stage or rolling behind the curtain, until a sole survivor remained. He cowered as the killers surrounded him, his spectacles shattered and his longcoat torn, exposing ashen flesh. He begged for clemency, hauling reams of parchment from his pockets, promising knowledge and secrets, anything if only they would spare his life. But the killers were unmoved by his pleas. As they raised their talons one last time there came a blinding flash of crimson, a final surge from the orchestra's pit. Then the debutantes were gone, abandoning the stage to the body of their final victim.

There was silence.

Then the auditorium exploded in thunderous applause. At that moment, Caleb slid into the royal box. Harrow's security moved to intercept him just as his entourage surged to their feet, pressing against the rails as they cheered and whooped. Caleb appeared to stumble in the press of bodies, slipping from the guards' grip. He fell forwards, his hands outstretched to Lord Harrow's throne. The switch took a moment, the oversized ring easily departing Harrow's finger, the replica just as quickly taking its place.

The guards pressed around him. He cowered before them, the pocket watch brandished like a talisman.

'My l-lords,' he stuttered. 'Forgive me, I entered the wrong box. I did not mean...'

He trailed off, aware that he was no longer their focus. From his prone position he turned, following their gaze.

Lord Harrow was staring straight at him.

Caleb made sure to tremble as he prostrated himself before the head of the Harrow family. He risked a glance at the old man's face. There was no malice there, nor anger or ill will. But a cold intellect resided behind those eyes, and a terrifying certainty of purpose. For a long moment Caleb thought that Harrow had recognised him for what he was: a thief and a liar. But then the old man dismissed the guards with a wave of his finger, as if wholly unconcerned by Caleb's presence. His focus returned to the main stage, where the debutantes had gathered for their encore.

The passageway was quiet bar the patter of Caleb's footsteps. He moved tentatively, waiting for the silence to be broken by gunfire, or some sophisticated death machine unfolding from the darkness. He glanced to the Harrow family ring on his finger, half expecting the ruby to glow. At least that would indicate it actually *did* something.

Kreep had been adamant the security systems were entirely automated, that the ring shielded its wearer from otherwise certain death. It was quite possible. Caleb had no doubt the nobles had access to such sophisticated technology, and there was some logic to the head of the family holding the keys to the vault. But only a fool would rely on a single means of protecting his legacy, no matter how secure the key. Caleb had looked into the man's eyes, and he knew Lord Harrow was no fool.

At the corridor's end lay the museum's main entrance. It

was rather uninspired, adamantium blocks seemingly carved into the walls of the corridor, separated by a stiletto-thin seam. The only adornment was a data-point on the left door, a small concave housing framed by the Harrow family crest.

Caleb raised his hand, the ring loose on his finger, and pressed his fist to the lock.

He felt it before he heard it, the distant whir of motors buried deep beneath him. With barely a moan the impenetrable doors slid open. Beyond lay an ebony corridor of polished stone lit by glass braziers.

He slipped through, hugging the wall as he followed the passage through the atrium. Aisles unfolded before him, but it was too dark to make out his surroundings. The walkways could be lined with snipers, or a regiment of Harrow's personal guard stationed behind the shadowy displays.

He slowed, hissing into his comm-link.

'Iktomi?'

There was no response. He'd known the signal would not penetrate the auditorium but he'd hoped that the museum would be less heavily shielded from the outer hive. He'd have felt better with her at his side. The ratskin's presence was always reassuring. For one thing she tended to be the target of the first few volleys.

From beneath his collar he unfolded his infra-goggles, slipping them into place. His view shifted from pitch-black to a dark green. He could make out the walkways and aisles, but the roof of the dome was beyond his vision. There were no heat signatures or other energy fluctuations besides the flickering braziers. The museum was as quiet as a tomb.

He moved faster now, either emboldened by the silence or because his fear overrode his caution. Kreep had provided the museum's layout, but Caleb had not grasped the scale of the place, the aisles stretching in all directions like the threads of a spider's web. He glanced briefly at the displays as he passed, but in the darkness it was difficult to discern their content. Most appeared to be paintings or textiles. He hoped that the Hand of Harrow was something a little more robust. As he moved, other braziers silently blossomed into life, presumably triggered by his passage.

There came a crackle in his earpiece.

'Iktomi?'

The only response was static.

Before him lay the access port, a lavish silver frame that glistened in the gathering light. Beyond lay a chamber of cold iron, at its end a plasteel doorway, the final barrier to the Ash Wastes.

He tried the comm-link again.

He could hear her now, but the words were garbled, broken by static and the roaring gale outside the hive.

'Iktomi? Can you hear me?'

More static. But then he heard it, the whine of a thermal charge. The chamber began to glow like a furnace. He turned his head, shielding his face from the heat, even as the silver frame warped and ran like wax.

It took a moment for the smoke to clear. Then a figure emerged through the twisted bulkheads, bound in a blood-stained leather duster, a keffiyeh tied around her head. She removed her goggles, wiping blood from the lenses. The fluid had a particularly unpleasant purple sheen.

'What happened to you?' he asked.

'Spiders,' she shrugged, removing the duster. 'There was a nest halfway up.'

'Are you all right?'

'I've seen worse,' she shrugged, nodding to her forearm,

where the long-healed welts from a dozen bites were still clearly visible. 'Help me with the rest of it.'

Between them, they hauled Iktomi's pack through the opening. The grav-chutes were laid out by the access port while Caleb secreted various cutting tools about his person, along with his laspistol. He was relieved to have his hands on a weapon again.

'Have you found it?' she asked.

'It's too dark to find anything,' he sighed. 'There must be a better lighting system. This is supposed to be a museum. How is anyone expected to appreciate the exhibits?'

Iktomi did not answer, her focus drawn to the dome's distant roof. She frowned.

'What is it?' he asked.

She paused. 'Something is up there.'

Caleb followed her gaze, scanning with his infra-goggles, but he could detect nothing – no heat signatures or energy emissions.

'I can't see anything,' he said. 'Do you want to try my goggles?'

She shook her head.

'Well I'm telling you there's nothing there. Are you sure you're okay? You didn't get bitten?'

'Only slightly,' she shrugged with a wave of her hand.

'There is no such thing as only getting "slightly" bitten by a giant spider.'

'You get used to it,' she murmured, still intent on the upper dome.

'Fine,' he sighed. 'You stare at the sky, I'll find the Hand of Harrow, and we can get out of here. Okay?'

She nodded, but her gaze never wavered, her hand curled round the handle of her hunting knife.

Caleb swore but turned away, scrutinising the displays. More and more braziers had blossomed into life, and the lower levels of the museum were now bathed in a soft blue glow. The paintings made little sense to him. Most featured members of House Harrow, recognisable by the insignias on their breastplates, engaged in savage duels with hideous troglodyte creatures emerging from the darkness. The armour and weapons were unfamiliar to him – presumably poetic licence on the part of the artist. He moved on.

The next display held a selection of artefacts: broken weapons, a breastplate torn by a trio of parallel slashes. He scrutinised the items for a gauntlet, or even a severed arm, but nothing stood out, and nothing seemed to be labelled.

'This is impossible,' he sighed, glancing to Iktomi. She was following silently, still intent on the dark above. 'You want to help me look?'

She didn't answer.

He strode to the next cabinet. More paintings, more celebrations of House Harrow's triumphant warriors slaying pitiful creatures. Except none of the warriors seemed in eminent danger. Their armour was impenetrable, their weapons bestowing death and ruin. The longer he looked the less it seemed like a battle. It was just a massacre.

His theory was proved fact by the next cabinet. It was full of skulls.

Most appeared human, or close enough if you forgave the odd fang or additional nose cavity. Some must have belonged to xenos creatures, or perhaps something foul from the depths of the underhive. A few were fitted with bionic enhancements, though these were corroded and worn.

'Well, I suppose this is progress,' he heard himself say, his mouth suddenly dry. 'All we need to do now is find the cabinet filled with severed hands.'

'We shouldn't be here. It smells like death.'

Her voice was calm, but Caleb could tell she was scared. Which, logically, meant he should be terrified.

'Then let's hurry this along,' he said, moving on to the next display. 'Since you have the exceptional eyesight maybe you should try...'

He trailed off. Before him was the display he'd first encountered on entering the museum. In the half-light he'd mistaken it for textiles. He'd been right to a point.

Human skins.

Most were mounted on the walls like the hides of beasts. Some had been fashioned into garments and ornaments. Here and there were features of their previous owners – empty eye holes, or the stretched remains of fingers. Though aged and worn, a few still bore distinct tribal markings: crimson scars across the eyes.

He whispered her name, but Iktomi was already beside him. She wore the same expression she'd had the day he'd first found her, bleeding from a dozen wounds but somehow still alive, the same cold, dead fury etched on her face. She'd been sprawled in rubble stained red by her family's blood. The skinless bodies of her tribe had been dumped in the water. The killer was never found. He'd presumed it was some terrible creature from the depths of the underhive. When he'd asked her of that day she'd spoken of daemons with steel wings, monsters who breathed death and laughed as they hunted her people for sport. He hadn't understood then. But that was before the debutantes' dance, before the museum.

He knew what they were now.

Caleb never heard it approach, but he must have sensed something. He'd already half-turned, pistol in hand, when it struck. The impact lifted him from his feet and sent him tumbling across the stone floor, losing his grip on his weapon. Iktomi was a shade faster, her knife already raised when she was seized, steel talons piercing her shoulder. A curse formed on her lips, but it was choked by the blood and foam frothing from her mouth. As Caleb struggled to stand she was hurled aside contemptuously, her body crumpling as it struck the stone. She convulsed once then lay still.

Standing over her was the daemon.

Its face was a multitude of sensors that glimmered in the half-light like the eyes of a spider, its body segmented steel. Its forelimbs ended in bloodied talons fed by an array of cables and tubes. Though hunched, it still stood a head taller than him.

'Your dog was impressive,' said a voice. Though distorted by the helmet it sounded human, almost familiar. 'This suit renders the wearer invisible to the most advanced auspex, and yet I swear she almost spotted me. These savages are quite remarkable in their own way.'

Caleb didn't reply, crawling towards Iktomi. She lay still, eyes half-open, her foam-flecked lips tinged blue.

'She won't have suffered much,' said the voice. 'The venom is quite potent.'

He hadn't heard the creature move but it was beside him. Instinctively he reached for his holster, but the weapon was gone.

'You, on the other hand, are something of a disappointment,' it continued. 'Caleb Cursebound. Vanquisher of the Badrock Boys. Slayer of the Unseen Beast. Ninth most dangerous man in the underhive.'

It laughed.

'You know me?' Caleb asked, buying time, his gaze darting around the museum, seeking his lost sidearm.

'I'm afraid not,' it replied. 'I'm just reading from your bio. I like to familiarise myself with my prey before the hunt. This list of accomplishments sounded very impressive. But you,' it continued, seizing his arm and effortlessly dragging him to head height, 'you seem barely worth the effort. Slow, clumsy. You couldn't even take the ring convincingly.'

Even with the distortion Caleb recognised the voice.

'Harrow?' he whispered.

'Lord Harrow,' was the response, as the creature tossed him aside. 'The Red Knight, the Lord of the Honoured, the Weaver of Legends. The greatest hunter of my line. Once upon a time.'

Caleb rolled on his shoulder this time, rising awkwardly, his hands rummaging through his overcoat for a weapon. His fingers fastened around a cold metal disc.

Harrow closed on him, hydraulic sinews propelling him forward.

'Sadly, I am now too old to hunt with the newbloods,' he sighed. 'That is my children's duty and privilege. I am reduced to luring greedy rats into traps.'

'Some rats bite,' Caleb replied, sweeping his coat aside and brandishing the metal disc.

'A pocket watch?'

'Yeah,' Caleb said, his gaze falling to his palm. 'That might have sounded better if I had something a little more intimidating.'

'You choose to mock me. Do you think that is wise?'

'No,' Caleb continued, his thumb sliding over the watch's stem. 'It's actually part of a plan. Well, a sort of plan. Maybe.'

'You're babbling. And I am now bored.'

Harrow surged forwards, his massive frame moving with terrifying speed. Caleb stood unmoved as talons were raised to deliver the deathblow. At the last moment he clicked the stem to the side, hurling the watch at the monster's face as he threw his arms over his head. Even with his eyes shielded he felt the blast burn into his retinas, the photon flash grenade flooding the chamber for a few scant moments with the light of a star.

Harrow screamed but Caleb was already running. He risked a glance over his shoulder and saw the monster clawing at its faceplate. At such close range the blast should have burned out most of the sensors, but the armour was beyond anything Caleb had ever seen. He had no idea how long the effect would last. He needed a weapon.

He turned, sprinting down the aisle, taking a left then right and slipping behind a display. There he squatted amongst malformed bone and flayed skin, his gaze hunting the relics for something that could penetrate Harrow's armour. Before him stood a winged statue, surrounded by the remains of a dozen victims. Behind it a painting depicting returning heroes clad in the livery of House Harrow ascending from the underhive back to the peaks of the Spire, their armour bedecked with trophies. Beside it a row of glass tanks displayed severed heads preserved in sickly green fluid. The furthest had begun to show signs of decay, but those in the nearer tanks were almost lifelike, and the closest was more than a little familiar. Caleb had wondered why Kreep had not recruited One-eyed Tippet for the heist. He now knew the answer: Tippet had already been recruited, he just hadn't been very successful.

There came a hiss, followed by a sudden onrush of dark

microfilaments, like spider silk. Caleb was already moving but the blast caught his sleeve, pinning it to the wall.

'So you do have a few tricks.'

The voice was no longer distorted. Caleb turned his head and saw Harrow approaching, arm outstretched, the wrist-mounted webgun trained on him. His helmet had been discarded and the old man's sallow skin seemed out of place amongst the nest of wires and cables, as though his head had been severed and mounted on some cybernetic monstrosity. Emerald fumes roses from the respirator situated just below his jaw, but his breath was still laboured.

'It would seem you have earned a spot beside the other thieves,' he smiled, nodding to the parade of heads. 'I must confess to an overreliance on sensors and targeting systems. Thank you for helping me address my weakness.'

He raised his taloned hand, the weapon poised to unleash a second blast, but as he moved Caleb slipped free from his overcoat, ducking through the display. He felt something sail over his head, tearing out hair by the roots, but he kept moving. Iktomi's body lay just ahead. She must have something on her besides that hunting knife. Without his helmet, one shot between Harrow's eyes could finish it.

He was a few yards away when the blast caught his legs. He staggered, tumbling forwards but never quite reaching the ground as the web constricted, suspending him in place. He was still scant feet from Iktomi. He stretched his hand as far as he could, but she remained out of reach.

'Our hunt is at an end.'

He heard Harrow approach this time, the wheeze of his breath and click of metal on stone. The old man strode into view, bending down beside Caleb.

'Something of an anticlimax,' he sighed, his expression

sour. 'Still, you weren't the worst I've faced. I suppose I should take some solace in that. Are you ready to claim your prize, thief? Are you ready to die at the "Hand of Harrow"?'

His face was inches from Caleb's own, framed by the emerald fumes wafting from the respirator. The smell was familiar, a cocktail of stimulants and combat drugs. Caleb breathed deeply and felt his own heart pounding as a red haze descended on the edge of his thoughts. The fumes seemed to emanate from a thin glass canister plugged into a side housing. It looked like a recent addition to the armour.

'Any last words before I add your head to my display? If you can think of something memorable I may add it to the plaque.'

'You need to do your research more thoroughly,' Caleb replied, keeping his voice steady. 'That bio was a pack of lies. The Beast of Sumptown, killing Bonesnapper – I never did any of that. I'm honestly not that much of a killer, I don't quite have the stomach for it. I'm more about misdirection and distraction to be honest – she always delivered the killing blow.'

'Your dog?' Harrow smiled. 'How did that turn out?'

'Were you part of the Blood River Massacre?' Caleb continued, ignoring him. 'I just stumbled across it. She had survived for days. Even fell in a spider nest and somehow crawled out again. Never seen anyone with that many bites. She was comatose for a week. I didn't think she'd pull through. Were you there that day? Did you make the river run red? Did you exterminate her people?'

'You'd need to be more specific. I've slaughtered a lot of vermin in my time.'

'They have markings around the eyes. Like scars.'

He nodded to Iktomi's body. Harrow tilted his head a fraction, staring down at her prone form.

Caleb's hand snaked out, tearing the canister from Harrow's face. It tumbled to the stone, smashing and engulfing the three of them in a noxious cloud. Caleb held his breath but still felt as though his blood were bursting through his veins. Everything seemed to move in slow motion. He glanced at Harrow; the old man was shaking, each breath a jagged rasp. His eyes had haemorrhaged, the whites stained scarlet, the pupils pinpricks. He swayed, almost falling, but the stabilisers in his armour held him on his feet.

His face snapped back to Caleb, eyes twitching, teeth bared. He made a sound, a guttural roar that might have contained words, and raised his taloned hand for the final time.

Iktomi burst through the cloud, screaming through blood-flecked lips, burying her blade in Harrow's eye socket.

He shuddered, teeth still bared, claw still poised. For a moment it looked as though he would somehow deliver the deathblow. Then his head bowed, his eyes rolling back in his head, his armour still.

Iktomi stood heaving, her lips tinged blue, her eyes bloody. Both hands were clasped around the handle of her blade, which was still lodged in Harrow's skull. From what Caleb could tell this was the only thing keeping her upright.

'Emperor's breath,' he whispered. 'How are you still alive?'

She swayed, glancing across at him.

'S-spider venom,' she stuttered. 'Y-you get used to it. It just took a m-moment.'

She lost her grip on the knife, falling to her knees.

'Hey, stay with me,' Caleb said, reaching awkwardly for her shoulder, his feet still webbed to the floor. 'We have to get out. Check his suit for a solvent or something. He must have a way of unsticking his victims.'

She nodded but didn't reply.

'Iktomi?'

'Not yet,' she said, her eyes fixed on Lord Harrow's armoured gauntlet. 'Not empty-handed.'

Kreep's office was fitted with a range of surveillance equipment. It gave enough warning for him to dive behind the desk before his door exploded, spraying the room with shrapnel. He was rising, his hand snaking into his longcoat when he felt the blade press against his throat. Fingers grasped him by the ear, dragging him to his feet.

'Hello, Kreep,' Caleb said, emerging from the smoke, a sack slung over his shoulder. 'I bumped into One-eyed Tippet.'

Kreep opened his mouth to speak but Iktomi hushed him with a slight twist of the knife, a bead of blood pooling on its tip.

'So, we had a difficult few days,' Caleb continued, perching on the blackened desk. 'It turns out that the Hand of Harrow wasn't so much an artefact as an opportunity to be flayed alive or decapitated by a geriatric psychopath in an armoured battle-suit. The whole thing has left my colleague and I at something of an impasse. We cannot decide whether you sent us to our deaths deliberately or you were just so damned greedy you failed to spot some very clear signs. Mr Tippet's disappearance for one thing.'

'Please,' Kreep whispered, 'I had no idea there–'

'See, I knew there had to be a misunderstanding,' Caleb grinned, slapping Kreep's shoulder. 'Just pay us our fee and we will say no more.'

'Fee?' Kreep said with a gulp. 'But you said there was no artefact.'

Caleb reached into the sack, retrieving a bloodstained gauntlet and slamming it on the desk. Half an arm was still attached to it.

'The Hand of Harrow,' he proclaimed. 'Now where's our money?'

A FIRSTBORN EXILE

Filip Wiltgren

Filip Wiltgren returns to the pages of Inferno! *with this engaging follow-up to* Volume One's 'The Firstborn Daughter'. *Having won the respect of her company, Lieutenant Ekaterina Idra of the 86th Vostroyan Firstborn continues her fight against the rebellious Tovogans.*

In this action-packed tale of human-on-human conflict, Ekaterina finds herself struggling to maintain her position within her regiment, battling the rigid doctrines of Imperial command as well as a heavily entrenched enemy.

The Chimera rumbles to a halt.

'Try again,' says Lieutenant Ekaterina Idra.

'Sir!' Sergeant Dalsik, Idra's vox-operator, turns the dials, aligning the runes on the vox-caster. '992nd Firstborn,' he says, 'come in nine-nine-two.'

Idra pushes open the Chimera's top hatch. Empty, grey Tovogan skies. Empty, grey Tovogan razorgrass plains. So unlike the ash wastes of Vostroya, yet so similar.

Except for the rebels. Vostroya's heart and loyalty is with the Emperor. Which is why the Firstborn are on Tovoga. Loyal troops to quell the rebellion.

'Do you read, nine-nine-two?' says Dalsik, his voice almost drowned out by the armoured troop carrier's idling engine. The antenna is solid, bending in a shallow arc over the Chimera's armour. It is only twelve miles to Salomar. Dalsik should have been able to raise the 992nd. He should have been able to raise them sixty miles ago.

Behind Idra, the rest of the Vostroyan 86th Firstborn Regiment is spread across the razorgrass. Two more Chimeras, the boxy, grey troop carriers painted with red Firstborn recognition markings. A Taurox, its triangular tracks clogging with mud. A wheeled Tauros scout vehicle, what constitutes Idra's outrider squad, making a lone shadow against the horizon. And a brace of grey, steel-wheeled trucks, captured from the Tovogans. Slow and unarmoured, the only transportation readily available to Idra. The 86th Firstborn is a regiment reduced to company strength, a bare hundred troops, plus walking wounded.

Nothing to be done about that until they get to Salomar, and the 992nd.

'Do you read, nine-nine-two?' says Dalsik. Idra closes the hatch, waves for her driver to engage the tracks.

The vox erupts with sharp pops. Heavy bolter fire.

'Who is this?' comes a voice. *'Identify yourself. This is a restricted military channel.'*

'Sergeant Dalsik, 86th Firstborn, under command of Lieutenant Idra.'

The vox goes silent, then returns.

'86th, by order of Colonel Gurlov, you are to proceed to Salomar with haste,' it says. *'Enter the city and relieve Command Group Gurlov, engaging and destroying any rebel forces you encounter.'*

'Gurlov?' says Idra. The name is vaguely familiar.

'Didn't he die?' says Sergeant Mathis Lokhov, Idra's second-in-command.

Rumours click into place in Idra's memory.

'Ramrod Gurlov?' she says. 'The one who had his entire regiment flogged?'

She taps Dalsik on the shoulder.

'Apprise them of our situation,' she says, but before Dalsik can engage the vox, a slow drawl comes through Idra's vox-bead. Wisniak, Idra's lead scout and head sniper.

'Sir, you'd better see this.'

The Chimera claws its way up the slope. Idra pushes open the hatch.

In the distance, a plume of black smoke stains the Tovogan sky.

Salomar is burning.

The city of Salomar is dwarfed by the factorum. A massive rockcrete box, three miles long and half a mile wide. Tall enough for its roof to disappear in the smoke coming from the burning petro-chem storage at the other end of town.

'Reminds you of home, doesn't it?' says Lokhov, stroking his drooping, grey moustache. Idra nods.

'Looks a bit like the miniature factorums you'd find in toy shops,' she says.

The Firstborn around her chuckle, even though the joke is ash-dry. Men will laugh at anything before a battle. It's either that or cry, and the Firstborn would rather shave their moustaches than cry before a battle. The crying they save for afterwards, when it is time to burn their friends and drink their fear away.

Idra scans the town's perimeter through her magnoculars. No motion visible. It looks deceptively calm, except for the fire and the occasional explosion or flash of las-blasts near the factorum on the east side.

'Any ideas, uncle?' asks Idra. Lokhov shakes his head.

'Cursed inconvenient,' he says. 'The moment we roll into those fields we become grox for the slaughter.'

The 86th's vehicles stand behind a low ridge, shielding them from view. Between them and Salomar lie rows of fields separated by shallow ditches. Beets, potatoes, what looks like poisonous ashberry bushes, but probably aren't. Not enough ash on Tovoga.

Idra drums her fingers on the magnoculars' steel casing.

'Too long until nightfall,' she says. 'But the west side of town looks calm. We move a bit north, then rush across the fields as far from the factorum as we can. Take them by surprise before they can organise a strong defence.'

'And if they already have a strong defence in place?' Lokhov says.

Idra gives the town another scan through the magnoculars. The houses look whole, no walls blown open to emplace guns, no camouflage netting or trenches. It looks peaceful, deceptively so. She chews on her lip.

'Not much choice,' she finally says. 'We'll have to storm across, using the Chimeras to shield the trucks. Lay down a barrage with the multi-lasers, launch the smoke grenades as soon as we're in range, and drive.'

'Dangerous,' says Lokhov. 'If there were any other way…'

Idra nods again, doesn't say what they're both thinking. A lieutenant does not challenge a colonel. Especially not a man like Ramrod Gurlov.

'Move out,' Idra says.

'Any other orders?' Lokhov asks.

Idra pauses, one foot through the Chimera's hatch.

'Pray,' she says.

Idra hates sitting in the confines of the Chimera. Outside, she has speed, power, control. Outside, she can fight.

Locked up in the troop carrier, she is useless. Her driver knows where he's going. Her gunner is more skilled at operating the multi-laser. Her vox-operator monitors any transmissions. All Idra has to do is wait, and sweat. The fingers gripping the hilt of her power sword are white with pressure.

'Don't scowl,' says Lokhov.

'I wasn't scowling,' says Idra, trying to force her face to relax. A commander should not give her men cause to worry.

'You looked like someone had poured ash into your ohx and stirred,' says Lokhov.

This gets him a laugh.

'Thank you, uncle,' Idra says.

The Chimera thumps with the dull sound of firing smoke mortars. Outside, out of Idra's view, the air will be filling with grey clouds. More grey on this grey world. Only the Firstborn's uniforms are red, like drops of blood against the Tovogan soil.

Blood about to be spilled. Idra's neck hairs stand on end. She feels like she's about to crawl into a blackwasp nest blindfolded, the swarming insects readying to drop on her. Why isn't the multi-laser firing?

Maybe the Tovogans haven't spotted them. Maybe they're pinned by the 992nd, unable to watch the perimeter. Maybe the 86th will make it through to Salomar unharmed.

The Chimera gongs, a giant blow making the armoured side ring like a broken bell. It is followed by multiple smaller pops, almost inaudible after the first crash. Autocannon, followed by heavy bolter or maybe a spate of light infantry weapons. The Chimera's walls flash rapidly, reflections from its turret-mounted multi-laser. Dalsik is shouting, his mouth moving, but Idra can't hear a thing. Acrid smoke fills the compartment, tasting of heated steel and burnt rubber. But the Chimera is still shaking, still moving forwards, shielding the following trucks from the fire.

Another crash, followed by a violent rocking, and stillness. The floor leans backwards at a sharp angle; the driver hangs from his seat belts, blood dripping from his slack fingers.

'Out!' Idra yells, forcing open the rear hatch, grabbing Lokhov and pointing down. They dive out of the carrier, its multi-laser still firing above them.

A wall. Grey rockcrete, the Chimera having smashed halfway up it and got stuck. More flashes from between the Chimera's treads, dark orange, not the bright white of multi-laser blasts.

Idra rolls out, ends up beside a stack of sandbags. The autocannon emplacement. She thumbs the rune on her power sword, sheathing the blade in dancing, blue haze. Jumps over the sandbags, her open, red Vostroyan coat trailing like a cape.

Grey uniforms, grey helmets, an empty grey patch where the golden Imperial aquila should be. The rebels gape in surprise. Idra cuts them down, the power sword slicing through flesh and armour alike. Two unarmed loaders fall, the autocannon's oversized magazine tumbling to the ground. A sergeant raises a chainsword, but Idra's powerblade cuts through both plasteel and man. She spears the gunner, ending the autocannon's flashes, then jumps across his falling body, cutting down another loader.

A las-blast lights up the wall beside her. She turns, kicks at the gun in the rebel's hand, cuts at his head. He ducks, and she decapitates him on the back stroke, the blood beading away from the coruscating blue power field.

A truck rolls out of the smoke, breaking as the driver spots the autocannon. Firstborn spill from the open rear grate, forming up around Idra, their eyes wide. Their mouths move, but all Idra can hear is the ringing in her ears, and all she can feel is the memory of her power sword, slicing through flesh.

* * *

Someone hands Idra a steaming cup.

'Sir!' Her driver, arm in a sling. Lignin, from Kolbach Hive. His moustache and the hair sticking out from beneath his tall, black, bearskin shako, are almost white. He's been with the 86th a long time.

Idra sips. Warm ohx, salty and spiced with ground black pepper in the low-born way. It burns its way down Idra's throat, filling her with warmth and making her smile. An acquired taste. Mother would have a fit if she saw Idra drinking the stuff.

'Thank you,' she says. Lignin tries to salute with his wounded arm, but fails and nods instead, before returning to the field medic station.

'They believe in you,' says Lokhov. He's picked up a scratch on his cheek.

'For leading them into a gun emplacement?' says Idra, nodding to the no-longer-concealed autocannon. Around her, scout teams are starting off into the town, their red coats like splashes against the rockcrete.

'You destroyed the gun,' Lokhov says. 'Without losses.'

'And him?' Idra jerks her chin towards Lignin.

'He'll live,' says Lokhov. 'Trina, they believe in you. You are the commander who slaughtered a monster, led them out of two deadly and well-executed traps, killed a traitorous superior officer, and got a commendation from the lord commissar of the entire Tovogan campaign herself. You are blessed with the Emperor's own Luck.'

Idra shakes her head.

'Not you too, uncle,' she says.

'I believe what I believe,' Lokhov answers, raising his hand to forestall her comment. 'But get us through this alive, and I'll stop saying it.'

'Good enough,' Idra says, clapping him on the shoulder. There is work to do.

Her sixth, and last, three-man scout squad moves into the city. They're well trained, the 86th, moving by leaps. Two men watching, ready to fire; one man rushing to the next position, bent over in that leaning, furious run that soldiers adopt in war, presenting a smaller target. No dishonour in that. This is what war does, even to Firstborn – has you always waiting for that sharp yank on the flesh, the bewilderment and the pain.

Six scout teams. Eighteen men. Almost a fifth of her entire force. Blessed indeed.

'We take it slow,' Idra says. 'Scout well in advance, probe until we manage a link up with the 992nd. No casualties today.'

One of her combat engineers is cutting apart the autocannon's loading mechanism with a portable plasma torch. They're leaving nothing for the enemy. The command Chimera is level again, Firstborn pulling it away from the wall. Its engine stutters, hiccups, rumbles to life. The armour is gashed and burned, but the armoured troop carrier claws its way out of the rubble.

'Sir!' says Dalsik through the hatch.

It's time to move out.

Salomar is deserted. Idra likes the quiet. Solid rockcrete beneath her boots, instead of the endless, cutting razorgrass. Reminds her of home. A Vostroya in miniature.

Without people.

Whoever lived here has cleared out. Only the sporadic, distant sounds of gunfire from the factorum, and the echoes of the Chimeras' engines, break the stillness.

The Firstborn march in half-squads, spread out along the

road, red coats brushing against the walls of three- and four-storey buildings, scanning the empty windows on the opposite side. Covering each other.

They are good men, forged in battle.

Something crunches beneath Idra's black, armoured boot. A porcelain doll, its face cracked and squashed by her weight. Civilians passed this way, not long ago.

A far-off lasgun salvo breaks the silence, the sharp cracks muted by distance. A split second later, it echoes through the Chimera's open hatch.

'Nine-nine-two, come in, nine-nine-two,' says Dalsik. '86th Firstborn to 992nd.'

'Err, you're a bit late for that,' says a thin voice through the vox. Idra grabs the hatch, launches herself into the Chimera.

'Who is this?' says Dalsik. The voice goes quiet for a moment. Then it returns.

'Acting Corporal Ninov,' it says. 'Command Group Gurlov.'

'Patch me through to the 992nd,' says Dalsik.

'Sorry, they pulled out two days ago.'

Dalsik glances at Idra, raising his eyebrow.

'Hello?' says the vox voice, Ninov, the acting corporal. '86th, are you there? We could use a bit of help over here.' A brace of las-blasts sounds from the vox.

Idra nods, curtly.

'We're coming,' says Dalsik.

The 86th rushes through Salomar. Empty streets blur by, scout teams rejoined and mounted in the trucks, Wisniak's Tauros in the lead. A las-blast strikes down from a warehouse window, and the Chimeras reply by blasting the entire facade with their multi-lasers. They don't stop to look at the half-burned body that falls out.

It is a crazy manoeuvre, relying on speed in a built-up, hostile environment. It goes against everything Idra believes in. But they are still miles away from the barracks, and a command group is counted in squads, a few platoons at most. Without the 992nd, Idra's depleted 86th is the strongest force in Salomar.

Except for the Tovogan rebels.

The 86th doesn't stand a chance of punching through. Not against a concentrated effort by a dug-in enemy. Successfully charging a single autocannon through a smoke screen to get into Salomar was luck. A full fire-support company would have decimated the Firstborn. Charging an enemy regiment would be suicide. Their only chance is to link up with Gurlov before the rebels find out how weak they are.

Speed and superior firepower. Sufficient amounts of one gives you the other. It doesn't matter if the enemy is stronger. They can't be stronger everywhere, and if they are, you're already dead, and, by the Emperor's Grace, haven't realised it.

But the 86th Firstborn have the Emperor's Grace. They have faith, they have experience, and they have speed.

The battle is short and brutal. Idra loses eight men and a Chimera to a lascannon. Another four to a heavy flamer. A handful wounded by small-arms fire.

They break through the rebel cordon, charging out of the cover of the grey tenements, then over the killing field outside Command Group Gurlov's armoured barracks, taking cover behind half-blasted dragon's teeth, the rockcrete tank obstacles leaving only a small road clear for the vehicles. An armoured gate clanks open steps ahead of the Firstborn. When the gates slam shut behind them, Idra realises her hands are shaking. She clenches her fists, counts her men.

They are inside. At least she didn't have to bang on closed armaplas while her comrades died around her.

The Salomar barracks are standard Vostroyan Mk III pattern, right out of the *Treatis Elatii*. A square, two hundred and fifty yards to a side, anchored by four squat towers mounting multi-lasers. Three of them are burned-out husks, but the fourth is still firing. Rockcrete bunkers capped with firing parapets. A dark, gaping maw surrounded by blast barriers that is the protected tunnel entrance to the underground vehicle bay. A twisted mess of broken steel where the anti-air battery should be.

Everything smells of sweat, gunpowder and the telltale scorched-ozone smell of lasgun fire. There are black las-blast marks on the insides of the bunkers, almost all the way to Colonel Gurlov's small office.

'Tovogans,' he says by way of greeting, crisply returning Idra's salute. 'No honour among them. Snuck in an assault squad among the wounded, the Emperor damn them.'

Gurlov is a squat man, with a fringe of orange hair around his bald head, and an impressive orange moustache obscuring his mouth. His uniform is impeccable: starched, bright red plas-weave jacket, crossed by polished, white grox-hide bandoliers. His golden officer's braid is thick, the gold and copper threads tied in the traditional, hand-made Nadalya's knot. Idra wonders if he's tied it himself, like she has with her smaller one.

Gurlov's face is closed, guarded, his chiselled chin thrust out. Even the bulky metal bionics, an arm and a leg, sticking out of his uniform, look polished. Except for the dusting of dried iron filings on his boot, and the smell of stale sweat in his office, he could have come from a recruitment poster. He seems affronted by the rebels' ruse, as if it were a stain on his own honour.

'No courage,' he says. 'Proves what forsaking the Emperor's word does to a man.'

'Sir!' says Idra. Gurlov isn't what she imagined. The rumours paint him as a giant, a hero and a tyrant, using the *Tactica Imperium* as his sword and shield. And the rebels have shown little cowardice that she's seen, often fighting to the last man.

'We lost twelve men,' she says.

Gurlov nods, his fringe of orange hair waving.

'They died with courage, in the service of the Emperor,' he says. 'No man can ask for more.' He pauses, eyebrows wrinkling. 'Or woman,' he adds.

Callous bastard. But he doesn't know the dead. Not like Idra did. Lukov. Orlik. Strelvin who played the harmonica. Or maybe Gurlov truly doesn't care.

'That's ten per cent of our regiment,' says Idra. 'Gone in minutes.'

'The Emperor demands, Vostroya gives,' Gurlov says. 'They died doing their duty, paying Vostroya's debt. And it was good that you had the wit to charge. The *Treatis* and the Emperor favour boldness, no matter what the *Tactica* says.'

He's got both in his office. The office is a tiny, windowless room, slightly longer than it is wide. Idra could probably touch both walls if she stretched out her arms. A single strip of pale lighting in the ceiling. An off-white plascrete desk; a pair of steel chairs; a shelf with the thick volumes of the *Tactica Imperium* and the two-volume edition of the *Treatis Elatii*, the Grey Lady's holy text. Even Idra's private chambers were more lavish. At least she had an arms locker, and a painting of Saint Nadalya by the Throne.

'Thanks to your acting vox-corporal,' Idra says. 'Without his information, we would likely have tried for a slow linkup and been overrun.'

'Acting corporal?' Gurlov says.

'Ninov,' Idra replies.

Gurlov stiffens, glances aside at the *Tactica*. When he looks back at Idra, his mouth is pursed, his nostrils flaring.

'Haugen!' he yells. 'Get me Private Ninov.'

It is an uncomfortable wait. Idra stands at attention, hands stiff at her sides. There's a mad scratching between her shoulder blades, as if an ash-mite is rolling around in her uniform. Why is she still here? Her men need her, to say the words for the fallen and to keep those still living focused on their tasks.

Gurlov paces. Outside, there's a dull thud, followed by the sharp cracks of a multi-laser. The water in the glass on Gurlov's desk ripples.

'Sir!' The man that rushes in and snaps to attention is no more than a boy, his pale, round face sporting the barest wisp of a moustache. He's tried to comb it longer.

'Ninov,' says Gurlov.

'Sir!'

'You impersonated a vox-corporal,' says Gurlov, 'contacting the 86th.'

'Sir,' says Ninov. 'Corporal Bagulbin was out and–'

Gurlov's hand slaps his desk with a crack like a bolter shot.

'You,' he says, 'impersonated an officer.'

'Sir!' says Ninov. He licks his lips, his hands shaking. Idra wants to clap the boy on the shoulder, tell him to buckle up. In battle, you do what you need to do, to win and save lives.

'This is a court martial offence,' says Gurlov. 'But in view of your age, I will use my prerogative and sentence you to administrative punishment.'

A slap on the wrist. Idra's been given more administrative

punishment than she can remember. Push-ups, pull-ups, kitchen duty. But Ninov is still shaking.

'Guard duty,' Gurlov says. 'Two months. Double shifts.'

Ninov's pale cheeks go white as untreated armaplast. Two months of guard duty in a combat zone, while double shifts wear you out and wear down your focus. It is a death sentence.

'Yes, sir,' he whispers.

'Sir!' says Idra. 'Permission to speak!'

'You are already talking, lieutenant,' says Gurlov.

'Sir, as we just discussed, without Private Ninov's intervention, the 86th would have moved for a slow linkup and most likely been wiped out.'

Gurlov runs a hand over his bald scalp.

'Impersonating an officer, breach of tactical doctrine, breach of vox conduct,' he says. 'Without discipline, there is no force, there is no Guard, and there is no Vostroya. A court martial would sentence him to hanging.' Again, he glances at the *Tactica*. Or maybe not the *Tactica*. The *Treatis Elatii*'s there too.

'Sir,' says Idra, 'the Grey Lady favours luck. As does the Emperor.'

'The Emperor's own Luck,' says Gurlov, with a grimace. He stretches, the servos on his bionic arm whirring. He is not going to budge, and if Idra isn't careful, she'll pull down Gurlov's wrath on the 86th as well. She's already lost twelve men today. She should salute and be done with it. What importance is a single private in a war?

'Sir!' says Idra. 'May I ask a favour?'

'Ask away, lieutenant.'

'The 86th will need a liaison,' Idra says. 'I would prefer one that is lucky. Calling us in certainly was that.'

Gurlov barks a laugh. For a moment, his closed face lights up like a lightning rod in an ash-storm. Then he grows dark and dispassionate again.

'Very well,' he says. 'You may take the private. But the punishment still stands. Carry it out.'

'Sir!' says Idra, saluting.

'Who's this?' says Sergeant Lokhov. He's cleaning his lasgun, sitting on a crate of melta bombs in the vehicle bay. The bay is an underground cavern, stretching under the entire barracks. Three hundred yards on each side, it's built to handle an entire regiment of combat vehicles. The 86th's surviving transports are dwarfed by it, Idra's Firstborn scurrying around like red-coated ants on the grey rockcrete floor.

'Ninov,' says Idra. 'The voice on the vox.'

'The 86th finally get reinforcements?'

'No,' says Idra. 'Gurlov had him up on administrative charges for impersonating an officer.'

Lokhov slots the lasgun's barrel into the sight block, clicks in the barrel retaining pin.

'Why is he here?' he asks.

'Two months of double line duty, uncle,' Idra says. She doesn't need to spell out the consequences. Lokhov lifts his hand to stroke his moustache, before realising that it's sticky with insulation fluid.

'Trina,' he says, 'why is he here?'

'He's our new liaison,' Idra says. 'Not officer.'

Lokhov doesn't answer. The nearest Firstborn stop their scurrying. Only the faint sound of distant gunfire from above disturbs the peace.

'He helped us,' Idra says. 'What would you have me do, uncle? Leave him to die?'

'By the Throne, girl,' Lokhov says. 'Get on Gurlov's bad side and we'll all be doing double line duty. Did you think of that?'

'The colonel isn't bad,' Ninov says suddenly. 'Corporal Bagulbin say he's a war hero.'

In the dim stillness of the bay, Ninov looks uncomfortable, like a school boy caught writing love poems about the Grey Lady.

'He is,' says Lokhov. 'He also had one of his companies doing push-ups during an artillery barrage for breach of regulations. Emperor's own Grace that nobody died.' He turns to Idra. 'I'm surprised he let the boy get away.'

'I'm supposed to administer the punishment,' says Idra.

Lokhov puts aside his gun.

'Do you intend to get the kid killed?'

'No,' says Idra. 'Do you think the order's another administrative mishap waiting to happen?'

Administrative mishap is their little joke, a laugh at what the powers in general command do to the 86th. Like the 86th not getting any reinforcements. Like the 992nd pulling out two days before the 86th arrives. Like Idra's orders from general staff getting mis-transmitted until it's almost too late to carry them out, and deal with it, lieutenant. Idra almost spits before she remembers herself. Unseemly, for an officer. Gurlov would probably have her up on administrative charges for dirtying the floor.

Still, it rankles. No other commander suffers these kinds of errors this frequently. But then, no other commander is a woman. If Gurlov is enough of a traditionalist, the 86th will be in big trouble.

'I doubt it would be Gurlov's doing,' says Lokhov. 'All the rumours say that he's rule-bound to a fault.'

'Um...' says Ninov. 'The colonel really hates rumours. Corporal Bagulbin says that–'

The howl of the alarm klaxons drowns out his words.

Colonel Gurlov's small office is cramped, with the colonel, a major, a captain and Idra. No adjutants though, nor non-commissioned officers. No room for them. Or maybe they're all dead.

'Ten minutes ago,' says Colonel Gurlov, 'the rebels overran Captain Kadarov's forward positions in the factorum's central hall. This puts the armoury and the void shield generators within their reach. Our orders are to hold the generators at all costs. If the rebels overrun them, and get them operational, they will be able to lock out any counter-attack long enough to start utilising the factorum. General command is very concerned with a fleet of rebel tanks appearing in our rear. We need to push them back, and secure Kadarov's positions.' He glances at Idra. 'The 86th will lead the charge.'

Idra swallows.

'Sir!' she says. 'Permission to–'

'Speak, lieutenant.'

Every eye in the chamber is on her. The cup on Colonel Gurlov's desk smells strongly of ohx, the low-born, peppery kind. The room suddenly feels even more crowded.

'Colonel Gurlov, sir,' Idra says. 'The 86th is severely depleted. Our current strength is ninety-one men and four combat vehicles. That includes walking wounded.'

Gurlov steeples his fingers in a tiny pyramid before him.

'I am aware of that fact,' he says. 'However, orders are orders. General staff requires us to retake the factorum. We have an entire regiment at our disposal.'

His face remains closed, serious.

'Sir,' Idra interrupts, 'you have to apprise them of the situation.'

The room's empty walls are more expressive than Gurlov's face. Even his bushy, orange moustache doesn't quiver.

'I have done so,' he says. 'General Krikovin's orders are to attack.'

Gurlov's officers exchange uneasy glances.

'I am aware of the difficulties involved,' Gurlov says. 'Two companies against what amounts to an entire regiment is bad odds. However, the Tovogan rebels have so far shown little evidence of training, and limited capabilities. Certainly, they are no match for our Firstborn, no matter how many of them there are.'

'Sir,' says the major. His name badge reads *Bulwa*. 'We'll need at least a company to hold the barracks.'

'You'll get two platoons, major,' says Gurlov.

'Wait!' blurts Idra. 'You're going to withhold troops to guard the barracks?'

Gurlov gives her a hard look. For a second, she wonders whether this is the administrative mishap that will crush her. Instead, Gurlov speaks.

'Let your heart be a well-defended fortified barracks, your mind a rockcrete pillar,' he says.

'*Treatis Elatii*,' says Idra. 'Fourteenth chapter, eighth stanza.' Gurlov raises an eyebrow, and gives her an almost imperceptible nod.

'Very good, lieutenant. Now go prepare your troops.'

He's going to send the 86th, plus two platoons of staff soldiers, to assault an enemy held factorum. Hard, but maybe not impossible. Idra's done hard before.

But the *Tactica* states that a force should always hold a link to their command post and base. Meaning that the Firstborn will be spread out in a thin line along the factorum floor. The hairs on Idra's neck feel as if someone's dragged a knife over them.

It's suicide. The rebels will pick off the holding teams one by one. Would Gurlov abandon doctrine? Not likely. Maybe if she could bend one of his officers.

'Sir,' says Idra. One glance at Gurlov's staff shows her the futility of the request. They're both staring ahead, at their commander. They're going to follow this man to hell, and beyond.

'Yes, lieutenant?'

Idra's mouth is dry, her hands shaky. A wrong word could send her to the stockade. But if she doesn't say anything, the 86th is doomed.

'Sir,' she says, stalling for time. 'The *Tactica* says to keep the lines of communication open. The Grey Lady preaches the values of a base of operations.'

A well-defended base of operations.

'This is hardly a well-defended barracks,' she says. 'With two platoons, it will be worse than weak.'

'Are you recommending that we abandon our post, lieutenant?' Gurlov says.

Emperor's Mercy, the man is going to doom them all. He isn't even trying to see the world beyond doctrine.

'If we defeat the rebels, we'll be able to retake the barracks,' Idra says.

'General Krikovin's orders are to hold our command post at all cost,' says Gurlov.

'Yes,' says Idra, 'but does the general say that it has to remain at the barracks?'

Gurlov blinks. He knows. He has to know. Yet he remains silent. Orders. He's going to follow his orders to the letter, even if those orders take them straight into the void.

A colonel does not contradict a general, and a lieutenant does not contradict a colonel. But there is always another way. All you need to do is find it. Idra takes a breath, exhales, draws another. Gurlov waits, his eyebrow ever-so-slightly quirked.

'The 86th command post is mobile,' says Idra. Which is true. She is the command post. She, Dalsik and Lokhov. 'May I extend an invitation on behalf of the 86th Firstborn to Command Group Gurlov to utilise our resources?'

The captain snorts. The major hides his mouth behind his hand. Gurlov nods.

'If we fail,' he says, 'it will be your head, lieutenant. General Krikovin has made it plain that he is not fond of you. My orders are to remove you from command at the first sign of incompetence or insubordination.'

Idra nods. Administrative mishaps waiting to happen have turned into orders. She is a woman, the first female Firstborn. Being first into battle is dangerous. Being first is always a danger, regardless of where. But Idra is accustomed to danger.

'Do you wish to rescind your invitation, lieutenant?' says Gurlov.

Her men would shield her from the danger, if they could. But a commander isn't there to be shielded. She is there to lead, and to protect her men from fools.

'No, sir!' she says. Firstborn hating her. It is a feeling she knows well.

They are ready. A hundred and fifty Firstborn throng the barracks' eastern gate. Weapons checked, sword-bayonets mounted, bandolier pouches stuffed with grenades and lasgun power packs. The eastern gate is the secondary one, a slab of plasteel painted grey to match the walls. It's large enough to let them run through eight abreast.

'Lieutenant, your commander will be Captain Suvarin,' says Gurlov. His bionic leg hisses with every step, making him limp, ever so slightly.

Idra snaps to attention and salutes. She knows how this game is played. But to his credit, Captain Suvarin doesn't attempt to wrest control of the 86th from her.

It's doubtful that he could. Her troops already mutter about following a staff officer into combat.

'Attention!' says Idra, the vox-beads carrying her voice to her companies. The 86th Firstborn stands to, backs straight, guns by their left legs.

'Firstborn,' says Gurlov, 'today we show this world Vostroyan might.'

His troops give a 'huzzah'. A moment later, Idra's do, too.

'Move out,' says Gurlov.

'Move out,' says Captain Suvarin.

'By companies, move out,' says Idra.

The gate swings silently open, the hinges well maintained. There's a three hundred-yard swathe of barren land between the barracks and the factorum, a stretch of grey filled with the spiked pyramids of rockcrete dragon's teeth. Two communication trenches zigzag between the teeth.

'Forward,' says Idra, her heart racing. 'Into the trenches, double time.'

As soon as her first squad, Wisniak and nine of his scouts, start running down the trenches, the air erupts with the crack of lasgun fire. White and pale blue bolts blast the ground around the trenches. Lascannons stab into the grey earth. At least a company firing, maybe more. The hairs on Idra's neck rise again, but none of it touches her Firstborn. The trenches are deep, and their zigzagging prevents clean firing lanes. The design is right out of the *Tactica*, and it works.

'How far do the trenches stretch?' Idra shouts to Captain Suvarin as they jog behind the 86th. The rebels' blasts dust the air with earth, and the dust smells of iron.

'All the way to the factorum, and beyond,' Suvarin shouts back. 'The colonel had them connected to the factorum's bunker system.'

It makes good tactical sense, but it would have been easy to leave the work for later. Gurlov's troops must have cursed him more than once, digging it all out.

A scream breaks Idra's reverie. The troops bunch up in front of her.

'Move aside,' she shouts, pushing forwards. Ahead, someone is shouting for a medic.

Her men make room, pressing themselves against walls. A stretch of the trench lies almost perpendicular to the tenements of Salomar beyond the killing fields surrounding the barracks.

Idra's shoulders clench, her breath fighting to escape her lungs. The angle creates a straight kill lane for the rebels, enabling them to fire down the length of the trench from their positions in the buildings. Las-blasts dig into the bottom of the trench, as more and more of the rebels realise there is a way to destroy the Firstborn. A death zone fifty yards long. She can't order her men to run through that.

At the end of the line, closest to the barracks, firing starts up. The rearguard, engaging approaching rebels. The rebels have figured out that the Firstborn are outside the protection of the barracks. They need to move.

There's always another way. A stanza from the *Treatis* flashes through Idra's consciousness. Open your heart for the Emperor's strength. Uncloud your mind and He will fill it.

'Smoke, then charge through,' she says.

'Smoke!' yells Sergeant Lokhov, waving for the Firstborn to make room for the 86th mortar team.

The mortar team consists of one experienced mortar loader, and three replacements, firing for the first time. They manage to situate their mortar at the bottom of a protected part of the trench. The loader flings a smoke shell into the tube. Idra presses her hands to her ears. The force of the bang hammers at her chest.

'Outgoing!' shouts Lokhov.

The first mortar bomb lobs high into the air, falling far beyond the trenches. The second hits the factorum roof. The third is a dud, the fourth disappears.

A lascannon finds its mark, burning a glowing hole through the trench wall. A Firstborn curses, yanking his burning shako from his head. Everyone hunkers down.

'86th, *advance*,' commands Gurlov, through the vox.

'Lieutenant!' shouts Suvarin, miming throwing.

Idra jumps at the mortar team, yanking a case of oblong mortar bombs from the surprised loader.

'Like this,' she says, bashing the trigger against the steel of the mortar base. She flings the bomb over the side of the trench.

There is a pop, and whitish smoke blows over the Firstborn. The mortar crew starts pulling and throwing bombs. Suddenly, one screams. A smoking mortar bomb rolls down the trench, between the legs of the crouching soldiers. Sergeant Lokhov snatches it up and tosses it over the wall.

'Nadalya's Mercy, man,' he shouts at the soldier, a grizzled grey-hair like himself, 'you want to kill us all?'

'Sorry, sergeant,' says the man, 'it slipped out of my fingers.'

'Hold tighter next time,' says Idra. 'Now move.'

They run through the covering smoke, and reach the factorum alive, to be greeted by a line of corpses.

They enter through the loading dock, a two hundred-yard stretch of roll-down gates, each one a hundred feet tall and seventy wide, several of them open. As she enters, Idra feels a pang of homesickness. The roof shuts out the grey Tovogan light. Inside, you could almost believe you were on Vostroya.

A single hall, wide enough to make the walls hard to see, stretching into the factorum's dark depths. Two parallel conveyor belts, lines of connected steel slabs, each capable of carrying a Leman Russ tank. Above them, steel gantries stretch into the gloom, pierced by the occasional window set in the ceiling. The factorum smells of scorched iron, oil fumes and welding gear. But it is eerily silent.

The floor is uneven, craters blasted into it. It is littered with debris, smashed, fallen gantries, overturned tool cabinets, vast chunks of rockcrete. The conveyors stand immobile, a single Medusa heavy artillery tank blocking the right dismount ramp. It lacks armour on the left side, and its heavy siege gun is missing the stabiliser, but shells the size of four men stand at attention in its internal storage space. Unfinished, as if the siege gun went through the production line in the middle of a shift change.

Or a battle.

The rockcrete floor by the loading dock holds a line of Firstborn corpses. The dead are waiting for burning, arms crossed over their bandoliers, hands tied together with a single string of wire, holding the Firstborn souls safe until the cremation frees them. Idra stretches to attention, raises her hand to salute the fallen.

A las-blast flashes past her shoulder, gouging a shining rent in the gate. Motion catches her eye. The shadows by the assembly line crawl with rebel soldiers.

'Cover fire!' she yells, yanking her lasgun off her back. She fires wildly in the direction of the rebels, then breaks right. 'First company, with me.'

She ducks into the lee of a massive chunk of rockcrete, a handful of Firstborn squeezing in with her. Behind her, lasgun fire drowns out the shouts of soldiers. The factorum lights up with their blasts.

From the assembly line, from the gantries, from the disabled Medusa, seemingly from thin air, an answering volley materialises.

A Firstborn by Idra's side cries out and falls. She pulls him deeper into cover, looking over the ground.

They're trapped by the loading docks, the rebels holding a solid line by the assembly line. If they stay here, the rebels will be able to pick them off at leisure, or flank them. By chance Idra's score of men have made it almost halfway to the assembly line. Idra's face twists into a wry grin despite herself. The Emperor's Luck.

'Valeriak,' Idra tells the corporal by her side, 'take five men and rush right. Set up a firing position and give us some cover fire.'

The man nods and races off. Her remaining men cover his team with concentrated fire. Even here, outnumbered and outgunned, their training shines through. Pride fills Idra. There are no better urban soldiers than the Firstborn. She shouts towards the open gates, waves her arms until Lokhov notices.

'Uncle!' she shouts. 'Covering fire towards the assembly line.'

Idra draws her power sword, not waiting for his reply. Speed and firepower. Enough of one will give you more of the other. The sword's power field flickers blue.

'Forward,' she screams. 'We stop, we die.'

Her men rush forwards into the half-open floor, dodging broken spars, jumping slabs of plate and pieces of fallen rockcrete. The assembly line is impossibly far, a hundred steps away, a thousand, a million.

Idra's boots pound the rockcrete, her pulse pounds in her ears. All she can hear is her pulse, all she can see are the flashes of lasgun blasts.

Forwards, always forwards. Speed and firepower. To stop is to die.

From her right, a brace of las-blasts slam into the rebel positions by the assembly line. Ahead looms the giant slope of the dismount ramp. Beside it, a pair of tool cabinets make an improvised shield. A round, grey rebel helmet pops up over the top. The man's eyes grow wide with surprise, his arms yank a lasgun upwards.

Five steps. Two. One.

Idra slaps the rebel's lasgun with her sword's whirling blue power field. It cuts the barrel, shearing it halfway through. The man fires. Idra ducks.

A las-blast illuminates them, exploding the broken barrel, sending flaming shrapnel outwards. The man screams. Idra stabs her sword through the tool cabinets and the scream fades to a gurgle.

A handful of Firstborn have made it to the assembly line. The hall behind them is littered with prone shapes, some firing, some crawling, some still. By the gate, a clot of

Firstborn is firing volleys upwards, trying to clear the gantries of rebel snipers. But Idra's squad has penetrated the rebel defensive perimeter.

'To me!' she yells, waving her sword. The blue power field trails a line of sparks in the air as it sheds droplets of molten tool cabinet.

The closest Firstborn converge on her. Five, eight, ten. The last one is Private Ninov, the not-acting corporal. He's breathing hard.

'Orders, sir?' he says.

'Yes,' says Idra. 'Don't die.'

They charge.

Grenade. Wait. Explosion. Charge. The ram of sword against steel, against armour, against flesh. Over and over again.

Around them, flashes from other parts of the battle. A man falls screaming from the gantries above. An errant rocket explodes deep inside the factorum.

Idra rushes, cuts, thrusts. Her squad becomes a sickle of destruction, running along their line, flanking it with every step. Through the litter on the factorum floor, a small group of Firstborn led by Sergeant Lokhov joins her team. She splits half of them off to cover their rear, keeps Lokhov with her, orders them on.

A Firstborn falls, clutching his leg. Another stumbles, collapses into a heap. Eight left, seven, six. Idra's small force clears one side of the assembly line, rushes across the top, boots clanging on the metal plates of the conveyor belt. Speed and firepower.

A grenade explodes nearby. Sergeant Lokhov slips. Idra grabs him, pulls him into the cover of a half-assembled tank. Five Firstborn left.

They reload their lasguns, charge to the edge of the belt, empty their power packs into the crouching rebels on the other side, then jump. One of her men stumbles, moans, grabs at a leg twisted the wrong way. Idra leaves him in cover, firing upwards, then charges. They've cleared half the circle of rebel defences.

Suddenly a shout goes up, and the rebels start running, a flood of men abandoning their positions, throwing down weapons, dragging away wounded. A few reach Idra, spy the flickering blue of her sword, the motion of red coats behind her, and raise their arms into the air.

'Please,' they say.

Idra jerks her chin, ordering one of her remaining troops to lead the prisoners to the gate. Then she turns, and goes looking for her casualties.

Four wounded, two dead. Kulin, from Tharkov Hive, and Martinov, a shiny recruit that came in on the same transport as Idra.

Lokhov is alive, and only lightly wounded.

'If you say the Emperor's Luck, I'll tan your hide, officer or no,' he says.

'Nadalya's Grace then, uncle,' Idra says.

Lokhov glares at her.

'I've got a medic digging around in my behind,' Lokhov says.

'Shall I order him to leave the shrapnel be?' Idra asks. 'It might make sitting an interesting experience, though.'

She tries to put a sting in her voice, but the edges of her mouth keep jumping upwards. She wants to laugh, to dance, to shake and to cry. Around her, each Firstborn reacts to the battle in their own way. Some sit, staring at nothing. Others weep over the bodies of fallen friends. A few share a flask;

someone sings, a low, haunting melody, a story of love lost and promises forgotten. Idra moves among them, offering a word here, a silent hand on the shoulder there, watching each manage in their own way. Each is alive, and that is all that matters for now. She is almost surprised to see Ninov amongst them.

He's sitting with his back against the conveyor foundation, his head lowered. As Idra walks up to him, she sees his hands shaking. He tries to hide them, shoving them into his armpits. Idra squats by his side, hands him a half-drunk cup of hot ohx somebody's handed her.

'Everyone's afraid,' she starts, and falters. What should she tell this stranger? He can't be that much younger than her, yet there is a gap of experience between them. Idra looks into his friendly, trusting face, and wonders if she was ever so open. Maybe, before her father tried to make a warrior out of her. Succeeded in making a warrior out of her.

'Lieutenant.' Captain Suvarin steps up to her side. 'The colonel wishes to see you.'

Gurlov doesn't look happy. A command post is taking shape behind a wall of broken junk, steel spars welded to overturned cabinets and slabs of discarded armour. An ad hoc bunker, in the middle of the factorum, braced by the broken Medusa.

The Medusa's engine is rumbling, one of the 86th's enginseers prodding the generator's machine-spirit to life with one of his serpentine holy tools, Dalsik exploring the tank's vox. Petro-chem stink covers the smell of scorched steel and spilled blood. The line of corpses by the gate is longer than before.

'Sir,' says Idra.

Gurlov grimaces in pain. He's got a scorch mark on his bionic arm, the uniform above it burnt away. The staff company medic is removing drops of slag from his cheek. Parts of the arm, blasted into his skin.

'Congratulations on your resolute charge, lieutenant,' says Gurlov. 'I would like you to know that I will write it up in my report. Now, your braid, please.'

'Sir?'

Gurlov taps the Nadalya's knot of his own braid, heavy with his officer's aquila.

'You are demoted, private.'

Idra blinks. The breath huffs out of her, as if she'd been punched. Her throat constricts, her nostrils flare, her fists clench. No Idrov has been demoted, ever. Killed, yes. Maimed, sometimes. Demoted? Never.

'Why?' she says.

'Orders, private.' Gurlov purses his mouth, as if he's eaten something distasteful. Then he nods towards the clumps of Firstborn, lasguns at the ready, in cover by the edges of the heavy conveyor belts. 'I note that Private Ninov is not among our guards,' he says.

Insubordination. Demotion.

'Oh,' says Idra.

Emperor's own Luck, indeed.

'You're our commander, sir!' Wisniak spits. 'I'm not going to fight for that desk warrior!' Around him, the men of the 86th nod.

'You will fight,' says Idra, 'because that is what the Emperor requires of you, what humanity requires of you, what Vostroya requires of you, and what I require of you – and by Saint Nadalya's Mercy, you will do your duty.'

The spot on her shoulder where her officer's braid hung feels empty. She resists an impulse to touch it. The cloth is cleaner there, more red, as if a phantom braid still swings from invisible hooks.

'Sir, it isn't fair!' says Wisniak.

'Nobody said war was going to be fair,' says Idra. She hates how reasonable she sounds. Like a training platoon teacher explaining things to her wards, when what she wants to do is scream and curse and complain. 'Your commander is Captain Suvarin, and you will follow his orders.'

At least that is good. Suvarin seems a competent officer. The troops don't seem convinced.

'By the Throne,' Idra roars. 'Are you Firstborn or are you traitors? Make up your minds, and either fight or walk across the line, because I will have no rebels in my unit!'

They spit and curse, but in the end, they grip their lasguns and form up for battle, every one of them. They are Firstborn, and well trained.

But it still hurts to see them follow someone else.

'There is at least a regiment of Tovogan forces in the factorum,' says Gurlov. 'Captain Kadarov estimates that at least four full companies are holding him pinned by the void shield generators.'

Idra is present at the gathering of officers. Not as a partner, but as Lokhov's aide. A message runner. The guard posts around the command Medusa are being fortified, Firstborn cutting away parts of the assembly line using melta bombs and plasma-cutters. The lights from the explosions paint the hall in blue and orange. The officers squint each time, but refuse to crouch in the cover of the Medusa. Gurlov stands straight, and so do they. Stupid pride.

If only Idra's heart wasn't as full of it. Being a message runner hurts, but being barred from the officer's meeting would hurt more. At least Gurlov tolerates her presence, even though the excuse is thin.

'Our orders are to relieve Kadarov, and throw out the rebels before they can restart the factorum.'

'Sir,' injects Gurlov's major, Bulwa, 'what about reinforcements?'

'Negative,' says Gurlov. 'The 992nd is bogged down in clearing the Tovogan traitors out of Rivanon Gorge. The 569th got ambushed and mauled. General staff is moving the 1055th Heavy Artillery Regiment closer. Should we fail, they will bombard the factorum, reducing it to rubble.'

A murmur passes like wind through the Firstborn ranks. To destroy such technology, even if it's Tovogan. It's almost sacrilege. Death comes to all men, but technology remains. It is what binds the generations together, what carries the Vostroyan traditions, the reason Firstborn collect the weapons of the fallen – to pass them on to further generations of warriors. Tradition. Faith. Duty. Those are strong words.

'You understand, gentlemen,' says Gurlov. 'Relieving Kadarov is more than our orders, it is our duty in the eyes of the Emperor.'

'Could we reach him through the bunkers?' says Bulwa, nodding towards the hatch bolted to the floor beside the Medusa. 'Our scouts report that the pathways beneath the factorum seem weakly defended, or even abandoned.'

'Perhaps the traitors are unaware of the extent of the tunnel system?' says Suvarin. 'It could work to our advantage.'

'It won't,' says Gurlov. 'Kadarov is pinned by the void shield generators on the upper levels, above the main magazine. If we start a firefight in the ammunition storage, we will blow up the factorum.'

His bionic leg sparks, twitching, the motion passing through his entire body, growing ever more violent, until he manages to force it away. Only the corners of his mouth keep quivering. His officers look away, impassively, hiding whatever they may be thinking. Idra forces away an urge to ask, to intervene in the conversation, focusing on her breath. In, out, in, out. What does this man have, that good men will follow him?

'We lack force,' says Gurlov. 'Nor do we have the luxury of outside support. Thus we need to substitute speed and surprise for men and firepower.'

He gives each officer a look. For a moment, his eyes linger on Idra, before moving on.

'We will take a small relief force of our best into the gantries, as close to the roof as possible. Our main force will launch a diversionary attack along the floor, letting the relief force speed by. Relief force reaches the void shield generators and attacks the traitor positions in concert with Kadarov. Together they break out, spreading to the side walls and flanking the Tovogans, while we keep as much of their forces tied up here as possible.'

Idra has to admit that the man is inspiring. It is a daring move, more out of the stories of Saint Nadalya's vengeance than the *Tactica*. From everything she's seen of Gurlov, and his cautious adherence to standard doctrine, this is surprising. It's high risk, but if it succeeds, the rebels will be broken.

But there are a lot of them, even though the ones the 86th encountered were not as highly trained nor as combat ready as the Firstborn. The plan is like shoving a stick into a nest of blackwasps in the hopes of spearing the queen. You'd better have a very long stick, and be prepared to run. But the Firstborn have nowhere to run. The holding squad outside the auxiliary gate reports rebel movements across the killing grounds around the abandoned barracks. But still, it is the kind of mission where reputations and fortunes are made. Where privates are promoted to officers. Or ex-lieutenants are reinstated. There is a chance.

'It is a dangerous mission,' says Gurlov. 'I will lead the strike force myself.'

Gurlov hand picks the troops, taking two full squads of his own. From the 86th, he takes Wisniak, the head sniper, an assault squad and both the remaining heavy weapons teams, leaving the regiment a light company without scouts.

He doesn't take Idra. She walks by his side while he decides, shadowing Lokhov and Gurlov's senior officers. They don't seem very happy at being left behind either.

'Sir!' she says to Captain Suvarin. 'I'd like to volunteer.'

'Noted,' replies Suvarin, without looking at her, continuing to walk away from Gurlov and the relief force.

'Sir!'

'Noted, private,' says Suvarin. He despatches the last guard changes to their positions. Idra is about to go, too, to lead the right flank ground assault squad.

The diversion assault squad.

'I can do a good job up there,' she says, nodding at the gantries. The Firstborn have been ordered to avoid pointing, in case the Tovogans have spotters nearby.

'I'm sure you would,' says Suvarin, 'but the colonel has ordered you to remain behind.'

'He hasn't,' Idra blurts. 'I mean, sir, he didn't order me to do anything at all.'

'Then you are supposed to stay behind,' says Suvarin. He puts up a hand, blocking Idra from speaking further.

'Private Idra,' he says. 'In my years with the colonel, I have never known him to do anything without cause, nor without thought.'

'Including having his entire regiment flogged, sir?' The words leave Idra's mouth before she can stop them. Suvarin is not one of her troops. He is Gurlov's, and Gurlov hates rumours.

'Ah, so it comes down to that.' Suvarin falls silent, ticking off the squad dispositions on his hastily scribbled map. The Firstborn's improvised defensive positions are crammed with the forward elements, the diversionary squads are ready. All except Idra's. At least she's been given that much, a private commanding other privates. Suvarin glances down at her. His eyes are the grey of a Vostroyan sky, cold and deadly.

'Yes, the colonel ordered the flogging of his entire regiment,' Suvarin says. 'Entire regiment, private. Including himself.'

'What?'

'The regiment failed to execute its orders. The reasons were not important. The penalty for misconduct under fire is flogging. It's in the *Tactica*.'

Idra's mouth opens, then closes, no sound emerging.

'That's–' she finally begins, but stops herself in time.

'Insane?' says Suvarin.

'A private would not say such a thing about her commanding officer,' Idra says.

Suvarin gives a tight, mirthless smile, almost hidden by the throat-mounted aquila raised on his armour.

'Or to her commanding officer,' he says.

'Sir!'

'How old are you, private?' asks Suvarin.

'Twenty-two.'

'Well, the colonel is sixty-eight. He fought at Pulveron. He's seen first-hand the treason and corruption that comes out of disregarding orders. So have the rest of us that chose to follow him into exile.'

'Exile, sir?'

'Exile,' says Suvarin, then raises his hand to the vox-bead in his ear. Idra turns off her own beeping alarm. 'But that is a story for another time. It's time to attack.'

Every time Idra has charged in battle, it's come about owing to momentum and position, by the simple fact that charging was less likely to get her men killed.

Now she prepares for it, studies the flat rockcrete floor ahead through a view-slit in the barricades, plans where to run, which obstacles to keep between her squad and the Tovogans waiting in the factorum's murky depths. She can hear them moving, the occasional clank of metal on metal, or the muted echo of a voice.

There's precious little light. None of the glow-globes work, and the factorum's roof is mostly intact, blocking the grey Tovogan sky. At least there will be no artillery barrage. The roof would stop it. Before it collapsed and buried everyone inside.

'Ready?' Idra asks her troopers. There are ten of them again, and only four from the 86th. But all of them are close combat specialists, lethal in their own ways. Four of them carry chainswords, another a hand-flamer, his pack stuffed with spare fuel bottles. The remaining Firstborn wield long, double-edged sword-bayonets atop their lasguns. A specialty of Tharkov Hive, the blades turn their guns into spears, equally deadly at long and close range. Idra's power sword makes up the eleventh position.

Eleven, a good, lucky number. The number of Saint Nadalya's Deeds, and the number of her companions.

'*Ready,*' comes Sergeant Dalsik's clear voice in their vox-beads.

'*Mark one.*' A barrage of mortar bombs thuds from static tubes, flying into the depths of the factorum.

'*Mark two.*' The mortar bombs detonate, flashes of light from deep inside the darkness.

'*Mark three.*' The Firstborn's positions light up with lascannon and plasma gun blasts, streaking light into suspected rebel positions, into the gantries above them, into the walls, into the roof, into the floor itself. Idra forces her eyes shut, blinking away after-images.

'*Advance!*' comes Dalsik's voice. Idra rushes from her position, rounds the armour plate that keeps it secure. Behind her, a hundred lasguns add their fire to the cannons and plasma streaking into the factory, a concentrated volley of heat scorching her skin and making the air hard to breathe.

She charges across the fifty yards to the nearest pile of debris, a shattered gantry that has crashed into a motorised loading crane, upending both. Her troops jump the jumble of pipes, shouting war cries and curses.

The area is empty, but there is motion behind another pile, twenty yards further into the factory. Idra points at it, her sword's blue power field turning the gesture into a visible line.

'Fire,' she says, and half her squad go down on a knee, levelling their lasguns. The first volley illuminates the rubble, and the pair of Tovogans behind it. The second flings a rebel backwards. By the third, Idra and her men are at the barricade, tearing into it with their hands and swords, climbing, swinging at the poor sod behind it.

The rebel dies without firing a single shot, his lasgun clattering to the ground. Idra hurdles the obstacle, and rolls into a crossfire from two Tovogan positions.

The battle has truly begun.

They fight, they kill, they die. The Tovogans are unprepared for the onslaught, a mere screen of men, a few platoons at most. Idra's squad overruns another two-man position without losses, charges the third, only to find it abandoned, the rebels running into the cover of the darkened main hall.

Idra is past the loading docks. The dim factorum stretches before her, flashes and screams coming from the assault squads on the other side of the seven-foot-high assembly line. Idra orders her men deeper into the building, running into a rebel half-platoon led by an officer with a chainsword. Both sides are equally surprised, but Idra recovers quicker. She swings, and the officer barely parries, Idra's power sword stripping the teeth from his whirring chain.

A Firstborn chainsword flashes beneath her guard, tearing into the officer's arm and ripping it off at the elbow. The man falls with a high-pitched wail. It is drowned out by Idra's power sword chopping into the Tovogan behind. A series of lasgun shots downs another, and sends the rest running. The Firstborn move deeper.

Idra's squad is fired upon from a position among the shadowy, half-built tanks on the conveyor belt. She dives into a darkened maintenance tunnel, emerges on the other side of the conveyor, charges the position from behind. Her men follow her, firing salvos into the unprotected backs of rebel defensive positions thrown up between the two conveyors.

It is easy, too easy. Where are the Tovogans that almost

threw them from the factorum? Where are the rebel assault companies?

Idra's vox-bead squawks, snippets of speech emerging. The words are clipped, lasgun fire and screams making them almost unintelligible.

'Sir, sir!' The heavy drawl is unmistakably Wisniak's. 'Man down!'

Around Idra, everything is quiet. At the end of the factorum, by the auxiliary gate they entered through, the only motion is the red of Firstborn uniforms. On her other side, in the deep gloom, flashes of lasgun fire and melta explosions light up the gantries. Too far to see clearly with the naked eye, almost too far for the vox-beads. Yet it's clear that the battle is intense.

Her men are fighting there, and even if they're not her men any longer, they're Firstborn. Firstborn do not abandon each other, no matter what their orders say.

'Squad, to me,' Idra says. Her men jog up, forming into an arrow shape.

'Sir?' says one of the gunners, a man from her 86th. Idra points to the flashes.

'See those?'

The men nod.

'We climb,' says Idra, pointing to the gantries. 'And then we charge. Anyone disagree?'

Nobody does.

From one hundred and fifty yards above the factorum floor, the half-finished Leman Russ tanks on the immobile assembly line look like oversized toys from a training simulation. Or a shooting gallery. The last man of Idra's squad hauls himself up, his breath wheezing from a face red and sweaty with exertion.

They run across gantries littered with chunks of rockcrete and broken-loose retainer bolts. Every step makes the heavy iron girders sway, causing Idra's stomach to clench, her heart to flutter. They jump a perfectly round hole in the gantry's steel-mesh flooring, still faintly glowing from the heat of a melta bomb. Every step takes them closer to the battle.

Twice they fight, once overrunning a four-man scout detail, then attacking a pair of heavy bolters from behind. The sounds of the battle raging ahead drowns out their steps, giving them cover. They reach the factorum's main support arch, a massive rockcrete edifice thick as three Chimeras set side by side, and emerge into the factorum's central chamber.

Ten cold rockcrete furnaces, each large enough to melt an entire Warhound Scout Titan in a single go, line the hall. Half-formed Leman Russ chassis and huge swaths of uncut armour plates hang from hooks the size of a grown man. Chains, with links thick as Idra's torso, connect the furnaces and workstations. An entire Leman Russ turret hangs suspended from one, swinging slowly. At the very top of two connected furnaces, the Firstborn of Gurlov's strike group are holed up.

They're hunkered down behind improvised barricades and hastily erected blast shelters. Around them, above them, even from the insides of the cold furnaces, Tovogan rebels fire on the Firstborn's positions. Three hundred, four hundred, five hundred, it is impossible to estimate the amount of rebels.

Across the hall, by the raised dais several hundred yards across, rages another battle. Captain Kadarov's positions, near the void shield generators.

This is not a lone traitor regiment; this is two, three, maybe four.

'Sir,' whispers a voice in Idra's ear. 'What shall we do?'

Her troops huddle around her, in the cover of a pile of severed chain. Idra's rescue force is pitifully small. A single well-placed rocket could kill them all.

She follows the patterns of the fire, identifies enemy positions. There, a lasgun platoon; there a plasma gun emplacement. Slowly, a puzzle starts to emerge.

The Tovogan commander is incompetent. Or, more likely, there are several commanders, unable or unwilling to coordinate their forces.

'There,' Idra points, 'see the line between the first furnace and that lascannon position? The flow channel for the metal to the plate moulds?'

'Sir?' says the Firstborn. Idra realises he's one of Gurlov's soldiers, calling her sir. It's a bitter-sweet realisation.

'There is no one holding that part. No las-blasts coming from there. Silence the cannon and we have a clear run to the second furnace.'

'But, sir,' says the trooper, 'the colonel is at the third furnace.' Idra nods.

'We drop down into the second furnace,' she says. 'There are slag tunnels between the furnaces. Standard pattern. We crawl into the second, emerge at the third. Ambush the Tovogans inside. Then all we've got to do is convince your colonel to run.'

The trooper looks like she's slapped him.

'The colonel would never do that, sir,' he says.

Idra gives him a mirthless smile.

'I never said it was going to be easy,' she replies.

The lascannon falls, the loader and spotter dying before the gunner even realises anything is amiss. The flow channel is black with encrusted steel. It tears at their hands and knees as they scuttle up, keeping as far down as possible to avoid detection.

A funnel of solidified slag greets them inside the oven. Most of it has drained through the tunnels. Giant outflow vents, really. The oven is still hot, still full of fumes, but the Firstborn are used to worse. They pull out their gas masks, calibrated for the poisonous ash wastes of Vostroya. The stink of slag and steel doesn't even strain their filters.

The masks limit their field of view, and each breath is still hard and hot, like running in a bakery kiln. Still, they make it into the slag tunnel, crawl, emerge in the third furnace.

There are Tovogans there, a lasgun squad spread around the edges, aiming upwards. They don't notice Idra's men until it's too late. None of them make it out of the furnace alive.

Idra thumbs off her power sword, presses her vox-bead. Nobody replies to her queries. They're still firing, up there. Maybe it is the furnace, blocking the vox signal.

Idra licks her lips inside her gas mask. She'll have to get their attention. From a spot where they expect Tovogans.

Emperor's Luck indeed.

'Colonel!' she yells upwards. The gas mask muffles her voice. No one replies through her vox-bead. Idra picks up her lasgun and fires a blast into the edge of the furnace's open top, well below the edge.

A second later, a small, dark object sails over the edge.

'Grenade,' Idra yells, her men scattering to the sides. The grenade bounces once, then falls down into the tunnel. The explosion sends up a cloud of slag.

'Colonel Gurlov,' Idra yells. 'Wisniak! By the Throne, anyone up there?'

A flash of light from the top, a mirror on a stick. It withdraws, and a Firstborn face looks down. A moment of shouting later, a chain-link ladder drops into the furnace.

'Nadalya's Mercy, sir, are we glad to see you!' The Firstborn is one of Idra's, one of the 86th's veterans. 'And sorry about the grenade, sir.' He gives her a guilty look. Idra claps him on the shoulder, and he seems to relax.

Their position is cramped, a child's blanket fort made out of broken girders and slabs of unpainted tank armour.

'Where's Gurlov?' she says, and the man points to the other furnace.

'Got ourselves surrounded,' he says, needlessly, but Idra is already pressing her vox-bead, calling for Gurlov.

'How many men have you brought?' Gurlov asks.

'Ten,' Idra says. There's a pause.

'That's all?' says Gurlov.

'That's all I've got,' says Idra. 'Sir, you've got to order the holding force to withdraw.'

Another pause. A lascannon drills a hole in the barrier across the furnace, melting the armour plate stapled there. It doesn't manage to melt the one behind it, and the follow-up shots all hit in different spots.

'Our orders are to relieve Captain Kadarov,' says Gurlov. *'With your men–'*

'Sir!' Idra interrupts. 'There are four rebel regiments here. We've got less than a platoon.'

Gurlov hesitates.

'Our orders–'

A gigantic explosion interrupts him, the flash almost blinding Idra. The Leman Russ turret that swung from the chain sits on a furnace across the floor. Its battle cannon is smoking. Gurlov's position has been breached.

Smoke flows across the covered walkway to the other

furnace. Screams sound over the vox-beads. Gurlov's position is torn open, a gigantic hole blown in one side. Dead and wounded Firstborn litter the furnace top.

Las-blasts crack across the covered walkway between the furnaces. Idra can hear her heart pounding in her ears. Her knees shake. But Firstborn do not abandon each other.

Idra rushes across, las-blasts bouncing off the girders and thin sheets around her. Grabs a screaming man, hoists him over her shoulders; grabs another by the collar and starts dragging. Bolter shots and lasgun beams crack into the inside of the position. The barricade has become a deathtrap.

Men flow in behind Idra, grabbing wounded and weapons. The weapons are as important as the men, heirlooms from past campaigns. By the time Idra is back in the first position, the other furnace is cracking with las-blast hits. She hands off her Firstborn to the medic. Only then does she notice that her arm hangs loose, the plascrete armour melted on her shoulder. The pain hits her, makes her gasp. She pushes it away. Later, there will be time for hurt later.

'Where's the colonel?' she asks. A man points to a prone shape.

Colonel Gurlov. He's lost his shako. Blood covers his bald scalp. He's unconscious, but his bionic leg keeps spasming.

'Who's in command?' says Idra.

'You are, sir,' comes Wisniak's drawl.

'What about Captain Kadarov?'

Wisniak jerks his chin towards a slim gun port in the barricade. Flames and smoke cover the Firstborn positions around the void shield generators. Tovogan rebels crawl among them. No more las-blasts illuminate that part of the factorum. Kadarov's position is overrun, his force gone.

'Orders, sir?' says Wisniak.

A platoon charging four regiments to recover the corpses of Kadarov's fallen? That's suicide, no matter what Gurlov would believe. A waste of the Emperor's troops. For Idra, there is only a single possible order.

'Climb down,' she says, pointing to the chain-link ladder into the furnace. 'Then withdraw.'

Gurlov lives. He's sitting, propped up behind the armoured barricades by the Medusa near the loading docks, a big bandage swathing his head. A dark red spot is slowly growing on it. The bandage is bleeding through.

The Firstborn engineers have blown off the girders in the assembly hall's roof. They lie like a giant's discarded crutches, blocking parts of the approach vectors. The remaining openings are crammed with barricades, manned by Firstborn. So are the tunnels beneath the factorum floor. The line of corpses by the gate is longer, the pile of Vostroyan weapons larger.

The Tovogans have launched probing attacks on the Firstborn positions, throwing companies forwards to claim yet another pile of rubble. Each time the Tovogans lose men. Each time they manage to come closer. It's only a matter of time before they reach good jumping-off positions. After that, they'll throw their entire might at the Firstborn.

Or starve them out. The Tovogans have the time. Minutes after Idra's force managed to get back to the loading hall, the factorum's void shields flickered to life. There will be no reinforcements, no surprises, no outside help. The shields are powerful. It would require days of bombardment from a heavy siege regiment to bring them down, and no such regiment is available.

Gurlov clears his throat. His voice is no longer the confident rumble Idra remembers from their first talk. At least he isn't objecting to Idra being present at the staff meeting.

'Our orders,' he says, 'are to retake the factorum to prevent the traitors from restarting the production lines. Should we fail to do so, general staff has ordered us to destroy the factorum.'

A murmur passes amongst the Firstborn. A few look roofwards, glancing around the gigantic hall.

Everything they've done so far has been repairable. To obliterate such technology completely, it would almost be sacrilege.

'Sir,' says Captain Suvarin. 'Could we retake the factorum?'

Gurlov leans back, closes his eyes. To Idra's eyes, he looks tired, a wounded, old veteran struggling to follow orders.

'Is there a chance to detonate the magazine?' asks Suvarin. 'Could we push our way through to Kadarov's old positions?'

For a moment, Gurlov remains silent. Then he shakes his head.

'No, captain,' he says. 'There is no chance.'

In that moment, both of Gurlov's officers deflate. His aide looks astonished. The assault trooper who followed Idra, and carried the colonel back, makes the sign of the aquila.

They all look lost.

Sergeant Dalsik sticks his head out the Medusa's open side hatch.

'Colonel Gurlov, sir,' he says. 'Movement between the conveyor lines.'

Gurlov nods tiredly.

'Another probing attack,' he says. 'Private Idra, can you handle it?'

'Sir,' Dalsik interrupts. 'Sniper Wisniak says there are more of them than blackwasps in an ohx pot. And tanks, too.'

* * *

The attack begins with a barrage from five Leman Russ battle cannons. The rebels have managed to reactivate parts of the assembly line at least. The cannons boom, shells scream in, shattering Firstborn positions on the front. Firstborn withdraw, to backup positions, shielded from the tanks' fire.

Yet the Tovogans are careful. Instead of launching an all-out assault, they keep probing, withdrawing into cover as the Firstborn return fire.

'Colonel, sir,' shouts Suvarin. 'We need to relocate the command post.' He points to the Medusa's half-armoured magazine. Idra agrees with his assessment. The shells are immensely powerful. Unprotected, they are easy to detonate. One shot from a battle cannon, and the entire Firstborn command will be wiped out. They should roll them away, maybe towards the Tovogans, if they can find a smooth part of floor.

'Nadalya's Grace,' says Idra. 'Sir, we can destroy the factorum.'

It is Suvarin who answers her, raising an eyebrow.

'We couldn't blast our way out of the tunnels to relieve Captain Kadarov,' she says. 'But this time we don't need to relieve him, just blow up the magazine.' Idra slaps the siege gun shell. 'With this.'

'We won't be able to get a crane into the tunnels,' says Suvarin.

'We won't need to,' says Idra. 'We'll roll it.'

Suvarin hesitates.

'Sir,' he says, but Gurlov is already on his feet, his eyes aglow.

'By the Throne,' he says. 'You have a point, lieutenant.'

Neither Idra nor Suvarin correct the rank.

They lower the shell through the hatch, twenty men with pulleys working while the remaining Firstborn hold off the

Tovogan attacks. Once down, the shell tips almost of its own volition.

In the hall, the Firstborn begin a fighting retreat. The holding forces in the tunnels attack, sweeping a few surprised Tovogans aside.

Side tunnels branch off the main route, to storage chambers, to generator halls, to bunkers and air-raid shelters. An entire division could hole up down here.

But the Firstborn aren't interested in holing up. They roll the shell, blasting doors wider, rigging traps in side tunnels. Fighting an ever-stiffening rebel opposition.

Far behind them, a powerful explosion rocks the tunnels. The Tovogans have found the rigged entrance hatch, detonating a brace of melta bombs and the remaining shells in the Medusa's magazine. A fitting funeral pyre for the Firstborn dead.

Major Bulwa is killed with the rearguard. Suvarin is wounded leading a charge against a Tovogan platoon holding a tunnel intersection. Idra orders him taken back to a side bunker, one that the Firstborn haven't booby-trapped. This is their fallback position, the one that will save them from the blast of the magazine. If they survive. Of the officers, only Gurlov and Idra remain in the vanguard, having left Suvarin commanding the rear action.

The tunnel's grey walls are shot traps, sending shrapnel and bolts ricocheting forwards. The Firstborn vanguard is somewhere beneath the furnaces, when Gurlov is hit.

A las-blast shatters his bionic leg. Idra's sniper takes out the Tovogan, but their progress is halted. The Tovogans are sending down more troops, trying to clog the tunnels from all sides.

'Have him taken back to the bunker,' Idra orders one of Gurlov's Guardsmen.

'Wait,' says Gurlov. 'I can still fight.'

His eyes are sharp, and the plasma pistol in his hand is steady. The Firstborn are exchanging las-fire with the Tovogans, blasts going past, over and around Idra.

'We'll need to charge,' says Idra. 'One more push to get close to the magazine.'

Gurlov looks up at her, an old, wounded veteran. Will he be given a command after this? Probably not. The factorum of Salomar is going to be destroyed, and someone will have to pay for it.

'Please?' he says.

Idra grabs him by the armoured collar, hauls him onto her back.

'You shoot,' she says, 'I'll run.'

They charge.

Around them, the Firstborn cry out and rush forwards in a red wave. The Tovogans fire one last volley, but the distance is short, and Idra's men near. A few Firstborn fall, the rest rush into the square intersection chamber beneath the magazine.

It is full of Tovogans, platoons of them, entering through the entrances on three of the room's four sides. Idra halts, Gurlov almost slipping from her back, and she grabs him, ducking back into the cover of the firing ports by the tunnel entrance. One of her Firstborn slams the heavy, steel door shut. Gurlov shoves his arm into the gun port, firing his plasma pistol. The replying volley lights the entire room and makes the blast door vibrate.

'There's too many of them,' says Idra. 'We'll need to detonate the shell here.' She waves for her troops to move the shell forwards. It clangs against the door. Two Firstborn have taken Gurlov's place, firing through the slim port as fast as their guns will reload. As soon as one lasgun pack is empty, another Firstborn sticks his gun into the port. A crude barrage, but it keeps the Tovogans away.

'Set the charges,' Idra calls, and a Firstborn ordnance expert rushes forwards. The middle of the door starts to glow with red heat. The Tovogans have got a lascannon or a plasma gun down into the tunnels.

'No time,' says Gurlov. 'Run, and I'll detonate it.'

He twists the dials on his plasma gun, setting it to overcharge.

'Sir,' says Idra, 'you are the ranking officer.'

Gurlov looks up at her, gives her a smile.

'I am a wounded, querulous old man,' he says. 'With a long history behind me and many enemies among my friends, and nothing to return to back home. This is my last command. We both know it. Let me end it in service to the Emperor.'

Idra pauses. Eyes him, a proud warrior, asking for a chance to die in service.

'Is that an order, sir?' she says.

'A request,' says Gurlov. 'Please.'

Idra salutes.

'Sir,' she says. 'Firstborn, back to the bunker!'

As the troops withdraw, Gurlov stretches out his hand. Idra clasps it. Something small tickles her palm.

'May you wear it in honour and service,' says Gurlov. 'Lieutenant.'

Idra opens her fist. There, rolled into a tight ball, lies her officer's braid.

She salutes again, and then she runs.

The Firstborn emerge from the tunnels. There is little smoke. Not enough is left of the factorum at Salomar to burn. Behind Idra, the bunker's buckled blast doors squeak as they slam closed for the last time.

The city itself is mostly spared, the void shields having contained enough of the explosion before they failed. On the horizon, a string of Firstborn Chimeras and Basilisks roll down into the Salomar valley. Reinforcements, days too late.

'Orders, sir?' says Idra.

'Nothing right now, lieutenant,' says Captain Suvarin. 'Although one request. I believe that I promised to tell you the story of Colonel Gurlov, and his exile. Would you like to hear it?'

'I'd be delighted to,' says Idra.

AT THE SIGN OF THE BRAZEN CLAW: PART 4

Guy Haley

Veteran Black Library author Guy Haley continues his story-within-a-story saga in the Age of Sigmar, as the aelven prince Maesa and other adventurers share stories in the tavern of The Brazen Claw during a fierce storm.

This time it is the turn of Hyshian sorcerer Pludu Quasque, who tells of how he came to leave his majestic Realm of Light and come to a backwater tavern in a desolate region of Shyish. It is a story of lost relics, the dangers of excessive pride and the machinations of nefarious skaven…

Prince Maesa and Shattercap have come to the hinter-
lands of Shyish in order to catch a Kharadron packet
ship through the Argent Gate to Ghur. Delayed by
stormy weather, they sit out the night at the Sign of
the Brazen Claw. As they wait, the travellers at the inn
swap stories. The first to speak was the innkeeper, Hor-
rin, who related the tale of how he came into his career.
Then Stonbrak the duardin told how his brother lost his
life because of a hasty contract. As the night wore on,
Prince Maesa took his turn to tell the story of how he
and Shattercap's association began. Now the eye of the
storm turns over the inn, and Pludu Quasque, last mem-
ber of the company, prepares himself to speak.

THE SORCERER'S TALE

The wind dropped to an irregular whispering. The sound of the storm now much diminished, many small noises crept out to be heard. Wood crackled in the fire. Beams sighed. The soft drip of Quasque's spilled wine was thunderously loud. Every scuff of movement from the travellers seemed amplified, and when Stonbrak the duardin scraped back his chair everyone but Maesa grimaced. Firelight danced over the common room, glinting from glassware and the magical amulets hung over the bar. Somewhere deeper in the inn, a clock chimed sixteen. The very middle of the night.

Shattercap leapt at the ringing. Maesa reached out absent-mindedly and patted the leaves on the spite's back, but his gaze was intent on the ragged Quasque. Maesa's pupils were black and deep, alight with soul sparks. Very few men could withstand their scrutiny for long, but Pludu Quasque looked at him dumbly, without fear, blinking like a sleepwalker suddenly awoken.

Stonbrak cleared his throat. 'You were going to tell us your story, lad,' he said gently. 'It's your turn.'

Quasque swallowed, a slow, heavy action that gave him a somewhat toad-like aspect. 'I was. My story. Yes,' he said.

'Go on then,' Horrin the innkeeper encouraged him.

'Yes,' Quasque said once more. He wiped his hands on his stained finery, and sat unsurely again, whereupon he took a deep, shuddering breath, and began.

'My name is Pludu Quasque,' he said, though they all knew this already. 'And I am from Hysh, the Realm of Light.'

Horrin raised an eyebrow. Quasque was pallid as any native of Shyish. Few dwellers in the Realm of Light were so pale.

'Though,' Quasque said quietly and hurriedly, 'I may not look it to you.' He patted at himself, almost as if he were checking he was still there, and smiled sadly. 'Once upon a time, my clothes shone with Hysh's light. My skin was golden brown, not this chalk you see now. I am filthy and poor, but I was rich, and respected.' He paused. 'And young. Very young.' His gaze remained downcast. 'We make such foolish errors when we are young, as Master Horrin's tale attests, but his youthful mistake gained him all this.' Quasque's frightened eyes swivelled about to take in the room. 'This inn, a foster son, a loving wife. My error brought me nothing but pain.' Anger hitherto hidden coloured his pasty cheeks. He looked up, shocked, as if he had been rebuked. The company waited silently for him to continue.

'I was born in Balshizzam, one of the Seven Cities upon the edges of the Brilliant Sea. You have never seen such a place, and never will. We of Hysh do not welcome visitors, and the empire of the Seven Cities is among the most secretive of all nations, for there we perform magic of such delicacy a stray thought can send all awry. You think Hysh rises and sets to light the realms by chance alone?' He pointed a grubby finger upwards. 'No!' Again, his anger showed itself. 'Since time began our peoples have tended the works of reality to ensure all is lit, from the swamps of Ghyran to the most wretched deserts of this benighted Realm of Death. The streets echo to the chanting of songs that have been sung unbroken since the realms came into being, whose words were taught to my ancestors by gods far older and more terrible than Sigmar and his pantheon.' As Quasque spoke, he calmed. A little regality stiffened his spine. 'I was noble once,' he said, directing a sharp glance at Maesa. 'The aelf is not the only one of good breeding. My lineage is as great as any prince's house, generations of wizard lords reaching back, back, through millennia of light...'

He trailed off. The wind sighed.

'That should have been enough for me, but no young man is content with what his family provides. The day I left for the Lyceum of Radiance to learn the higher arts, my father came to speak to me. He and I had argued much as my youth passed and my majority approached. All fathers and sons do. Young Barnabus here will fight with you soon enough,' Quasque said, gesturing at the boy cuddled into his foster-mother's side. She kissed his head.

'Not yet,' she said softly.

'It shall come,' Quasque said. 'His last years of childhood shall be a blight on your house, a shaking as great as this storm, and when it blows out, he shall be away, off on the path of manhood, leaving the shivered timbers of fond memories behind. That is childhood's curse.' He took a swift sip of wine. 'My father and I argued more than most. I, in my arrogance, would not listen to him, and he, filled with an elder's superiority, would not hearken to me. So it was we avoided each other until the day I left, he descending from his tower of mirrors only when I stood in the cab of my chariot, my rods of control grasped so.' He crossed his arms and held his fists upright. 'I stared ahead, over the glowing manes of my stallions. The horses were his gift to me, worth a fortune. I never thanked him.

'"My son," he said. "Remember you that the Wind of Hysh is the finest, most delicate of all the eight magics."

'"I know this," I said to him, curt as only a son can be to his father.

'"And that it can only be controlled with great concentration. True mastery takes many years."

'"This I know too." I wished he would go. Why could he not just glower from his high study as I set out. This is what I had envisaged – the noble son putting his unjust father's ire behind himself. The tears of the women of my house were shining in the constant light of our realm. I wore my finest make-up, black kohl about my eyes, my beard beautifully oiled and my hair concealed beneath a golden conical crown. The scene was perfect except for him. He embarrassed me.'

Quasque sighed. 'Embarrassment is worse than a sword cut to the young. Father would not relent. The day was getting on, I was late leaving being sluggishly out of bed. The heat of the Brilliant Sea was rising.

'"Know also that the Wind of Hysh cannot be manipulated by one man alone." He put his hand on the rail of my chariot. "Son, son. Look at me."

'I would rather have not, but I did, and the look on my father's face almost broke my youthful arrogance. How I wish it had.

'"No man is a fortress," he said. "You are young, sure of

yourself, but the way of our people is to work together. To sing the songs of dawning and of evening. We are of ancient stock, well blessed, and that comes with certain responsibilities. You must listen to your teachers. You do not know everything that you think you know."

'"I will make my own way, my own name," I said proudly. I was so sure of myself!

'"You will, but listen to me. You–"

'"I have heard enough!" I said. "Farewell, father." I set my face forward, and spoke the words to set my stallions in motion.

'The animals we have in Hysh are nothing like the beasts of lower realms. They are beautiful, made of magic as much as flesh. They are more glorious than the creatures of Azyr, even. My horses shone like suns, with skins of lemon light and manes of lustrous gold. Rados and Solio they were called. They leapt as swift as beams of light, pulling my chariot from its resting block. The wheels, also of pure light, ignited, and I roared from my home, out through the gates, down the hills of shining crystal and then straight out, over the Brilliant Sea, whose glories the hoofs of my horses trod as easily as solid ground.

'I did not look back.'

'I like not the talk of all this light. Tell me, Master Quasque, does the light burn the trees?' asked Shattercap.

'In Hysh, the trees are made of light,' said Quasque.

'But what of the moss, does it not dry?'

'The moss? Also suffused greatly with light,' said Quasque. 'For Hysh is the Realm of Light.'

Shattercap frowned. 'Does it not blind the birds?'

'No, master spite,' said Quasque. 'For their eyes shine more brightly than Hysh does in the sky here. Everything is light.'

'The ferns, the moths, the katydids, the bats, the owls, the blooming flowers,' chanted Shattercap, creeping forwards, 'the soil, the water and fish? Are they not scorched then by such dry brightnesses?'

'All these are made of light, in part or in totality,' Quasque said tersely. 'It is Hysh!'

Shattercap picked at his teeth with one of his long nails.

'I think I would not like this place. Too much light.'

'It would not like you,' Quasque said. He drank his wine in a single gulp, slammed down the cup and gestured for more.

Horrin poured, but as he did, he asked with a small laugh, 'You do have coin, sir?'

Quasque's agitation returned. Maesa spoke quietly.

'I will pay for his drinks, innkeeper, and I assure you I do have coin. Pray continue, mage of Hysh.'

'Perhaps you are a prince after all,' said Quasque. Horrin refilled his glass. 'I arrived at the Lyceum of Radiance full of pride, but my father was right. The study of light magic is hard. It is good we are blessed with longevity in my realm. I thought myself the better of any man. It soon appeared that was not so. I regarded myself above the choruses of acolytes, whose songs form the foundation for our magic, focusing Hysh's insubstantial but powerful winds so that greater mages might manipulate it. When tested on the lower stages of proficiency, I found the basic chants beyond me. During incantations my voice stood out for its roughness. I fumbled my words. I forgot the true forms. A humbler man than I would have recognised his shortcomings. He would have worked harder. He would have sought more teaching and forgiveness. Not I. I was much too arrogant for that. I placed the blame on everything and everyone. I blamed our servants. I blamed my classmates.

I blamed the hour of the day or the weather. The one person I did not blame, and who was most obviously at fault, was myself.

'Our master, Hepeknek, took me into his study to speak with me. He offered kindness, but my pride heard only rebukes, and he received the same disrespect as my father. I applied myself to the higher incantations, neglecting the lower. I reached too high, too fast, and so I always failed.

'But eventually, close to expulsion, I began to understand. I learned a little humility. I abandoned some of my pride. I redoubled my efforts.'

'Another short tale?' said Shattercap. 'Like beardy's? Is that it? You were bad, but then good, then all over?' He blew a raspberry. 'Boring!'

'My tale was not short, imp!' grumbled Stonbrak. 'You mistook the beginning for the whole. You heard the matter of my brother's betrayal not an hour gone by!' The duardin shook his head, his thick white beard rustling over his clothes with loud disapproval.

'You must learn to wait to hear the whole of a tale, Shattercap,' said Maesa.

The spite shrugged. 'I think I learn quicker than quack-quack here. I am small, but if I were to be as tall as he, then he would still be the bigger fool.'

Quasque looked ashamed. 'You are right. Pride trips a man. Envy ruins him totally.'

'Envy?' said Ninian.

'Yes,' said Quasque. 'There was another student at the Lyceum, whose name was Hamanan Kekwe. Were this a parable, he would be my exact opposite in humility and diligence. But he was not. Kekwe was as arrogant as I. He was also more talented. He had an easy way with people.

The acolytes liked him. Women liked him. The masters liked him. All my efforts were outdone by him.

'I hated him. I envied him.' Quasque's timidity was being washed away by the wine. Some of the youth from his story emerged from beneath the frayed man in the inn. 'Arrogance, pride, hatred. Three of the twelve forbidden urges, as we enumerate them in Hysh, but I had more than that! I was rash. I was thoughtless.' He shuddered, and hunkered over his goblet.

'Hyshians are by reputation aesthetes. But youth will behave as youth does wherever it blooms. We drank. We caroused.

'In the Lyceum's collection of magical wonders is a statue of a lesser god – Adembi, the weeping sage. In ages past, he gave counsel to the Septarchy and the Grand Luminance. Adembi would answer truthfully any question put to him in good faith, and would also verify oaths, his pronouncements making any promise binding on pain of ejection from the shining realm. Truth was his domain. But like many small gods, Adembi was limited in his power. Having lost his body in some celestial war I cannot recall, his spirit took refuge in the statue. Therefore, the statue was Adembi, and Adembi was the statue. There was great magic in its warm marble, but the greater part of it was invested in tears of Hyshian realmstone set into his carven cheek.'

'Now gems,' said Stonbrak, jabbing the stem of his pipe at Quasque. 'This is more my kind of tale, though as we've seen, one must be careful, if one is to profit from them.'

'A desire for profit was not the effect of looking upon them!' protested Quasque. 'These gems are the very essence of light. Hysh is poor in realmstone. Our magic is airy, and not given to crystallisation. What little exists is valued for its beauty and its power. Alas, it is coveted not just by our own people. Some centuries ago a sneak-thief of the ratkin dared the halls of the Lyceum to steal the gems. He was found out, and slain, but not before he had prised free one of Adembi's tears. He perished half in his rathole leading from the realm, struck down by spears of light. But when the clutched paw of his corpse was opened, the gem had gone. This story I knew to be true. The skeleton of the creature was kept mounted in a crystal case, and the hole he had gnawed into the skin of reality remains, half-closed, a puckered wound in the masonry of a minor hall, now locked and barred and set under constant guard in case the ratkin return.

'They say the Chaos-tainted soul of the thief took the gem with him when he died, down into whatever realm of death the ratkin call their own.

'Adembi's power was broken by the loss of his tear. He spoke no more. Only one oath would he verify, or so the stories said, and that was if anyone pledged to retrieve his tear and replace it in the empty socket upon his cheek. No one dared say those words near the statue, just in case.

'Our tradition was to drink at Adembi's feet and pledge promises to one another. The intention to pass our examinations, to be faithful to each other as friends, to achieve new heights of power, better the world and bring honour to our school. Foolish things, youthful boasts.

'I remember the night. Brass lamps shone along the hall in the twilight that passes for dark in Hysh. A few of my fellows played harps strung with moonbeams. Hysh's lowlands are never cold, and the night was balmy. Our realm is a paradise of logic and serenity and I yearn for it still.' His face hardened. 'Kekwe was there at this celebration. We took it in turns to make our boasts and promises to the silent god. Kekwe's turn came.

'"Oh, great Adembi!" Kekwe called up to the statue. "I swear most faithfully to study hard and rise through the hierarchy, to find fame and fortune as one of the high hierophants of light! Hurrah!"

'The group responded, "Hurrah!" and drank, sealing the promise.

'Kekwe bowed with a flourish, a little unsteadily, and another student got to his feet. We were all drunk, though none as drunk as I. Kekwe was accompanied by a beautiful girl named Messana, of the School of the Shining Snake. I lusted for her myself, and hated that Kekwe and she were part-bonded, and had drunk much in anger.

'"Only one of the high hierophants? Why not the highest!" I roared, waving my drink like a sword, interrupting our fellow student before he could begin his oath. "Why not pledge to become the Grand Luminance himself?"

'Kekwe's good cheer fled. I had challenged his honour in front of his friends, and insulted the most revered mage in our empire, our leader himself! Of course, he could not pledge to become the emperor. That was as near a blasphemy as one could get in the Seven Cities.

'"Then what will you pledge, Pludu Quasque, small lord with the mighty opinion of himself? Why do you not pledge to be the emperor? Surely," Kekwe said mockingly, "with all your talent and all your wisdom, you are better equipped for the role than I?"

'His barb stung me. I was drunk. I was young. I was foolish, and I hated Hamanan Kekwe with my very soul.

'"I will do better than that!" I said. I raised my goblet to the god, my wine slopping in luminous waves from its rim, and looked into the god's stern face, where three tears shone and the empty socket of the fourth glared blackly. "Oh, mighty

Adembi, I swear solemnly upon your sacred visage, and upon my heart and the immortal light of my being, that I, Pludu Quasque, shall not rest until I have ventured from this realm, recovered your missing tear, and restored it to you!"

'The group gasped as one. Messana put up her hand to her mouth at this rash oath. Kekwe was horrified. "Stop! Pludu, you should not!" But it was too late.

'"Hurrah!" I called, sealing the oath.

'Not one of my fellows responded. The music and laughter stopped. They looked at me with absolute disbelief.

'"It's just a story," I sneered. "You're all fools."

'The temperature dropped. The lamps flickered in a sudden breeze.

'"THE OATH IS JUDGED FITTING! THE OATH IS ACCEPTED!" boomed a divine voice, the first time Adembi had spoken since his tear was taken. "PLUDU QUASQUE SHALL RETURN MY TEAR UNTO ME, SO I, ADEMBI, RATIFY."

'So I was doomed.'

Rain pattered softly. The wind had dropped to nothing. Thunder rumbled but quietly, far away from the inn.

'I will not dwell upon the shock that went through the Lyceum,' said Quasque, 'or the reaction of my tutor, Hepeknek. The old man intervened on my behalf, but the oath could not be unsaid. I was forbidden from travelling while our teachers debated what to do, but already the city was in uproar, with some demanding I fulfil my promise – others said that disaster would befall the city if I were not sent out immediately or even killed. I was confined and my parents were sent for. Before they arrived and the scandal spread I escaped the Lyceum and left for another nation where I was not known, and whose Realmgates were not barred to me. There I realised the scale of the task I had set myself. I surmised the ratkin must have an underworld within the realm of Shyish, and that the gem must be there. It was not so simple. Minimal research told me no one knew where the skaven go when they die, and even if the location were known, one cannot simply come to Shyish and enter any afterlife one chooses.'

'We know this,' said Shattercap. Maesa sipped at his wine, his almond eyes still fixed on Quasque.

'There are underworlds where the living are not welcome, or cannot go at all, and in all of them the Lord of Undeath's jealous eyes are everywhere, seeking out interlopers or thieves. The perils inherent to this realm alone would see me fail a thousand times over. I had so much to learn – much, much more than I would have needed to gain my accreditation from the Lyceum. But somehow I found the application I lacked while in school. I left Hysh, and my education took a new path.

'From a shaman in Ghur I learned how he peered into other realms without leaving his hut. From a wizard whose soul was half-lost to Chaos I learned some secrets of the ratkin – that they call themselves skaven, that they are everywhere, and that their capital is a miniature realm to itself, but not much more than that. I consulted necromancers, daemonologists, thanatothurges, cartomancers, hedge wizards, high mages, academics, historians, adventurers, tomb robbers and more. From most of them I had to keep my purpose secret. All of them discovered what I intended, sooner or later. Some urged me to break my oath, others drove me away. Two tried to kill me, fearing that the very idea of my quest would bring the Lord of Undeath's attention on them. To venture into Nagash's lands is foolhardy, but to take anything from his kingdoms, even something as ephemeral as knowledge, or a kiss, is suicidal. It matters not to the God of

Death how he came by his possessions, only that he keeps them. He is a jealous god.'

Shattercap cringed. Maesa stroked him.

'Hush,' he said.

'Little by little, my power grew,' said Quasque, 'though the magic I wield is a long way from the pure energies of Hysh. I learned a little of all, from the purest, to the most debased. From each of the eight paths of magic I took something, and from those outside the established colleges too, the corrupt, the prohibited, the evil. I can never be a mage of light. Step by step, I became a sorcerer.'

'Did you ever find the tear?' asked Barnabus quietly. All at the inn were enrapt.

'Quiet, Barnabus,' said Ninian. 'Let him tell his story.'

'The darkest tale yet,' muttered Horrin.

'Yes!' piped up Shattercap. 'Do you have it? Did you get it? I like jewels. They are so pretty!'

'I am coming to that part. More wine, please, if you will, master innkeeper. I am sorry, Prince Maesa, I abuse your generosity, but this part of the story is hard for me to tell. I...' His hand shook as he held up the goblet to be filled. 'I have never told it before.'

His glass recharged, he took a long sip to steady himself before continuing.

'It was years before I was ready to come to Shyish. When I arrived, years more effort awaited me. I had still not learned the location of the skaven death realm, or even if it existed, but was sure the answer must be here. I travelled from the living kingdoms to afterlives of all kinds – those that throng with souls as corporeal as you and I, ones that were faded places serving kingdoms long since gone to dust, and whose last inhabitants were mindless shades shrieking on the winds.

Others were overrun by Chaos and twisted into perverse form, and many, many more fallen under the sway of the Great Necromancer and become part of his unliving imperium. The saddest though were those where only ruins remained, haunted by spirit scraps who gibbered lost tongues into the wind.

'I saw kingdoms where the living and the dead lived side by side. Places where the living hunted the dead, or the dead hunted the living. I witnessed the heavens and hells of men, duardin, aelves and many more races, both good and ill. But never once did I see a shade of the ratkin, or hear any notice of where they go when they perish. I had no news of the tear of Adembi either.

'The years rolled by. I had already grown from youth to man before I came to this realm, and here my early manhood passed by in dark places. I was embittered by my quest. I came close to giving up more than once, and would have done had I not found a reference in an obscure grimoire to the Library of the Forgotten.

'A passage in a book written by a madman, a dead one at that, but it gave me hope. It described a library towards the centre of Shyish where all things that have been forgotten are recorded. Not only living things die, but dreams, and hopes, and knowledge – they too have lives and deaths.

'This was it, the only place I might discover where the soul of the ratkin thief had gone along with Adembi's tear. After a year of searching, I found it. What I saw there I will not speak of. There were many things too terrible to describe, but wonders also. The library is a place of infinite capacity, where all things that were known might be rediscovered. Perhaps it was once a place of learning, but the Great Necromancer's domain has overtaken it. The black pyramids and obelisks

built around it appalled me. Shyish there lives up to its reputation as an inversion of Hysh, a place of cold instead of
warmth, of gelid shadow rather than soothing light. Surrounded by buildings of lifeless realmstone, the wondrous
library moulders, unattended, more silent than a grave, yet it
is not uninhabited.' He shuddered. 'I will not speak of that.

'I was there for nine years. Eventually, in a wing dedicated
to the history of a lost world, I found tome after tome con-
cerning the ratkin. These are not selective histories as written
by men, but the tiniest detail of every life that was ever lived
and every thought ever had. It is maddening to read the lives
of skaven. They do not think like us, and their recorded
beings scratched madly inside my skull, but my obsession
drove me on, keeping me sane, until I happened on a single
book detailing a place unlike any other.

'In the book were details of the realm of the skaven beyond
this one. Not a true country of death at all, but a place
outside the Mortal Realms entirely. The tome named it as
Ruin, and called it among the principal kingdoms of the
ratkin's verminous deity. There, upon the marches of Ruin,
are the myriad different afterlives of the skaven dead, terrible lands that their vile god calls his dead children to dwell
in forevermore.'

This information escaped his lips as little more than a hiss,
but its speaking brought an awful, watchful silence. Quasque
took another drink.

'There were several books on Adembi that hinted at the
great secrets of the realms. Had I wished to follow the trail
of those references, I would be the most learned man alive.
But I needed to know where the tear was. I had to have it,
and free myself from my oath. Another year passed, until I
found that too. The tear was in the tower of a rat daemon

whose name I cannot pronounce and dare not try. I was tempted again to abandon my quest and remain, for anything that has been known is there, and more than once I came across the remains of scholars who had entered the library, and died drunk on knowledge. Again my obsession with the tear saved me, and I departed.

'From the library I had learned spells of the direst sort that would allow me to quit Shyish proper and make my way to this realm of Ruin. I prepared for the journey, forging a dagger of a kind certain sorcerers use to cut their way through time and space. My essence was too bright for the place I had to go, so one half of my soul I burned out with fire stolen from a change daemon I lured into the library and imprisoned.' His eyes dropped. 'I am almost as dead as I am alive,' he said quietly. 'The last stages required sacrifices I could not bear to make. I needed magic, lots of it, and it was there in the person of my horses. They knew what evil I meant to work. I could not bring myself to do it, until brave Solio gave himself nobly to the cause. I shed my last tears when I plunged this sword through his noble heart.' His hand, still shaking, rested on his hilt. 'Those things done, I was ready. With the dagger of Chaos-tainted realmstone I cut a slit in the world, mounted Rados and plunged into the secret ways.

'I left the realms, galloping through a place between. I was not in the heavens, those that we see in the night skies of every realm, but some other place. The underside of sky, that is the only way I can describe it. From my vantage I could see each of the realms floating by, gargantuan islands in oceans of magic, and other places beyond, most dread of all a glow far away where evil gods live. It was like a sky of light, with stars inverted black, but it was at the same time a swirl of sorcerous colour, an ocean of possibility – but I tell you gravely all, my friends, that the skaven riddle the place between the realms with their networks of tunnels, green-black burrows stretching in spreading nets to snare the cosmos.

'I followed a map stolen from the book that spoke of Ruin. It led to a tunnel unlike the others used by living ratkin. They were dread passageways, from the little I saw, and I doubt I would have survived them. The tunnel of the dead was separate from the network, accessible in few places, and once entered vast and black, full of streaming shades, uncountable millions of them, a tide of rats running before a flood, all heading down, down.'

'To the realm of Ruin!' squeaked Shattercap.

'Just so. The shades were skaven dead, scurrying to whatever fate awaits their kind. The numbers were staggering, an infinity of rat-souls, pouring on, on, down the great tunnel, which grew and grew, becoming the throat of a vortex, marbled with green and crackles of purple lightning. The rushing swarms filled every surface.'

'Didn't they attack you?' asked Ninian.

'I have some art in the routes of the deceased, and though the way was different to that of other races it was still a road of the dead, and I was safe enough there. Besides, the creatures all were ghosts, hardly aware of me, and they recoiled from the light of Rados, so we flew untroubled down the endless tunnel,' said Quasque.

'The end came suddenly over a tossing sea. The rat-souls tumbled from the tunnel, falling down into water, where they squealed and thrashed, until forced under by the torrent of others following them. Their flailing pushed them into roaring whirlpools, at whose bottoms glowing lights suggested ten, twenty, a hundred other tunnel throats, perhaps more, going where I knew not – and down them the dead went again. I saw only a little of these other tunnels, and only a little more of the exit from the tunnel I was in, which was huge and shaped like the bell of a black trumpet, for Rados bore us away quickly, his glowing skin a glare in that gloomy place. Away from the roaring whirlpools, the sea was grey and covered with rubbish of every conceivable kind. We reached the shore, and Rados set down, his light illuminating a desolate shore crammed with trash.

'I patted my horse's steaming neck. Alarmingly, his light appeared to be fading. Flight is within the gift of Hysh's golden horses, but too long aloft drains them. I had pushed him hard. As we rode across the desolate land, he grew dimmer, and for the first time in my life, I saw shadows on a golden mount of Hysh. His skin beneath was dull, like unpolished brass. He was dying.'

'You didn't come with your horse, master. I did not stable him for you,' said Barnabus.

'Quiet now,' said Horrin softly.

Quasque gave Barnabus a sorrowful look, and drank some more.

'The realm of Ruin is a terrible place. Mounds of stinking refuse are heaped as far as the eye can see. Every rise is a mound of rubbish. Distant mountains reveal themselves to be yet more rubbish. The map dictated we follow the shore of the grey sea. The water was scummy, and had an oily, chemical scent. It was gloomy, but never truly dark, the clouds troubled by green bale lights. More tunnels opened in the ground, leading down to worse places yet. I am glad I did not live and die as a ratkin beast. Theirs is a terrible fate.

'The worst thing about the refuse clogging that place was its nature. It appeared of uniformly brown, rotten, midden shades, but look closer and riches can be discerned. Once seen, they are everywhere. In that place are the broken glories of thousands of races, millions of nations, perhaps even the gnawed loot of worlds. Huge rat daemons stalk the valleys between the mounds and sometimes, with no predictability, a vision of a sprawling city appears in the sky. Its appearance lights up the realm of Ruin starkly green – then just as quickly as it arrives, it is gone, plunging the land back into the dark.

'Scavenging things came against us. I despatched them with my sword, not daring to use my magic in case I exposed us.

'So it was we came in time to the tower the book said held the tear of Adembi. I rode up onto a hill to better survey it. The tower was situated close by the shore, but even there half its considerable height was buried in stinking rubbish. I saw a swarming of figures off to the tower's west, inland away from the sea. My eyes were drawn towards it, and I beheld the flash of magic between a plain bracketed by twin Realmgates, small as coins from my distance, but immense. The clash of metal and discharge of great guns sounded on the edge of hearing.

'War had come to the realm of Ruin.

'I dithered a little. My path would take us close to the battle. I had no choice. I urged my faltering Rados on towards the tower, my eyes always on the conflict. One Realmgate was of seething amethyst magic, the other a ragged tear green with skaven sorcery. From the skaven side poured a legion of armoured ratkin, urged on by the scourges of their rat daemons into a horde of undead I cannot properly describe. Vast armies of skeletal remains animated by the will of the Great Necromancer. Huge clouds of spirits soaring over them. Opposing the rat daemons were giant constructs of bone and flesh, and the corpses of monsters raised to a semblance of life. The forces on each side appeared to be limitless. The front lines of the battle stretched on for miles, engulfing Ruin as far as I could see. My path took me up a rise made almost entirely of potsherds of dizzying variety. From there I watched the battle.

'There were dread generals of the deathless legions riding the sky. They cast magic from their staves and wands. Squadrons of vampire knights charged freakish beasts. Skirmish lines of ghouls loped ahead of ranks of skeletal archers, who fired mechanically without tiring. Protected by phalanxes of armoured undead guardians, soul syphons fashioned from the bones of godbeasts extended fleshless jaws, racks of lead pipes sucking up the souls of the skaven as they died. I was witnessing a war not over territory, but spirits. I had been warned that the Lord of Death regards all dead things as his by rights, and it seems even the souls of so mean and tainted a race as the skaven lie within his claim.

'On their side, the skaven responded with alchemical cannons and strange machines. Monstrous beasts stitched from the flesh of many creatures waded into the armies of the undead. Steam-powered weapons scythed down swathes of the foe. Both sides suffered terrible casualties, but more warriors poured from the holes in space to join the fight. I would have been noticed were the two sides not so absorbed with each other's destruction. Certain I would not remain undetected for long, I rode off, down the slithering heap of shards, towards the tower by the sea.

'When I reached the grey beach the battle was out of sight, though the clamour continued loud enough to hear, if not enough to drown out the rush of dirty surf. Bright pollutants swirled in the water, and all along the beach foam made extravagant, quivering heaps between lines of tide-washed treasure. I urged the dying Rados up the slopes of refuse clinging to the tower, hoping that if I were quick, I would be able to leave that terrible place and save his life. It was not to be. I dismounted to search for a way in, the entrance being hopelessly buried. The sound of Rados falling down had me rush back. At my return he opened his eyes a final time and whickered softly. The last of the light left him, his body heaved and his coat dulled to mundane flesh. I stroked his muzzle as he breathed his last, whispering that his trials were over. If only that were true! I was in an uncanny realm, and so witnessed his gallant soul rise from his body. It shone with a measure of the light he had in his life, and he climbed upwards, heading I was sure to a just rest in shining fields.'

A tear slipped down Quasque's nose, and plinked into his wine. 'Something grabbed at him as he went skywards, and yanked him ferociously across the sky towards the battle. His soul, so serene a second before, screamed in terror, then he was gone behind the mountains of filth, certainly consumed by the soul syphons of the undead.'

Quasque's narrative ceased. He broke down, and wept silently, his back heaving with refreshed grief. Ninian put her hand on his. Horrin got up, and rubbed his back.

'This one is on the house, good sir,' Horrin said, refilling Quasque's goblet. But Quasque would not be consoled, and the party had to wait for his weeping to subside before the tale continued. The wind began to blow again, and the rain fell harder. Lightning flashed around the shutters, followed by a boom of thunder, very loud, that came close behind. Shatter-cap squealed and scampered up Prince Maesa's arm, fidgeting around the aelf's neck until Maesa plucked him up and set him back on the table. The fire bellied in the grate. Wind shrieked, then again, and set once more to a constant moaning.

'The eye of the storm is passing over,' said Maesa. 'That is all, Shattercap. The tempest returns.'

'Don't like it, wicked prince,' growled the spite. He sniffed suspiciously. 'Smells wrong.'

At this, Quasque recovered his dignity, and said, 'Then I should be quick and finish, for it means there is not much time.' He gulped hard at his wine.

'The tower was made completely of iron, without any way in, and though it was heavily rusted its walls were unbroken. Dark shapes high above I took to be windows, but they were beyond my reach. I thought myself defeated at the final hurdle, until, on the very far side overlooking the sea, I found a balcony. It was above my head, and I was obliged to haul myself up to gain access, but in this way I arrived within the tower, covered in filth and streaked with rust.

'The book in the forgotten library told that the tower was made by a rat daemon, whose name I cannot pronounce and dare not attempt, to house the treasure brought from the Realm of Light by his infiltrator – the tear of Adembi that I sought. I expected resistance in the tower, and primed myself for battle magic, but there was none. No sign of souls, living or dead, only the sickly smell of slow rot, and the crash of waves upon the beach.

'The centre of the tower was taken up by a spiral stair. On each level was a room. I peeked into them as I passed upwards. They were all empty, save one, wherein lay sprawled the immense skeleton of a rat creature crowned with horns and dressed in corroded armour. Beneath an outstretched claw a second skeleton was pinned, this one human and armoured in a style I did not recognise. Everything in there was rusty, covered in dust, except a sword, still bright with magic, jammed in the ribs of the creature, and the cause of its death. This must have been the owner of the tower, slain by a hero long ago. I had not read the story of this encounter in the library. Perhaps the library did not contain all knowledge, and a terrible thought took me, that the treasure was gone. I hurried on to the uppermost room.

'In a chamber lit by thirteen tall windows was a chest of greened bronze between two thrones. In the thrones sat the mummified remains of ratkin warlords aglow with dormant magic. I dismembered these quickly with my sword, threw their limbs out of the windows and placed their heads away from their bodies. This done, I turned my attentions to the chest. It was locked, but nothing to the magic I had learned, and I opened it easily with a minor cantrip. Immediately the heads began to chatter their jaws, and the bodies roll about. Had I not dealt with these things first, I would have had to fight them.

'Inside the chest was a rotting leather pouch that fell apart the moment I lifted it. Out tumbled a single drop of exquisitely carved Hyshian realmstone – pantherine, yellow as a tiger's eye. I sobbed with relief, but could not delay. Time was of the essence. I heard the battle's roar coming closer to the tower. Neither undead nor skaven would forgive my taking the tear.

'There was too much solid iron around me to attempt to flee magically, certainly the builder's purpose in using the material, so I fled down the stairs to the balcony and back out onto the grim shoreline. I believe my opening of the chest had alerted the death lords to the tear's presence, for from over the horizon came the moaning of phantoms. A charge of luminous cavalry, aethereal and alive with corpse-light, galloped soundlessly up and over the mountains of refuse. I had but moments to escape. I sliced at the weft of reality with the tainted knife. The edges of the beach sucked inwards, and a hole opened onto another place. I had no clue where it headed, but threw myself headlong within. The gap closed over my head. I had escaped.'

Quasque took a shaking breath. The storm built again in ferocity, approaching the power it had earlier in the evening again.

'I was lucky,' said Quasque. 'The land in which I emerged was one of the gentler parts of Shyish, many thousands of leagues away from the terrible places of that realm's centre and edge. Though alive, I was alone and impoverished. My horses were dead. My possessions were lost. The dagger disintegrated with the last cut. All I had you see here, these clothes, sword, small pouch, a tiny amount of coin. My troubles were far from over.' He smiled. 'But I finally had this.'

He reached for a pouch by his side, and withdrew a shining gem of yellow stone. He set it on the table with a gentle click. Gentle, golden light shone into the inn, soft as a summer's day.

Shattercap's eyes widened. Involuntarily he reached for the stone, then self-consciously snatched his hands back. The company leaned in, except for Maesa, who remained impassive as always.

'Now that is a pretty stone, and no mistake,' said Stonbrak, his eyes glittering.

'Pure realmstone of Hysh,' said Quasque. 'With this, I could purchase a kingdom. It is a shame I will not have the chance to fulfil my promise.' He picked up the stone and put it back into the pouch.

'What do you mean?' said Stonbrak. The wind shrieked outside. The inn trembled.

Quasque looked up defiantly. 'In Ruin Nagash warred over

what he regarded as his, this gem included. I regret to tell you that since retrieving the tear, I have been pursued across Shyish by the agents of the Lord of Undeath. He wants it for himself. Nagash!' Thunder boomed. 'I thought I had finally managed to outrun them. From the Argent Gate in Ghur it is only a short journey to Irb and the Realmgate to Hysh there, but this storm…' He smiled and waved his hand over his head. 'The sky-ship's early departure… It has delayed me just long enough.'

Another shriek came from outside.

'That was not the wind,' said Maesa. He was on his feet, sword in hand before the next scream blasted around the inn. Shattercap scampered up his arm. A third shriek cried.

The protective amulets Horrin had hanging above the bar jumped twice, then set up a constant jangling.

'By the gods!' breathed Horrin. 'What have you brought on us?'

'I am sorry,' said Quasque, 'they are here.' His smile became crazed. 'The Hounds of Nagash have come.'

JOURNEY OF THE MAGI

Jonathan Green

*Jonathan Green's first story for Black Library appeared in the
very first volume of the original* Inferno! *magazine back in
1998, and we are thrilled to see him return to* Inferno! *with
this mind-warping tale of that most psychically gifted of Chaos
Space Marine Legions, the Thousand Sons.*

*Three sorcerers converge on an ancient necron structure in
the hopes of retrieving something of great value to all three of
them. But they will find that though dormant, the necrons do
not give up their treasures easily...*

The orb designated as the Godstar tumbled through the void as it had done for countless aeons. More artefact than world, it was not bound to the gravity well of any one celestial body. The light cast by dying suns barely penetrated the oily green corona surrounding it, painting the monolithic structures covering the comet-sized construct's surface with their suffused luminescence.

Below the protective shield, before a smooth obsidian pyramidal edifice, space-time deformed and buckled. Strands of coral-coloured warp matter and aquamarine etheric energy bled out from a rent in reality. Forming into tendrils, they behaved like the tentacles of some deep-sea cephalopod testing the limits of their new habitat.

The writhing corona of kaleidoscopic colours widened, as the hole opened in front of the pyramid. With ice crystals frosting the void-black stones of the processional avenue onto which they stepped, three figures emerged from the portal.

First through was Prototokos the All-Seeing, warp-mage of the Thousand Sons Legion. Eerie green light cast by carved channels in the blockwork of the pyramid reflected from the greaves and vambraces of his turquoise battleplate, while the shimmering cloth-o'-gold icon banner tied at his waist undulated in the unseen breezes of the warp as he walked. So too did the blood-red cape that hung about his shoulders. In one gauntleted hand Prototokos carried a heavy, curse-bound, star-matter blade, which seemed to draw light into itself.

Second, and more impressive still, came Sorcerer-Magister Opados. He was clad in an elaborately ornamented suit of Terminator armour that had survived the fall of Tizca and the burning of Prospero, its myriad battle scars and subsequent repairs adding a gravitas that only age and experience could bring. The crimson cape secured to his auto-reactive shoulder pads flapped in the warp wind. A pair of flattened golden horns, inlaid with platinum and lapis lazuli, rose from his turquoise helm. These features were echoed in the projections that crowned the force stave he carried, the emerald eye-stone set within the tip of the staff rolling and blinking erratically. Standing ten feet tall, Opados was still dwarfed by the edifice that rose before him to more than twenty times his height.

Arch-Magister Tritos, the last of the three, did not step from the portal but glided through it, his feet placed firmly on the back of a thing that was a warp-born amalgam of impossible flesh and gold-chased steel. It resembled a circular platform but with nine great gilt blades rising at equidistant points from its rim, while between those, nine watery eyes bulged and blinked – every part of them painted in shifting shades of blue, from their fleshy lids to their whites and malformed irises.

And the master of the daemon was no less awe-inspiring

than the warp beast he had tamed. The sorcerer was clad in a turquoise war-suit, trimmed with gold and inlaid with precious gems, the serpent sigil of the Thousand Sons Legion that adorned his left pauldron turning slowly as it chased its fiery tail. The pauldron protecting his right shoulder bore the Cult of Time's own writhing icon, a swollen snake pregnant with the possibilities of myriad futures.

Great golden horns, so intricately detailed they looked as if they had grown from the sorcerer's head rather than having been cast by an artisan of the forge, rose from the crown of his helm, while other antler-like growths curved downwards to frame the front plate of the exalted one's visor.

His ornate armour was half-hidden by the heavy robes he wore. The gold-embroidered scarlet chasuble gave him the appearance of a scholar or a priest, as much as his battle-plate marked him out as a formidable warrior.

Adorning the plastron of his war- and warp-scarred armour was a scarab beetle as large as a man's head. Sculpted from a single piece of red alabaster, it seemed to cling to the front of the sorcerer's carapace, looking like it might suddenly crack open its wing cases and take flight at any moment.

During the Faronic Age of ancient Terra, aeons past, the primitive peoples of that dim and distant time had believed the scarab god renewed the sun every day, rolling it above the horizon and continuing to carry it through the underworld after sunset, only to renew it again the following dawn. And so it continued day in day out, season after season, year after year, for all eternity.

It was no coincidence that the beetle had been claimed by the Cult of Time's Sect of the Crimson Scarab. The magisters of that faction treated time as if it were a tapestry, to be unravelled and resewn as they saw fit, striding through the warp to unpick the past and reorder it in a manner that would echo down through the centuries and aid them in their conquests in the future. To an exalted sorcerer-magister of the Crimson Scarab, past, present and future were mutable and interchangeable, if circumstances so required.

Behind the three magi the immaterial vortex contracted and closed. The echoes of the concussive boom of displaced air that followed the sealing of the rent rippled across the surface of the comet world like laughter, while a shock wave of ethereal spectra swept across the underside of the flickering green force field that stretched from one horizon to the other.

Arch-Magister Tritos of the Heralds of Destiny regarded the angular pyramid before him with a disdainful eye. As he did so, the dragon-head exhaust ports which rose from the power pack that energised his armoured suit turned to regard it too, with unblinking golden eyes.

The processional avenue leading to the edifice was a grand affair, precisely incised geometric channels running on either side, pulsing with the same intense emerald light that writhed in a sickly aurora above the artificial Godstar.

Without a word being spoken, the three sorcerers set off down the stone throat of the avenue. The arch-magister astride his disc led the way, the daemonic entity leaving a trail of iridescent ether stuff in its wake, while gold-embroidered sigils adorning the hem of Tritos' rippling robes performed a strange, esoteric dance all of their own.

As tall as a Battle Titan, the pyramid's entrance was constructed of a smooth onyx broken only by a series of circles and lines that formed the demarcation glyph of the impossibly ancient dynasty that had constructed the comet. It was a symbol Tritos had seen again and again, from Kovarian IV to Port Stormshield, etched upon the wraithbone ruins of the aeldari in the Shifting Deserts of Osiris Primus, and inscribed in blood throughout the myriad volumes of the writings of the mad prophet Mortsafe in the dusty libraries of Kelock on the dead world of Narthax. And in its form he now understood its meaning, although that had not been the case the first time he had beheld it in the mirrored waters of his scrying pool.

Consisting of three overlapping circles, superimposed upon one another in green-black stone and near-white light, as well as other emanating rays and discs, it was the symbol of the Nephrekh Dynasty of the aeons-old necrontyr.

The thin light of the Halo Stars struggled to penetrate the flickering gauss defences that surrounded the necron-constructed comet craft. The verdigris glow of the sky shield bathed the sorcerers' gold and turquoise armour, the light reflecting from their polished battleplate casting rippling reflections on the onyx walls of the processional avenue, making it appear as if they were moving through the pelagic depths of some ocean world rather than across the surface of a deep space fastness.

None, beyond the immortal phaerons of the necron race themselves, knew how many such celestial engines and timeless artefacts there were adrift within the vastness of the galaxy. The name 'World Engine' was still spoken of in hushed tones in star systems across a hundred sectors, from the Reefs of Melanoptera to the tribal territories of the T'au Empire offshoot septs in the Damocles Gulf. But it hadn't been the only such manifestation of the necrons' world-shaping mega-technology.

The Godstar was another such ancient artefact, unknown to the myriad intelligent species that populated the galaxy. Indeed, it was unknown to all outside the necron race, other than for these three sons of the Crimson King, these three who had discerned its location by studying the cuneiform script pressed into baked clay tablets on arid Za'handra. These three who had scoured the mind of a t'au ethereal having boarded the xenos' Gal'leath-class explorer vessel seeking more information, and left it to the mercy of void-devourers when they departed. These three who had journeyed across countless battlefields and warzones, across great gulfs of time and space, to reach this place, in what, for the time being at least, they would consider to be 'now'.

'The way ahead is closed,' said Prototokos, regarding the entrance and its Titan-tall warding glyph, as the three magi halted before the cyclopean doorway at the end of the descending defile.

'Indeed,' agreed Opados, scouring its surface with his eyes, even as his psychic senses probed its defences, searching for a means of ingress, 'but there is always–'

'Another way,' finished Tritos.

The arch-magister's hands began to twist and dance in the air before him, manifesting esoteric gestures of serpentine sorcery as he sought to fold time and space with what appeared to be no more than a snap of his fingers.

To look upon the cerulean flesh of his left hand was to look upon the armoured skin of his gauntlet, the warping effects of millennia having merged flesh and bone and ceramite into one, to form a new and unique warp-made amalgam.

As he began to unknit the fabric of reality, the air before them seemed to jerk and twist and extrude itself in obeisance to his flexing fingers, while glowing warp runes became visible, crawling up and down the vambrace of the arch-magister's left arm. The threads that made up the matter of the universe were loosed into thin strands of pink and blue warp-stuff, which clung to his dancing digits like sticky cobwebs.

What started as a few loose strands soon became a gaping hole. And through that hole, superimposed upon the sealed gateway, could be seen a dusty darkness that was spared the attentions of the flickering aurora of the sky shield.

Taking hold of the edges of the hole, Tritos pulled and stretched the limits of the portal until it was large enough to admit even Opados, cocooned within his Terminator armour.

'This way,' Tritos said, pointing. 'This is our other way.'

'Will it take us straight to the heart of this place, and the prize we seek?' asked Opados.

'No,' admitted the arch-magister. 'The deeper levels of this sphere harbour warding technology that prevents it.'

'But this is enough,' stated Prototokos. 'Where our powers of sorcery will not suffice, we will turn once again to bolter and blade to clear a path to the prize.'

In one stride, the warp-mage made the translation from the surface of the artefact-comet to the tomb's silent interior. He was followed by Sorcerer-Magister Opados, with Arch-Magister Tritos passing through the portal last, carried on the back of his warp steed.

The hole healed itself again and the tomb was briefly illuminated by a flash of witch-light. As the boom of the portal's closing faded fast, lost among echoing sepulchral halls, the rows of golden warriors were for a moment made visible, before fading back into the shadows, and the all-pervading hush returned.

Not that the sorcerers needed any light to make out the serried ranks of the tomb's occupants. The optical enhancements of their helms enabled them to pick out every detail of the motionless figures.

They were almost skeletal, not unlike mortal men in form

and size, but with limbs made of metal, their bodies encased in gold.

But where the souls of mortal beings would have burned with fierce fire to the witch-sight of the sorcerers, these endless ranks of necron warriors were dull and dead, the brightest thing about them their tarnished armoured body-shells.

They looked like they would not have appeared out of place standing upon plinths within the statue-lined galleries of the twisted silver towers of Tizca.

'Are they dead or merely dormant?' Prototokos asked, as if addressing the darkness.

'Does it matter?' grunted Opados, his voice distorted by his helm into a daemonic growl.

'We are here to release the prisoner, nothing more,' said Tritos. 'Which way does the vault lie?'

Prototokos scanned the gloom, slowly turning his head from left to right and back again, like a near-blind old man seeking the glow of a lumen-globe. He stopped abruptly, facing what was not so much an archway as a gap in the far wall of the tomb-chamber that ran from floor to ceiling, fully tall enough to admit a Battle Titan god engine.

'This way,' he said.

'Then lead on,' said Tritos. 'Our prize awaits.'

The three magi advanced, passing through hall after hall, and gallery after gallery, built around the dimensions of gods rather than mere mortals.

In each one it was the same: sterile, lifeless, with barely even any dust on the floor to be stirred by the sorcerers' passing; rank upon rank of motionless warrior-constructs clad in tarnished golden armour, packed into crypt-like vaults in their thousands; looming walls adorned with the broken glyphs of the Nephrekh aristocracy, from lords and overlords to the obscure sigils of individual phalanx groups. The only sounds that accompanied the Thousand Sons' advance through the tomb was the ringing of their armoured feet on the echoing stone floors, and the incoherent whispering of the arch-magister's disc.

Every time they left one chamber and entered another, they descended a flight of ancient steps, cut from something akin to black basalt, which led them ever deeper into the God-star's interior.

Descending a much longer and steeper staircase into another vaulted space, Prototokos saw that where the other galleries had held the sleeping soldiers of the revenant race, this chamber – bluntly cruciform in shape – was no more than a parting of the ways within the labyrinth. And where the other halls had been dead and free of moisture, an oily mist covered the floor of this intersection, shot through with motes of twinkling green light, like an inverted star field.

As Prototokos and Opados reached the bottom of the staircase, their boots sinking into the soupy green fog, they stopped to take in the dimensions of the space. While the warp-mage replayed the visions he had witnessed in the waters of his scrying pool, so as to determine how they might best continue their journey, the trio waited in silence. And that was when the echoing clatter of automaton claws and the hum of gravitic engines reached their ears.

They were not alone.

'There!' Arch-Magister Tritos said, gesturing with the golden cobra-head of his force stave at a black shape emerging from the square hole of a maintenance conduit.

The thing bore the characteristic armour plating, and green-glowing sensor arrays and power coils, of a necron automaton, but in every other way it resembled a multi-limbed arachnid.

Tritos regarded the ancient robot with the intense scrutiny of one who sought to know everything there was to know about the entity. For if he understood it, he would then know how best to destroy it.

Unlike their necron masters, ancient robotic constructs such as this one never slept, tirelessly tending to the tomb, servicing its stasis systems and maintaining the fabric of the Godstar's structure, down through the centuries, aeon after aeon.

The spyder scrutinised Tritos in turn, drawing level with the sorcerer's elevated position and subjecting him to a barrage of sensor sweeps, broad beams of muted jade light playing over his robed and armoured form.

The disc shuddered under him.

'And so it begins,' he said. 'There is no hiding our presence here now.'

The hum of the spyder's motive systems abruptly increased in pitch and the construct assumed a more threatening posture, its pincer-limbs raised to strike.

With barely a thought, Tritos lashed out with a lance of psychic power at the automaton, sending it hurtling across the intersection to smash into one of the black stone walls with catastrophic force. There was a sharp crack, followed by a dull boom, and the spyder was consumed by the ball of green fire that emanated from within its carapace, its power core having suffered terminal damage and vaporising the guardian drone in an instant.

'Brothers,' Tritos said, his tone having acquired an urgent edge, 'we must move. Now!'

'This way,' said Prototokos, leading the trinity along the left-hand spur of the intersection and down another precipitous stair, the sound of more clacking mechanical manipulators carrying to them through the stillness of the tomb.

As they descended, the mist tumbling over the steps in a slow cascade of condensing cryo-vapour, the black shaft of the stairway fanned outwards to become the walls of a vast hall. Columns like elongated obsidian geodes rose fully one hundred and sixty feet from floor to ceiling, their glassy black faces reflecting the strobing, molten green light-pulses that coursed up and down them, loudly sparking arcs of emerald lightning crackling between the columns in irregular discharges.

It was the echoing tapping and scraping of metallic claws on the pulsing pillars that alerted the sorcerers to the arrival of more of the tomb's guardians, since their witch-sight was blind to the approach of the soulless alien techno-entities.

They were multi-legged spyder-forms as well. Such constructs didn't only act as repair-servitors and watch over their sleeping masters. They could also be formidable foes, if called upon to defend the tomb from anything they caught trespassing within the sepulchral complex.

Unlike the first drone the Thousand Sons had encountered, which had only approached them with wary interest – at least at first – this cluster was ready to defend the tomb and its slumbering occupants from the invaders, fabrication arrays snapping open and closed, like the pincers of hungry crustaceans, while particle beamers energised.

Prototokos could only surmise that the first spyder had scanned them and passed on what it had found – and experienced in its final moments – and so the rest of the tomb's guardians were now on a war footing, expecting an invasion and ready to resist it.

But of course Tritos had anticipated this. 'Obliterate the arachno-forms!' commanded the arch-magister.

Before the robots could open fire, the favoured of Tzeentch

lashed out with magicks and raw psychic power, accompanied by intermittent yet devastatingly accurate shots from Prototokos' Inferno-pattern bolt pistol, and withering salvos of fire from Opados' combi-bolter.

With a furnace roar, like one of the Changer of the Ways' fire-spewing servants, Tritos' own ornamented weapon hosed a trio of drones with rippling warpflame, sending them plummeting to the floor of the hypostyle hall, trailing snaking tendrils of fire.

The trajectory of one of the downed spyders sent it hurtling towards Tritos. The arch-magister didn't even blink as the construct came within arm's reach of his position.

The sorcerer's steed rose sharply. Intercepting the spyder's plummeting dive, with lightning-flash reactions, the disc snatched it from the air and set about rapidly dismantling the automaton's body with its semi-organic golden blades.

One wave of spyders fell, then another, and another, but all the while other things congregated in the pulse-shot shadows, the occasional flash of an energy discharge briefly illuminating glassy eye-lenses, oily exoskeletons and scythe-sharp reaping blades.

'We have to keep moving. We cannot fall back,' stated Tritos with grim finality, even as constructs with exposed spines and tails of articulated metal appeared, clinging to the pulsing pillars or descending from the vaulted roof space of the colossal chamber.

Prototokos looked. The way ahead was choked with hordes of robotic entities, some of them giving birth to other, smaller swarming metallic things. The beetle-like constructs scuttled across the floor of the chamber in their thousands, each following a simple set of subroutines, avoiding each other and all obstacles in accordance with a preprogrammed set of rigid algorithms, but moving as one undulating carpet of irides-cent alien alloys.

'Virus-riddled vermin,' hissed Opados in irritation.

'Fear not, brother,' replied Prototokos. 'I know how to deal with vermin like these.'

Taking a bejewelled cylinder from a hook on his belt, Pro-totokos twisted the enamelled crimson scarab cap and hurled the object into the seething mass of robotic beetles rapidly closing the gap between them.

A new sun burned away the sepulchral darkness, hurling the disintegrating cinders of shattered scarabs in all direc-tions. But as the glare of the plasma blast faded, it became clear that Prototokos' assault had barely decimated the robotic ranks.

The three advanced, Prototokos making continued use of psi-targeted grenades – his witch-sight helping him predict where the bombs should land, moments into the future, to cause the most devastation – while Opados and Tritos helped clear a path through the metal tide with judicious flashes of focused psychic energy, channelled through their shining force staves.

And all the while they suffered the assaults of a whickering hail of emerald energy pulses, as the necrons' slave-machines continued to resist their advance. Most of the automatons' beam-blasts were repelled by the wards of protection with which the sorcerers had girded themselves, dissipating in ripples of unctuous magenta light against the surface of the invisible sphere that surrounded the Thousand Sons. But still the occasional pulse of focused light found a way through, only to spang from the ceramite of their sigil-wrought armour.

The reservoir of warp energy they had drawn to themselves

was in ever-greater danger of running dry, the more the magi were called upon to bolster their psi-shields and cast their conjurations of devastation.

The tide of scarabs and thrumming spyders parted as rank upon rank of golden warriors, marching in lockstep, advanced from the far end of the vast hall.

'The sleepers wake,' said Opados grimly.

Where the gold trim of the Thousand Sons' suits blazed sun-bright in the light of the necron weapon discharges, the gilt body-shells of the advancing warriors were discoloured and dulled by the endless aeons, just as the minds of their mad masters had been degraded by the remorseless millennia, and who, in their insanity, had taken prisoner the one the magi intended to free from captivity.

Slicing beams of light cut through the gloom of the chamber. The warriors were among the lowliest of the necrons but the weapons they brought to bear, to repel the tomb's raiders, were potent artefacts born of another age, when star gods had warred across the heavens.

'The Bringers of the Dawn seek only to send us into the darkness,' Tritos announced. 'But we shall enlighten them and teach them that their time is over. Do not falter, brothers, and we shall teach the fearless to be fearful!'

Prototokos lobbed another of his red scarab plasma grenades over the heads of the advancing warriors. It landed in the midst of them, launching two dozen necrons into the air as it detonated. Opados doused the humanoid machines with fire from his combi-bolter, the magical energies bound to the inferno weapon imbuing its shells with the power to melt their soulless robotic bodies. Still more were hurled between the geode pillars as Tritos smote the horde with potent psychic shock waves.

Riding over the heads of the implacable phalanx, the arch-magister focused his sorcerous power through the glittering ruby eyes of his force stave's hooded cobra's head. Where his focused magicks struck, warrior after warrior was reduced to its component parts, as metal and crystalline matrices were unmade, time was reversed, and the necrons were turned back into the base elements from which they had originally been formed.

But even those necrons smashed to smithereens by the other magi's attacks were not out of the fight for long. All along the trail of destruction left in the wake of the sorcerers' advance, dismembered limbs clawed towards shattered torsos, while eyes of disembodied steel skulls crackled with green fire, as if willing their headless bodies to recover and reattach them. Broken forms that appeared to the magi to be beyond repair were tended to by spyders, the arachnoid robots' fabrication claws reconstructing motive units and articulated joints damaged during the Thousand Sons' assault.

The sorcerers' progress felt slow to Prototokos now. A journey that had taken them across the stars, covering unimaginable, incalculable distances, had almost ground to a halt here in the tomb, within striking distance of where the prisoner was held captive, its furious, star-bright spirit straining to be free.

Prototokos focused his gaze on the far end of the hall, still a third of a mile away – if his measuring reticule was to be trusted in this dead space – and saw something huge move within the shadows there. It looked like one of the ancient statues of Tizca come to life, taking form from the suffocating darkness. The warp-mage could feel the thud of its ponderous footfalls, heavier than a Helbrute's, through the boots of his own heavy, armoured suit.

As one, without a word of warning from the warp-mage, the Terminator-sorcerer and arch-magister saw it too.

A beam of light, like a blade of green flame, shot the length of the hypostyle hall, focused on Tritos, exploding the sphere of magical protection around him. The daemon-disc gave a high-pitched shriek of pain as its warp-formed flesh and bone-metal blades were unmade by the lethal gauss cannon salvo.

'Magister!' Prototokos cried out in cold shock. But he and the Terminator-sorcerer Opados could do nothing but watch, in appalled horror, as a second dissembling beam followed the first to its target, this time hitting the arch-magister himself.

And as they watched, the lower portion of his right arm disintegrated. At first it was only the gauntlet and vambrace that crumbled into nothingness. But then the skin and flesh and bone beneath were shredded at a molecular level too. Gauss beams ate at Tritos' corporeal form, stripping it away, layer by layer, mitochondrial strand by mitochondrial strand, unmaking him, even as his transhuman constitution and warp-wards battled to reconstruct the fractally fragmented flesh.

'You must be gone from here and finish our mission!' the arch-magister commanded, even as he shaped what Prototokos sensed could be his final spell.

Tritos stretched out his left arm, cerulean fingers splayed wide, and in that instant it was as if the very air about him froze – not with ice but in time. The inbound disintegrating beams of the necrons halted a mere moment from making contact with the sorcerer's armoured form.

But the time-freezing spell did not stop there. It spread outwards from the arch-magister's position in a crackling sphere of cyan energy.

Anything the expanding bubble touched froze where it was. Spyders hung suspended in mid-air. Necrons became immobilised mid-stride. Searing pulses of gauss energy became glowing green icicles, transfixed to the muzzles of the warriors' weapons.

And still the spell-sphere swelled and grew.

Flashing beams of gauss-light striking the coruscating barrier suffered the same effect, becoming trapped in time, like fish frozen in a pond in winter.

'Run!' Opados commanded Prototokos, and the two sorcerers sprinted for the elongated archway that marked the exit from the vast chamber.

'He would sacrifice himself for us?' Prototokos gasped.

'Is that not what you would do in his situation?' Opados challenged him.

And then the necron colossus was before them. A titan of metal and lethal intent, it turned synaptic obliterators towards the sorcerers, intending to blast them with a concentrated burst of subatomic particles. Such an assault could tear apart the molecular bonds within the very cells of the intruders' metahuman bodies.

But Opados had already intoned the incantation that would save them. Out of the corner of his visor-feed, Prototokos saw the red-veined alabaster scarab that clung to the front of Opados' armour twitch and shake itself, wing cases opening, revealing a fluttering of bejewelled plumage beneath as the sorcerer-magister's bond familiar awoke at the behest of its master.

The vulture-form of Opados' pet Tzeentchian spirit freed itself from the esoteric workings of his arcane armour and shook itself, ruffling its feathers and opening its beak in a screeching yawn. Taking wing, it flew straight towards the construct. The daemon-thing's iridescent down shimmered, as if alive with dancing flames, and then in the next moment it was consumed, phoenix-like, by the hungry azure blaze.

As the familiar was destroyed by the flames, it confounded the colossus' targeting arrays and alighted on the construct's insectile cranial command unit.

A hurricane of psychic fire exploded from the daemon-spirit's immaterial body, consuming the giant necron's head. As the firestorm raged, still chased by the time-freezing conjuration, Prototokos and Opados passed between the colossus' multijointed legs and crossed the threshold of the exit archway.

The warp-mage heard the buzz of a force field activating behind them, and a shimmering gauss field filled the portal. But it was too little too late as far as the necrons were concerned.

Turning momentarily, Prototokos saw the cyan shock wave of Tritos' chronomancy strike the warding shield and there stop. Everything inside the hall had become subject to his time-lock spell, including the arch-magister himself, and all were now as flies imprisoned within amber.

Beyond the hypostyle hall, Prototokos and Opados passed through a now empty vault and from there descended yet another staircase, which led them, eventually, to a bridge of onyx stone. The structure spanned a chasm between two towering walls of exposed circuitry and more of the black metal architecture of the tomb's interior.

They stood together at the edge of the abyss. The walls of the chasm rose above them as far as Prototokos, or his suit's optical sensors, could measure, and dropped away below them beyond the range of sight as well. The bridge had no handrails or enclosing cage, such considerations of safety or damage prevention being irrelevant to the unsleeping servitor machines that made use of the causeway during their scurrying maintenance of the tomb.

Halfway across the unnatural canyon stood a lone pillar, twenty yards in diameter, its insides carved out where the maintenance accessway penetrated it, and Prototokos could see a pulsing crystalline power node contained within. The causeway passed through the other side of the impossibly high pillar and ended at an angular platform jutting out from the wall on the opposite side of the chasm, in front of a sealed security hatch.

'The vault!' Prototokos exclaimed. 'It is as I saw it in my vision.'

'I know,' said Opados with something like exhilaration colouring his words. 'We are close to completing our mission at last.'

Without another word, the warp-mage and the Terminator-clad sorcerer-magister set off across the bridge, the door to the vault now in their sights.

It was quiet here at the heart of the Godstar, eerily so after the clamour of the battle in the hall.

Prototokos took in the ominous structures of the deep tomb. The smooth black walls were adorned with more of the geometric glyph patterns of the necrontyr that also brought a certain level of dim illumination to the unplumbed depths of the comet construct. But the closer he looked the more he began to pick out signs of decay – inconstantly flickering icons, the strange metal-stone surface of the pillar they were approaching pitted with corrosion – while oily substances oozed from a hidden network of rusting pipes.

They entered the power node chamber within the pillar,

and felt the air thrum with the machine-heart pulse emanating from the crystal.

Exiting the chamber containing the relay, as the two of
them set out across the bridge once more, Prototokos became
aware of movement at the far end of the causeway. Batteries
of gauss flayers, mounted within alcoves in the archway –
and that had, prior to their arrival, been pointing at the
entrance to the vault itself – responded to their presence now
by rotating to target them. And due to the fact that neither
of them was transmitting the correct override protocols, the
weapons opened fire.

Forced back by the dread power of the gauss batteries, Prototokos and Opados rapidly retreated to the sanctuary of the
power node chamber.

The gauss batteries ceased firing, but remained on alert,
trained on the bridge and ready to resume their barrage of
beams, should the Thousand Sons return.

From opposite sides of the exit archway the two magi
regarded one another.

'Rest easy,' Opados said, as if reading Prototokos' anxious
thoughts. 'There is always–'

'Another way?' offered the warp-mage.

'Indeed.'

The Terminator-sorcerer took a moment to observe the
relay and assess how it connected to the circuits of nearby
systems.

'Destroy the node and we take out the gate's defences,' he
said at last.

'And how do we do that?' Prototokos asked.

'How else? Using the same means that have helped us penetrate this far into the tomb. Through indomitable strength
and with an implacable will.'

Spreading his armour-plated arms wide, Opados seized the pulsating crystal with both hands, the faceted faces of it fracturing under the crushing pressure of his gauntlet-guarded fingers, and heaved.

With a groan of suit-servos and the tortured rending of metal, the node began to tilt forwards as Opados pulled it towards him. There was a sudden snap and the crystal jerked forwards again, as some vital connector buckled.

Sparks fountained from the disrupted coupling with a crackling buzz, like a swarm of electrified mosquitoes, strewing the floor with pieces of fried alloy.

Opados heaved again and with a shearing crash the crystal broke free of its mountings altogether. Without pausing, the sorcerer cast it to the floor, where it exploded into fist-sized quartz-like chunks.

Arcs of energy erupted from the shattered power node, subjecting the chamber's other systems to what was, to all intents and purposes, a self-contained lightning storm that wreathed everything in corposant, including the two sorcerers.

Prototokos luxuriated in the energising thrill of it. Even though his arcane armour insulated him from the worst effects of the high-voltage discharge, he could still feel it dancing over his skin as his battleplate burned crimson for a moment.

And then the energy discharge died, the sensation passed, and the chamber was claimed by the preternatural darkness of the tomb.

The warp-mage tore his eyes from the ruptured power node and turned his attention back to the entrance to the vault, on the other side of the chasm. The illuminated barrels of the gauss flayers blinked off and drooped in their gun pods.

'What did I tell you, brother?' exulted Opados. 'With indomitable strength and an implacable will, anything can be achieved!'

'I will remember that,' Prototokos replied.

Suddenly sensing the presence of another nearby, the warp-mage tracked something flitting through the pools of oily darkness that lay beyond the suffused glow of the gigantic dynastic glyphs.

Perhaps it had been a subliminal awareness of its gravitic suspensors, or a subtle shift in the air currents of the tomb that had alerted him. It certainly hadn't been his psychic senses; in this deathless place his witch-sight was as blind as a Prosperine cave salamander. The interloper was yet another of the necrons' soulless servants.

It moved like an apparition, sometimes there and sometimes not, as it phased in and out of three-dimensional space. It was composed of a mechanical insectile head, crablike claws and a snake-like spine of a body that ended in a cruelly spiked tip.

As Prototokos took aim with his inferno bolt pistol, Opados brought his bewitched combi-bolter to bear, the runes on its artisan-worked casing pulsating as if alive, as he opened fire.

But the sons of Magnus were shocked when, a split second later, they observed their shots pass straight through the phasing entity.

'It is a wraith,' Opados said, 'primarily a probe mechanoid, but a dimensional destabilisation matrix enables it to phase-shift in and out of reality. It can even modulate its matrix so as to keep different parts of its body in different states simultaneously, although this drains its energy reserves more rapidly.'

Prototokos fired his gun again and stared as the robot's carapace became as immaterial as a warp ghost, his enchanted bolter shell blowing a chunk out of the pillar behind it, rather than harming the construct creature itself.

'I encountered them during the enacting of the Great Undoing rite at the height of the Scythe Stars campaign.'

'And did you defeat them then?'

'Yes.'

'Then how do we kill it now?' Prototokos demanded, as he continued to fire on the flickering entity.

Whatever wisdom the sorcerer had been about to impart, his advice was abruptly choked into silence as the spectral form of a second wraith materialised around the Terminator. The invisible assassin already had Opados in its clutches. As it took corporeal form, so too did the cluster of writhing wormlike silver tendrils and gleaming claws that had, in their phased state, penetrated the sorcerer-magister's vital organs. Now that they shifted back again they were destroying Opados' genhanced body from within, and blood poured from the grille of his helm.

As Prototokos watched, the image of the Terminator-sorcerer that was being relayed to him through his visor's sensor array flickered like a corrupted pict-feed. And then he could see the details of the far chasm wall behind Opados as the sorcerer blurred and became as transparent as a warp ghost.

As immaterial now as the wraith had been when it first laid claws on him, Opados simply took a step backwards, freeing himself from the tomb keeper's clutches with that one simple action. In response the wraith phased out of reality again and the two began a dance in and out of space and time, their motions leaving a trail of phantom images behind them as they blinked in and out of existence.

As the ethereal Terminator and the unreal wraith grappled with each other in the spaces between dimensions, Opados sent the near-hypnotised Prototokos a final command, making his intentions plain to the warp-mage with a burst of psychic projection.

+Finish it. Free the prisoner.+

At the same time, the first wraith materialised and flung itself from the pillar, angling its gliding flight towards Prototokos. But as it passed the wrestling wraith and Terminator-sorcerer, Opados stepped back through the veil of reality. Wholly real once more, he reached out a hand, grabbed the necron's lashing tail, and hung on.

The wraith recoiled, writhing and twisting as it fought to be free, but the remorseless Terminator maintained his hold, both his hands bursting into flame, the canoptek creation catching fire within his grasp.

And then the wraith phase-shifted, as did Opados, and the three combatants continued their dance of death through the dimensions.

Opados had bought Prototokos the time he needed.

Continuing across the bridge, the warp-mage did not stop running until he reached the great black door of the vault. The gauss guns hung limply within their recessed alcoves, giving Prototokos ready access to the lock panel.

After centuries of meticulous planning, the culmination of his quest was now within reach. But there was still one last obstacle to overcome before the prisoner could be freed.

Placing his left hand against the black metal-stone of the arch, Prototokos focused his thoughts on the locking panel. Opening the well of his soul, tracing the skeins of time back into the past, in his mind's eye he saw beyond the alien alloy composite of the portal's surround to the arcane mechanisms buried within. He saw the pattern the moving parts had formed the last time the vault had been opened, decoded the path the electrical impulses had followed through the near-neural network of the arcane circuitry and, transforming his thoughts into telekinetic actions, forced them to assume those positions again now, in what passed for the present.

With a hiss of cryogenic gases, the vault door ground upwards into the wall.

At first, all Prototokos could see were the clouds of roiling stasis mist that filled the chamber. As his helmet's esoteric systems penetrated the obscuring fog, they registered the presence of a series of plinths within the chamber. But it was what he saw with his witch-sight – utilising senses that were neither natural nor artificial – that caused hope to flare within his twin hearts once more, that he might yet complete the mission that he and the others had set out upon, so many years before... Or had that time yet to come?

Taking his hand from the door frame, the hidden locking mechanisms realigned once more and the door began to descend again as Prototokos crossed the threshold.

The vault closed with a dull boom. A moment later a sound like a roar of pain or fury, or both, reached him from the far end of the chamber in which he now found himself. Prototokos hesitated as the enormity of what he was about to do settled about his shoulders like a mantle. The echoes of the roar died to be replaced by a bestial grunting, and the sound of something enchained struggling against its shackles.

The stasis mist had settled on the floor of the tesseract chamber, oozing around the bases of the black stone plinths, upon each a prize, frozen within a beam of flickering green light that Prototokos knew was more than just a source of illumination.

The treasures kept safe within the vault had been wrested from the younger races of the galaxy. He took them in as he passed: the fractured helm of a witch-seer of the aeldari; the blunt, thick skull of an ork warboss, a crude optical implant still embedded within one eye socket; a recon drone that was clearly t'au in origin; a power sword bearing the heraldry and honour ribbons of the Adepta Sororitas; even a tyranid spore mine, frozen at the moment of detonation.

This place was as much a museum as a prison. A mausoleum archive of treasures collected by the eccentric archivists of the Nephrekh Dynasty.

But his steps carried him ever onwards. For in the darkness of the catacomb a soul burned brightly, revealed to his witch-sight now, the blistering flare of the enraged caged spirit imprisoned within the vault. The archivists' ultimate prize. And his.

His footsteps rang from the onyx floor of the chamber as he neared the prisoner, with something approaching reverence.

The architecture of the vault, with its metal ribs and black stonework between, had something of a skeletal aspect about it, so that Prototokos felt he was walking through the fossilised remains of some long-dead star beast, reconfigured by the passage of time and the esoteric technologies of the necrontyr.

At the far end of the vault, beyond the endless rows of plinths bearing the alien artefacts and lost treasures of a thousand empires harvested from a million worlds, atop a platform raised from a series of gauss-quarried, concentric circular stones, and smothered by a haze of cryo gas, Prototokos could see a hulking shape. The vapour cleared, as his approach disturbed the air of the vault, and he saw the prisoner with his own eyes for the first time.

Locked within a wheel of living metal adorned with more of the necrons' glyph circuitry, and held within a sphere of crackling sea-green light, was the Godstar's prisoner, the one Prototokos had travelled so far, and for so long, throughout so many lifetimes, to find. To find and to free.

Doubtless alert to danger, upon hearing the sorcerer's footsteps suddenly stop, the prisoner gave voice to another bellow of rage and pain.

Three times taller than the warp-mage and more than ten times as heavy, the bulk of its body barely contained by its metal hide, the thing was a monster in the truest sense of the word – a grotesque amalgam of flesh and armour.

The distended ceramite of its body-shell had the same turquoise lustre as Prototokos' war-suit, edged with gold, while a carved scarab of red alabaster clung to its chestplate.

Above that same chestplate, visible within a metal maw of silver steel teeth, and framed by arching golden horns, was the furious face of the prisoner. The legionary's gold and turquoise skull visage looked not unlike the mechanical face of one of the Godstar's woken warriors.

But Prototokos also knew that the sculpted likeness was only a death mask, and not a true representation of the son of Magnus entombed alive within the enormous machine body. The physical form of the captive was now no more than a pulped mass of organs, bones and nerve ganglia, the body of the sacrificial offering having been flensed of its skin and subjected to the mutagenic effects of unsullied warpflame, before being placed inside an amniotic sac. This in turn had been inserted into the coffin-like maw of the Helbrute where, once inside, it became the motive force of the warped Dreadnought armour, the unendurable torments of the damned soul imprisoned within fusing with the Helbrute's motivators and driving the war colossus into battle.

But that had not been the end of the wretch's flesh-life, for within the mechanical frame of the Helbrute, that flesh had found new forms, bubbling forth, swelling to fill every empty conduit and claim every motive system of the monstrous mechanical creation for its own. Pulsing, veiny muscle had grown with cancerous enthusiasm to cover the manoeuvring joints of its massive piston legs and encase the armoured vambrace of the huge claw fist that formed the Helbrute's right arm.

On the left side of its body the thing had no arm, but instead a writhing nest of tentacles, that were as much mechanical prosthetics as they were fleshy appendages of mauve meat.

And yet both the Helbrute's fist and its scourging whips were held fast within great metal clamps that formed part of the framing ring to which it was bound, as were the hooves of its massive metal feet. Despite being fuelled by the never-ending rage induced by the agony of its continued existence, and an unquenchable hatred for those who had been the architects of its fate, the psychotic organism was unable to free itself.

A walking engine of war, what worse fate could there be for one such as the Helbrute than to be kept caged here, denied the opportunity to fight when it felt the ache of the siren call of combat within every iota of its being?

Resuming his march towards the platform, with a mere gesture the warp-mage deactivated the last of the security systems, the sphere of sea-green light melting away.

Sensing the change in its environment, the Thousand Sons Helbrute began to shake at its bonds with renewed vigour, grunting like a bull grox as it did so.

'Calm yourself,' Prototokos said, keeping his voice low, 'for I understand your pain.'

The beast-machine continued to jerk and pull at the restraining clasps, the sorcerer's words merely seeming to aggravate it.

'I know you. You are the End of All Things. You are the Death of Souls, and the fate foretold. And I name you Thanatos.'

The Helbrute suddenly became still, the only sound it made the snorting of its bullish breath.

Prototokos hesitated. He was so close to the beast now that he could pluck the memories from its damaged mind, and remind it of who it had once been. In his mind's eye he watched those recollections jerk and dance, as if viewing a degraded pict-feed.

He let out a shuddering breath as, in that moment, he experienced what Thanatos had experienced – the pain, the rage, the betrayal.

'I see it now!' Prototokos gasped. 'I see how you were deceived by Sutek of the Brotherhood of Dust, and how at Bav'ilim you fell before the Mosac Gate, only to be dug from the ruins by the Bringers of Dawn, the necrons of the Nephrekh Dynasty, a hundred years later and brought to this place.'

The Helbrute remained still, its actions, or rather lack of them, convincing Prototokos that it was taking in the words that issued from his mouth like a mantra. A cluster of eyes, protruding on short stalks from beneath its chestplate, watched him approach the dais with keen interest, blinking in a random, staccato pattern.

He felt his body tense at the prospect of doing what fate had prescribed he must.

'And you know me too,' Prototokos said. 'You have heard my voice in your stasis slumber. You have heard me calling to you down through the aeons, across the gulf of space and time. For I am Prototokos the All-Seeing, the first, and I am here to free you.'

The hulking monster remained still as the sorcerer began to climb the steps of the dais. Taking in the clamps bolted tight around the brute's fist and scourge, he hefted his star-matter blade in both hands, as snakes of psychic power began to wrap themselves around the keen cutting edges of the curse-bound weapon.

With a force of will, Prototokos leapt high into the air, his crimson cloak streaming out behind him, sorcerous teleki-netic manipulation carrying him higher than the Helbrute was tall. As he descended, he rammed the tip of the force sword down between the silver fangs of the maw-like open-ing in the front of the daemonic Dreadnought.

The energised blade screamed as it sliced through ceramite substructures, severing power cables and artificial fibre-bundle muscles. And then Prototokos felt the resistance lessen as the sword's diamond-sharp tip penetrated the amniotic sac containing the mortal remains of the wretch bound to the weaponised prison-machine.

The Helbrute's scream reverberated around the vault as the imprisoned son of Magnus felt the dark oblivion of death begin to seep into its own organic components.

Oily blood and viscous matter welled up around the life-ending blade, as they flooded from the wound Prototokos had dealt the Helbrute, while the one known as Thanatos bucked and twisted within its bonds, railing against the all-consuming darkness and an end that had been predes-tined ten thousand years before.

'Do not fight it,' Prototokos told the beast in a soothing tone. He hung on to the blade, his feet planted firmly on the Helbrute's chestplate. 'I bring you merciful release. I came here to free you, and freed you I have.'

The Helbrute roared again, determined not to give in to anything so easily, ever. Prototokos was aware of a sharp crack, as something within the ancient shackle-wheel, degraded at the atomic level, gave way.

'I understand, brother,' the warp-mage said, trying to maintain the same calm tone as he clung to the pommel of the blade that acted as a conduit for the furious force of his blazing psychic fire. 'Within what is left of your madness-ravaged mind you are wondering why? Why is this happening to me? I know this because it is happening to me as well. And in the hope that it might relieve your tortured psyche, I will do my best to explain.'

The Helbrute continued to lurch within the binding ring and with a metallic groan of protest, something else came free, allowing Thanatos a greater range of movement.

'I understand because we are the same, you and I.'

But the brute wasn't listening now; it had been taken over by its wracking death throes. And yet Prototokos persevered regardless, for his own sake if nothing else.

'Three of us set out upon our quest and penetrated the defences of this necron tombworld construct, this so-called Godstar. Only three. But that was still enough, to do what had to be done.

'It was I who first discovered our doom-laden destiny, whilst conducting a scrying ritual, although I doubt you remember any of this now. But I had not the power to act and avoid such a future. And so I planned to seek the power, perform the required rituals and achieve the mastery of magic over time that I might intervene and save my future self – you, Thanatos – from such a hellish fate.

'But it was not until my future self became an exalted brother of our Legion, and achieved the necessary mastery of warp magic, taking the name Tritos in honour of his accomplishments, that he was able to manipulate time and bring together his younger selves, those sorcerers that I had yet to become, that we might begin our journey and free you from your torment. Although, as I perceived it, he appeared to me only a matter of months after I made my discovery and set myself upon this path of fighting fate.

'But you do not remember any of this, of course, which is why I must release you from your tortured existence. The others have bought me the time I needed to complete my task. For as long as I endure, they can be saved. *We* can be saved.

'I have sifted through the remnants of what passes for your mind, and have discovered from the few memories that remain how you fell into this state, how you were tricked by Sutek the Deceiver and entombed within this accursed armour-form. And so I will no longer walk that doomed path. I will not share your fate.

'And now, Thanatos, the End of all Things, it is the end for you.'

With a screech of rending metal, the Helbrute tore its mighty fist free of its restraining clamp at last. With the crackling energy sphere deactivated, the Helbrute's bonds were no longer strong enough to hold him by themselves.

In one swift movement, the monster seized Prototokos with its crushing claw. The sorcerer cried out as his battle-plate crumpled in the Helbrute's grip. Flanged plates of turquoise and gold cut into the very flesh they were supposed to protect, rupturing veins and arteries and puncturing myriad enhanced organs. Auto-muscles and servo-motors shorted out, and the resulting jolts of electrical discharge pulsed through Prototokos' cardiovascular system, setting up an arrhythmic ventricular fibrillation within his dual hearts.

'Thanatos, stop!' Prototokos spluttered through blood that bubbled up from his lungs and into his throat. 'You will unmake us both!'

But Thanatos of the Thousand Sons – nothing more than a brute beast now – was no longer listening, or no longer cared.

In that moment of crystallised time, Prototokos realised that his quest to free himself from his ultimate fate had been a fool's errand all along. One way or another, it was his destiny to be slain by the madness that beset his soul upon being imprisoned within the Helbrute armour.

Its power scourge alive with energy again, now that the dampening shield was down, Thanatos flexed its mechadendrites and tore them free of their restraints.

The snaking metal and muscle tentacles whipped around the warp-mage's neck and began to tighten their grip.

'Stop!' Prototokos the All-Seeing protested. 'You know not what you do!' And then he could say no more as the gorget of his armour fractured and the tentacles began to constrict both his spinal column and his windpipe.

With one final squeeze of its huge hand, the Helbrute crushed the sorcerer's suit of armour as if it were no more than an empty ration tin.

At the moment of his death, denied his physical voice, Prototokos' death rattle was reborn as a psychic scream of agony and frustration, the raw, untamed energy of it finding an outlet through the star-matter sword. White fire blazed the length of the black blade into the amniotic sac of fluid and genhanced flesh, boiling what little remained within of the once mighty sorcerer of the Crimson Scarab sect.

The Helbrute's dying screams echoed from the walls of the necron vault, while the sorcerer hung lifeless within its huge fist, the vital spark of his life having already been snuffed out and passed on in silence.

Bathed in the unreal rainbows of coruscating warpflame, the Helbrute's body began to unmake itself. Flakes of turquoise lacquer and thin slivers of gold leaf drifted away from it, like burning pieces of parchment rising from a funeral pyre. At the same time the crimson scarab adorning its chestplate crumbled, turning to glassy dust, while the warped flesh that covered much of its lumpen limbs began to dissolve and mingle with the stasis-gas still clouding the containment chamber, before evaporating altogether.

With Prototokos' life cut short, he would no longer become the Terminator armour-clad Opados of the Nine Kings thrallband who, in turn, could now never ascend to the rank of exalted arch-magister of the Cult of Time. With the tapestry of his life unravelled, the future became malleable again, mutable, unwritten.

The unmaking accelerated, as first the near-impenetrable shell of the Helbrute's armour and then, as they were exposed, sinews and power conduits, nubs of bone and auto-reactive servo-motors, exhaust stacks, twitching nerve ganglia, coolant feeds, metastasising lumps of gristle, mechanical claws, fibrous connective tissue and carbon-fibre muscle-bundles, all dissolved into threads of potentiality and were carried away on the unseen warp winds of unformed futures.

And as the Helbrute was expunged from reality, its body dissipating into a state of non-being – having never existed at all – there was now no reason for the magi having made their journey to this time-cursed place at all. And so, alone now, the body of the warp-mage began to unravel as well.

The Godstar tumbled through the silent night as it had done for countless aeons, the light cast by dying suns penetrating the chthonic-green corona that surrounded it, picking out the monolithic structures covering its surface. Before one obsidian-smooth pyramid, space-time warped and buckled, and a portal opened.

First to step through it, onto the ice-frosted void-black stones, was Prototokos the All-Seeing, warp-mage of the Thousand Sons Legion, arrayed in his turquoise battleplate. Second – and more impressive still, clad in an elaborately ornamented suit of Terminator armour – came Sorcerer-Magister Opados. Last through the portal, riding upon the back of a warp beast formed of blue flesh and gold-chased steel, came Arch-Magister Tritos of the Heralds of Destiny, master manipulator of the warp and weft of the fabric of time itself.

As the three moved towards the pyramid, following the sloping path of a grand processional avenue, behind the three magi the immaterial vortex closed again, the echoes of the concussive boom of displaced air rippling across the surface of the comet-world, like laughter.

The Beginning.

THE SERPENT'S BARGAIN

Jamie Crisalli

*We are pleased to welcome Jamie Crisalli, who came to
Black Library via the open submissions window, back to the
pages of* Inferno! *With her penchant for bloody violence and
melodrama, it feels only natural that Jamie turn her hand to
the deadly and capricious Daughters of Khaine.*

*Tormented by the followers of Slaanesh, Laila is forced to seek
out the help of the 'Fair Ones', aelven maidens with a grudge
against the Prince of Pleasure. But she soon finds that these
strange beings drive a hard bargain.*

Laila wriggled into the hole dug deep under the hut she called home. The hole was little wider than her hips and she yanked the stone cover over the opening, sealing her in a womblike darkness. Small holes the size of an old Pelos coin let in air. Thin roots tickled her freckled skin and the smell of Ghyran loam smothered her nose. A cache of water and bread in a sealed clay pot sat between her bare feet. In her shaking hand, she clutched a small leather bottle on a string around her neck.

Raw screams and exultant roaring filtered down to her in that tiny hollow. And other, more obscene sounds as the fiends went about their horrid joys. Of all the places in Ghyran, the followers of the Needful One had come to her village of Varna. The new palisade had not kept them out, nor had any fighter that they possessed.

Up above, the hut door banged open and she started, her heart racing.

A man moaned and licked his lips.

'Not much sport here,' he said, his voice melodious.

'This is the first settlement in weeks not tainted by those reeking pus-bags,' said another. 'So, I'd enjoy yourself while you can. These little people are entertaining enough.'

Something crashed over, shards of pottery scattering across the floor. And they talked about what they had done and would do if they found someone. Shuddering, Laila clamped a callused hand over her mouth and pressed herself deeper into the dirt. Her mind shrinking away from the memories of her husband's tortured last moments years ago, Laila worked the stopper out of the bottle and a dusty smell like dead flowers filled the air. She would not die as he had.

Inside was a poison called Blood of the Wight; it was not painless but it was lightning quick. Her mother had given it to her when she was a child and told her to keep it with her even when she slept. There were numberless things worse than dying.

With a hiss, the raiders went quiet. A shadow crept over the breathing holes, sniffing. Laila put the bottle to her lips. Then a shrill hollow tone wended over the town, reverberating in her head.

'Is that a retreat?' one asked in disbelief.

'I would watch your forked tongue unless you want to be the cure for Lord Zertalian's ennui,' said the other. 'Clearly he wishes to save this place for future amusement. So let's go.'

Ceramic crunched under foot and the door banged shut. Yet, Laila could not move. She stayed, holding the poison to her lips, staring at the dirt wall, trying to breathe quietly. Only a buzzing tension remained, as if her head were full of bees. What if it was a trick and they had not left, instead waiting to pounce? No, it was better to stay in here with poison than risk that fate. Even as her sturdy legs cramped and her lips went numb, she held still. Then a familiar voice called her name.

'Stefen!' she called, her voice ragged.

Laila crammed the stopper back into the bottle and clambered out of her sanctuary. Then she paused.

Her home was wrecked, her meagre belongings tossed about and broken, her food stores spilled and trampled. Still, she was lucky – only her things had been touched by the seekers. She would burn it all as was tradition with tainted things. Hopefully the elders would spare the hut itself or she would have to move in with a neighbour during winter.

Stefen rushed in, his dark eyes wide.

She embraced him, trembling and choking back tears. He was an old childhood friend; they had gone on to their separate lives when he had become a hunter and she had married Jonas.

'It's all right, they're gone,' he said, pulling her close. Stefen was tall and well built, though the Rotskin pox had left him with scarred, pallid skin, ruining his good looks. A clutch of scrawny birds swung over his shoulder, along with his snares and bow.

A wash of cold fear rolled through her as the gossip of the raiders rattled in her brain.

'Are the elders still with us?' she asked.

'Yes, they were spared,' he said.

'They need to know,' she said.

Without waiting to see if he followed, she rushed out into the bright light of the Lamp. The palisade gate dangled as men worked desperately to wrench the doors back into place. Homes burned, releasing sweet smoke and pale flames as ashen-faced neighbours watched, making no move to put them out. Others wandered aimlessly, their clothing torn and eyes utterly vacant, while some desperately called out for missing loved ones. Horror seeped through the very air as if some malign spirit had made a home in every hut and heart, a final curse bestowed by the fiends. No doubt it would linger for years.

Laila walked, eyes seeing but unable to understand it, same as it had been then. The horrid memories edged into her mind and she forced them away. Jonas was long dead, praise Alarielle.

By some miracle, the stone elders' hall had not been touched. Some speculated that it was once a temple devoted to a forgotten storm god. Perhaps that was why the fiends avoided it.

Inside, the place was stifling hot, the fires burning high to warm old bones. Yet, the crowd was more meagre than Laila had expected. The hall guards were gone to help with the gate. At the far end, sat in a loose half-circle, were the elders, some hunched and withered, some grey and still robust. The old altar loomed behind them.

'We will rebuild and mourn as we have always done,' Uma said, her voice like a creaking door. 'The dark ones never stay. The seekers will move on and leave us be.'

The other elders nodded. As always, they acquiesced to the ancient crone. Laila suddenly hated the old woman and the sycophants that surrounded her. Of course they felt that way; they sat in the heart of the village surrounded by stone and armed guards. Did they even know what happened out there? No more than they had after the last raid by the seekers.

'No, they won't,' Laila said, her tone cold. 'They're coming back.'

The silence sharpened and Laila blushed as all eyes focused on her. Uma's face crumpled, her eyes narrowing.

'What do you mean?' Uma said.

'They're coming back?' another man said.

The crowd bubbled with alarm, looking around as if the dark ones were going to lunge out of the walls.

'Two of them came into my house while I was hiding,' Laila said, wrapping her arms around herself. 'They were summoned by their leader early. They said that they would return.'

Another rumble of discontent. If Uma could have killed Laila with her gaze, she likely would have.

'I agree with Laila, we can't wait and do nothing,' Stefen said behind her.

'What would the youngsters suggest?' Uma said. 'That we fight them?'

Laila stammered, her thoughts churning. She had no solution to the problem that she had presented. Then an idea popped into her mind. A dangerous endeavour but better than the alternative.

'The Fair Ones in the Valley of the Oracle's Eye,' Laila said. 'They help people if the foe is right. Is that not correct?'

The crowd murmured. The Fair Ones. Some said they had earned this name because they were beautiful. Others claimed they were hideous, with snakes for hair, and cursed those who did not flatter them. What the legends did agree on was that the Fair Ones hated Chaos more than anything else, especially the followers of the Needful One.

Uma snorted. 'You are not serious,' she said. 'The valley where they dwell is a place of madness and they are themselves not remotely human. The Fair Ones fight on their own terms and no one else's. You are a fool.'

'Says the old woman who counsels that we wait for those beasts to return and finish what they started,' Laila snapped.

Uma blanched, her thin skin turning whiter than the wisps on her head.

'Out! I will not tolerate your stupidity a moment longer,' Uma said, snapping a finger at the door.

Laila spun on her heel and pushed through the crowd, out into the smoky air. Inside the hall, the arguing escalated. Although there was a harvest to bring in, no one wanted to go outside the walls if there was the slightest chance that the fiends were waiting for them. Cries echoed, questioning why they did nothing. Others called for the villagers to resettle elsewhere. Uma shouted back with all the ferocity in her old bones.

'And she calls me stupid,' Laila muttered to herself.

'She's afraid, nothing more malicious than that,' Stefen said. 'This isn't like the pox walkers. It's worse. I should have been here.'

'You would have just got yourself killed, or worse,' Laila said. 'We need to get help from people that can fight. Uma is right, we can't defend ourselves against that.'

'I can lead us to the valley,' Stefen said. 'I've been to the borders anyway.'

'Really, you've seen it?' she said. 'That's forbidden.'

Stefen blushed sheepishly and nodded. 'Once.'

'You will not get there alone, especially if the fiends are still out there,' a stranger said in a hard, growling accent.

They both spun about. A man stood before them in leather and bronze plate. His skin was tanned and aged and he was built heavily with a round gut that spoke of a steady diet of beer and meat. That he was creeping into middle age indicated either luck or skill, likely both.

'Who are you?' Laila asked.

'Ano,' he replied, as if that explained everything. When they continued to look at him in silence, he added, 'I worked for the merchant, Antton. I hope that if I help you, your village will let me stay over the winter.'

'What we're talking about doing is dangerous,' Laila said, suspicious.

'I heard, but what that old woman is suggesting is worse,' he said. 'What you described sounds like something that the fiends do. They wait for your guard to fall. And they can wait a long time. Then they strike.'

While Laila did not trust the stranger, when standing against the Chaos hordes all pure humans had to stick together. What few untainted humans remained.

'The real question is will Hadlen let us out?' Stefen said.

Laila winced; the reeve was stubborn at the best of times. 'We have to try,' Laila said. 'He might be persuaded.'

Stefen smiled tightly. 'Yes, and lightning men will fall from the sky and kill our enemies.'

They snickered at the old child's tale and made their plans. They delayed as much as they dared, speaking to the few close friends that they knew would keep their peace. With the watch so tense, sneaking out would be a challenge. Carefully, they gathered their supplies – a few loaves of hard bread, dried beans and smoked meat. Then at the light of dawn the next day, they walked to the back edge of the village where the midden heap lay next to the wall. It smelled of rotten grain and human waste; however, there was a gap in the palisade where the beams had rotted and they slipped out into the greater world with no one the wiser.

'So this is how you kept escaping,' Laila said.

Stefen grinned as he brushed off his hands. 'No one ever looked.'

As they walked around the village and onto the road, they

saw not a single corpse. Just dried bloodstains and spatters of clear fluid like the trails of slugs. Strange perfumes lingered in the air, faded but potent enough to tickle the nose. Crows fluttered out in the fields, squawking at each other.

Stefen took them off the road towards the east, into the thinning forest. A deep layer of leaves rustled underfoot. Overhead, the skeletal trees rattled in the wind. The glow of the Lamp dimmed with the evening, while the Cinder Disc glimmered, already small and red with the autumn.

It felt almost unnatural to be moving away from Varna. The trees seemed to hide sinister threats, and Laila waited for some pale horror to come pelting out at them. Out here, the urge to leave struck her as impulsive while in the town it had felt brave. Had she misheard the raiders? Was Uma right? With a start, Laila realised that she had never been this far from the walls.

'Second thoughts?' Stefen said.

'How do you do it?' she said. 'Leave Varna I mean.'

'One step at a time,' Stefen said, smiling.

They walked on, the shadows growing long. Stars flickered into being and the night birds started to warble to each other.

'What about you?' Laila said to Ano. 'How did you come to travel?'

'It's tough to do,' Ano said. 'But there are advantages.'

'Like what?' she said.

'Being paid in coin is good,' Ano said.

It was practical, yet there was a mercenary attitude to his response that she did not like.

'We can't pay you in coin,' she said, hoping to gain a clearer sense of his motivation.

'No, but a bed for the winter is priceless,' he said. 'Besides, I could not help my employer.'

192

She let the subject drop when he looked away from her with a cough.

They travelled for several days, the forest twittering and breathing around them. It had not always been so. Once upon a time, this entire woodland had been a mire of maggots, rot and corpses. Then something had changed. Some said it was just the way of nature to reassert itself after a time. Others said it was a blessing from Alarielle, waking from her long slumber. Still others whispered that it was the Fair Ones that had freed the region of its decay.

Laila found herself dreading the night. Her sleep was long in coming and when she finally drifted off, nightmares haunted her with horrifying blends of past and present. The fiends, all wearing the manic sweaty face of Jonas, chased her through the fields. They always caught her and then cut her apart, ecstatic breathing echoing in her mind. The shadowy pain remained after she bolted awake, lingering in cramping muscles and unmarked skin.

Just as Laila began to think they were going the wrong way, Stefen spotted a coiling vine growing under the dense boughs of a great tree. It was black, like the night void when no other heavenly bodies lit the sky. Laila had never seen such a colour in nature before and marvelled at the glossy black leaves.

'Don't touch it,' Stefen said. 'Most things in the Valley of the Oracle's Eye are venomous.'

'Are you sure you can get us there?' Ano said, shifting his weight.

'Normally this is where I turn around,' Stefen said. 'If we just keep walking, the landscape will guide us. Though it will be dangerous in ways that are unfamiliar to us.'

'We should be more cautious now,' Ano said, gripping his spear. 'Pay attention. Watch your backs. I will take the rear.'

'Why?' Laila asked.

'Because I have the feeling that the beasts out here do not attack from the front,' Ano said with a sardonic smile.

Laila shivered. The shadows seemed even deeper and more threatening than before. As they moved eastwards, the land grew bleak. The trees shrank, their limbs struggling upwards. Blood-red leaves coated the earth, filled with worms that slithered alarmingly under Laila's bare feet. Above them, the Lamp grew fat and orange as if seen through a veil of ashes. Animals became quiet and unnatural, with deep black coats, bloated white eyes and long spidery limbs. The world of Ghyran changed, tainted by whatever miasma leaked from the Oracle's Eye.

They trudged onwards until the Lamp suddenly winked out and darkness fell, a blackness so complete that it hurt the eyes. Laila stifled a scream. The night had never come on so fast back at Varna, not even in the depths of winter. A clammy chill rushed in, cutting through their clothes. The sort of cold that would slowly kill if allowed to.

'Light,' Ano hissed. 'Now.'

Leaves rustled under foot as Ano shifted around.

The shadows watched them. This she knew. She felt their gaze lingering on the skin. Something whispered past her and she flinched. Shadows touched her hands, coiled around her legs and brushed her cheeks, light as cobwebs. She stayed still, even as a scream threatened to escape her throat.

Instead, she focused, her ears straining. The whisper of cloth, a soft grunt, a light rattle of stone. Something fell into the leaves. Stone clacked against stone. Sparks flared, stinging her eyes. Then the crackle of fire. The hiss of retreating things.

'Hold this,' Stefen said, handing her the torch before putting an arrow to the string of his bow.

'Where is Ano?' she said, looking around.

Their hearts hammering, standing in the little circle of light surrounded by blackness, they realised that their best fighter was gone without a struggle. How could he have not made a sound? Neither dared to call for the man. Laila crept to the edge of the light, as if she were looking over the side of a boat into a dark sea.

'Ano, say something,' she hissed, then her toes brushed something heavy and wooden.

Ano's spear lay where he had dropped it. There was nothing else. Not a drop of blood, nor a shred of cloth. Not even the leaves were disturbed. With a start, she looked up, expecting some beast but there was nothing but blackness.

'Don't make a sound,' Stefen said, then turned his back to the light and walked out a few paces. Unblinking alien eyes peered from the gloom, disappearing and then reappearing somewhere else. He raised his bow, drew and waited. Then he loosed and something hissed in pain out in the darkness. That he could see anything amazed her.

'We should move, that's not the only thing out here,' Stefen whispered. 'We may be in some creature's territory and it will leave us alone once we're gone. At least that's what I hope.'

Some might have called her and Stefen cowards for not looking for Ano. However, death came quickly or sometimes not fast enough. He was already lost and she would not risk her own life for a corpse.

Laila nodded jerkily, shaking from the fear and cold. She picked up the heavy spear though there was no way she could wield the thing. The idea of fighting was not comforting:

more than likely she would die. Still, better that than simply giving up. They moved on, searching for shelter of some sort.

Laila wrapped her cloak about herself. She had thought the greatest danger was the fiends waiting outside Varna; once past them, she imagined that the venture would go smoothly. Guilt crept over her. This journey was her idea. Ano would not have been out here if they had not gone. But what choice did they have, given what they knew?

They needed an army, and if Ano had died to give them that, then his death was not in vain. Yet if the darkness could take Ano, what hope did they have of reaching the valley?

Eventually, the pair found a small ditch within which they took shelter, building a roof of branches over the top and then a fire to stave off the chill. Laila did not sleep, every noise emphasised by the unnatural darkness. The rustling of her clothes, every small cough, even her breathing seemed loud enough that all the world heard.

Dawn came on weak and cold, the air thick with grey vapours. They helped themselves to some beans and bread, then moved on. The earth became hard and stony, the trees shrivelled and the undergrowth thickened with pale white plants that shrank back when touched.

'We're definitely moving down,' Stefen said.

Grey hills rose on either side, shrouded in mist. Laila felt she was walking into a prison that she could not escape. Yet, her nightmares whipped her on. What dangers compared to what the fiends promised?

They walked on and then the rocky earth gave way to a smooth stone street, like the ancients had made before the Plague Times. Tall statues of women loomed on either side. But their proportions were strange, too tall and thin as if they had been stretched out. They wore scandalously little clothing and brandished swords as they silently charged towards an unseen enemy. Laila shuddered at their screaming faces and wild hair. The place seemed abandoned, yet every eye followed them as they passed.

Ahead of them, impossibly tall towers hove out of the mists, clawing up towards the heavens like a clutch of brambles. Laila had never seen anything so vast made by the hands of mortals. Set in the side of the nearest was a huge set of doors that stood open, guarded by another pair of stone warrior women. From over the doors, an idol with a screaming face watched them, grasping a downturned sword in one hand and something small and dripping in the other.

'Maybe this was not the best idea,' Stefen said. 'We should not be here. This place is not for us.'

She found herself nodding in agreement.

'We can't,' she said, more to herself than him.

'That statue is holding a heart in its fist,' he said, drawing an arrow from his quiver.

Laila paced around on the threshold, her fists balled up, trying to summon up her courage. One part of her wanted to yell at him for strengthening her fears, while another part wanted to leave and never return.

'I know what they will do,' she said, her voice shaking. 'I can't let that happen to me or anyone else. This place is terrifying, but not as bad as being in that hole, knowing what they do.'

She looked at the black opening and steeled herself. With a deep breath, Stefen stepped forwards.

'No, not you. Just her,' a hoarse man's voice floated to them out of the darkness.

They both froze like rabbits caught out by a fox.

'And no weapons in this holy place,' the voice said.

Laila swallowed. Reluctantly, she handed the spear to Stefen and then stepped over the threshold. A stifling silence enveloped her and when she looked back, the outside world was hazy and dark. Stefen was little more than an ink blot on a sheet of paper. Pale blue torches guttered, merely enhancing the deep darkness that settled in every corner. The ceiling loomed far above her, arched and covered in sharp, jagged runes. It made the old temple at Varna seem like a hovel.

'Go on,' the voice said.

She caught sight of a gaunt face in the dark, the eyes two black pits. Then it vanished into the gloom.

What kind of place was this? How could a darkness this deep exist? And was this one man all there was? No place this grand stood empty and unprotected. Yet the silence was so deep, and the place so empty. What if this was merely another grandiose ruin?

As she walked deeper, her eyes started to pull phantasms out of the black air, leering faces, flying serpents and skeletal men riding gangling horses.

A glutinous bubbling sound caught her attention and she moved towards it. As she walked closer, the air grew thick with incense and a sweet, coppery stench like cooking blood sausage. A strange altar revealed itself – at least, she thought that it was an altar. Two flights of stairs wound their way up to a vast cauldron held by a statue of a straining man. Steam rose from within the huge vessel. Looming over it was the same idol she had seen above the door. Yet this one was covered in thick red enamel, burnished gold and glittering gems. Its eyes burned crimson and seemed to follow her with predatory focus.

Something stirred in the cauldron, fluid sloshing over the side. A great coil rose, like a leviathan breaking the surface of the sea. Then a small green snake crept over the side, black tongue flicking. She cocked her head, puzzled. Another serpent and then another slipped over, peering at her with unnerving, single-minded interest.

Laila took a step backwards. Why would anyone put a snake colony in a cauldron? And what else was in it? Instinct rattled through her, the overwhelming need to run. There was a predator in here, one large enough to kill her.

Then a bright light leapt to life from her left, stinging her eyes. A woman's voice, deep and rough with wisdom, spoke softly. Whatever was in the cauldron settled back like a dragon lulled to sleep.

'I would come towards the light, young one,' the voice said. 'My sister is not friendly to the curious.'

Laila blocked the light with her hand and stepped towards it, feeling her way with her toes. She stumbled when her feet touched earth and a soft fragrant wind sighed through her curls. With watery eyes, she looked around at an outdoor garden, the surrounding walls gleaming like black glass.

All the plantings, neatly laid out in vivid clusters, were venomous: Strikeweed, Neolinem and Grave-eye. And those were just the ones she recognised. Other plants and trees whispered in the wind, dark and spiky or pallid and ghostly. Even the grass under her feet had a purple cast to it. Above her, the Lamp was shrouded, though still brighter than the blackness within the temple.

In the centre of the garden stood the most beautiful woman she had ever seen. Now Laila understood why they were called the Fair Ones.

The woman resembled a human being only loosely. Long and thin as a blade, she moved with an airy grace, like a great cat. Her pointed ears peeked through her black hair and her skin was dark as a doe's eyes, without blemish or scar. A jewelled leather cloak hung off her slim shoulders and underneath she was nearly nude, though Laila doubted she felt any shame in it. Two strange blades hung from her hips, more like torture instruments than weapons of war. Yet it was her face that was the most unnerving. While her expression was gentle, it was at odds with her sharp black eyes and thin cruel lips.

Next to the aelf was an elaborately carved table, upon which rested a stone bowl etched with sharp runes and the familiar idol in miniature.

'We have not seen one of your kind in many years,' she said, her accent hissing through the human words.

'Generations, ma'am,' Laila said, her voice scratchy with nerves. 'I am Laila. I represent the village of Varna.'

The woman's eyes narrowed and her smile deepened. No human expression, that. It was like seeing a sicklecat smile.

'I always forget how short-lived you humans are,' she said. 'So, Laila of Varna, do you know who we are or have even your legends forgotten us?'

Laila opened her mouth but then realised that she could not in fact answer the question. Certainly, not to this woman's satisfaction.

'Only in the vaguest terms,' she said. 'We know that when the great enemy comes, you will fight for us.'

'For a price,' the woman said, with a tremor in her voice as if she were trying to repress some strong emotion. 'Let us move beyond simple legends, shall we? My name is Cesse, and this is a temple of the Khelt Nar, a sisterhood devoted to the defeat of Chaos under Khaine's holy guidance.'

'So you are a holy order?' Laila said warily.

'Precisely,' Cesse said, her voice bright with fervour. 'We are dedicated to our faith and that is enough.'

'And if you operate on faith, what is this price then?' Laila said, sensing something was off.

'The price is that of blood. Blood buys blood,' Cesse said, drawing a dagger from her belt.

Laila took a step back.

'Please, I will not kill you,' Cesse said, flicking her hand dismissively. 'You have a need of our skills. You need us to kill your enemy. What is this enemy?'

'They worship… um… they worship…' Laila started, then she took a breath and looked up at the sky. 'The Needful One. The Beckoning Prince.' Cesse looked at her, one thin brow arched in confusion. '*Slaanesh,*' she mumbled finally, looking at her feet.

Heat crept into her face at her blasphemy, at speaking that abominable name. She looked up and recoiled. Cesse stared at her, every muscle standing like a cord under her skin. Seemingly unaware, the woman slowly drove her blade deep into the table, the wood creaking. The pleasant mask was gone, leaving a hate that shivered through the aelf's limbs and etched her face into a scowl of furious cruelty.

'Hear my words, human. We will not rest until your dread enemy is slain,' she snarled, her voice a terrible rasp. 'We will kill them without mercy. None of them can be allowed to live.'

Laila fought the urge to run, holding herself still as Cesse wrenched the dagger from the table. Seeing Laila's expression, Cesse's eyes narrowed in suspicion as if sensing some weakness.

'Do you not want them all dead?' Cesse said, her black eyes feverish.

'Yes, of course I do,' Laila stammered.

Cesse smiled. 'Oh, I see. To be as ignorant as you are now.

You do not know what they do. You do not know the thing that lurks in the darkness and eats at their souls.'

Cesse's focus turned towards some inner turmoil, her eyes dark and dull. A profound hate flickered there, a self-loathing that was all-consuming and burned eternally. A shame that ever boiled, a pain that never eased, a hurt that never healed. What caused it, Laila could not guess. However, she did not want to be around when that storm of emotion turned outwards.

'You will kill them for blood?' Laila prompted. Now that she said it out loud, it seemed insane. What would a holy order want with blood? What was the significance?

Cesse tossed her head, her black hair shimmering, coming back to the present.

'Of course, that has always been the agreement,' Cesse said. 'And what is blood compared to the tortures that await you if you do nothing?' Cesse leaned across the table. 'Trust me when I say, the agonies and slow death that you envision are only the beginning. It is not just the body that they devour.'

'Whose blood is it?' Laila asked.

'Yours, I assume,' Cesse said. 'Who else's?'

Laila blushed. It seemed easy enough.

'Why?'

'All of creation moves at the beating of a heart. All things from the strongest godbeast to the stars themselves. Nothing can be outside it. The heart and the blood it moves are the most sacred of things.'

Laila nodded. 'I agree on behalf of Varna. You will kill the raiders in return for blood.'

'Excellent, now we can begin,' Cesse said, gesturing that Laila should stand opposite her at the table. Then she began to chant, her words like the rattling of swords and spears.

The aelven woman sliced the dagger across her palm without even flinching, as if she had done this many times before. Blood leaked into the bowl. Then she crooked a long finger at Laila.

Yet Laila hesitated. Then she shook herself. What was a little cut compared to what those creatures did to their victims? She thrust out a hand. Cesse took it, her skin feverish, and then quickly slashed open Laila's palm. It burned like hot iron and Laila tried to jerk away, but Cesse held her fast until her blood fell into the bowl. At last Cesse released her, still chanting.

Now the blood began to seethe, filling the air with coppery smoke. Shadows crept among the shrubs and flowers. Cesse's voice rose to a shout, darkness seeping around her body like a serpent. Then she clapped her hands together, the sound like thunder. Laila stepped back towards the door. The air became dark, vile and oozing, catching in her throat and lungs, crawling over her skin like spiders. Cesse's eyes were pits of the blackest spite, her hands dripping blood and gloom.

'It is done,' Cesse said. 'You will have our blades, our magic and above all our hate. All is yours for blood yet spilled. Now go, this place is no longer for you!'

Laila did not need to be told. She fled, the shadows hurtling after her. As she burst through the hall, something hissed and roiled up on that dread altar. Laila ran on, things catching and plucking at her clothes and hair. She bolted under that fearsome archway out into the sickly light.

'Stefen,' she yelled, slowing her breakneck pace only slightly. 'We're done. We need to go!'

He was not there. Only the spear, a broken arrow and an ominous spatter of blood remained.

'Stefen!' she screamed, looking around frantically.

The shadows boiled out of the temple, hissing like vipers.

Laila ran as fast as she could. Like any nightmare, it could not catch her if she did not look back at whatever it was that snarled and snapped at her heels. She reached the edge of the forest and hurled herself through the trees without pausing. The seething shadows grew distant and then retreated as if the brilliance of Ghyran was not to their liking.

Once she was certain that she had left the creatures far behind, she dropped to her knees and wept. Never had she imagined that Stefen would perish. She had always thought that it would be her, that Stefen would be the one to carry back the news of their success. After all, she was just another farmer and he was a hunter that went out in the wider world.

Why had she lived while he had not? As if in answer, the cut in her palm leaped to life, stinging like an envenomed lesion. The wound seeped a clear fluid, and the skin surrounding it was a sickly grey. She tore a strip of cloth from her frayed tunic and tied it around the torn flesh.

This done, Laila set off towards home, tormented at night by nightmares and pain, and driven on by terrors of fiends and predators during the day. Sometimes, out of the corner of her eye, she glimpsed thin pale men on dark horses slipping through the shadows. She wondered if she was going mad.

It was twilight on the third day when she came within sight of Varna, long shadows reaching across the fields. A familiar sickly-sweet smell tickled her senses. Had she been too late? Was that grim bargain all for nothing?

Exhausted fear leaped through her and she pelted out across the fields of red-tinged grain. She half expected some terrible shriek or that shrill tone to echo from the trees, but there was nothing.

The gate was already closed when she reached it. She banged on the wood and called out for someone to have mercy and open it, though she knew that they should not. They would leave her out here to survive the night as best she could before opening that door.

Then the gate creaked, opening just enough to let her in. She rushed through the gap and crashed into something solid.

'Laila,' Hadlen said, slowing her down. 'Where have you been? Where is Stefen?'

One of the other warriors took off, running towards the great hall, shouting that she had returned.

She shook her head and told Hadlen what had occurred in a soft voice. Yet, she found herself obscuring details, even as the story spilled out. She lingered instead on Stefen, on his skills, on his calm. As she finished, she noticed a commotion coming towards her.

Uma. Of all the people in Varna, the last person she wanted to see was Uma. Laila had no stomach for the crone's displeasure after everything that she had seen.

'You were forbidden from doing this, Laila,' Uma snapped as she shuffled up to them.

'What would you rather have happen?' Laila said. 'That we just sit waiting to be slaughtered by the worst that this world has to offer? By those beasts. You know what they were going to do to us.'

Laila glanced around. To her surprise, some of the others crowded around rumbled in agreement. Still, many clearly sided with Uma, their faces set hard as stone.

'You know not what you have done,' Uma said. 'Time will tell. The legends say to be cautious of the Fair Ones. Who knows what they will do in the end.'

'They are going to kill all those fiends for us,' Laila snapped, jabbing a finger in the old woman's direction. 'We might learn that we don't have to be so afraid any more.'

It was an empty thing, grasping at surety in the face of Uma's doubts. It was as if the old woman were plucking Laila's own secret worries from her head, when Laila desperately wanted the bargain to work out. Uma had not seen Jonas' body or heard his last wheezing breath. Sometimes the lesser evil was all that remained.

'I doubt that,' Uma said, turning away from her. 'There is always something to fear.'

Uma shuffled away, her back bent more than Laila remembered. Her supporters went with her, scowling.

Exhausted, Laila excused herself when the others pressed in with urgent questions. She stumbled into her house and hurled herself into bed. Yet her nightmares continued, dreams of shadows chasing her through endless halls while the aelves' bloody-handed god loomed over her with burning eyes. Sometimes, Ano and Stefen were with her and they were always devoured by whatever beast ran in the shadows.

As Laila returned to the familiar rhythm of her old life, she remembered the bargain with ever greater unease. She was missing something. But what? Cesse was sinister certainly, but had given her word in front of her god. While that god was no Alarielle, he was still a deity that had rules that were binding. So why did it feel like something had gone horribly wrong?

The days turned into a week and then two, autumn cooled and the rains started in earnest. Fear of famine set in; their stores were lean as much of the harvest had rotted in the fields. Stefen and Ano's funeral came and went, bleak and routine like all the others before it. Normalcy never returned. The cut in her hand would not heal; instead it constantly broke open and bled, the skin ashen and dry. Likewise, the vivid nightmares also continued, an unending torment.

Her neighbours treated her differently, either greeting her with cool politeness or pointedly avoiding her, making holy signs as they did so. Rumours that she was cursed began to circulate. Never had she felt as alone as she did now, surrounded by familiar faces, none of whom trusted her as they had.

Then late one night, a high musical tone sounded through Laila's dreams, reverberating through her bones. Dazed, she opened her eyes as another call went out, louder than the last. Laila clamped her hands over her ears as the sound pierced her skull like a butcher's pick. The horn-blower was real; worse, it was out in the fields. The fiends were outside the walls.

The cut began to itch, then to throb. She clutched her hand tight and felt warm blood. She stripped off the soaked bandage and searched for another. As she looked, another horn call went out, different than the first. Brassy and eerie, it shivered up the spine and set the heart racing. Then there was a high, keening howl.

The Fair Ones had come.

She wrapped her hand and glanced at her bolthole. Disgust at her fears and nightmares rose. She had to see the creatures die. Maybe then she would be free from the monsters that stalked her dreams and the memories of her husband's death. The Fair Ones had promised to kill them all, why not see them fulfil that promise?

She paused. The sounds from the battle filtered through to her, high ululating screams, roars of elation and the metallic bang of weapons meeting. It was almost musical in its own way, rising and falling by some rhythm that she could not discern.

Even as the pain crept up her arm like venom, she stepped outside and looked up at the cloudy sky. No, not clouds. Shadows. They weaved through the sky as though they were living things, tinting the Cinder Disc into a colour like heart's blood.

She climbed the wall to where Hadlen and a couple of warriors stood and looked out with them.

The scene was grim.

Out amongst the rotten grain, a great jewelled chariot lay crumpled like a dead beetle. Clustered about the wreck was a group of heavily armoured men, if one could call them such, bunched up with weapons turned outwards. At the centre was a tall, lithe creature with an elaborate helm, shouting in a silvery voice. All about them, shadowy women probed at the raiders' defence, thin spears piercing through hardened armour, others tearing at shields with hooked blades. A final, bloody last stand.

Something flew out of the trees on the wings of a drake and circled above the battle. Then it dived down into the heart of the raiders like a hawk. The defensive knot broke apart, revealing a flickering dance between the Chaos leader and a monstrous winged aelf. Blows lashed between them and for a moment, it looked as though they were equal. Then the aelf skewered the leader through his jewelled breastplate, ending the beast's life.

The winged woman was not the only monster. Other aelves with the bodies of serpents weaved among strange crystalline statues that glittered in the half-light, frozen in mid-flight. Still other warrior women flickered after their fleeing enemies, snaring them with barbed whips or lopping off limbs with long daggers. The crack of breaking bones, the chanting of women and the screams of dying things drifted out from beyond the trees. A strange fire burned out there, throwing up dense, ruddy mist. The stench of blood was so thick on the wind that it gummed in the eyes and throat.

Never had Laila imagined that their defence would be so ugly. Yet did those creatures not deserve it? Did evil deserve evil? Yes, they did. Maybe now, Jonas would no longer haunt her dreams with his screams and pleading.

As they looked on, a shadow walked down the road. It was Cesse. Below them, she stood, strong and cold. A bloody sickle gleamed in one of the aelf's hands, while in the other was that magnificent crested helm. No, not a helm, a head in a helm. She lifted up the gruesome trophy, blood dripping from the severed neck.

'We thank you for this glorious slaughter, which we have carried out in your name,' Cesse said, her voice quivering with a cruel elation. 'This creature will trouble you no more. Now, whose blood shall it be?'

'What? I gave you what you wanted,' Laila said. 'I gave you my blood.'

Cesse blinked and dropped the head into the dirt. All the other aelves stopped and looked towards the village as one. The shadows paused in the sky as if frozen and then seeped downwards like black snow. Out in the forest, something rumbled and that dread altar rolled forwards of its own volition out of the trees, the cauldron the source of that terrible smoke. Around it slithered some terrible thing, a vast serpent.

'It pains me that your kind are so forgetful,' Cesse said, a hint of amusement in her voice as if she were revealing the punchline of a joke. 'You spoke for all, therefore you are all.

Your blood stands for your village's obligation to us. Do not worry. We will not take the strong from among you, only the weakest from each household. The ones that you will not miss. Given the state of your harvest, you would not be able to feed them anyway. In time, you will be grateful for the lack of useless mouths. Just as it was before.'

'She cannot be serious,' Hadlen said. 'Laila, you could not have agreed to this.'

'I didn't,' Laila stammered. 'That was not what we agreed to.' She leaned over the wall. 'I gave you blood.'

'No, you sealed the agreement with your blood,' Cesse said. 'A few drops is not enough. Did you really think it was?'

Laila frantically searched her memory for some misstep, some loophole, something. Then a single moment leaped out at her.

For blood yet spilled.

It had been right there in front of her face. She had thought that the phrase referred to the enemy. But no, it had been her own people. That could not be right. She looked at the others, who glared at her with the frightened anger of those dragged into a situation not of their making. She had to fix this.

'The whole point of this was so that the defenceless would live,' Laila said. 'If we could have done it ourselves, we would not have needed you.'

Cesse cocked her head, her sharp brows furrowing. 'I do not understand your motive. We have laws. We do not move our forces on behalf of the weak without payment in blood. The weak must be culled from the strong so that the strong may continue unburdened. If you do not give, we will take what we are owed, no more, no less.'

Cesse did not – no, she could not – understand. She wasn't

human. It was inevitable now. Dozens were going to die because of Laila's naïveté, her idiocy. There was now nothing that she could do. There never had been. Someone was always going to kill them; she had merely chosen a different foe.

'You are like the fiends, like a reflection of the Lamp in a lake,' Laila said.

Cesse's face twisted into a depthless fury that no human could know. All the self-loathing and hurt turned outwards. She leaped into the air with a shriek, her cloak falling away, wings like those of a great dragon snapping free. The monstrous aelf crashed into Laila, slamming her off the wall. Laila experienced a long moment of weightlessness before she hit the ground, the breath blasting from her body. Breathless and throbbing with pain, she lay there.

Shadows flitted past her, the gate groaned open and the aelves shrieked in. They bolted right for the hall and the villagers scattered like startled birds from a nest, fleeing in terror. It mattered not, they died all the same: the infirm, the aged, the injured and the unlucky.

Cesse crouched nearby, a fleshy tail flicking, her wings loose over her back, watching the slaughter.

'Please understand, this is not purposeless or merciless,' Cesse said, calm as if the screams mattered to her not at all. 'We build a better world. One that is strong enough to stand against not only the destruction of the flesh but also the entropy of the soul. Illusions like justice and fairness allow weakness to fester. Killing the weak is merciful to the strong.'

Laila pressed herself onto an elbow, still trying to suck in a breath. Pain flared in her palm and then was gone as if it had never been. She looked down. A thin scar was all that remained of the wound.

'The bargain is complete,' Cesse said, straightening up. 'Now you are strong and will survive.'

Cesse leaped into the sky, her wings hitting the air. In the space of a breath, she was gone. They were all gone as if they had never been. Light washed over Varna as the shadows lifted, revealing a village of sorrow and corpses, of wailing and death, of curses and recrimination.

And Laila wept.

SALVAGE RITES

Thomas Parrott

Continuing his journey with Black Library, science fiction enthusiast Thomas Parrott brings us another tense, haunting story from the 41st millennium, this one following a diverse crew of void-salvagers.

Captain Ved Tregan and his crew discover a small, warp-capable vessel drifting in orbit around the planet of Effandor. For scavengers accustomed to sifting through space-junk, this valuable piece of tech could turn out to be the find of a lifetime. Or, setting foot inside it could be the biggest mistake any of them has ever made...

Even with the ship hanging there in plain sight, he had a hard time believing in it. It was a little over half a mile long. Though their scrambled scans hinted at the presence of a Geller field, he'd never heard of a warp-capable ship this small. Still large enough to dwarf their tugboat, much less the shuttle they were in now, of course. The derelict gave off nearly zero emissions; the only reason they'd been able to detect it was because it was damaged. Even now that they had it in visual range, it kept threatening to slip off their augurs completely. It was, in a word, exceptional, and it was going to make Captain Ved Tregan a rich man indeed, if he had his way.

'*Starting final approach, captain.*' That was the steady voice of Petin Hite, pilot extraordinaire.

Tregan thumbed his vox-rig. 'Thank you, Hite. Everyone get strapped in.' He moved to the nearest restraint couch and followed his own advice. Cracking his skull on an errant manoeuvre would be quite the spoiler for his moment of triumph.

Effandor, home sweet home, was a hive world groaning under the by-products of millennia of development. Its orbit had not been spared this pollution, either: it swarmed with millions of fragments of debris hurtling along at high speed. Even a tug like their own vessel needed a quick hand to avoid the worst of it. The big interstellar bulk freighters, loaded down with priceless food and raw materials, would shred like a man caught in Adric's shotgun spray were preventative measures not taken. That was where Tregan and his crew came in.

The planetary government paid a bounty for each piece of orbital debris cleared, which was all the incentive necessary for the dozens of scrapper crews roaming Effandor's orbit. The task was too large for the work to be finished in even a dozen lifetimes, so most chose to carve out narrow paths through the treacherous void. This doubled their income as a beneficial side effect: the big ships still had to be guided along the safe routes. They were the expert pathfinders of the hazardous spaceways, roughnecks who kept the lifeblood of commerce flowing to and from their world.

Sometimes, of course, what they retrieved wasn't merely trash. Battles had been fought in Effandor's local space, and mixed in with the usual refuse they'd found everything from intact shuttles to the desiccated dead still garbed in their wargear. It could all be sold at a premium, and the money was desperately needed. Tregan's debt payments to House Orend were perpetually due, and most months it was all he could do to scrape together the bare minimum.

As if summoned by the thought, Celia Vanar ducked through the hatch and headed for one of the other restraint couches. Her dark hair and eyes marked her out from the rest of the crew as being of noble blood, though it was far from pure. The bastard child of some wayward scion who'd mingled a little too closely with their lessers, Tregan had heard it said. She wasn't a bad sort as blue bloods went; she carried her weight on their salvage ops. Yet every look at her reminded him of her real purpose. She was the house's watchdog, here to keep them in line and make sure the money kept rolling in.

'It's hard to believe we're the first ones here,' she said as she buckled in.

'We barely picked up the signal trace ourselves, and nearly lost it on the way in even then. We may very well be the only ones to find the ship.' He held up a forestalling hand before she could say anything else, before reaching over and patting the weapon rack next to his seat, where several autoguns were laid out. 'I don't plan to count on it, though.'

'Ready to risk it all over this thing, then?' Vanar's words seemed innocent enough on the surface. It was easy to read criticism into it, though. She was always happiest when the crew quietly did their 'real jobs', working the safe routes through orbit.

'It's a find worth fighting for.' A find that could mean freedom. The scrapper operation wasn't a cheap one. He'd had to find someone to pay for the tugboat, the void suits, all the equipment they needed. Enter House Orend, hive nobility. They called themselves his 'sponsors'. The boot on his neck, more like. Salvaging a ship like this would pay off everything he owed and then some, enough to set him up for the foreseeable future.

Anything further Vanar might have had to say was cut off as the tug rattled and lurched. The sudden turbulence slammed

Tregan hard against his restraints. Judging from her wheezing gasps, Celia was doing no better. Coughing, he hit the vox. 'Petin, what in the warp was that?'

Her voice was reassuringly cool. *The ship is trailing a debris cloud following its orbit, probably from whatever damaged it. We should be through the worst of it now.*

A scream echoed from the next compartment, jolting Tregan. 'Damn.' He hastily released his harness and dashed in that direction. Another, smaller, tremor threw him against the hatch but he caught himself and staggered on through, saying sharply, 'I swear, if one of you didn't strap in like I ordered, I'm going to cut your shares to nil.'

Adric Cale was seated on the right in the next hold, eyes wide and the old gang tattoos on his shaved scalp glistening with sweat. He held his hands up defensively. 'We were both strapped in! She just started squalling for no reason! Another one of her fits.'

Tregan shot a look at the woman Adric was indicating. Eusalia Zand was lolling against the straps of her seat, shaking uncontrollably. He hastened to her side. 'What happened?'

Eyes ringed with vivid dark circles locked on his. 'We shouldn't be here.' Her pale skin and silver hair marked her as no native of Effandor; indeed he'd recruited her off a starship passing through the system. Her hunches were often eerily accurate and had led to some of the best finds of his career.

Tregan frowned. 'What's wrong?'

She was looking right through him now. 'Who are you? What are you?' Unnerved, he glanced over his shoulder. Nothing there. Abruptly she grabbed his wrist, 'We have to go.'

'What?' He gently pried her hand free of his wrist. 'What does that mean, Eusalia?'

Scrubbing her hands over her face, she shook her head. 'I don't know. We just can't be here. This place is dangerous.'

Tregan looked to Adric, but the other man only shrugged helplessly. Returning to Eusalia, he sighed. 'You fell asleep. You had a bad dream. It's nothing.'

She reached up and grabbed his wrist. 'Captain, please. We can still turn back.'

No sooner were the words out of her mouth than a thud vibrated through the hull of the tug. He gave her a wry smile. 'That's docking. We're there.' He gently pulled free of her grip. 'It'll be fine, Eusalia.' Another look between the two. 'More than fine. This is the find that makes us. The find of a lifetime. You'll see.'

Adric nodded appreciatively. 'Right there with you, boss. Stacks of gelt and easy living here we come, right 'Sal?' Tregan was always struck by how protective of them all the man was. Not exactly what you expected from a hardened gunhand plucked from the underhive. Yet the crew was Adric's gang now, and he had bonded to them fiercely.

There was a trapped look in Eusalia's eyes. She tried to muster a smile. 'Right. Easy living.'

Tregan nodded. 'That's the spirit. Now gear up and meet me at the airlock in five.'

They both nodded and he strode from the one hold back to the other, where Celia was freeing herself from her restraint couch. She gave him a raised eyebrow as he walked in. 'No blood on the deck already, I hope.'

He snorted and shook his head. 'Eusalia got spooked.' As he spoke he took his void suit from a rack and began to pull it on over his jumpsuit.

'Eusalia might as well be a ghost haunting us for how often she spooks.' Celia rolled her eyes and began to prep for the boarding as well.

Soon thereafter, the five of them were walking down the shuttle's ramp. The bay they'd landed in was an echoing expanse, empty save for their ship. All the lights were out, so the darkness was only broken by the dust-filled beams of the stablights on their helmets. Pitch-black corridors branched off in every direction.

Tregan cleared his throat. 'Everyone stay alert out there. There's no sign of other ships in the area, but you never know if someone dropped off a team and withdrew out of augur range.'

Adric put on an over-the-top sinister voice. 'Plus if you don't tread lightly the tanglemouths will bite.' He elbowed Eusalia, who smirked and shook her head.

'Enough.' It came out sharper than Tregan had meant for it to. Bad memories. 'Joke all you want, but be careful all the damn same. Stay in vox contact too.'

Celia raised an eyebrow. 'And suppose we do, in fact, run into someone else out there?'

Tregan gave her a flat look. 'I don't intend to share this stake.' He paused. 'And this isn't a rescue mission.' He glanced back to where Petin lingered in the hatchway. 'You stay here and keep an ear to the vox, just in case we need to warm up and get out of here quickly. Everybody got it?'

Petin nodded with clear relief. 'Solid copy. I'm no footslogger.'

Adric patted his shotgun contentedly. 'I am. Time to put in work.' The others nodded.

Everyone set off down one of the corridors to begin exploring the ship. Truth be told, Tregan regretted the need to split up like this, but there was no choice. They needed to evaluate and get control of the derelict quickly, and even in a relatively small ship like this one there was a lot of ground to cover. In spite of his brave words to Celia, a stampede might be headed this way, and if enough competition showed up this ended badly, no matter how you sliced it.

He picked his way along the corridor, his breath loud in the void suit's helmet. The stablight's beam glimmered off the polished surfaces of the walls and ceilings. He'd never really seen anything like this construction before. It was worlds away from the ships and city streets he was used to. They were all dripping pipes and rattling vents. This place was smooth. Austere. Sterile. Not to mention silent. The stillness was almost oppressive. He snorted a laugh at himself. 'Letting Eusalia get to me,' he muttered.

Just a short time later she came on the vox as if she'd heard him think about her. *'Found something.'*

'Care to be more specific?' Tregan asked.

She gave a short laugh. *'I'd love to, captain, but it's difficult. They're blast doors. Military grade – looks like you'd need charges, multiple, to get through. I guess I could try to get started with a cutting torch if you wanted.'*

'No. There's no telling how long that will take or what you'd set off if you did. Just keep looking.'

With their conversation concluded, Celia spoke up. *'I have something too. I'm not sure what to call it though. A gallery, maybe?'*

He frowned. 'What, for art?' There were possibilities there, at least. You never knew what some highbrow noble would pay for the right wall decorations.

'Not exactly. There's a couple of full-length mirrors, but the walls are covered with data-slates showing picts of people.' There

was a pause as she investigated further. *'I think I might even know a couple of them. People from my house and the planetary government.'* She sounded unnerved. He couldn't blame her. *'How would they have these pictures if this was some old derelict?'*

Tregan reached up to scratch his head, only for his fingers to *thunk* against his forgotten helmet. He shook his head. 'I don't know. Not what I expected.'

Celia snorted. *'Yeah, me either. What do you want me to do with it?'*

'I… Hold that thought.' There was light up ahead in the corridor. He'd found something himself. Carefully, he moved ahead right to the edge of the doorway, light leaking through the gaps around the frame, and listened for a moment. The same complete stillness. The door controls were right next to him. Best to do it swift. He palmed them, opening the door, and swept around in a rush, weapon at the ready. There was no one here.

Instead, it was filled with an array of arcane devices. A terminal sat in the middle of the room, and around it were six deep niches. Five of them were empty, but the sixth was filled with some sort of elongated box. 'Some kind of storage room, I guess?' he muttered. Blinking lights marked the side of this crate, though the lid was already open and any contents removed. 'Damn thing's big enough to store a body.' There were odd indentations within. He stepped closer and leaned in a bit. The imprint of something. The longer he stared at it, the more he became convinced it had once held a person. His skin crawled.

Something rustled behind him.

He whirled, heart pounding. Still empty. The door had shut. Some sort of automatic timer, presumably. He stepped over and tapped the controls just to make sure, and it cycled open again to reveal the hallway beyond.

'*Tregan?*' prompted Celia with a note of concern.

'Yeah,' he said. He took a shaky breath. 'This room's just as bizarre as yours. I don't know what's going on with this ship.' Their discussion came to an abrupt end as the sound of a shotgun blast echoed through the corridors.

'*Throne! I got a problem!*' cut in Adric with clear alarm.

'Adric?' Tregan whirled. There was no clear answer, but grunts came over the vox and more gunfire rang out. 'Emperor's blood!' Tregan set off at a sprint towards the sound. 'Everyone get to Adric's position as fast as you can!'

Tregan was the first one to reach him. He found Adric slumped against the wall, panting. He scanned the area quickly, ready for a fight, but there wasn't any threat visible.

The underhiver managed to gasp out, 'It's gone. Ran off.'

Tregan asked, 'It?'

His crewman gave a shaky laugh. 'Yeah. Dunno what the warp that thing was. Shaped like a person, but it had… pitch-black skin and red eyes. Then it cut me.' He held out his arm, a bleeding gash drawn right through the void suit and the clothes beneath. 'I tried to blast it and it scampered.' He pointed towards a vent up near the ceiling. 'Ran right up the damn wall and slithered into that vent like it was nothing.'

The other two came running up with weapons raised, and Tregan held up a calming hand. 'It's gone. Something attacked him and got away. Went into the vent.' In spite of his reassuring words, he glanced up and down the dark corridors.

Celia glanced around at the shotgun blasts marking the walls. 'You didn't get it?' she asked, surprised. Eusalia just looked nauseated.

Adric gave another of those unsteady chuckles. 'Warp take me, but I don't think I even hit it. It was so fast.'

Celia looked astounded. 'Could it actually be a tanglemouth?'

'No,' Tregan said flatly. They all looked at him.

'How can you be sure?' Eusalia asked.

'I've seen them before. Seen what they do.' They all looked surprised. It wasn't often someone claimed to have met folk tale monsters, he supposed. The memory threatened to well up again. The towering figure lunging from the shadows with lightning speed. Bullets sparking off alien carapace. Claws shredding flesh to ribbons. The ungodly slurping as the nest of tentacles on its face pulled Indrid up and it feasted on her. She'd screamed the whole time. He'd heard her as he ran headlong through that ruined ship, leaving her behind. He swallowed. 'No. This sounds like something else.'

'Like what?' asked Celia.

Tregan shook his head. 'I don't know. Nothing about this place makes sense. Tanglemouths and their kin hunt the old wrecks, leftover from the war. Those pictures you found say this ship isn't from then. Some kind of spire enforcer maybe?'

The house agent's jaw tightened. 'Not every evil in the world tracks back to the nobility, Tregan.'

He gave her a cool look. 'Not everything, no. Just enough.'

Adric cut in, 'Warp take your politics right now! Can we focus on the damn thing that sliced me?'

Eusalia was staring at the vent. 'He's right,' she said distantly. 'You said it went into the vent. What if it's still there? Listening to us.'

The rest of them exchanged uneasy looks. The vent was beyond the reach of any of them. Adric was hurt, Eusalia was Eusalia. He looked to Celia.

She sighed deeply. 'Fine. Let's get this over with.'

Tregan stepped over to the vent and crouched, making a stirrup with his hands. Celia stepped onto it and hoisted herself up, then slowly craned to peer into the darkness. Everyone was silent for what felt like an eternity as she shone a light into the gap.

Then the vent rattled and she jerked back. The shift in weight caught Tregan off guard and he staggered. Both of them went down in a heap and he desperately grabbed for his rifle, aiming it at the gap as fast as he could. The others were scrambling for their weapons too, Adric trying to raise his shotgun in an awkward one-handed grip.

Hastily, Celia called, 'Calm down. It was just the ventilation system turning on. Caught me by surprise.' She looked frustrated and staggered to her feet, dusting herself off. 'Nothing in there. And that space is tiny. Barely fit a person inside at all.'

'It must be moving like a snake to get around. Slithering around up there.' Eusalia shivered after she said it and hugged her arms.

Tregan took a deep breath, rising as well. 'Not helpful, Eusalia.'

Celia shook her head. 'That system must connect to the whole ship. Assuming it actually can move around in there, it could be anywhere by now.'

Petin's voice cut in over the vox, sounding uncharacteristically rattled. *'Uh, we got an issue, folks.'*

'Throne dammit, of course we do.' Tregan gritted his teeth. 'What is it?'

'I heard the ruckus you were having out there, figured it'd be smart to get the shuttle warmed up just in case. Someone's sabotaged it. From the inside.'

They all exchanged worried looks. 'I thought you were in there with it buttoned up,' observed Adric.

'I was. I am. Still here, still in the docking bay. I don't know

how they did it. They cut cables right through the wall, without even removing the panels. None of it makes sense.'

'If they got on board, check the map case. Make sure nothing happened to it,' Tregan instructed.

'The what?' Petin asked.

He sighed. 'Focus, Petin. The safe in the cockpit with the orbital maps in it? Is it intact?'

'Oh! Sorry, captain. Preoccupied with the sabotage. It, uh, yeah. It's still there. It's fine.'

'Forget the maps. Are we dead in space?' Celia asked.

'Well, we can't take off like this. If we could replace the severed cables somehow we might be able to get going again.'

'We have a whole ship to salvage here. Surely we can find–'

Tregan was interrupted again by Adric giving a low, pained groan. With a wheeze the man slid down the wall, clutching his arm. Eusalia darted to his side, crouching next to him and reaching out a hand to touch his arm. 'Let me see it.' Reluctantly, he extended his arm, and she scrambled back retching.

Tregan stepped forwards to see what had provoked this response, grabbing the man's hand before he could retreat again. The wound was necrotic. The simple cut had already turned into a widening pus-filled sore with the centre blackening.

'I seen things like this before,' whimpered the man. 'It looks just like a jumpcrawler bite down in the underhive. It poisoned me.'

'All right,' Celia snapped. 'This is out of control. We need to get back to the shuttle and hunker down, put out an all call for help.'

'No!' Tregan snarled. They all looked at him, startled. 'I will be damned if I cede this claim just because things have got a little rough.'

'A little rough?' Celia barked a laugh. 'Are you kidding me? He's hurt, and the shuttle's crippled. We're in over our head, Tregan!'

'He'll be fine, and we'll have the shuttle fixed in no time.' Tregan's tone brooked no argument.

Nevertheless, Celia fired back. 'Do you really care more about this claim than your crew?'

'This claim is going to secure a future for my crew, and I'm not going to let you take that away from them. Not you or your house. We're done being your indentured servants, and you can't stand that. That's the problem here.'

'The problem here?! The problem here is that–'

'Stop!' Eusalia hissed. 'Both of you, stop! This isn't helping.' Carefully she pulled Adric up and put his good arm around her shoulders. 'We need to get him back to the shuttle and you're standing here arguing.'

Petin's voice cut in over the vox-rig, *'Also, hate to say it, but the long-range comm is sabotaged too. We couldn't call for help even if we wanted to.'*

'That would have been useful to know before now, Petin,' Tregan bit out. Celia and he glared at each other for a moment before Tregan gave a sharp nod. 'Fine. Let's get him back to the shuttle, and then we'll organise a search for parts.'

Celia's lips were tight. 'I guess we don't have a choice.'

Caught between caution and haste they made their way back to the shuttle as fast as they could. The trip passed for the most part in worried silence, save for moans of pain and fear from Adric.

Tregan glanced back at a particularly sharp groan. The underhiver was dragging now, a heavy weight on Eusalia. He fell back a step and took Adric's other arm to share the weight. 'Holding it together, lad?' he asked with forced joviality.

The answer was unintelligible, flecks of foam clinging to Adric's lips. It worried Tregan more than he wanted to admit to see the state the underhiver was in. He'd known the man to shrug off bullet wounds with a curse and a snort. The poison was eating at him rapidly.

By the time they arrived, Adric had lapsed completely into a feverish delirium. They carefully strapped him into one of the couches and Tregan took the chance to remove his helmet and sweep a hand through his sparse, sweaty hair. He regretted it almost immediately, Adric's wound filled the air with a pungent stink made worse by a hint of sickening sweetness.

Fighting down the urge to vomit, he looked to the others. 'All right. We have to find the parts. That means going back out into the ship.' No one looked excited at the prospect. He couldn't blame them. He'd fought his fair share of claim battles, but this was something else. Something beyond his understanding. A tremor ran through his hands, and he clenched them tight to hide it.

'I should go with all of you,' Petin said abruptly.

Tregan looked at her in surprise. 'What happened to you not being a footslogger?'

She offered a lopsided smile. 'You're down a man, and I want to get out of here same as the rest of you. Besides, I know what we're looking for better than anybody.'

Celia seemed pleased. 'That gives us enough to pair off.'

Tregan hesitated. She was right, and his instinct was to avoid sending anyone out alone this time. A low moan of agony escaped Adric and drew his attention. The man was writhing against his restraints, sweat running off him. He made up his mind. 'No. We have to split up.'

Whatever relief Celia had momentarily felt when Petin volunteered evaporated into anger. 'You can't be serious. One of us already got hurt.'

'I know. That's exactly why we have to. He's dying, Celia. The longer we take, the worse his chances. If we split up, we can cover more ground and find these cables we need faster.' He looked around the group. 'We'll stay in the same general area and keep in contact. Anything happens, we'll be there.'

No one would meet his eyes except Petin, who gave him a reassuring nod. I can't just let the man die while we take the time for a careful sweep, he told himself. This is how it has to be. As for this thing waiting for them on the ship, whatever it was… His hand shook again and he clenched it even tighter, nails digging into his palm. They would have to deal with it however they could.

They spread out into the ship once more, a frantic search this time by contrast with the earlier cautious exploration. Everyone checked in occasionally, but the early finds weren't promising. A training room with quiescent combat servitors as dummies. A one-bed medbay with an array of arcane instrumentation.

At last, Petin voxed in with relief in her voice. *'Got 'em. Perfect cabling. Just–'* Then the transmission cut to static.

Tregan started up from inspecting a storage chamber full of crates of concentrated nutrient paste. 'Petin? Come in, Petin.' His stomach lurched. 'Everybody find her, now!'

Nobody sounded off. His heart lurched. They're already running, he told himself desperately. No time for the vox. He set off as fast as he could. Once more he found himself running through corridors desperately to reach one of his crew. His heart sank as he darted into the chamber Petin had been searching. It looked like a planning room of some kind, with a projector in the centre and a few benches arrayed around it. The cabling was laid out neatly on one of those, but the pilot was nowhere to be seen. 'Hite! Petin Hite, can you hear me?' he called. Not again, please, he prayed. Not this crew. Not like Indrid.

A low groan answered him from the corner of the room and he hurried over. Instead of Petin, however, he found Celia laid out there, dazed and holding her head. He knelt beside her quickly. 'Celia, what happened? Are you all right?'

She shook her head in confusion. 'I don't know. I was nearby. We heard the call, so I ran here. When I came in, I saw...' She swallowed and looked at him. 'I saw Eusalia. She was dragging Petin away. I called out, and she whirled and hit me.'

'What?' Eusalia said from the doorway, seeming bewildered.

Celia scrambled to her feet in fear, causing Tregan to hastily stand as well. 'You took Petin! What did you do with her, you freak?' she demanded.

'I just got here, you blue-blood lapdog! What are you talking about?'

The whole thing was spiralling out of control. Tregan looked back and forth between the two, both people he had known for years. At each other's throats while Adric suffered and Petin... who knew. 'Calm down, both of you,' he demanded.

Celia raised her gun instead, prompting Eusalia to do the same. 'We should never have trusted you. We all knew it. We allowed a monster into our midst, and now we're paying the price.' She shot a look at Tregan. 'This is what happens when you shelter a witch!'

Everyone froze. It was the unspoken secret of the crew. Odd.

Curious. Weird. Those were the words they used, because you protected your own, and other words brought dark fates. Especially this word. Witches meant Imperial law. Imperial authority. Tregan spoke up, 'Let's not be hasty. This doesn't have to be a matter for the Arbites. We're all friends here.'

Celia's face showed a moment of regret before it hardened again. 'You know the teachings of the Creed as well as I do, Tregan. Suffer not the witch to live. We brought poison into our lives, and thought to profit from swallowing it.'

'I-I'm not! How dare you! You always thought you were too good for the rest of us!' Eusalia turned a desperate look on Tregan. 'I've been with you for years, never hurt any of you! I would never hurt Petin!'

The captain looked between them uncertainly. It was all crumbling now. No matter how this ended, his crew would never be the same. The life he'd thought to build was burning to ashes. 'Look. I don't know what's happening. None of us do. But we're falling apart, and Petin's nowhere around. We have to get out of here.' There was desperation in his voice. He didn't care any more who heard it.

'I'm not going anywhere with this filth ready to stab me in the back. Drop your gun, witch,' said Celia.

'If you think I'm going to disarm and let some delusional idiot murder me, you've got another thing coming.' There was a grim determination forming in Eusalia's eyes.

'No one's murdering anyone, but you are going to disarm,' said Tregan. Eusalia started to protest and he hurried on. 'Both of you are.' He put his shaking finger to the trigger of his own weapon. Don't do this, he prayed. I can still save you both. I have to be able to.

'What?' snapped Celia.

'I told you. I don't know what's going on. So I'm going

to walk behind both of you with my gun, we're going to go back to the shuttle, and we're going to get the warp off this ship. Then we'll sort everything out back on board the tug.' He put iron into his voice. 'That's an order. Not a suggestion.' *Please.*

Reluctantly they both lowered their guns and tossed them aside at his indication. He scooped them up carefully, slung them around his shoulder. Then, collecting the cables, they hurried back through the dark corridors. There was no doubting the oppressiveness of this place now. All of its mysteries apparently amounted to horror. He could live without those answers.

They reached the shuttle again without further incident and boarded quickly, closing up the ramp behind them for whatever good it might do. Tregan's heart sank even further as he looked in on Adric. The man was completely still and foam covered his lips, his eyes gazing blankly into nothing. Black veins crawled up his neck. He stepped over and sat next to him, weariness dragging him down. Years of faithful service ending in a vile death. He'd deserved better. They all did. 'I wish we'd never found this Throne-damned ship.' Eusalia sank down next to him, staring at her friend with tears streaking her face.

Celia must have found some compassion, as she held out her hand and said gently, 'Here, give me the cables. I'll hook them up and fly us back to the tug.'

'You'll need the maps, too,' he said wearily.

'Right,' she said quietly. 'What was the passcode again?'

He felt hollowed out. '*Gather the Lost.*'

She nodded and departed the hold. The two of them sat in silence for a moment. It was strange for Celia to forget the code. The maps were what the house valued most, really.

This day had taken it out of all of them. Tregan took a deep breath and reached forwards, closing Adric's eyes. 'He was a good worker. A good man.' The words felt lame and empty, but Eusalia just sniffled and nodded.

Then she froze. She whispered something to herself and he looked at her in confusion. 'What?'

'The mask. It's dropping the mask.' She turned on him with terror in her eyes. Then stood and whirled this way and that desperately like a cornered animal. 'It has what it wants and it's dropping the mask. It's coming!'

He stood, staring at her. 'What? You're not making sense.' She locked eyes with him, and in them he saw a fear that touched on madness. Then she lunged for the gun rack. In that moment, all he could think of was Celia's words about Petin's fate. 'Eusalia, stop! Stop now! Don't!'

She came up with the weapon, and he fired. One, two, three times. Craters carved themselves across her torso, and she toppled to the floor. Her chest hitched once in a convulsive breath and she was still. He stared in horror. 'No. I didn't... Eusalia, why?'

His crew all dead, save one.

She was in the doorway.

'Celia...' but it wasn't her. There were traces of her, but Celia's features ran like hot wax, rearranging even as he looked. It was something else, some nightmare thing. The thing from the ship, the ship they should have never disturbed. It was human in shape, a woman, but painfully skinny and wrapped in corded muscles. Its flesh was swathed completely in a matt-black substance that clung to it like a second skin. Knives and blades slotted into sheaths along its arms and thighs. One knife in particular was held loosely in its hand, the blade shimmering oddly. Yet somehow it was the eyes that carried the threat. They were nothing but gleaming red lenses, offering no emotion and no hope.

'Who are you? What are you?' he rasped out. There was no answer.

Desperately he raised his gun as it came for him.

Hours later, the shuttle left the tug in orbit around the planet and came down to the space port. It settled into place amidst others and the sky shield closed back up, sealing out the bitter acid rain of Effandor's ruined atmosphere. The ramp lowered and Ved Tregan came walking down. He looked around thoughtfully. The lifts that went to the Spire and the governing districts were that way. He set out walking.

He hadn't got far when a technician called out, 'Tregan! Where's the crew?'

Tregan smiled. 'We needed fresh rations, so I dropped them off at the starch manufactorum to pick up a few pallets. Then I headed over here to get some work done on the shuttle.'

The technician nodded amiably. 'Well, don't work too hard. End up in an early grave at this rate.'

Tregan's smile widened. 'I'm afraid my work's only just begun.' He set off for the lifts once more. The governor's mansion awaited.

GREEN AND GREY

Edoardo Albert

Edoardo Albert is a London-based writer and editor, and the author of several books on a variety of subjects. 'Green and Grey' tells the story of Lucius Stilo, an Astra Militarum tanker, the only survivor of the catastrophe that killed the rest of his Leman Russ tank's crew.

As a greenskin horde descends upon his position, Stilo must remember all of his training in order to survive, and use the ruined tank's limited capabilities to destroy as many of the orks as possible, while he awaits rescue. This tense, compact story gives us a unique perspective on what happens when battle plans fail, and the nature and value of a soldier's courage.

Tick, tick, tick.

That was what woke him. The regular ticking of cooling, contracting plasteel.

Tick, tick, tick.

He'd heard that sound before, growing up, the son of a tanker. He'd heard the sound during his training, when the squadron pulled up for the night, the tanks parked in rows ready for a pre-dawn start, their engines cooling, the cylinder blocks ticking out the day's accumulated heat.

Tick... tick... tick.

The ticks were slowing down. The engine was near enough cold now. He could not remember command telling the squadron to make camp for the night.

His mind was fogged, as dull as the dawn on...

He could not remember where he was.

He could not remember who he was.

It did not seem to matter.

He began to drift.

It was the pain that dragged him back. As the tick of the cooling tank died away, it was replaced by a rhythmic pain, pulsing down from the front of his head.

He did not want to move but the pain forced his hand into motion. But as he tried to reach for his forehead, his hand stopped. There was something in the way. It felt firm but not metallic, with a lingering warmth.

He did not want to open his eyes to see what it was.

Lucius Stilo.

That was it. That was his name.

Lucius Stilo. Loader. Leman Russ *Sancta Fide*. Third Squadron. Fifth Alphard Tank Regiment.

He knew who he was now, but he could not remember where he was.

He still did not want to open his eyes.

Lucius Stilo would have drifted away then, if he had been able to, but the pain would not let him. It throbbed through his head, an arrhythmic counterpoint to the cooling engine.

The engine was quiet. Stilo knew that it shouldn't be.

He still did not want to open his eyes.

But he knew he had to. It was his duty. He was a soldier of the Astra Militarum, a member of the Fifth Alphard Tank Regiment. Although his eyes were still closed, he could suddenly see his father leaning down to him, telling him, 'Yes, it's true, the Emperor protects, but first, the Emperor expects. Expects every man to do his duty.'

Stilo opened his eyes.

He opened his eyes to darkness.

But it was as if opening his eyes, even though they could see nothing, opened wide his other senses too. He could suddenly smell Leman Russ: the throat-clutching stink of human sweat, the acrid bite of the cannon propellant, the sulphur of the heavy bolter and, overlaying everything, the overwhelming smell of promethium. Although his lips were closed, he could taste it. Had the fuel tank ruptured?

'The Emperor protects, but first the Emperor expects.'

The words sounded louder than memory, so loud that Stilo turned his head to see if there was someone speaking them in the tank. But the dark was Stygian: he could see nothing.

Without light, he could do nothing.

Stilo began fumbling in the dark. He was searching for the emergency lumens. His fingers found things, but he could not relate what he found to his training – everything seemed wrong, twisted somehow. Then he realised the problem: everything was twisted because he was lying on his side. Stilo turned his mental map through ninety degrees and as he did so, things began to snap into place. There, the bin for the armour-piercing shells; here the bin for high-explosive shells in between the chute for spent shell casings; and on his left, the bank of kill switches.

Yes.

And beneath the kill switches, another console for the backup systems.

First, second, third along.

Stilo pulled the switch.

The emergency lumens came on, red, lurid, pulsing. He could see.

What he saw was the face of his tank commander.

'Captain Bartezko?'

Bartezko made no answer. He was hanging above Stilo, dangling in his webbing, the standard position for a tank commander going visual. His power sword hung from his belt. Bartezko loved his sword. It had been a gift from the corps commander for his bravery in the Battle of the Machengo Rift.

'Captain?' Stilo reached for Bartezko's webbing and twisted it, so the tank commander's face turned into view. What was left of it. The captain would not be giving any more orders.

'Emmet, Vanhof. Klee, van Thienen.' Stilo called out the names of the rest of the tank crew. 'Emperor, let them answer,' he whispered. But the names fell into the thick air and were swallowed. No one spoke, no one answered. The body of Captain Bartezko hung limp in its webbing. Stilo frantically tried to remember what had happened. The captain announcing he was going visual, clipping on his webbing, standing up, reaching for the turret hatch… There. That was when his memory whited out. Air burst, maybe? An ork shell exploding above the tank just as the captain unsealed the hatch, the shock wave thrashing Bartezko against it, then slamming it shut, the pressure change in the confined volume of the tank incapacitating – killing – the crew. Except for him.

'*Come in, Third Squadron. Do you copy? Third Squadron, do you copy?*'

The voice, the first that he had heard since regaining consciousness, sounded thin and tinny and far away, but it was coming from the vox-panel. Turning from the corpse of his commander, Stilo twisted past scattered cases to the panel.

'Third Squadron, receiving. Over.'

'*About time, Third Squadron. We've been trying to raise you for the last hour. Report.*'

As the voice came through on the vox, Stilo fiddled with the controls, trying to turn it up so that he could hear better. Stilo touched his ear. His fingers came away wet and sticky. His ears were bleeding. The pressure shock of the air burst.

'This... this is Third Squadron, *Sancta Fide*, sir. Loader Lucius Stilo reporting, sir.'

'Put on Captain Bartezko.'

'I can't, sir. He's dead. They're all dead, sir, I'm the only one left.'

The vox went silent for a moment. Stilo heard the vox-operator whispering to someone.

'The corps commander wants to speak to you, Loader Stilo.'

A different voice came through: warm and generous, the voice of a kindly, rich uncle.

'Loader Stilo?'

'Y-yes. Er, sir.'

'I need you to call up the auspexes and give me a report.'

'The auspexes are all dead, sir. Everything's dead. The fuel tank's ruptured. I'm standing up to my ankles in promethium. I don't know what to do. You've got to get me out of here.'

'Stilo.'

The name dropped into the loader's increasing panic and stilled it, like oil on water.

'Yes, sir.'

'The vox is working. Try to raise the auspex. You're a tanker, Stilo. Act like one.'

'I-I will.'

Stilo reached for the auspex panel. It was unresponsive. All its screens were blank. He banged on it in frustration.

'Machine-spirits are temperamental creatures – hitting one rarely works. Try restarting it, tanker.'

Stilo stared at the panel in front of him.

'I-I can't remember what to do, sir.'

'Remember your training, tanker.'

Stilo knuckled his forehead. 'I-I can't, sir.'

'This is your first combat patrol, isn't it, Lucius?'

'Yes.'

'No one wanted for it to go like this, but you're still there, still alive. The Emperor protected you. Now the Emperor expects.'

Hearing the litany coming through on the vox, remembrance settled upon Lucius Stilo. His training took over, moving his hands over the panel, keying the relaunch sequence. The screens flickered into life.

'They're coming online, sir.'

'Good, good.'

'Frek! They're all showing static.'

'The sensor array must be damaged. Loader Stilo, I'm going to have to ask you to make a visual report.'

'L-let me try again, sir.' Stilo began keying the cut-out sequence.

'No time for that. I must have a report. Now, tanker. Remember, the Emperor expects.'

'Y-yes.'

'Yes, sir.'

'Sorry, sir. Yes, sir.'

Stilo looked at the body of Captain Bartezko, dangling in his harness, his face a livid red wound scored through with white lines of exposed bone, his power sword hanging uselessly by his side. The loader felt the physical revulsion of the living at the prospect of touching the dead. He was going to have to release the captain from the webbing so that he could get to the hatch.

'Sorry, sir.'

Stilo unclipped the webbing. Bartezko's corpse fell forwards, wrapping its arms around Stilo in the embrace of the dead.

The vox-channel was open. Stilo just about suppressed a

scream and pushed the body aside so it flopped against the breech of the cannon, sprawling over it like a dead fish. Bartezko's slack body slumped, slowly, before dropping down off the turret cradle into the pool of blood and promethium at the base of the tank.

The way clear, Stilo scrambled up to the turret hatch.

Skratch, skkkratch.

The noise came from outside, from the other side of the hatch.

Stilo's hands froze in the act of opening the hatch.

Skkkkratch, skkkkkratch.

Something was outside.

It was the sound of nails on glass, of a knife scraping over plasteel.

Of claws scratching up the hull.

Stilo pushed the turret lock shut.

Bang, bang, bang.

The impacts were so loud that Stilo's teeth rang in his skull. But this was not the sound of rounds bouncing off the hull of the tank.

Bang. Bang, bang.

Something was hitting it. Hitting it with a hammer or a rock.

'*Lucius, what's happening? Report, Lucius.*'

Stilo dived to the panel and turned down the gain.

'S-something's outside,' he whispered. 'It's hitting the tank. You've got to get me out of here.'

'*Don't worry, Stilo. Just hold on.*' The voice of the corps commander was barely audible over the sounds coming from outside the tank. '*Try the auspex again.*'

'I-I don't want to see what's out there.'

Bang, bang, bang.

'Try the auspex, tanker!'

Stilo mumbled a brief prayer to *Sancta Fide's* machine-spirit as he keyed the restart again. It had been more hurt than him. As the screens lit up, the banging intensified, coming now from at least two different places on the hull: one set echoed down the battle cannon while the other was coming from the port sponson.

Despite the damage, the pict-feed from the outside red-lit, steadied, flickered, then the pixels slowly began to come together.

Bang, bang. Bang.

The screen cleared. Outside, Stilo could see a vast, dusty plain. Calleva. He remembered, now. That was the name of this Emperor-forsaken planet. The smoking shells of two other Leman Russ tanks told him that none of the squadron had made it to the extraction zone. The ground around them was gouged with craters; for once, the orks had managed to range their artillery. Far off, he saw the curving arch of the Infinity Bridge spanning the continental abyss, its curve as elegant as the drop-off to the shifting magma sea was sudden.

Even as he saw it, Stilo knew that was wrong. The bridge should have been blown by now. His squadron had been detailed to delay the enemy while demolition charges were set, then head to the extraction zone. Either the charges had failed, or the engineers had not made it to the bridge.

But that was for the brass to worry about.

Bang, bang, bang.

He still couldn't see what was making the noise. Stilo tried tracking the pict-feed around, but it did not move. Whatever had killed *Sancta Fide* had broken the motors. It was only by the Emperor's grace that he could see anything at all out there.

'Report, Stilo.'

'I-I can't see...'

A face appeared in the screen, staring at Stilo. It opened its mouth. Its tusks and tongue were the only things that weren't a livid, fungoid green. Then, it bit down. The sensor went dark.

Lucius jerked back from the screen.

'Orks.' He leaned over the vox, whispering into it. 'Orks, outside *Sancta Fide*. They're what's banging and biting it.'

'Orks loot as readily as they kill,' said the corps commander.

'I've got *Sancta Fide* locked down, sir. They won't get in here.'

'That's good, tanker. What else did you see?'

'What? Oh, yes. I'll try to get another pict-feed running. But the plain looks clear, sir. Only ork I saw was the one trying to get in here. Surprised they're not heading for the bridge.'

'What? What did you say, Stilo?'

'I'm trying to get another pict-feed up.'

'No, no. The bridge. It's still up?'

'Yes, sir. It's still up.'

'Hold there, tanker.'

The vox went quiet. But outside the tank, Stilo could hear movement. Lots of movement. He fiddled with the auspex, switching to another sensor array, and the screens gradually cleared.

'There's... there's dozens of them around me,' he whispered into the vox. 'Hundreds. If I keep quiet, maybe they'll go away.'

'Confirm, the bridge is not down.'

'What?'

'Loader Stilo, get visual on the bridge. Is it down?'

Bang, bang, bang.

Stilo started as the banging began again, flinching from the port sponson.

'*Stilo, confirm.*'

'Confirmed, sir. The bridge is still standing.'

There was silence on the other end of the vox, then Stilo heard the corps commander talking urgently to someone else.

Bang, bang, bang.

'Throne, they're trying to get in, sir. What should I do?'

'*Stilo, listen to me. Are any orks closing on the bridge?*'

Bang, bang, bang.

They were hammering at the starboard sponson now. Creaking, groaning noises came from the plasteel, as if someone were trying to peel it off, layer by layer.

Stilo glanced at the pict-feed. The long plain that led to the Infinity Bridge lay there, dusty, bare and empty. 'No, sir.'

'*Copy that.*'

Bang, bang, bang.

'They're trying to get in, sir. What do I do? Tell me what to do, please.'

'*Remember your training. There's a flight of Valkyries on its way, tanker. The Emperor protects.*'

Bang, bang, bang.

'How long before they get here?'

Stilo was staring, with horrified fascination, at the port sponson. The plasteel there was bending and flexing, like a sheet of paper held in the breeze. 'I don't know how long before they split *Sancta Fide* open.'

'*Are there others, tanker? Are they all focused on you?*'

Stilo could not move. The heavy bolter in the port sponson was banging backwards and forwards like an engine piston.

'*Lucius!*'

Stilo dragged his gaze away from the heavy bolter to the screens. On them, he could see the greenskins getting on their warbikes and warbuggies, the engines belching smoke. Even through the layers of plasteel that separated him from them, he could hear the roar of the engines firing up.

'They're leaving, sir, they're leaving!' Stilo remembered his training. 'Heading two-six-five.' They were making for the bridge. That was the big prize that opened up the rest of this world to them.

That was for command to worry about. He wasn't going to die after all.

'*Loader Stilo, open fire.*'

Stilo stared at the vox. He made no answer.

'*Stilo, do you copy? Open fire.*'

He looked at the pict-feed from outside. The first of the warbikes were already accelerating away.

'*Stilo, this is an order. Open fire.*'

'B-but I want them to go away, sir.'

'*Open fire, Stilo! The Valkyries are on their way, they're nearly there, but they won't be able to find you unless you start shooting.*'

'They're leaving, sir. I don't want to attract their attention.'

'*Don't you think there will be more? Shoot them, now, while they've got their backs to you. The Valkyries will finish off the rest and extract you. They're nearly there.*'

'ETA, sir?'

'*Ten minutes, tanker. You've just got to hold out for ten minutes. Now, open fire. Use high-explosive shells on them – warbikes are soft targets.*'

Stilo stared after the departing cloud of dust that told of the rapid progress of the ork vanguard across the plain. It was true what the corps commander said: out on that dust plain, riding warbikes and wartrikes and warbuggies, the orks had no cover. They were ripe for the killing.

But the basic animal desire to survive, to hunker down and play dead stopped Stilo's hands from moving.

'*That's an order, Stilo.*'

The words activated something even deeper in Lucius than his instincts: they fired up his training. The hours, days and weeks spent running through the same sequence of actions over and over and over again. He could no more switch off that sequence, once activated, than he could stop his heart beating.

'Loading main cannon, sir.'

'*Good, lad. Good.*'

'Th-thank you.'

'*By the book, son. Do it by the book.*'

Stilo opened the high-explosive ammunition bin, manhandled out a round, slid the door to the bin shut and pushed the round into the breech of the cannon. He was trained as a loader, so this was what he knew to do: during training he'd got his time to load a round down from nine seconds to four point five.

But that was the problem. He'd done almost all his training as a loader; the cross-training as a gunner and a driver had only lasted for an afternoon.

'*You'll have to track the cannon manually, tanker.*'

'Yes, sir.'

Stilo took a quick look through the sights. The cannon was thirty degrees off. Grabbing the handle, Stilo began to crank the turret round.

The turret groaned as it moved.

'Three turns for one degree of rotation, three turns for one degree of rotation,' Stilo muttered, sweat breaking from his skin as he hauled the crank round.

Slowly, the turret turned.

Stilo checked through the sights. Nearly there. The orks were a moving dust cloud, heading west across the plain towards the bridge. Another five degrees. Fifteen turns.

He counted them off.

'...four, three, two, one.'

Stilo jumped to the sight. The reticule was lined up with the heart of the dust cloud. He set the auspex to heat. The dust cloud lit up red.

'Elevation, elevation,' he muttered, checking the vertical calibration. 'Up, two degrees.'

Stilo grabbed the cannon elevation crank and turned it, counting off six revolutions before checking the sights again.

The crosshair was aligned in the deepest red of the heat source.

Stilo pushed the ignition lever.

'Fire.'

The battle cannon jerked backwards. Propellant fumes, thick and throat-clutching, swirled into the main turret.

Stilo's training took over once more. He pulled open the breech block, released the spent high-explosive shell, letting it fall into the cartridge bin, then slid the ammunition bin door open, hauled out another high-explosive shell and shoved it into the breech.

Stilo took another quick look at the sights.

The dust cloud had stopped moving but its heart still glowed red and the crosshair sat in the centre of it.

'Fire,' he muttered, not even realising he was talking to himself.

He hardly heard the sound.

Round after round. Without thinking, his body running through its training.

Load, aim, fire. Load, aim, fire.

Load, aim, fire.

Stilo paused.

The vox was crackling but he ignored it. He checked the auspex. It was all red – but then he had just fired Emperor knew how many high-explosive shells into the dust cloud. He switched to motion sensor. There were no movement traces.

The vox was squawking.

'Stilo. Report.'

'Can't see, sir. Flare out on the auspex – heat from the shells.'

'You'll have to go visual, Lucius.'

'Unlock? Now?'

'It's the only way to tell if you've got them all. Besides, you'll have to unlock when the Valkyries arrive.'

'What's their ETA, sir?'

'Sub-ten. They're on their way, tanker. Now get me that visual.'

'Sir.'

Stilo pushed up into the turret again and began to unlock the hatch. But then he stopped. He dropped back and cycled through the remaining sensor arrays, checking the area around *Sancta Fide* was clear of greenskins. With nothing showing on the auspexes, Stilo checked his rebreather, then finished unlocking the hatch and, slowly, began to lift it.

The first crack to the outside world opened and the ochre-yellow light of Calleva flooded into the tank. Stilo's goggles blacked, then adjusted.

He peered ahead, eyes squinting against the glare, searching into the dust cloud. There was no sign of any of the ork vehicles. He turned his head slightly to try to hear. Nothing, apart from the dull ringing that was the aural aftermath of firing shell after shell of high-explosive. In the thin air of

Calleva, the dust cloud thrown up by the barrage was already beginning to settle. Stilo pushed the hatch further open so that he could see better.

As the dust drifted down out of the sky, he saw the mangled remains of the ork patrol scattered over the plain: ripped-up warbikes, warbuggies blown into pieces and eviscerated greenskins, some of their severed body parts still flopping with the reflex to war, but no longer able to do anything apart from scrabble in the dust.

He had killed them all.

He, Lucius Stilo, loader, Third Squadron, Fifth Alphard Tank Regiment – on his first combat patrol, with all the rest of the crew of *Sancta Fide* dead – had done this. He was blooded. He was a proper soldier, a proper tanker now. Like his father.

Lucius Stilo threw back his head and roared his triumph at the yellow sun that hung, fat and bloated, in the thin, dark atmosphere of Calleva.

By the Emperor, and through His Grace, he had done it.

Stilo slapped the slide of the battle cannon, the plasteel still hot.

'We did it,' he said. 'We did it.'

Down in the crew compartment, Stilo could hear the vox squawking but, for the moment, he ignored it, taking in the sight of his first battle. But as the dust settled further and the distance came into view, he saw emerging from the cloud the arch of the Infinity Bridge.

It was still standing.

Even as he watched, he saw distant flares light up on it – light up and die away. Darting round it, reduced to little more than mayflies by the distance, were the silver shapes of Imperial aircraft. Stilo squinted: Marauders, maybe Thunder-bolts or Valkyries. Those could be for him, dropping engineers at the bridge before coming to evac. The bridge shivered, moving like a giant snake, but then it settled. Stilo could see parts of the bridge falling into the continental abyss that it spanned, but still it stood.

He'd heard rumours that the Infinity Bridge was xenos built; if they were true, it might explain why it was proving so difficult to bring the structure down.

The distant reports of explosions reached him, echoing past into the vastness of the continental plain. Then, coming through the receding rumble of the explosions, he heard the sound of engines behind him. Lots of engines.

He froze.

Stilo knew he had to turn and look, but his muscles would not obey. They had locked in place, keeping him staring ahead, ensuring his eyes stayed firmly to the front.

This was Lucius Stilo's first combat patrol. He had thought the greenskins who had surrounded *Sancta Fide* constituted an ork warband. He had thought he had saved himself when he saw their corpses littering the plain. He had thought the thirty or so bikes and buggies were all the orks were sending his way.

Stilo forced himself to turn around. Now, looking back over the plain, he saw what an ork warband really looked like.

Clanking, smoking, rattling towards him was a tide of scrap metal pockmarked with green, tusked faces, screaming and laughing and yelling.

Stilo could hear the war cries of the greenskins even above the clank and rattle of the Battlewagons and wartrukks, as harsh and guttural as barking dogs.

He dropped back into the tank, frantically locking the hatch behind him, before seizing the vox mic.

'Where the frek are those Valkyries? There's thousands of them.'

'Report, tanker, report.' The voice on the other end of the vox remained as calm and implacable and unhurried as ever. It made Stilo want to reach through the mic and throttle the commander. But, instead, he made his report.

'Ork patrol destroyed. Ork warband approaching, ETA about two minutes.'

'The bridge. What about the bridge?'

'Still standing, sir.'

There was a moment's silence at the other end of the vox.

'What's the ETA on the evac, sir?'

'The Valkyries will be there in three minutes, tanker.'

'The warband will get here before that, sir.'

'Then you'll just have to hold them off until the Valkyries arrive.'

'Yes, sir.'

Stilo dropped the vox and began frantically turning the crank to rotate the turret. As he did so, he could hear, even through the plasteel, the whoops and howls of the approaching orks.

Using the crank, the turret rotation speed was one hundred and eighty degrees in fifty seconds. Stilo began counting, under his breath, turning the crank handle while watching the desperately slow rotation of the turret.

'...thirty-nine thousand and one, forty thousand and one, forty-one thousand and one.'

Without even checking the auspex, Stilo dragged open the ammo bin and loaded a high-explosive shell into the battle cannon.

Then he checked the auspex.

The greenskins were nearly on him.

Stilo frantically turned the elevation crank, bringing down

the barrel of the cannon, until it was pointing at the ground just in front of the oncoming horde of revving, racing trukks, wagons and trikes.

'Fire.'

Recoil, clear, reload, fire. Recoil, clear, reload, fire. Recoil, clear, reload, fire.

Bang, bang, bang.

It was coming from the starboard sponson.

Bang, bang, bang.

From the port sponson.

Stilo looked up.

They were on the turret.

The greenskins were trying to peel *Sancta Fide* open.

Stilo wasn't thinking now. He was doing.

The hull rang with the reverberations of orks bashing at the hull with hammers and axes and clubs. Even as he watched, he saw the plasteel bulge inwards.

This was close range now.

Stilo grabbed the port heavy bolter and started firing. He didn't even need to aim, he just sprayed bolts; it was like hitting locusts. Spent cartridges clattered round his feet. Greenskins appeared in his sights and were splattered. It was like driving at speed at night on a bug-ridden road.

The sound of greenskin bodies exploding under the impact of a heavy bolter fired at point-blank range echoed over the concussive blasts of the bolter itself.

Stilo kept pressing the trigger, turning the bolter this way and that, but it was for nothing. Through the sights, he saw the orks gather themselves, kick aside the body parts that were in the way, and come running back at him.

'Out!' he yelled, as he'd been trained, just as the wave of orks reached *Sancta Fide*, hitting it like a green tidal wave.

The tank rocked under the impact of a hundred ork fists and axes. The plasteel squealed and screeched. The tank began to rock, back and forth, back and forth.

They were trying to tip the tank over, to get at its belly.

'They're all over me!' Stilo yelled towards the vox, throwing himself at the starboard bolter. 'I can't hold much longer.'

Stilo sprayed bolter rounds from the sponson. The rapid click of the spent shell cases falling onto the hull around his feet triggered a fleeting sound memory: the tick of the cooling engine block when he had first woken into darkness.

There weren't so many greenskins on the starboard side of *Sancta Fide*. After Stilo had traversed the bolter, there were even fewer.

But the orks came. At the sound of bolter fire, at the smell of seared flesh, they came, swarming over and around the stricken tank.

One of the orks grabbed the barrel of the bolter in its hands. Smoke rose from its fingers. But still it began pushing the barrel up, away from its fellows.

Stilo yelled out and, unholstering his laspistol, he took aim through the viewport of the bolter and put a round between the ork's eyes. Then another, when the ork didn't seem to register the first. The third did the trick. The ork went cross-eyed, as if trying to figure out why a hole had suddenly appeared above its nose, then began to sink down. It didn't get far. Another ork slammed it out of the way.

Stilo grabbed the heavy bolter again, squeezed the trigger.

That ork evaporated into a mist of green slime as it took three heavy bolter rounds at point-blank range; its teeth drummed into the side of the tank like ivory knives.

The roar of the bolter ran underneath the sound of Stilo's

screams of rage and triumph as he killed greenskins at zero range, vaporising the ork vermin in the hail of bolter fire.

But even as he killed orks on one side of the tank, it started bouncing on the other side, rocking left to right like a ship in a storm.

The warboss was here and he was directing the show now.

The tank began to rock, higher and higher on each bounce.

With every upward motion, more orks got a handhold, pushing the tank higher each time. Inside, Stilo grabbed tight, trying to stop himself being thrown around helplessly.

'Where are the frekking Valkyries?' he screamed into the vox. 'They're going to turn me over.'

'Hang in there, son,' said the colonel. *'The Emperor protects.'*

With a final heave, the orks pushed *Sancta Fide* over onto its side. Stilo crashed down against the starboard spon-son. Under the weight of the tank, the sponson housing cracked open. The smell of propellant mixed with spilled promethium.

One auspex was still working, flickering grey and red. On it, Stilo saw the ork warboss click its massive neck, flex its huge fingers, then stride up to the tank.

The warboss grabbed the turret hatch. With the tank on its side, the massive ork could reach it easily.

'It's trying to get in,' Stilo whispered into the vox.

The hatch creaked, the lock straining.

It held.

The warboss backed off.

Suddenly aware it was being watched, it turned and stared into the sensor array.

Stilo saw the guile in its eyes.

The warboss reached out, grabbed an ork and held the struggling greenskin in its hands.

Without warning, the warboss pulled its head off. The greenskin's body collapsed to the ground.

The warboss held the dripping ork head up in front of the sensors.

Then it turned back to the hatch and grabbed hold again.

The warboss was trying to tear the head off *Sancta Fide*.

Stilo heard the tank. It was dying. Its machine-spirit moaned and whispered as it leaked away.

He turned to the vox.

'There never were any Valkyries, were there?'

The vox was silent.

'Y-you don't need to sugar-coat it. I'm going to be dead soon.'

The voice, when it came through, was thick, heavy with an emotion that could not be spoken.

'The Emperor is sending His very own Valkyries, son. They'll bring you to His side.'

'Tell the Emperor I'll bring Him a present.'

While he spoke, Stilo was busy jamming open the remaining ammunition bins for the battle cannon. The armour-piercing rounds were still in there, as well as a handful of high-explosive shells. So long as the bins were locked shut, even if they were pierced and detonated by enemy ordnance, the machine-spirit of the tank would ensure that most of the blast was drawn outwards through explosion vents. But with the bin doors open, the destructive force of all the remaining ammunition would be channelled up and out through the turret.

The hatch was bulging outwards.

The locking mechanism was creaking, creaking. Cracking.

Stilo checked his laspistol.

It was on ten per cent charge. He might as well throw it at the warboss.

He needed a weapon. Stilo looked round frantically. There were a few flares, for signalling if the vox failed, but they wouldn't even make the warboss blink.

Then, in the depths of the rocking tank, Captain Bartezko's body shifted and turned. In the dull red of the lumens, Stilo saw the hilt of the captain's power sword. He scrabbled for it, desperately pushing tank debris out of the way.

The hatch broke open.

The warboss shoved its huge head into *Sancta Fide*.

Stilo thumbed the activation on the power sword. The ancient blade hummed its eagerness and, turning, Stilo thrust the sword into the middle of the ork's forehead. The weapon, hungry for greenskin flesh, bit deep, burrowing into the ork's skull. The warboss screamed – a surprisingly high-pitched sound, Stilo noted, as thought fragments spilled through his mind – and fell back out of the tank.

Outside, through the circle of the open hatch, Lucius Stilo saw the warboss staggering, then falling to its knees as it pawed at the sword sticking out of its skull.

But the warboss did not fall. On its knees, it managed to find the hilt of the sword with both hands. Slowly, it pulled the weapon out of its skull.

Stilo could see right through the hole.

The warboss sniffed the blade, licked it, then looked up. It looked into the tank. It looked at Stilo.

Slowly, it got back up onto its feet. For a moment it staggered, then the warboss steadied itself. It looked at Stilo again. It bared its teeth.

Stilo realised the ork was smiling.

The warboss tossed the power sword aside and began walking back towards *Sancta Fide*. Behind him, the other orks followed, gibbering in fear and excitement.

Stilo shrank back into the depths of the tank.

'Are the Valkyries on their way?'

'They are with you now.'

Stilo nodded.

'I know.'

This time the warboss reached in through the hatch, its fingers grabbing for Stilo. Lucius pulled back, out of reach.

'Come and get me,' he yelled, taking a flare from the rack.

The warboss pulled its arm out and looked into the tank, green blood running down into its red eyes.

From where he sat, scrunched up as far from the hatch as possible, Lucius Stilo, loader, Third Squadron, Fifth Alphard Tank Regiment, pointed the flare at the pool of promethium, and the armour-piercing rounds and high-explosive shells piled in the bottom of *Sancta Fide*. He fired it.

For a moment it flared brighter than anything Lucius Stilo had ever seen. Then it shone out even brighter.

He never heard the sound.

Sancta Fide's turret exploded outwards. From out of the belly of the tank flared a jet of purifying, white fire that scoured the surface of the plain, charring to blackened stumps the warboss and the orks clustered round it before igniting the engines and ordnance of the idling trukks and wagons, the explosions leaping from vehicle to vehicle as if blown by the spirit of a young tanker on his first, and final, patrol.

In the HQ of the Fourth Armoured Corps, the general staff were silent.

The vox had gone dead. Before it cut out, they had heard a sound unmistakeable to all tankers: the gushing *whoosh* of a Leman Russ brewing up.

Colonel Markus Stilo, commanding officer, Fourth Armoured Corps, stared at the silent vox. Then he turned to another of the vox-stations.

'Report.'

'The Valkyries have landed the demolition charges on the bridge. Engineers laying them now.'

'Tell them to remain on station to evac the engineers when the bridge is down.'

The comms officer turned back to his vox, passing on the order.

Colonel Markus Stilo stood up slowly.

The general staff looked upon their commanding officer in silence.

'Our mission was to destroy the bridge. To achieve victory, it is sometimes necessary to sacrifice that which we hold dearest. The Emperor calls upon us to make that sacrifice – so long as we are willing do so, the Imperium of Man shall never be defeated.'

The colonel turned slowly, looking around the room, but his eyes were blank.

'My son always dreamed of being a tanker. He died one.'

The colonel reached out a hand, steadied himself, then turned to leave.

'Sir, do you want me to send a Valkyrie to collect... to collect your son's body?'

Colonel Stilo did not look round.

'The Valkyries will carry out their orders. Inform me when the bridge is down. Carry on.'

THE FOURFOLD WOUND

Eric Gregory

American author Eric Gregory makes his first Black Library appearance with this epic story of betrayal and revenge from the Age of Sigmar. With his distinctive style, Eric weaves an engrossing narrative that spans a lifetime and takes us to the farthest corners of the Mortal Realms.

Providing a new and unusual take on the Stormcast Eternals, 'The Fourfold Wound' asks a simple question: how can you take revenge on what is essentially unkillable? The story of Shinua Gan shows us the dangers of obsession and dealing with powers beyond your understanding.

I

Across the realms, heads drew together in forgotten places.

The God-King, they said, gave out the gift of immortality as he saw fit – sometimes to the brave, or in the wake of great works, but sometimes to the ill or to spinsters or to layabouts.

You couldn't work or worship your way into the graces of Sigmar. Not reliably. There were those – everyone had a daughter, a cousin, a father – who gave themselves to service in the armies of the free cities, then died a hard death and were gone.

Across the realms, resentments boiled over into talk, and talk bound comrades into enclaves of spite.

The God-King, they said, wasn't fair.

They met in the cellars of public houses, in stables, in bathhouses. They met in every realm – in Shyish and Chamon and Ghur, even in Azyr. Human and duardin and aelf, they shared grievances and whispered and watched. They tracked the landfalls of Stormcast Eternals, read patterns in their deployments, studied the characters of the Stormhosts.

You learned quickly when you travelled the realms: there were forgotten people everywhere, and they were watching.

Shinua had travelled a long time and a long way to learn what they saw.

This far north, the guild-chartered maps of Ghyran still weren't as reliable as they might have been. Ice caps jutted from waters that were drawn on cartographs as tundra; old settlements dotted coasts that the last surveys had marked as empty.

Shinua wondered whether it was the maps that were unreliable, or the geography. Out here on the edge of the Realm of Life, where even the Jade Kingdom's verdancy retreated from the cold, even the air felt tentative – a frozen fog liable at any moment to give way to something impossible.

But she found what she was looking for. The northernmost island, Ark'non – called in some tongues 'the Land of the Valorous' – announced itself to ships with the red glow of a lighthouse lantern. She tied her sloop to a dock that moored only two other ships, started into the village without encountering another soul.

Night was falling quickly over the village's precise grid of squat hovels and yurts. The roads were silent and empty except for a sledge pulled by three woolly, ivory-tusked beasts of burden. The rider was bundled so tightly into his sledge that Shinua didn't see him at first, took the beasts for pilots without direction. Her breath clouded before her like a spirit familiar guiding the way, and she blinked against the frigid air, half-scared of her eyes freezing shut.

If she understood the cipher, she was searching for a smithy beneath an icon of eight crossed tusks. A longhouse under a sign of tusks stood before her, precisely where it was supposed to be.

Shinua raised a frost-stiff fist and rapped on the door.

No answer.

She pounded on the door again, more urgent this time, more careful to strike the heavy wood in the pattern described by her despatches. Two raps, a pause; two raps, a pause. And then the cadence repeated.

So I'll freeze to death here, she thought. *Knocking on the door of an empty house.* She hacked out a painful laugh. Behind her, the neighbouring longhouses were quiet. The sledge was gone, and now the street was empty, lit only by the red glow above.

It would be a fine joke, surely: to track the despatches this far, to wrestle her sloop across cold seas, only to die frost-bitten in an abandoned village at the edge of another land. The type of joke only a god would tell.

She started to knock again, but the door creaked open before her knuckles reached the wood. The face that stared back at her was sunburnt and serious and younger than her own. The girl – no older than ten – was bundled in grey pelts and rested a palm on the knife-sheath at her waist, holding the door open only a narrow gap.

'Yes?' said the child.

Now that she was here, facing someone much shorter than she'd expected, Shinua wasn't quite sure what to say.

'Are your parents here?' she asked.

The girl shook her head. 'They were beheaded and thrown into the sea.'

Her northern Ghyranese dialect lent the words a peculiar musicality, but Shinua felt sure she'd heard correctly.

'I'm… very sorry,' she managed.

The words turned to fog between them. The girl nodded once.

'May I… may I come inside?' Shinua tried.

'You are welcome here by Guest Right,' the girl said gravely. Shinua doubted the words had ever sounded less welcoming.

The girl stepped aside to admit Shinua, but kept her hand conspicuously at her sheath. The warmth inside the smithy was a wash of fire against Shinua's face. She brushed frozen hair from her eyes, breathed as she felt blood traverse her limbs, and tried not to seem too desperately relieved.

If she'd worked out the chronology correctly, she had only hours left. The guild maps' errors had eaten her time, and now this was becoming too near a thing.

The interior of the smithy was a sort of mandala, with every fur and tool and furnishing arranged around the centrepiece of the hearth and anvil. The forge shone with the same hue of crimson as the lighthouse – a red richer than flame. The glow seemed to cast no smoke, though there was an acrid smell to the air.

Seated by the hearth was a woman of at least seventy, who smiled uncertainly from beneath layers of ornately patterned blankets.

Shinua made a hasty bow. 'I am Shinua Gan,' she said. 'I am here to–'

'She's quite a strong-looking girl,' the old woman said.

Shinua hesitated.

'A hard worker, I'd wager.'

'Grandmother is called *Hesh-yeh* to one housed under Guest Right,' said the girl, hand still on her knife with all the discipline of a palace guard. 'I am called Nor.'

Shinua spread her hands in a display of harmlessness.

'Thank you, Nor,' she said. 'Thank you, Hesh-yeh. I am here to–'

'Would she like some soup?' asked Hesh-yeh. 'She looks hungry. We have a mighty lot of soup. Leek and salted eel.'

Shinua forced a smile. The old woman by the hearth didn't look like a purveyor of anti-Azyrite intelligence. Shinua's own grandmother would have been a more likely suspect: ninety when she died but still lean and shrewd and entirely capable of slitting a bull's throat. But Shinua had met many unlikely dissidents in her travels; she pressed on, speaking more quickly now.

'I am here to speak in the circle of the eye,' she said, drawing up her sleeve to reveal the tattoos on the inside of her forearm: her old Freeguilder garrison tattoo, cancelled with a jagged line of red ink. And above it, closer to her heart, an eye encircled by radiating arrows. 'I have questions.'

'She has tattoos!' said Hesh-yeh.

'Yes,' Nor agreed.

'So lovely.' The old woman leaned forwards to admire the ink-work.

Nor sidled behind her grandmother and discreetly, without moving her palm from her sheath, lifted the sleeve of her knife-hand. The tattoo on her arm wasn't quite the same as Shinua's – it was more finely drawn, and the circle around the eye was a sort of sunburst halo. The ink was red. But the meaning was the same.

'I will show the guest to her bedroll and dry clothes,' said Nor, and hurried Shinua up a ladder to a cramped loft. The bunk was lit by a brazier that shone with the same crimson as the hearth below. The girl sat on the bedroll with crossed legs, her head bowed slightly so as not to hit the crossbeams of the roof, and Shinua attempted to echo the position.

'The question,' Nor whispered.

'You're... the Watcher of Ark'non?' Shinua asked, careful to keep her voice low. 'You wrote these?' She drew the Watcher's reports from her satchel.

Nor inclined her head. 'And so?'

She was a child. How was this possible? Shinua steadied her thoughts. 'I compile Watchers' almanacs in Shyish. I received your reports a fortnight ago. The original dating is some time earlier.'

Every sighting of the God-King's Stormcast Eternals, every known station and deployment, the name and biography of every claimed hero known to the recorders across the realms. The Watchers shared what they knew in a web of vellum and ciphers and post – information that wasn't even secret, most of the time, but that told stories or posed questions when stitched together into an almanac.

What lands had the celestial armies claimed?

Who was hallowed and chosen?

Why?

This account that had started with Nor had come to Shinua from a Watcher in Ghur, who had it from a Watcher in Hysh. It had passed through many hands before hers, which made the document all the more puzzling.

'The question,' Nor repeated.

'If you have the cipher right, if I do, you date a deployment of the Hammers of Sigmar to this night. This village. Is that what you intended to write?'

The child nodded in the red light. 'Yes.'

'How can you know that they will deploy here before it happens?'

'Why do you wish to know this?'

Shinua weighed the prudence of honesty. At last, the

tattooed eye shared between them swayed her to tell the truth. Or most of it.

'One of Sigmar's warriors wronged me. I will find him and make him answer for the crime.'

Nor brushed a strand of hair from her eyes and gazed appraisingly at Shinua.

'What crime?'

Four oilskins arrayed in the blackened earth of the farmstead. They should have been too small to hold bodies, never mind three generations.

'He betrayed my family to killers,' said Shinua. 'He betrayed my family while he lived, but the God-King claimed him as a hero.'

That seemed to satisfy the girl. She nodded.

'I suppose,' she said, 'you must meet my brother, the Lord-breaker. He is the one to tell you about futures.'

The spikes of Shinua's boots crunched ice as she and Nor hurried down the empty street, their breath rising like chimney-smoke into the red-black sky.

Smoke, Shinua thought. The hearth in Nor's home had burned, but there was no smoke, and the air was clear. The forge had burned with the same crimson light as the brazier and the village's vast lighthouse.

The girl wore a small mountain of grey-white furs that hunched over her head and amounted to an armour, trimmed with figures in black and gold. The pelt, Shinua realised, must have come from the little sledge-bearing mammoth-beasts.

If the bulk of the coat slowed Nor down, it didn't show; she seemed more urgent in her stride than Shinua, darting gracefully across the ice. Or perhaps she was simply more accustomed to the cold. Shinua struggled to keep up, and was relieved when the girl stopped at the base of the light-house. Beyond, the tides spoke their cold, hushed language. The signal-light above flickered, like a guttering candle in the night.

Nor pounded on the lighthouse door: twice, a pause; twice, a pause. And then the pattern repeated. But no answer came. The girl fumbled in her furs for a skeleton key, unlocked and heaved open the door. It opened into an unadorned stair-well not much warmer than the street.

'He lives here?' Shinua asked. 'Your brother?'

'Yes,' answered Nor, only a little breathless, taking two steps at a time.

'You called him the Lordbreaker. Who did he break?'

'Our village...' she took a breath, '...is built on pelt and bone and blood. The tusks of *marmut*, mostly. Some whal-ing – in the season. Before, the Old Lords kept my people in thrall. They commanded the hunts and the smithing and they took the coin. They ate the fat and we ate the meat that rots. Anyone who opposed them was beheaded and thrown into the sea.'

'So your brother broke the Old Lords,' she said.

'The horns of our whales and the tusks of our marmut and the blood of our veins – they are of great value. The Old Lords sold our labour to the Kharadron of Barak-Laskar, and to the Azyrite free cities.' Nor turned her back to Shinua and started up the stairs again. 'The free world was happy to have their custom. But we ached and ate rot and died. My brother raised a revolt. Ark'non loves him for it.'

Shinua's muscles burned as they climbed. As they approached the top of the lighthouse, Nor began to call what must have been her brother's name: 'Sgon, Sgon.' Her tone was between a warning and a question, but no answer came.

They reached the tower's apex. A wave of heat struck Shinua as they entered the room – welcome, but *wrong*, smokeless and subtler than it should have been. In the centre of the space was a hearth much larger than the forge in the smithy – this was a sanguinary pyre, piled high with obsidian bones. There was a pattern in the architecture of the pyre, a shape that Shinua couldn't quite name. Small, unburnt bones were scattered on the floor, knuckles or digits or ribs.

Before the pyre lay a young man's form, pale and bled from the wrist.

Nor took a hesitant step towards the dead boy, glanced back at Shinua. Her older-than-her-age composure was gone, replaced by incomprehension. Her wide eyes darted fearfully around the room. 'What happened?' she asked.

Sgon the Lordbreaker's right hand held a knife, the blade brown with blood that had nearly dried. He was dressed in a robe of black and gold. A trail of his blood ran from the rim of the pyre to a pool around his arm.

For a moment, the light turned black. Not a darkness, but a shadow-light. Then it was red again. A guttering candle.

'You should be with your grandmother,' Shinua said quietly. As far as she'd come, as hard as she had fought to be here, she wasn't prepared to see a child through loss. Nor knelt by her brother, but didn't touch him.

'He did this... to himself?' she asked.

Shinua looked out the aperture of the lighthouse at the emptiness of the night sea. Snow had begun to fall.

'He saw visions in the fire,' said Nor, nodding to the lighthouse pyre. 'That was your question. He knew the Hammers of the God-King would come to raze Ark'non because he saw it in the fire.'

This boy wrote the future, and then removed himself from it. The thought made her shiver.

'Why would the God-King want to raze this place?' Shinua asked.

'Sgon taught us rage as a catechism,' she said softly. 'He taught us to hone our wrath and blood into pure and liberating fire. The God-King does not sanction rage other than his own.'

The room's curved walls bore vellum maps of nearby islands. Stone-scrawled ideograms that Shinua couldn't read, racks upon racks of obsidian tusks carved into fine bladed weapons. In one corner, a small cot by a desk messy with papers. The home of a revolutionary.

The pyre flashed black again.

'Do you know how he saw his visions in the fire?' Shinua asked softly. Her conscience twisted uncomfortably at this pressing of the grieving girl. She thought of her own brother Hsien, burned. *The charred remnants of a life, gathered and wrapped in oilskin.* As a boy, Hsien had looked up to the man Shinua hunted now; he would have loved that the bastard became a Stormcast Eternal.

Nor looked up at her, wet eyes reflecting a warbling light.

'The oracle bones. And fire and blood. That is how everything is done here. The bone of the beasts of the ground and sea. Horns and tusks and limbs. Lacquered with the blood of...' She looked down. 'One of us. One born of the old families of Ark'non. The Valorous. Lacquered until the bone is black...'

Her voice failed her. She stared at her brother's sprawled form. Shinua was silent, and after a moment, the girl recovered her words.

'When it burns,' Nor said, 'the fire is holy. The kiss of the flame twists metal, but its glow is a small warmth. It spoke to Sgon. Tongues of fire. It told him what was to pass.'

The tusks on the racks around her. The skeletal construction in the lighthouse pyre. The bones of Hesh'yeh's forge. All black with the blood of the Valorous.

Who had bled? How much wrath and blood had Ark'non given itself over to? Shinua kept the question to herself, stared into the fire that seemed liable, now, to speak. Then her gaze travelled past the fire to the night sky beyond, and the breath caught in her throat, and all the warmth of the pyre receded.

The stars were falling.

She rushed to the aperture. Above, dark thunderheads parted like mouths and an army of light spilled from the sky.

The descent was silent at first. Then, a shock of sound buckled the atmosphere.

'Gods,' said Shinua, startling herself with the words. 'They're here.'

Nor climbed to her feet. The fear and grief and exhaustion written across her face made her painful to behold.

'Grandmother,' she said. 'They will kill her.'

'Her?' Shinua asked, then felt foolish.

She knew the stories of the God-King's annihilations. She had compiled the accounts in the almanac.

Nor heaved a carved black tusk from the racks, struggling to lift it by its one leather grip halfway down the blade. 'She is the armourer,' Nor said, sounding panicked. 'She lacquered every wartusk. They will kill her.'

The weapon was clearly meant to be wielded one-handed, slung under the forearm of an adult warrior. It was a sad burden in Nor's hands. The girl strained to raise the tip of the blade into the pyre.

Outside, the points of light in the sky brightened and grew larger, like sudden morning was dawning.

It's real now, Shinua thought. The anger of Sigmar was falling towards her.

'I'll carry it for you,' she said. 'Stay with me. I'll protect you.'

Nor appraised her for a moment, then held out the war-tusk. Shinua hefted the weapon and dipped it in the signal pyre. Crimson flame danced up the length of the blade with a whisper of ignition.

She grabbed a clutch of oracle bones from the floor and stuffed them in her coats.

'Down,' she said. 'Run.'

Nor spared a last glance for her brother and then ran down the spiral stairway, taking three steps at a time. Shinua was behind her, desperate to descend and desperate not to topple Nor, straining to hold the tusk aloft. The blade scored the stone of the wall.

Breathlessly, they tumbled out of the lighthouse and into the cold. She could make out shapes in the radiance now: humanoid forms, some winged; hammers and standards and great bows in silhouette, a luminous judgement.

Around them, the Valorous left their yurts, eyes turned to the lights above. Women and men dressed in black-trimmed furs like Nor's. Many carried tusks that glowed crimson. Every blade black with blood, lacquered by Hesh'yeh. The people of Ark'non gathered in clusters outside their homes, and they stared at the sky not in awe or bewilderment but in defiance.

They knew. They knew this was coming.

The first blaze of golden light struck the lighthouse. A concussion, a shattering more primordial than thunder. The ground quaked. Shinua risked a glance over her shoulder. Stonework toppled in a flare of auric wash, and the signal

'How are you here?' Halas asked. 'Are you real?' He paused. 'Sometimes I see you when I close my eyes.'

The snowflakes turned to steam when they fell on his face. But he was flesh, right there in front of her. His skin flush and wet with sweat, the old scar still on his brow.

'I'm real,' she said. 'I was looking for you.'

And it was true. But she wasn't prepared for the moment to be now. She'd expected months – maybe years – of scrying and searching.

'I'm sorry,' he said. 'I know that's worthless to you, but it's all I have. I am so sorry.'

'Tell me what happened,' Shinua said. Her voice was level; a peculiar calm had settled on her.

Halas inhaled. 'I disgraced myself.'

'You were drunk.'

'I was drunk on my post. You've known me a long time. You never saw me drink on watch, did you?'

For twelve years of his mortal life, he had been posted as a solitary watchman in the Freeguild outpost on the Gan farmstead. An eye and sword against the bandits and predators of Ghyran. She had seen him every day of her childhood, and he had been kind to her and her brother Hsien, taught them swordplay and taken their enthusiasms seriously. He was too eager to be liked, perhaps, or to share unlikely tales of his old wars. But he was neither a drunkard nor a shirker of duties.

'Why, then?' she asked.

'I don't know. I was stuck in melancholy and felt my years. Your parents kept a cask of Azyrite wine and the sky seemed heavy. I...' He hesitated. 'I had felt a weight over me in dark hours for some long time.'

The Halas she had known – the Halas who had been her teacher and friend – told his tales eagerly. He had spun out a myth of himself facing down orruk cavalries, felling undead gargants.

She had believed in Halas. She had idolised him.

'And what happened when you were drunk?'

'The outlanders,' he said quietly.

'The bandits from the outlands. They came for the cattle. The grain. They burned everything that remained.'

He was silent.

'When one of your mates in the garrison leaves his post,' she said, 'or breaks his oath, or turns tail, he loses his sash and his life. Soldier's justice.'

'I'm so sorry,' he said.

She saw Halas as he was when he came to them, a decade younger and stubbled, a scar across his brow but his face somehow childish, soft with a capacity for awe. The Gans had welcomed him and fed him their bread; her father had helped build furniture for the soldier's quarters in the watch-station.

'They trusted you,' she said.

'I know.'

He was barely audible. He couldn't meet her eyes.

'Look,' she said. 'Look at me.'

He looked up. Shinua showed him the scratched-out garrison tattoo on the inside of her forearm: a skull with skeletal hands over its eyes. He had the same tattoo.

'I left home to be like you. Someone who could keep watch. I trusted you to keep them safe while I was gone.'

'I'm so sorry.'

He was right. His sorriness was worthless to her.

'Four lives you owe me,' she said. 'This one is for Hsien.'

She reared back and swung the wartusk up and into his throat.

II

In the years since she left home, Shinua had lived alone and as she pleased, or near enough. She travelled the unmapped or faintly sketched places of the realm, and she sent her reports by courier to the free cities' surveyors' guilds. The pay was meagre, and the existence was humble; she slept in ruins or dunes or goatskin tents, rarely lingering on any frontier long enough to do more than render its topography. She mapped cavern systems and desolate mountain ranges, but all the while her life had been simple. She was alone, and her only real purpose was vengeance.

Now Nor was in her care.

The girl was hardier than Shinua had been at her age; she knew how to skin game, how to tie the net of a hammock in high branches. Talents Shinua had learned either from Halas or in training with the Freeguild. But she was another will, another knot of needs and whims. In the night, she sometimes cried out for her brother or grandmother. Sometimes she wept over dreams that she didn't understand: *'A horned god. A raven. A mountain upside down, burning to death.'* She refused to eat any meat she had not hunted herself.

At first, Shinua had considered leaving her with an orphanage or holy order. But Nor spoke regularly and matter-of-factly about her plots of violence against the God-King, and about the rituals of blood and bone that her brother had employed, that she would employ herself one day. 'I will burn down the heavens,' she said once, unprompted, over breakfast. The girl would have a difficult time, Shinua suspected, in the orphanages and academies of the free cities.

After cutting Halas' throat and securing a skin of oracle bones from the Valorous, Shinua had indulged herself briefly in some giddiness of triumph. But that thrill faded quickly. She owed her old mentor three more deaths. Worse, the holy fires weren't speaking futures as they had done for Nor's brother, the Lordbreaker. After the first two little bones burned down voicelessly, without a word of prophecy, she had grown wary of wasting the entire supply.

So she watched, and she recorded – for a year, and then another. As they travelled, Shinua shared her maps and accounts with others who bore the tattoo of the eye. In the cellars of public houses, in stables, in bathhouses, she exchanged journals and ledgers. She compiled a more current almanac. From a bitter-mouthed swineherd outside Hammerhal Ghyra, Shinua learned the true names of an entire company of Hallowed Knights – and realised with mixed intrigue and discomfort that she might track down those immortal warriors' surviving families, if she wished. She learned the heraldry of the Stormhosts; she learned to chart their organisation into chambers and companies, to read the symbology on their pauldrons and banners. She studied the sketches she had made of Halas' armour – the scrollwork and icons; the awful, empty face of a mask – and she knew where he stood in the armies of the sacred.

Finally, with his company named and numbered, she found him. In the dim-lit backroom of a muggy tavern, Shinua learned that Halas' company of the Hammers of Sigmar were reported in the fields of the Sog, embroiled in a campaign against the armies of the Grandfather of Plagues. The report was two months old, but the campaign was said to be a slow, brutal weathering of bodies and spirits, a grind with no evident end.

Shinua smiled.

On the north-west frontier of Ghyran lay a metropolis that no citizen of the free cities named as home, that was discussed – even in taverns with no love for the God-King – only in grim whispers. A city built in swamps, its pillars raised over centuries by slaves and then toppled in a day of epidemic.

In some tongues, the place was called the City Bereaved. In others, darkly, Abundance. To most, the agglomeration of mossy stone and ruined towers was known as Plaguespire. Even glimpsed on the horizon, any mortal eye could see that it was a place where reality thinned and sickened, where some other cosmos loomed. Vast winged sacs – what might have been gargantuan flies – circled the crooked towers, and the sky above was always tinged a feverish pink-purple.

The city belonged to the Plague God.

Far to the south-east, across leagues of marsh and rotwood forest, the Stormcast Eternals and their sylvaneth allies laid siege to the outer bastions of the Plague God's influence. They were an endless march from Plaguespire, but perhaps they didn't mean to take the city itself – only to contain

it. Reality strained out there on the front: the holy lightning of Sigmar scorched air made squalid by the breath of
daemons. Creatures not of these realms marched in sickly
legions – nearly humanoid, but not quite, they might have
been mistaken for walking corpses, moaning inscrutable
numbers in voices from outside time. Above the legions
towered great flesh mounds like rotten, living mountains.
And there were mortal worshippers of the Plague God, too –
bulked by the gifts of their deity, sweating in sick-green
armour.

Shinua wasn't foolhardy enough to make for the front,
especially with Nor in tow. The daemonic city seemed a
similarly deadly destination. Instead, she studied the latest
consensus maps of the surveyors' guilds and found an operational centre that the pair of them might hope tó survive.

Her maps called it the Abbey of the Twined Root. Half-
forgotten and cradled in creepers and moss, the ruins of the
aelven monastery were closer to the front than the city. The
construction was vaster than it first appeared: underground,
a network of catacombs and tunnels ranged far beyond the
obvious walls, emerging now and then into swamp brush
or quiet hillsides.

Shinua could fit in the catacombs, but only just, which
meant she couldn't have stopped Nor from exploring the
place if she had tried. Watching over the girl required her to
cultivate a careful disinterest – not to worry whether a tunnel
had collapsed on her, whether she had hunted some game
that got the better of her.

While Nor explored, Shinua waited on the old, neglected
road that ran between Plaguespire and the front. She sat
cross-legged by the side of the road and unfolded her book-
binding tools, committed her more current almanac to

leather. For three days, she waited. And on the third, they arrived: the mortal troops of the Plague God, walking the supply line.

They sang a merry marching song that collapsed often into phlegmy guffaws at their excretory rhymes. Their music travelled most swiftly, followed by the stench of shit and rot, and the sight of them. Swollen and unsteady, they were giants of men in armour of vomitous metal. Some of their limbs were inhuman, unruly suckers and feelers; every man looked simultaneously vigorous and on the edge of death. *The Rotbringers*.

'Hail,' said Shinua.

The Rotbringers' emissary was a man named Baslaergh. He was good-humoured but not quite so loud as his comrades, and Shinua thought it was a mercy that he came to the monastery alone. The gaiety of massed Rotbringers was trying, but the odour was deadly. He arrived at the monastery gate at precisely the appointed hour. Nor spotted him first, through the tiny window of the cramped cell where they slept.

'He's hideous,' the girl said.

'He is very ugly,' Shinua agreed.

The Rotbringer wouldn't fit comfortably in the narrow corridors of the abbey, so they met him in the vine-strangled courtyard. In one hand, he carried a stave crowned by a tremendous bell. He was even larger than a Stormcast Eternal, but he wore little armour beyond greaves and a helm; his bulk was a function of impossible, divine bloat. He seemed at ease in his flesh, even as his flesh seemed not entirely under his control. Cysts squirmed just beneath his pallid skin, and small bluish cilia grasped from his gut. He bowed his oversized, cyclopean helm in greeting to Nor.

'My lady,' he said. 'I am Baslaergh, Blightking of the Rot-bringers. Pleased to make yer acquaintance.' And to Shinua, 'A pleasure to see yer again.'

'And you,' Shinua lied, smiling too broadly and trying not to breathe through her nose.

'You're a king?' asked Nor.

'We are many of us kings, lass, if we live in the god's favour.'

'Are there Blightqueens, too?' Nor asked.

'The god welcomes all in the Garden.'

The air was heavy with humidity. Shinua slapped a mosquito from her arm and tried to position herself upwind of the stinking mass of the soldier. Nor perched on a half-tumbled statue of an aelven monk.

'You look ill,' said the girl.

Perhaps, Shinua thought, Nor wasn't the best partner in diplomacy.

Baslaergh smiled down at the girl. His teeth were rotten and sparse, his eyes hidden behind his helm. 'I expect I am! I've all manner of beasties livin' in me. Livin' *with* me. I choose to make myself a home for 'em. What yer call illness, I call hospitality.'

'Is that why your god makes you so big? So you can be a home?'

'That's enough, love,' said Shinua.

The Rotbringer was untroubled. 'Could be, at that! Or else to smash the false God-King.'

Nor grinned, satisfied with that answer. Baslaergh turned to Shinua.

'My masters,' he said, 'reviewed yer proposal with interest.'

Rusted and worn as it was, Shinua could make out a muddy reflection of herself in his helm. 'I'm pleased to hear it. What did they think?'

'They think yer would make a fine servant of the god.'

She craned her neck to stare up at the Blightking. The representative of daemons, of a fell god. Was he threatening her, or evangelising? With beings like this, what was the difference? Her stomach knotted, but she breathed and willed her face into a mask of confidence.

'I don't scare easily.'

'Aye! Fightin' spirit, very good. My masters were *intrigued* by yer scribblings on the God-King's armies. They've already diverted forces as yer suggested, and they'll continue the manoeuvres so long as ye provide the rest of the book. But... are yer sure it's what ye want?'

Shinua exhaled. In her mind's eye, on the front of the war in Ghyran, a line of the plague legions began to – ever so slightly – give ground.

After months of attrition, a line of Stormcast Liberators started to push forwards. Funnelled along a path.

'I'm sure,' said Shinua.

'And it's revenge ye want?'

She nodded.

'*I* want to burn down the heavens,' said Nor gravely.

Baslaergh looked back and forth between the pair of them. 'I'll warrant yer fearsome. But I don't ken how ye propose to kill one of the golden bastards.' He reached into the pouches of his belt and produced what looked like a snail shell, a bone-coloured spiral with a stopper of cork and ivory.

'I do not give ye this lightly. It is a flask of the Grandfather of Plagues' own breath, stoppered in the Garden itself.'

Her stomach curled at the sight of the spiral.

'I can't accept that,' Shinua said.

'It is not yers to refuse.' With absurd tenderness, the Blightking kneeled and placed the gift at her feet.

'If ye find yer want his favour... break the flask. Breathe his holy breath, accept his salvation.'

Shinua said nothing.

'And if ye will not... be ready. They are coming.'

'Look,' said Shinua. 'This is how you thread the needle.'

They had exhausted their preparations. They had mapped the whole of the Abbey of the Twined Root, the countless bolt-holes and the veins of secret passages that ran through the walls, through the rafters, beneath the floor. Now they each sat cross-legged on the cool stone of the vestry. Nor watched Shinua bind up the spine of a book of secrets for the daemon generals of the Plague God. The bone needle had belonged to Shinua's mother before her – it had sewn cloaks and shawls before it bound almanacs. She held out her needle and awl to Nor.

'Here. Try. The needle was my mum's.'

Nor took the needle. 'Sgon was the one who made furs. My parents were always on hunts. Before they were dead.' She tested the sharpness of the needle against her thumb. Drew a bead of blood. 'It breaks skin,' she said approvingly. Then allowed a small smile, which Shinua returned.

'It breaks leather, love. It breaks space and time, with enough work.'

She watched the work of Nor's mind behind her eyes – the unanswerable hurt of loss after loss. For Shinua, grief had meant one great annihilation of the people who loved her, all at once. For Nor, it had been twin concussions. After growing up on the promise that you were an instrument of others' yields.

Most days, there was a distance in the girl's gaze, as if she weren't quite present in herself. Here and now, her eyes focused. 'How do you mean?' she asked.

'You weave,' Shinua gestured at a sheaf of Watchers' accounts, 'words into a form that will endure, that carries visions from one mind to another, one age to another. You can work the needles, too. You understand?'

Nor nodded once, mulling the words.

'You'll need a trade to make your way in the realms,' Shinua said. 'I can teach you.'

'I wish to fight. I will fight for pay.'

'Then you'll spend your whole life fighting other people's wars. You need a trade if you want to be really free.'

The distance returned to Nor's gaze. 'I see,' she said.

Outside, a bell tolled. Baslaergh stood in the courtyard, ringing his bell-stave.

'It's time,' he called.

There were two armies at the Blightking's heels.

First, a procession of the plague legions in retreat. They marched in an organised riot down the supply road: cavalry on vast, squamous toads or gargantuan flies. The one-eyed infantry like dreams of corpses, sag-skinned and bloat-bellied, swords dragging in the dirt. Rotten throats droned enumerations. Then there were the walking mountains of flesh, horned and grinning...

Shinua tried to focus on Baslaergh's empty helm, to ignore the chants and gongs of the daemonic legion beyond the monastery gates.

'They're an hour behind,' said the Rotbringer. 'An hour at most.'

'Thank you,' Shinua said. Her stomach threatened upset, but she swallowed spit until it settled, and proffered the half-bound book of Watchers' secrets. 'I didn't finish the binding on the second folio, but I think you care more about the contents.'

The skin behind his helm creased to suggest a smile. Delicately, a hand the size of her head reached down to grasp the book. His nails were yellow and dirty with dried blood. Baslaergh briefly evaluated the volume and slipped it into a pouch on his belt. Her stomach twinged as she thought of the Hallowed Knights' true names, the surnames of surviving families all lined up in rows like gravestones.

'Yer sure ye won't embrace the god?' he asked, his tone allowing that he knew the answer already. 'There's such joy in it, lass. The sight of the Garden, the death and birth and death and birth, the *bigness*. The Grandfather might ease yer mind.'

Shivers ran along the skin of her arm, even in the humidity of Ghyran's midday. She shook her head.

'Ah, well.' He turned away and made for the monastery gate. 'But a word to the wise. Not just as a servant of the god, but... survivor to survivor. En't no point in livin' if it's only for yerself. Yer got to believe there's something beyond ye to make any meaning out of it all.'

'Why are you telling me this?' she asked.

He shrugged vast, sweat-slick shoulders. The cilia of his gut grasped at nothing. 'Revenge is an indulgence, lass. If ye make yerself a means of yer own satisfaction, what'll ye be when yer done?'

The second army marched in radiance.

Through the fug of Ghyranese noon: a golden company, thunderbolt banners borne high. In precise rows the Liberators walked, rows of shields and hammers and impassive face masks. Above, spear bearers and archers circled on wings of light, describing arcane patterns in the skies.

This was a company of immortal warriors who took the name of their Stormhost from the God-King himself.

First among the Stormcasts: the Hammers of Sigmar.

The company encircled the gate of the Abbey of the Twined Root. Liberators massed along the supply road and took up position by the gate. An advance guard fanned out through the halls of the monastery.

From her bolthole in the north-western wall of the courtyard, Shinua watched. Her window was only a crack in mislaid brick, but it was enough: she watched the Stormcasts assemble in parade discipline on the same ground where she'd splayed her weapons and plotted the previous afternoon. After a time, a figure somewhat grander than the others – its armour filigreed, a cloak around its shoulders – emerged to inspect the ranks of Liberators.

Here was a Lord-Celestant, commander of immortals. In the warlord's retinue was a bodyguard of Stormcasts in bulkier armour, wielding massive, light-puissant greathammers. The Lord-Celestant paused before a rank-and-file Liberator, bowed its head in some confidence. The leader's voice carried through the courtyard as it ordered the Liberator: 'Hearthguard. With me. Now.'

Shinua scrabbled from the bolthole up into the rampart passages, taking care to stifle her breathing, wincing at the scrape of her boots on the gravelly stone in the hollows of the walls. The tunnels were narrow; she had to arch backwards to work her way up and through the arteries of the abbey.

She wiped dust and stray spider-thread from her face, drew herself forwards handhold by handhold. The dark was total now; she had to rely on touch and count. Her packed shoulder bag scraped the walls. *Seventeen, eighteen, nineteen* – she should be over the sacristy now. Right, square shoulders to squeeze around the corner, then *twenty, twenty-one, twenty-two, twenty-three–*

She emerged into a cranny that overlooked the nave. The worship space was circular, a kind of enclosed amphitheatre with a lectern and stone altar at its centre. The altar was raised an arm's length from the floor. Shinua looked out across the nave through the open jaw of a statue embedded in the wall, some placid aelven icon.

Shinua unlatched her crossbow, crawled forwards and settled into a firing position.

On the altar, Nor sat with her legs dangling off the edge, her feet not quite touching the ground. She kicked absently, as if she were bored.

The Stormcast vanguard took up posts at intervals around the nave, levelling strange Azyrite pistols. Behind them came the slow, heavy march of the warriors in bulkier armour, the Retributors. Finally, a trio of Stormcasts:

The Lord-Celestant, revealed as a woman around fifty with grey hair braided to her scalp.

A man with heavy robes draped over his armour, thick-bearded and bearing a stave that shone with blue flame.

And a Stormcast in Liberator plate, walking a hesitant step behind the Lord-Celestant, as if he were unsure of his place.

The Lord-Celestant looked down on Nor.

'Child,' she said. 'How did you come to be here?'

Nor shook her head. 'Only Halas. I will only speak to Halas.'

'The one you have asked for by his true name is here.' She gestured with an armour-plated hand to the nervous warrior beside her. 'Liberator Hearthguard. *Halas.*' She turned to him. 'Do you know her?'

'No,' Halas said quietly. He removed his helm and crouched to speak to Nor. 'What is your name?'

'I am called Nor.'

'Why do you ask for me? How do you know my old name?'

Shinua fixed the sight of her crossbow on Halas' right eye. Tried to summon her mother's face into the fore of her mind. In memory, her mother's features were hazy, indistinct. Mixed with the image of bone needles. An oilskin of ashes, a hole in the world.

He took the clarity from my mother's face.

Her fingertip grazed the metal of the trigger. The sight described a black halo around Halas' head.

'I am bait,' said Nor. 'She is here to take a life from you. Price for your debt-of-mother.'

Halas and the Lord-Celestant exchanged a glance.

Behind her back, Nor gave the hand signal that she was ready.

'Now!' Shinua called, and fired.

Nor hurled herself from the altar and under its belly, into the monk-tunnels.

And Halas frowned.

The bolt from the crossbow hung suspended in the air, halfway between hunter and prey, captive in cobalt flame. The robed and bearded Stormcast held his stave aloft, eyes and hands and weapon blazing with the same aethereal fire.

Shinua's limbs went cold.

Slowly, the bolt spun around in the air. One hundred and eighty degrees, like a compass needle, to point at her.

The pistols of the guards followed the guidance of the bolt, all directed at the open mouth of the limestone saint where she crouched with her crossbow.

She didn't have time to fire another bolt. The Stormcast sorcerer gestured with a blue-burning hand, and the statue of the aelven saint collapsed. Shinua toppled to the floor yards from the altar, her knees and elbows cracking against the stone. She lost her grip on the crossbow and it clattered out of reach.

She coughed, climbed to her hands and knees. Her eyes teared against limestone dust. As the cloud parted and settled, Halas stood before her.

He looked more tired now than in Ark'non. More tired than he'd ever looked in life. The sight of her seemed to exhaust him, to dull his eyes.

'Oh, Shin,' he said. He kneeled and extended his hand. 'I am so sorry. I am so unutterably sorry for what I've done to you.'

She glared up at him. Made no move to take his hand.

'Some part of me was... relieved before,' he said. 'When you killed me. In the snow. I thought... perhaps you had done what you needed to do. But I see that isn't true. I've warped your life. I've taken years from you.'

'Will you protect us?' asks Shinua, a child who lies awake each night in terror of ghouls and daemons and necromantic bandits that raid from the outer darks.

Halas drops to one knee, right there in the kitchen. Her parents smile.

She is a child, and he is a hero, and he smiles beneficently in the morning light of her kitchen, his knee bent, his smile the bearer of all his legends. 'I always will watch over you,' he says. Even sixteen years later, the contours of that smile will remain with her; even as her mother's face fades, she will see him with perfect clarity–

Shinua spat on his golden boots. There was a bit of blood in the spittle, and it stained the gold. Behind him, the pistols of the Stormcasts stared her down with their dozen empty eyes.

'The worst day,' Shinua rasped. 'Do you know what the worst day was?'

Regretfully, Halas withdrew his hand.

'Not when I saw their corpses. Not when I learned they were gone. The worst day was when I learned *you* had died. The garrison captain called me to her tent and told me you had been assigned to a penal detail on the front. She said you died in single combat with a Chaos warrior. She said Sigmar claimed you. And all I could think was, *That death was supposed to be mine.*'

He was quiet for a time. 'I don't know if you can truly hear me now,' he said. 'But your anger – it's eating your life. It's eating the life of this girl in your care.'

'She wants to see you dead, too,' Shinua said, low and ragged. 'All of you. I couldn't turn her away if I wanted to.'

He frowned.

'I'm going to make a last promise to you,' he said. 'We will never speak again. You've let this… rage and rot into your soul on my account, and it's going to eat your years if you allow it. So I will be gone for you. From here on, I may as well be dead. You will have to spend time in gaol, but even when you are free, you won't find me. Let that be the end. Will you?'

For a moment, there was silence. The sorcerer and the Lord-Celestant loomed over his shoulders.

The sound that rolled from her throat started as a growl, an unsteady moan of defiance in confinement. Then it rose to become a scream – a hatred and a fury and an answer to an unanswerable question. Perhaps she howled *No!* into the echoing stonework of the nave. For an instant, her mind was unknowable even to herself.

Halas flinched. Shinua held her breath, grasped the flask in her shoulder bag and flung it with all her strength into the breastplate of Halas' armour. The bone spiral shattered against sigmarite.

The pistols of the Stormcasts barked; she hurled herself away and rolled behind the altar. A shot grazed her bicep, a streak of agony.

Behind her, a smog unfurled around Halas, the Lord-Celestant, the sorcerer. The breath of the Plague God filled the nave – a mustard-hued cloud that seemed to *want* to grow and grasp and consume everything it touched.

Shinua spared only a moment's glance. Through the yellow cloud, the skin of Halas' face erupted in boils and growths. Cilia lashed from his mouth like a dance of tongues, then from his eyes, his throat. His jaw opened until it cracked, his skull distended. Halas screamed even as he choked on growth, an awful, strangled sound. The Lord-Celestant choked. The sorcerer choked.

The Stormcasts' bodies *burst,* and their armour clattered to the stone. The lightning of Azyr pierced the stone of the monastery, lit the nave in holy blue. Shinua swallowed vomit and hurled herself into the opening of the monk-tunnel under the altar, shut the trapdoor behind her. Nor's anxious face waited for her in the darkness.

'Go!' Shinua hissed. 'Go, go!'

They had a long way to crawl before they reached the ends of the tunnels, where they opened into the swamps.

Her old mentor's words reverberated in her ears:

I will be gone for you.

III

In his last promise, Halas was true to his word.

For a year, and then another, Shinua and Nor walked the trade roads and pilgrimage paths and half-blazed frontier trails, sleeping in inns and high, tree-borne hammocks.

He was nowhere to be found.

Halas' company of the Hammers of Sigmar was easy enough to track. Mere months after the killing at the Abbey of the Twined Root, Shinua found a Watcher's report describing the company's assignment to a refugee camp on the Numinous Shore of Hysh. She read stolen troop manifests; she scoured the compound with her spyglass. She searched for Halas' face, for the markings of his pauldrons, for that cruel joke of a name, *Hearthguard*.

Nothing.

I will be gone for you.

In an inn, Shinua tried burning oracle bones in the

hearthpit. Asked her question and waited. But once more, the fires didn't speak.

'I will try,' said Nor. 'A blood prayer.'

The girl unsheathed a skinning knife. Cut her palm with a grunt of pain, her mouth set in a serious frown. Gingerly, she dripped the blood of her palm into the firepit.

A tongue of flame rose to lick her palm, and the fires darkened into a surreal crimson. Nor did not withdraw her hand. Her face was cast in a chiaroscuro of ruby and shadow. The girl murmured softly to the fire, so softly that Shinua couldn't make out the words, and the fire lapped at her hand.

'Louder,' Shinua hissed.

Nor ignored her. The pupils of her eyes glinted with the light of the flame.

'*The Raven*,' said Nor. Her voice was her own, but tripled – three of her seemed to speak at once. '*You will find the Raven.*'

Nor blinked. When she spoke again, it was with one voice. Slowly, a little reluctantly, she drew her hand from the fire, pressed her wound closed and winced.

'I saw you,' she said.

'Saw what?'

'You and the Raven. It was great and small at the same time. It had too many eyes. It opened its gullet and ate you whole.'

Between them, the crimson bled from the blaze and left an ordinary hearthfire, crackling softly. Shinua exhaled.

'That was it?' she asked.

'That was it.'

They had used eight of the oracle bones. Eight remained. Shinua turned one of the unburnt bones between her fingers, studied the shape.

'What do we want with a raven?'

Nor frowned into her bleeding hand. 'Perhaps...'

She hesitated to finish.

'Yes?'

'A raven may stand for death.'

Shinua was silent.

'It may be a sign,' Nor said, gathering confidence, 'that death lies along this path.' She saw that Shinua was about to interrupt and pressed forward, undeterred. 'It may be a sign that we should turn our eyes towards others. Towards a greater justice.'

All at once she sounded older to Shinua. She *was* older – not a girl any more, really. She was choosing her words with fear and care, like a woman weighed by responsibility.

'What justice?' asked Shinua.

'We might stand for all the serfs and field-hands that mortar the God-King's cities with blood and sweat and shit. We might cast down all the parasites like the Old Lords of Ark'non.' She turned her arm to display the tattoo of the eye on her skin. 'We can write books of revolt,' said Nor. 'We can do more than watch.'

There was a force of conviction in Nor that Shinua found she didn't share. Perhaps *couldn't* share. The thought made her sad.

'I thought you understood the use of vengeance,' said Shinua.

Nor shook her head. 'Wrath is a means to justice. I do not mean to burn the heavens for my own satisfaction.'

'You bind the library one book at a time,' said Shinua. 'This justice begets others.'

Nor looked uncertain, but nodded.

'We must find the Raven. Whoever it is, whatever it is. And you're right – we need to turn our eyes towards others.'

* * *

In the cellars of public houses, in stables, in bathhouses, they raised their sleeves and spoke the shibboleths. *I am here to speak in the circle of the eye.*

In each village or city or hamlet, the mark of the Watcher was in some small way unique. The shape of the pupil, the nature of the circle – halo or spiked crown or radiating lines. The artistry of the ink was different in every place. The people were different in every place: an elderly duardin woman, poor and self-possessed; an angry young man, wealthy and insecure.

The grievances were different: a child enslaved. Immortality denied. A crop blighted. A lover lost.

The grievances were all alike. *Suffering.*

Why does the God-King allow us to suffer?

In the public houses and stables and baths, Shinua and Nor asked the same questions: *Do you know where to find a Stormcast called Hearthguard? Do you know where to find someone or something called the Raven?*

Many Watchers knew nothing. But the eyes of some grew guarded at the mention of the Raven. Still others muttered names they might seek to learn more. *A collector of secrets,* they said, *a Watcher of Watchers. Ask in Aqshy.*

Finally, an innkeeper in a Great Parch township said he knew the Raven personally: it was the codename of a magister in the Callidium Academy. The professor compiled the Watchers' almanacs out here in the desert of the Parch.

Shinua bought brown scholar-aspirant robes from a pilgrim. Aspirants would have free entry to the academy, but not with weapons on their backs; she risked only a fire-striker blade under her robes, an oracle bone – too precious to leave to a secret cache – around her neck. Nor took her skinning knives.

* * *

The academy was a new construction, a project of renewal in a middling city that seemed eager to equal Hammerhal Aqsha or Bataar. The colonnade in the courtyard projected antiquity and Azyrite majesty, but the school was younger than Nor. An observer only had to search briefly to find labour-teams laying new brick paths, or erecting public art – a vast mobile of concentric rings – that Shinua supposed was designed in Azyr.

The magister's office was at the end of a long, sunlit marble hall, empty of students or sound. Shinua and Nor's approach was announced in loud, echoing footfalls.

The door to the office was open – inside, a darkness in stark contrast to the bright marble hall. They paused at the threshold, glanced at one another.

'Please do come in,' called a genial baritone. 'I don't suppose you'll be in this wing unless you're looking for me, or lost.'

'You're Magister Set?' asked Shinua, stepping into the office. As her eyes adjusted to the darkness, she could see the outlines of a cramped, shadowed library. Bookshelves heaved with tomes in the dark.

'Indeed!' said Set. 'I apologise for the dim light. My eyes are sensitive. Here, on your left.'

Nor nearly tripped on a stack of thick, leather-bound volumes; books were piled haphazardly on the floor, along the walls.

Set was hunched in his magister's robes behind an ornate desk that barely fit in the office. His beard was a blend of red and grey, his long hair tied back. It took her a moment to notice his eyes – dominated by too-large pupils, almost entirely black.

On his right shoulder, eerily still: a raven. The bird regarded her through eyes as black as the magister's.

'My name is Shinua Gan,' said Shinua. 'My friend is Nor of Ark'non. We're here to speak in the circle of the eye.'

'Ah, wonderful! Then today is the day. I lose track of time. You can imagine.' Magister Set rested his elbows on the desk and steepled his fingers. 'The girl will have to leave, I'm afraid. She is... claimed by another Power. She'll spoil the work.'

Nor's expression was outwardly impassive, but it said everything to Shinua. *This is wrong. We should leave.*

'Go back to the inn,' Shinua said softly. 'Wait for me there.'

Nor answered in a murmur. 'We should both go.'

'Wait for me, love.'

'I'm afraid,' Nor whispered.

'You'll be fine.'

'I'm afraid for *you.*'

'If you want your justice against Heaven,' Magister Set said, 'she must go.'

At the word *justice*, they both froze.

'Go,' said Shinua.

Reluctantly, Nor turned her back to Shinua and left the office. The raven watched her go. Her footfalls echoed down the marble hall; Set didn't speak until the echoes silenced.

'Her sort,' he said, not unkindly, 'will always obey in the end. They are creatures of prayer, and prayer is a submission, like any pleading. She is a fine instrument for you, but she mustn't spoil the work.'

'I don't understand,' said Shinua.

'No matter. I forget what you know.' He took a quill from the inkwell on his desk and began to scratch some note.

'I think it was her prayer that told me to find you,' Shinua said.

'Did it?' That seemed to amuse him.

She tried to read what he was writing, but the longer she

stood in this office, the less clearly she saw. The darkness seemed to shift around her, like an invisible tide lapping over the dim features of things.

For a moment, she imagined that the raven on his shoulder stared at her with nine eyes; that it was not *on* Set's shoulder but a part of him. She blinked and the vision receded.

'What do you know about what I want?' she said. 'How do you know?'

He paused his writing. Looked up at her with those vast pupils. For a moment, she imagined that he was nine-eyed, too.

'*What* I know is that you seek your justice against the immortal called Hearthguard or Halas. He is hidden. You would have me make him plain. *How* do I know? I am a Watcher of Watchers. It is my lord's work to know what is unknown.'

The words chilled her. She felt known and seen when she had believed she kept her own counsel.

'Your lord?' she asked.

Set ignored her. '*Your* sort,' he said, 'are not given to prayer, or to submission. You will always question, even down to the foundations of answerlessness. That is why my lord favours you, I think. That is why my lord will aid you.'

A wash of invisible tides. The darkness roiled around her, seized her with a vertigo. Set's face receded into shadow. His words made her nauseous.

'You want to render the hidden into the plain, the immortal into the dead, the impossible into the real. My lord is a lord of rendering. But it requires a sacrifice, a substrate for your alchemy.'

Shinua felt dizzy. 'I don't... have anything to give.'

'You will.'

Now she saw the raven again; once more it was nine-eyed. But the bird had grown vast as a cathedral, vaster than the academy around them. The great beak opened. The gullet opened. Inside was infinitude.

'When the time comes,' Set said, 'you will light a great hecatomb of souls, and then my lord will return you.'

The Raven consumed her.

Another darkness.

Cold sweat soaked her skin. Her head throbbed; her stomach felt as if it were straining to fold in on itself. Shinua doubled over and vomited, and that relieved some of the agony.

Wet drops. At first she thought it was her own sweat, but no, this was warm and falling from above.

Below, uneven stone. Not the flat marble of the academy, or anything hand-carved, but the floor of a cavern.

Some primal sense told her that she had *moved* far from where she had been. Worlds away. The air had changed: it was cool and carried an acidic tang.

Carefully, she climbed to her feet. She had mapped enough caverns for the surveyors' guilds to know the dangers of darkness like this.

Ahead, points of blue light like fireflies bobbed in the dark. Indistinct voices accompanied the glow.

Low murmurs and the steady drip of water into water, echoing in a tight, narrow space. The blue lights grew closer and began to illuminate the cavern. Fang-like stalactites loomed overhead; the walls were moist, the ground a path of shallow pools in the rock.

The two forms that approached out of the darkness were broad-shouldered and bulky with full body armour, standing as tall as Shinua's chest. Small glass chambers were affixed to their helmets, and inside the chambers fluttered bioluminescent moths. Their armour was crafted to resemble exaggerated duardin forms – one with a stylised moustache engraved into the faceplate, the other with a winged helm. In her right hand, the second duardin carried a staff tipped with many glass vials. They looked like Kharadron, but their armour was subtly different, adapted to some work that Shinua couldn't quite discern.

The pair paused, and the one in the winged helm raised the staff to collect a drop that fell from a stalactite. Then they noticed Shinua.

'Who are *you*?' came a muffled, bewildered voice. The Moustache.

'Please,' said Shinua. 'I'm lost. I need help.'

'Lost,' said the other duardin, the Wings. She sounded incredulous. 'You're... you can't be here, can you?'

'I don't know where I am,' said Shinua. She didn't have to work hard to sound scared. The best deception was the truth. 'Please, is there someone who can help me? Any soldiers? Stormcasts?'

The duardin exchanged a glance.

'I expect we had better get you out of here,' said the Wings.

'I can barely see,' said Shinua. 'Do you have a torch? I can light it if–'

'*No*,' barked the Moustache. 'No fire. Ever. First rule. Only rule. No fire. Understood?'

Shinua let herself sound shaken by his vehemence. 'Y-yes.'

'It's all right, dear,' said the Wings. 'Safety is paramount. Fire and the Living Mountain don't mix, and all of us miners will be the sorrier if they do. Come, stay close to me. And... maybe cover your mouth with the sleeve of your robe. Try to breathe through the cloth. I'm Ylgra.' She glanced back at the Moustache. 'It's not the *only* rule, Olreg,' she chided. 'You were complaining about the partner rule just yesterday.'

'That was more about you than the rule,' said Olreg. 'So "no fire" is the *golden* rule, then. Is that better?'

'The golden rule is don't tease the people with the very large hammers.'

The pair led Shinua through the tunnel, which gradually widened into a subterranean chamber. All around her, a vast labour was underway. Hundreds of tiny blue moth-lights – perhaps a thousand, perhaps more – marked workers on the walls of the caverns, applying delicate instruments to stone. In the centre of the chamber, a great, dark lake, the limits of which extended beyond Shinua's sight. Moth-lights marked miners on the lake, too, working some arcane machines that softly churned the water. The low whir of obscure devices echoed through the chamber.

Shinua felt light-headed. She wasn't sure if that was down to the nausea of her travel, or some quality of the underground air.

'This way, then,' said Ylgra, leading her onto a catwalk that wound around the edge of the lake.

'What is this place?' ventured Shinua. 'Where am I?'

'Not to worry, not to worry. This way!'

As they walked, a wind stirred in the chamber, like a storm-warning breeze. A great sigh passed through the cavern, and a fine mist rose from the lake.

'That sounded like a breath,' said Shinua. 'What was it?'

'No matter,' said Ylgra.

They crossed the catwalk, crossed the chamber, and passed into another tunnel. At the end of this tunnel was a brighter light, daylight. Shinua quickened her pace, hurrying through puddles that soaked her feet.

Outside: fresh air. She dropped the hem of her sleeve, breathed. Then she looked up, and vertigo gripped her.

The sky was earth – a great cascade of craggy, snow-peaked mountains. There were rivers, above, that fed into a sea on the horizon's edge. There were canyons etched in what should have been sky; her surveyor's eye wondered at the topography above, at the world writ in the distance.

Beneath her feet was a vast, rocky mountain that stretched into an expanse of cloud and sky. The mountain hung from the heavens. Sky-ships anchored here and there, and some colossal machines were built into the farthest reaches of rock, where the base of the mountain gave way to cloud. Tiny, distant figures were tethered to the engines, whirring in a mechanical flight that looked, from Shinua's vantage point, like the play of fruit flies.

On the cliff's edge beyond the mouth of the cavern was a sparse watch-station; it reminded her of the fire-towers that overlooked forests in Ghyran. Spyglasses peered from the windows of the cabin, some fixed on the landscape above and some on the clouds below.

In the watch-station, eye to the lens of a spyglass that faced the world above, was Halas. He glanced sidelong at her, returned to his observation. Then looked again. He started, stood up.

'You,' he said. 'You shouldn't be here.'

He seemed annoyed by the disruption. He pursed his lips and appraised her.

'No,' said Halas. 'No, I *know* you.'

'Hunter-Prime,' said Ylgra, 'I don't rightly know what to make of this, but we–'

'*Weapons!*' Halas shouted abruptly, as if coming to some sudden realisation. '*Unsheathe your weapons!*'

Ylgra and Olreg looked one to the other and then, more

swiftly than Shinua had expected, produced wicked hooks from their belts.

'Don't take your eyes from her,' commanded Halas. 'She's more dangerous than you know. More dangerous,' he breathed, 'than she knows, I think.'

The duardin shifted into fighting stances, curved hooks gripped tight in their armoured fists. They were not, Shinua thought, to be underestimated.

Faster than she could follow, Halas was in front of her.

His armour was lighter in frame now, scuffed and muddy. The grey pelt of some beast draped over his shoulder. He carried a handaxe rather than a hammer, and the symbology on his left pauldron named him – if she read it right – as a soldier of the Vanguard Chamber. One of the God-King's lone wolves, posted on long assignments outside the bounds of heavens or battlefronts.

The light in his eyes was guttered.

'*Here*,' Halas said. 'What kind of wretched compact did you make to get *here*?'

'There is no coward's escape,' she said quietly. 'It is justice. Justice follows.'

A bitter laugh, like a cough.

'No escape,' he said. 'That's certain. I see you in dreams. Out of the corner of my eye. Sometimes I forget your face, and sometimes I remember, and sometimes the dreams are true. You come here in, what, a scholar-aspirant's robes? With death and Dark Gods in your eyes.'

'I told you,' she said. 'Justice.'

'For my crime, you punish the world.'

'Only you.'

'No.' He took a book from the satchel at his waist. The spine was only half-bound.

'Recovered in Ghyran,' he said. 'At great expense. Written in your hand. I carry it to remember you.'

A bile rose in Shinua's throat.

'And so?'

'You gave the names of innocents – the children and spouses and descendants of Stormcasts – to a Ruinous Power. What do you think happened to those people?'

She was silent.

'Do you want to know what happens when you die, Shinua?'

Again, she didn't answer.

'When *you* die, you will be eaten. Your soul will be subsumed by the gods you've given yourself up to. That's what they are, Shinua. Eaters of eternities, and they start the feeding while you're still alive. Make you part of them. They're a part of you now. A wound in your soul. You're not just complicit. You are ruin.'

Shinua realised she was shaking. Halas took a step closer, careful now.

'You're the plague you spread. You're wrath. You're this impossible thing flitting at the edge of vision. You used to want to protect people. Who are you protecting now?'

'Bastard,' she growled.

'Repair your soul. Please. Let me help you. Let anyone help you. You're going to break yourself and leave suffering where you used to be.'

What she wanted to say was, *You're the hand of an arbitrary god. You are the receiver of unjust gifts.* But she didn't have those words. Instead she had the one moment in time that wouldn't fog or dull, the one moment that she was still somehow living: four oilskins arrayed in the blackened earth. Three generations.

And you call me ruin.

'You are a debtor,' she said. 'You owe me a father.'

What she felt then wasn't the tempered purpose that had borne her through years, but hatred as grace. She relaxed into the grasp of the grace, into a freedom from choice and decision, and another power bore her limbs.

Shinua turned her back on Halas and moved, more quickly than she had known she could move. It felt like ease; it felt like drifting. As though she were carried by the beating of countless impossible wings. The duardin shifted to stop her, to catch her, and they were fast but she was faster. As Olreg swung his hook, she met the swing, took hold of the weapon, seized the momentum and swung the duardin bodily; he flew one hundred and eighty degrees and into Halas. The duardin's faceplate cracked against the golden sigmarite of Halas' armour, and Shinua was still moving, hardly wondering at her strength, hardly wondering at the grace.

A vision: her father carried her through the air in a field of Shyishian grain, a moment that never happened. The man had never in her memory held her, hardly kissed her head. Old Tsien Gan wasn't given to physical affection – wasn't given to his family, really. He was always going to market, going to the pastures – going out of care for them, yes, but out of fear of them, too, not really knowing how to speak to this family he had made.

Shinua pressed a foot on the winged helm of Ylgra and leapt over her, soared into the cavern mouth of the Living Mountain. Into darkness, but there was no doubt in her mind now, no fear. In its place, certainties:

Halas was behind her, moving with aether-striding swiftness himself–

The mountain's living breath exhaled through the cavern,

an exhalation of mist and crisp air, and it should have pressed her back but it didn't–

The chamber loomed ahead, and the lake; the darkness was almost total but she knew they were there, and she knew she shouldn't reach it before Halas but she was going to nevertheless, because the Raven said, the Raven said–

She passed into the chamber, lit in dim blue by moth-light, and she plunged into the black waters of the lake.

The Raven said–

The lake was cold, and it wasn't water. It smelled like storms. Now Halas reached her; hard metal gloves gripped her shoulder. Another certainty: he wouldn't strike her with his handaxe, even now. He thrashed and tried to con-strain her, tried to seize her limbs, but something stronger gripped her arms and moved them. She reached inside her scholar-aspirant's robes, ripped the fire-striker knife from its sheath on her leg and scraped it across the collar of Halas' armour.

A spark.

The particle of heat and light caught on the dew or oil or blood of the Lake of the Living Mountain.

The Raven said: You will light a great hecatomb of souls, and my lord will return you.

Halas' golden armour erupted. She caught a glimpse of thrashing realisation in his eyes, and his face crumpled like paper in a pyre. There was a thunderclap, and he was yanked into the upper dark as if strung to an invisible line.

And Shinua was drawn away, too, as though she dangled from her own strings. Out and away, plucked through the aether at impossible speed.

She fell from the mouth of the Raven, tumbled onto the marble of the magister's study in Aqshy. But the gullet of the vast bird-that-was-not-a-bird gaped wide, and she could see the place that she had left.

In the Living Mountain, a ripple of white fire spread across the lake. It engulfed the workers on the lake's strange machines, ignited the air, danced along the cavern walls and ceiling. In an instant, the conflagration consumed hundreds of miners, turned light-bearing moths to ash. Hundreds of souls, more than hundreds.

A mountain hung in the sky and burned with white light and died.

Shinua stared into the mouth of the Raven and watched.

IV

Out past the farthest reaches of Aspiria, on the western frontiers of Aqshy. Beyond Passion's Gate, on the tidelines of the Disintegrating Shore. Waters from the wild edge of the realm itself crashed on beaches of black sand, the tides carrying – now and then – the husks and shells of creatures born to impossible geometries. Past the beachhead, under the grey skies and under the churning seas, ordinary logics strained and sometimes snapped.

Near the realm's edge, the laws changed. Reality thinned, and its more improbable children lurked just under the surface.

On the Disintegrating Shore, black dunes towered, and the beach was empty of settlements or beachcombers. Almost empty: now and then, you might catch – out of the corner of your eye – roving fauna not quite of this realm, or any of the Mortal Realms. Lithe and equine, these sinuous spawn of a lost god tasted the air with long tongues and strolled in the breakers.

They wandered here as if masterless, as if bereft of guidance. If you were wild enough, if you *wanted* them enough, you could master those steeds, or have them master you. The allure had drawn – and ended – enough would-be tamers that some functionary of Azyr had requested a small outpost of Stormcasts to discourage thrill-seekers, daemonologists and believers in absent gods.

It was a remote, quiet outpost – a good assignment for warriors of Sigmar who had suffered some trauma in the course of their Reforgings, who needed to rest. If you found the right perch in the dunes, you might watch the routines of the Stormcasts posted there on the Disintegrating Shore; you might keep time by them.

In the morning, a Liberator would leave his bastion and walk down the beach, leaving heavy footprints in the sand. His gait was slow, as though he were weighed down with more than his armour. He would walk at water's edge and stare out into the grey distance of the realm's edge, uncharted and unchartable. He would stand there, utterly still, for longer than you could bear to watch, and only then would you see the deathlessness of him.

He wouldn't fidget, or shift his weight, or sit in the sand. He would stand like a statue and stare out into the emptiness for a morning and then an afternoon, fixed and motionless in a way that no living soldier could have matched. A quiet sentinel at the edge of the world.

You could almost pity him, he looked so remote from life.

Halas wasn't hiding any more. He wore his old Liberator plate again, and the scrollwork on his pauldron named him *Hearthguard*, and every morning he walked along the beach where he stood in plain sight for hours.

The finding was simpler than it had ever been; placating Nor was harder. She insisted on accompanying Shinua, constantly wore an expression that alternated between the mournful and the anxious. She had been increasingly uneasy since she peered into the oracle fire and saw the Raven; Shinua began to wonder what else the girl had seen.

Every day, Nor urged her to return to life as a Watcher. To speak to those who suffered in the realms. To organise them against the dictates of Azyr. The girl put her in mind of Baslaergh. The Rotbringer's exhortations to belief.

Even as they crouched in the scrub of the dunes – Shinua watching Halas through her spyglass as Halas watched the waves – Nor tried to turn her back from her path.

'You're pressing fate,' she whispered. 'You've made him answer for so much. You've been lucky to survive this far. You might do so much more to help those who suffer in the God-King's realms.'

Shinua kept her eye on the spyglass. 'Sorry, love. The balance is the balance.'

In truth, she'd had the same thoughts. For once – for the first time, really – she had hesitated. The pair of them had not taken the shortest path through Aspiria to the Disintegrating Shore, but instead – and to Nor's initial satisfaction – made for Shinua's family farmstead on the outskirts of Hammerhal Ghyra.

Another family lived on the Gan farm now. They had tamed the pastures, built another home over the ashes of the last one. The granary and the barn still stood, same as they always had. Shinua paid an old garrison mate to manage the property, though she hadn't seen him in years, had only met her tenants once. The poor family didn't recognise her at first, seemed nervous of these hard-looking women on their doorstep. Shinua wanted the sight of the farmstead to enrage her, to stoke the fire. It hadn't.

She stood over the patch of dirt where the four oilskins had lain and felt a distance. The world had left her behind. Children she didn't know screamed their play out in the pastures, and strange hands tilled the soil of the garden. The realms had moved on.

Now she crouched in the dunes, and her debtor stood there unmoving on the beach, and she was almost finished. All these years, and soon there would be justice, and then she would be done. She stood up.

'It's time,' she said. 'Nor, love, you're to stay here. You're not to follow me. You understand?'

Nor stood, too. She looked like she wanted to move closer, but she did not.

'Please,' she said.

Shinua turned away from her and walked over the dune. She took her old Freeguilder's spear from her back and used the pole as a walking stick, dragging haphazard lines in the black sand. The sea breeze batted at her hair. After a moment, Halas turned, perhaps hearing the sound of her footsteps. That impassive golden mask fixed its eyes on her.

'You're not supposed to be here,' he said, not unpleasantly. 'This beach is restricted.'

The voice was unmistakably his, but it was also wrong. Too matter-of-fact.

'Hello, Halas,' she said.

He took a step closer. Raised his left hand and unlatched his helmet.

The face was his. The receding hairline, the jagged nose. But it was all… off, somehow. His eyes had hollowed. He reminded her, somehow, of her family's faces in memory, all blurred and blank.

His brow furrowed; he peered at her in confusion.

'I haven't heard that name in some time,' he said. 'Do I know you?'

'You know who I am,' she said.

'I'm afraid you must have me mistaken for someone else.'

A wave crashed and the voice of the tides was like her pulse in her ears. The dullness in his gaze, the placidity – it wasn't feigned.

He'd lost too many lives. Something in his head was corroded. And there was no satisfaction in that, no pleasure, because it was a mercy for him.

You don't get to forget what you've done.

Shinua took a step towards him. 'I know your name, Halas. You know mine.'

'My lady, I'm afraid I don't–'

'You have to remember,' she hissed. 'It's not right if you don't remember.' She tried to shove him, but he was too heavy. Her left hand gripped the spear so tightly that her knuckles were white. 'You don't get to forget me. You see me when you close your eyes. At the corner of your sight.'

'I'm afraid–'

'I flit around at the edge of your vision. I am wrath and rot and impossible things, always your shadow, always with you.'

His voice was a whisper. 'I'm afraid.'

'*I am Shinua Gan,*' she said, and raised her spear. '*I am ruin.*'

What Halas saw then, she didn't know. But a change wrote itself on his face. His eyes widened, and he remembered *something*. A nightmare with the contours of her face, perhaps. A Shinua-shaped horror that lurked in the recesses of his memory, that had dogged him across reincarnations. He grasped his warhammer and howled an abject, immortal terror that could only be cultivated through a succession of lives. The head of the hammer crackled with static and charged the air as it swung.

The hair on her forearm raised. She staggered backwards to avoid the swing and thrust her spear between the joins of his armour, caught him in the armpit and shoved.

Halas screamed. His hammer hand slackened.

But he didn't slow.

He had never really fought her before. She saw that now. His eyes were terrified and empty at once; light and steam spilled from his mouth as he cried out his immortal agony. Halas' entire form seemed to vibrate. He drew back his good hand and struck her above her heart.

Her ribs shattered. She was hurled backwards and skidded through black sand to the base of a dune. Shinua was broken before she touched the ground.

She lay face up, eyes on the grey sky. *Oh*, she thought, and struggled to shape a clearer one. Her mind was a fog. Someone screamed. *Oh*. She wanted to turn her head. She wanted to curl her fingers in the dirt. But her body wouldn't obey her.

There was pain, but it was distant. Almost pleasurable in its distance. Everything felt *far*. The world was leaving her behind, and quickly.

Nor eclipsed the sky. Tears fell from her face to Shinua's. 'I asked you not to leave,' Nor was saying. She knelt in the sand and cradled Shinua's head. 'I asked you not to leave me and you left.'

I am dead, she thought. *I am dead.*

But that was wrong. The life was still leaving her.

When you *die*, Halas had said, *you will be eaten. Your soul will be subsumed by the gods you've given yourself up to.*

He loomed above Nor, aghast at the work of his own hand. He'd said there was a wound in her soul, and she could feel it now, a cavity of the heart. Out past Nor, out past the grey sky and somehow inside of her, too, intelligences vast and predatory and unfathomable circled to regard her, to welcome her.

'It's all right,' said Nor, her mouth at Shinua's ear. Labouring to master her own fear, to make a benediction. 'It's all right that you are leaving. I will carry on.'

Shinua wanted to say, *no*. She wanted to say that this wasn't how it was supposed to be. Her own life was supposed to be different to this, better than this, and she wanted to make the loss worth something, to tell Nor that it wasn't too late–

'*Bastard!*' Nor shouted at the Stormcast. Even as she cradled Shinua's face and murmured reassurances, her voice was fierce. 'He won't have any rest. I'll carry on killing him. I swear to you. I will find him and kill him and find him and kill him. I will take *all* of his lives. All of them. He'll have no rest in the heavens. No rest anywhere.'

The girl stood and drew her skinning knives and advanced on Halas – the big, dumb automaton staring down at her wild-eyed and bewildered.

Shinua wanted to call, *no*. She wanted to tell Nor that there was no use in the killing, that there were only insatiable mouths in the sky.

She wanted–

She wanted–

She wanted not to have wasted her life on granting Halas the mercy of forgetting.

Beyond her sight, a cry of fury and the screech of metal on metal.

She wanted to have given Nor a good life, to have protected her, to have said she was sorry.

A pained grunt. A tremor of armoured weight in collapse.

The distance was too great. It was all too far, and too late.

A thunderclap.

So she wanted, at last, to be past suffering, to finally be done. But she understood now: she would not have respite after all. Like Halas, she would never be finished.

Shinua thought she felt her soul wrench itself from her mouth and towards the maws of the gods, and she thought she saw the truth of herself. The truth that would be bound in eternity. This last moment, this person she had become.

She was rage and rot. She was her ambition and her obsession, and she would always be what she had been.

She was ruin.

WHERE DERE'S DA WARP DERE'S A WAY

Mike Brooks

Mike Brooks' first Black Library appearance was in the first volume of Inferno! *with the Necromunda story 'A Common Ground', and since then he has written a novella and a full-length novel with us. Here, he moves away from humanity and brings us a story focused on the galaxy's most belligerent, violent green-skinned aliens...*

Ufthak of the Bad Moon clan is an ork with ambition. When boarding a vessel belonging to the Adeptus Mechanicus in search of valuable plunder, he sees an opportunity to prove himself and rise to greatness. 'Ere we go!

"Ere we go, 'ere we go, 'ere we go!'

Ufthak Blackhawk, Bad Moon warrior and definite second-biggest in Badgit Snazzhammer's mob, no matter what that zoggin' idiot Mogrot thought, raised his voice in the rolling, rollicking war cry as they piled into the 'Ullbreaker. Outside in the cold vacuum of space, Da Meklord's warfleet was busy crumping the humie ships, but that wasn't Ufthak's fight. Blowing stuff up from a long way off was fine in its way, but he preferred getting up close and personal. Let the gunboyz have their fun: Ufthak was on his way to the *real* fight.

The last few boyz piled in, along with Dok Drozfang and various grots, and then came Da Boffin. A Bad Moon like Ufthak and Da Meklord himself, and one of the warboss' most trusted meks, Da Boffin had replaced his own legs with a single wheel, powered by a fuel made of concentrated squig dung. Ufthak had never worked out how Da Boffin stayed upright on it, since even warbikes needed at least two wheels, plus either a kickstand or the rider's leg – or a kickstand made from someone else's leg – on the few occasions they were stationary. When Ufthak had asked, Da Boffin had just started talking about 'whirly bitz inside it', as though that made any sense.

The last hatch slammed shut and the flyboyz in the cockpit whooped, firing up the engines and vaporising anything immediately behind the shuttle. Ufthak had been on boarding missions before, so he knew what to do: grab on to one of the handholds roughly welded into the walls, and hang on like a grot on a warboar.

The flyboy kaptin stamped down on the lever which released the mag-clamp fastening them to the deck of *Da Meklord's Fury*, and they were away. Immediately, all the boyz who hadn't been in an 'Ullbreaker before went flying back to the rear of the ship, where they were crushed into a painful and indignant heap against the metal bulkhead. Ufthak laughed uproariously as they tumbled past him with expressions of confusion plastered across their faces.

'Ullbreakers got up to full speed quickly, and so it was only a few moments before the G-forces subsided enough for the newbies to untangle themselves from each other and start the important process of working out whose gun was whose. It only took a few moments more for fists to start to fly as they began bad-mouthing each other's shootas.

'If you gitz don't settle down den I'm turnin' dis fing around!'

Boss Snazzhammer stormed down the shuttle, spittle flying from his gob as he kicked boyz out of his way. He was a huge ork, head and shoulders taller than the rest of them, and bedecked in the most ostentatious finery that teef could buy – and, since he was a Bad Moon, he had a lot of teef. There was barely a surface of his armour that wasn't decorated with loot, whether that was medals taken off the corpses of humie bosses, those little bits of wax and paper from the armour of dead beakies, or even some of the fancy gems the pointy-earz wore. In his right hand he carried the massive weapon that had given him his second name: a metal shaft the height of a humie with its legs still attached, with a hammer on one side of the head and a choppa blade on the other. The entire head could be engulfed in a crackling power field with one flick of Snazzhammer's clawed thumb, and Ufthak had seen the boss smash right through a humie tank with it.

The boyz ducked their heads, grabbed their own shootas and tried to avoid the boss' eye. No one wanted to end up like that tank.

'Dat's betta,' Snazzhammer growled. He turned on the spot, addressing the entire 'Ullbreaker. 'Right, we ain't da only 'Ullbreaker wot's flyin' today...'

Boos and jeers.

'...but we got da most important job!' Snazzhammer continued. 'Da Meklord 'imself told me wot we gots ta do, so you all best listen.'

The mob quietened down, as much as they ever would. If Da Meklord had told them what to do, they'd probably better do it. Da Meklord was no ordinary warboss, if there was such a thing: he was Da Biggest Big Mek, and his gear was legendary. He'd gone toe to toe with rival warboss Oldfang Krumpthunda, and after one hit with Da Meklord's shokk-hamma no one had found any part of the Goff larger than a finger. Da Meklord's personal force field could shrug off hits from a humie Titan's cooka kannon. His supa-shoota could cut a Deff Dread in half before you could say 'Gork and Mork'. He was what any Bad Moon wanted to be: massive, 'ard as nails and carrying enough weapons and armour to kit out a small warband in his own right.

'Now,' Snazzhammer declared. 'Humies don't got Gork 'n' Mork ta guide dem froo da warp, ta take dem to where da next fight is. Dey gotta use some fancy worky bitz wot dey keeps in da middle of dere ships. Wot we gots ta do is get Da Boffin dere, where he's gonna do some mek stuff. Got it?'

There was a general muttering and nodding of heads, and Snazzhammer beamed. 'Good. Now den. *Who are we?*'

'SNAZZHAMMER'S MOB!' the assembled mass of orks bellowed, Ufthak amongst them.

'Are we da biggest?'

'YES!'

'Are we da baddest!'

'YES!'

'Are we da shootiest?'

'YES!' the mob yelled, and everyone waved their shootas, which were almost all kustom jobs with extra dakka. No one pulled their trigger yet, though, which was good: Ufthak had once been in an 'Ullbreaker where some git with a kannon had managed to crack the flyboyz' seeing-window, and it turned out there was a reason why these things weren't open-topped.

'Dat's what I fort,' Snazzhammer said with grim satisfaction. He reached up and grabbed a handhold overhead. 'Now, everyone hold on to sumfing.'

Ufthak had known this was coming, and reached up with his other hand. 'Ullbreakers flew quick.

There was a shudder as the shuttle's short-range torpedoes all fired at once, concentrating on a small part of the enemy ship's hull to weaken it. Ufthak began counting down.

Five…

Four…

Free…

Two…

One…

He frowned.

Bit of one…

The 'Ullbreaker smashed into the humie ship, its specially reinforced nose cone taking the brunt of the impact and punching them clean through into the interior. The force of the sudden deceleration lifted Ufthak's boots from the floor and nearly wrenched his arms from their sockets, but he held firm. Some of the new ladz who hadn't minded the boss' words enough went flying the other way down the shuttle. One of them collided with a support strut hard enough to snap his back clean in two, much to the disdain of the other boyz who'd managed to remain upright.

'Leave 'im!' Snazzhammer bellowed as a few of them started putting the boot in. 'We got humies ta paste! Get out dere, and get clobberin'!' He aimed a kick at the downed ork's head as he acted on his own words, and his steel toecap hit hard enough to knock it right off. Dark blood sprayed out across the nearby members of the mob, while the flying head caught a lurking grot clean in the chest and knocked it backwards into the wall.

'WAAAAAAAAGGGGHHHHH!'

Ufthak drew his weapons and surged forwards with the mass of green around him. This was life; this was what it meant to be an ork. Enemies in front of him, ladz around him, ammo in his slugga and a good right arm to swing his choppa. What more could anyone ask for?

The fore hatches burst outwards and the boyz spilled out. Ufthak shouldered his way forwards and forced his way through, looking for something to kill.

They'd busted through into a vast chamber of metal, the ceiling of which arched up overhead into gloomy shadow. The walls looked to consist largely of pipes, cables and contact points, some of which spat blue-white sparks, but Ufthak couldn't see much of them. That was partly because of the strange humie machines which loomed throughout the chamber – strange even to him, who'd fought a lot of different humies in a lot of different places – and partly because the humies that crewed this ship had decided they wanted to fight.

They were already swarming inwards, like buzzer squigs converging on an intruder into their nest. Ufthak saw the red-robes and the first flashes of gunfire and grunted in recognition: humie mekboyz! No wonder Da Meklord had his eyes on something fancy; humie tek could do some pretty wild stuff so long as you didn't hit it too hard.

The red-robes slowed, setting themselves to shoot, and Ufthak groaned. Why did humies never want to fight properly? Only beakies ever fancied a real rumble, and they didn't even taste good once you got them out of their armour. The rest of them got close enough for you to smell 'em, then hung back to shoot like Mork-damned Deathskulls.

They also always seemed to think that da boyz would just stand still.

'All right, ladz! 'Ave 'em!' Snazzhammer bellowed, and the mob surged forwards. Ufthak could feel Mork urging him on, and time slowed. His strides seemed to eat up the metal deck beneath him, and the figures in the humie gun line grew larger with each step. He saw an individual barrel track towards him, saw the humie's finger tighten on the trigger, but he took his next step at an angle and Mork smiled on him, because the bolt of spitting energy flew past his head instead of taking him full in the face. The next shot hit him in the shoulder, a white-cold shock that staggered him for a moment, but Ufthak had taken worse in the past, and the humie had gone for the kill instead of turning to run while it could. Not all of its fellows had done the same; some of them were already fleeing in the face of the unstoppable green tide bearing down on them.

Ufthak bared his fangs, bellowed his war cry and cannoned into the humie line with the rest of the mob.

The humie who'd shot him tried to parry his choppa with its rifle; Ufthak gave it respect for the effort but nothing for the execution, because his heavy blade smashed through the spindly weapon and split its torso from neck down to the middle of its chest. Like most humies, it died after one hit, sagging to the floor as he wrenched his choppa free and fired his shoota into what passed for the face of another, although this one was wearing a lot more metal there than most humies did. The metal didn't help it: Ufthak's slugga shots blew its head apart, metal face and all, and it dropped as well.

A humie lunged at him, wielding some sort of spear. The blade buried itself in Ufthak's chest and he bellowed in pain, then booted the wielder in its stomach. It flew backwards, disappearing with a despairing wail into the rolling maul of bodies around Boss Snazzhammer. Ufthak wrenched the spear out – it turned out to be one of the electro-guns with a knife stuck on the end – and threw it after its owner. There was a roar of anger, and Ufthak grinned as Mogrot Redtoof whirled around and clobbered a humie which had had nothing to do with the fact that there was now a knife in his back.

Next to Ufthak, Deffrow had lost his choppa – probably stuck in the ribcage of a dead humie somewhere – and so was using the next best thing: a stikkbomb. He battered one humie aside into the path of Dok Drozfang, who carved it apart with the power klaw he called Da Surjun, broke the skull of another, then wound up and took a swing at a third–

The world went white, very loud and extremely sharp.

Ufthak realised he was on the floor, along with everyone else within three yards of Deffrow. Deffrow himself was on his back, staring stupidly at the handle clutched in his somewhat shredded fist.

'Dey go bang, squigbrain!' Ufthak yelled at him as he got back to his feet. 'Dat's why we frow dem!' Deffrow's idiocy had left him with a bunch of shrapnel in his right-hand side, but it was nothing he couldn't deal with later. The humies, on the other hand, hadn't fared so well. The one Deffrow had hit most recently had taken the brunt of the impact and was now rather red and squishy, and even those further back weren't in a good way, rolling around, wailing and crying like a grot that had swallowed a fire squig.

'Seems like a design flaw t'me,' Deffrow muttered, pushing himself up. He winced and shook his mangled hand, and a finger that had only been attached by a shred of flesh pinwheeled off. 'Ow, dat smartz...'

'Now look what you did!' Ufthak complained at him. 'Dey're running away!' Sure enough, the remaining humies had clearly decided that enough was enough, as they were turning tail and fleeing from the slaughter. Or at least, they were trying to: those of Snazzhammer's mob who hadn't still been picking themselves up because their idiotic neighbour had blown everyone up were jumping on the humies from behind and sending them to see their Emprah. Humies liked to yell about their Emprah a lot, but Ufthak had once heard a bunch of really tough beakies in spiky black armour shouting that the Emprah was dead. With worshippers like this, he could see why. He raised his slugga and shot one in the back, but his heart wasn't in it.

A high-pitched whine grabbed Ufthak's attention. For a moment he thought it was just the after-effects of Deffrow's stikkbomb going off, but then he saw a crackle of blue power, and one of the machines lurched into life. It was a big trukk of some sort, with wheels taller than an ork, and if the blue-crackling thing on the top of it wasn't some sort of gun then he, Ufthak Blackhawk, was a Blood Axe.

'Oh *zog*,' he muttered fervently. 'Boss! You got ya hammer?'

'Don't worry about dat,' Snazzhammer retorted confidently, spinning his hammer and casually decapitating a stray grot with the backswing. 'Dat humie stuff breaks if you look at it funny.'

Ufthak had his doubts. Humies might not be much good in a proper scrap, but their guns tended to be the business. The dirty little gitz also had a nasty habit of aiming, instead of pulling the trigger and letting Gork and Mork decide what would land where, as was right and proper.

The big trukk-gun fizzed noisily, and glowed brighter. Ufthak braced himself: he had a feeling this was going to hurt more than a carelessly detonated stikkbomb.

There was a tremendous sound of tortured, tearing metal from behind them, and a huge shape came sliding across the chamber's floor, careering off humie machines and leaving the wailing red-robes it struck as mere red smears. It collided with the gun trukk, which exploded in a ball of blue fire, and came to a halt. Hatches popped open and boyz emerged, bellowing in anticipation.

'Told you we wasn't da only 'Ullbreaker flyin' today!' Snazzhammer said with satisfaction. He raised his voice in a mocking shout. 'What 'appened to you gitz? Got lost?'

The other mob's boss responded with a rude hand gesture, and Snazzhammer laughed. 'Right, on wiv da job. Boffin! You know where we're goin'?'

Through a lot of doors, as it turned out.

'Beats me how dese humies ever get anywhere,' Mogrot commented, as Wazzock fired up his burna to cut through yet another sealed hatch.

'Dey know how to open 'em,' Ufthak snorted.

'We know how to open 'em!' Mogrot protested, pointing at where Wazzock was dragging a white-hot line down the hatch.

'Open 'em wivout burnas,' Ufthak said patiently. Mogrot was hot squig dung in a fight, no doubt about it, but he wasn't what you'd call a thinker. That was why Ufthak was second-in-command, even though they were more or less the same size. 'Dey're lockin' us out, right?'

'Don't seem too bovvered we're here, den,' Mogrot countered. 'We ain't 'ardly 'ad no one to fight since dat scrap when we got out da 'Ullbreaker!' He nudged a red-robed corpse with his boot, but the mob outnumbered this bunch of humies, and they'd barely been worth the effort.

'Dere's a whole buncha ladz on dis ship by now,' Snazzhammer put in. 'So da humies don't twig wot we're up to. Dey're what da humies call a "destruction".' He raised his weapon and activated the power field. 'All right, outta da way!'

The ladz parted, and the boss stepped forwards. He swung his hammer and, with a *krakka-boom!* like thunder, the burna-bisected door caved in as though it were made of sticks. It revealed a long corridor, wide enough for five orks abreast. A few yards down it were another bunch of red-robes, aiming their guns somewhat shakily at the gaping hole where their door had been.

Snazzhammer lunged forwards, swinging his weapon two-handed by the very base of its handle to maximise his reach. The powered head smashed through their squishy humie bodies and killed most of them with a single blow. The other two turned to flee: Snazzhammer let them get a few steps before hurling his hammer after them, decapitating them both, one after another. The mighty weapon skidded to a halt, slippery with red humie blood, and Snazzhammer turned to look at Da Boffin.

'Def'nitely dis way, right?'

Da Boffin held up a clicking gizmo, and revved the motor of his mono-wheel excitedly. 'Yup! We got supa-strong warp stuff down da uvver end. Dat's where we needs ta be.'

'You heard da ork!' Snazzhammer bellowed. 'Get to it!' He turned back towards his hammer and began to stride down the corridor. Ufthak was just taking his first step after the boss when the door at the other end of the corridor slid open, not thanks to the destructive activities of some other ladz but with the smooth action of a machine operated by someone who knew how to work it properly.

A huge shape stamped into view, blocking out much of the light behind it.

'Now *dat*,' Mogrot said from behind him, 'looks like a proper fight.'

It was on two legs, but it was no humie. It wasn't an ork, either. Ufthak reckoned it was twice his height at least, and nearly the same across. It sort of looked a bit like a humie Dread, the kind the beakies sometimes had, but not quite. It had two power klaws, the weird round humie ones instead of a proper pointy klaw like any self-respecting ork would have, and some sort of 'eavy shoota looming over its right shoulder.

'Tinboy!' Da Boffin exclaimed with what sounded like real excitement. 'Always wanted ta see one up-close!'

The 'eavy shoota opened up just as Badgit Snazzhammer broke into a roaring charge. He got three strides before his head exploded in a welter of gore and pulverised bone, and he dropped as dead as a swatted squig.

'Zoggin' 'eck!' Ufthak yelled. 'Back round da corner, ladz, sharpish!' The tinboy was tracking its shots towards them, and in the confines of the corridor there was nowhere to take cover. He shouldered Deffrow aside and scrambled back out of the line of fire, and a moment later the rest of the mob joined him, hunkering down on either side of the doorway. More thuds of shoota fire sent gouts of blood spraying across the corridor's floor and over the threshold of the ruined door, as a couple of stragglers got well and truly crumped. As soon as there were no more orks in view, the tinboy's gun fell silent.

'Why'd you run for?!' Mogrot demanded from the other side of the gap. Ufthak found faces turning towards him, red eyes focusing on him. He'd given a command, and the boyz had followed him. The only problem was, he'd told them all to run away.

That wasn't going to wash for long, if he wanted to stake his claim as boss. He had to prove himself once and for all as the bigger ork.

'Dat wasn't runnin',' he declared firmly. 'Dat was a... strateejik wivdrawal.'

'If it looks like a squiggoth, an' it smells like a squiggoth...' Mogrot began menacingly. He drew himself up, fingering the activation switch on his chain-choppa. 'I don't fink you'z proper boss material, Ufthak. Don't fink you should be givin' orders.'

'Yeah?' Ufthak shot back, making a rude hand gesture. 'Why don't you walk over 'ere an' say dat?'

Mogrot growled, deep in his chest, and took one step…

…then paused, frowning distrustfully at the gap between them. Ufthak tried not to look at the same bit of floor, but it was no good. Even Mogrot's brain had remembered why they were hiding in the first place.

'Gimme a grot,' Mogrot grunted, reaching out behind him. One of the mob's hangers-on was seized and passed forwards with a squeak of protest, and Mogrot tossed it into the corridor.

The tinboy's shoota opened up immediately, and the sad, mangled remains of the grot thudded to the floor.

Ufthak cursed inwardly. That would have been *hilarious*, as well as useful. Nothing for it, then.

'We need to kill da tinboy,' he declared, as though Mogrot had never challenged him. 'An' we ain't doin' dat from here, an' we can't get to it ta kill it easy, coz it knows we'z orks, right?'

The ladz nodded. All of that seemed logical.

'Wot you finkin'?' Da Boffin asked, scratching one ear and looking at him thoughtfully as he rocked back and forth on his monowheel.

Ufthak beamed.

'All right, ladz, I'z 'ad a great idea…'

"Ello, I'm a humie!"

Humie spaceships, it turned out, had a lot of decent metal sheeting lying around if you had access to a burna to cut it off the walls, so Wazzock had been put to work. Before too long, the mob had several large chunks, to which they'd strapped the more intact of the red-robe corpses they'd made on the way to the door.

'We'z just humies, walkin' down dis corridor!'

Ufthak's plan was proper cunning if he said so himself, which he did, so that was okay. The tinboy must be able to tell humies from orks, or the humies would never let it walk around their spaceship. Therefore, it stood to reason that if it saw humies in front of it, it wouldn't shoot.

Into the corridor they went, a few boyz behind each metal plate, with dead humies on the front to confuse the tinboy. Simple, but genius.

'Wot if it don't work?' Deffrow hissed.

'S'gotta work,' Ufthak argued. 'I'm talkin' in humie, ain't I? An' makin' my voice squeaky an'–'

The shoota opened up again. The three boyz behind the foremost plate leaned into the impacts on what had suddenly become a makeshift shield, but the metal sheeting wasn't designed to stand up to firepower of that magnitude. One of them came apart as a shell punched right through, and Ufthak suddenly had guts over his steel toecaps.

'Zog it!' he shouted. 'Next plan!'

The boyz hadn't got far down the corridor before the tinboy had rumbled them, but they'd reached Snazzhammer's body. They dropped their apparently useless humie-shields and opened up, pouring fire into their enemy.

Which stopped short of reaching it, swallowed up and destroyed by some sort of force field.

'I've 'ad enuff of dis,' Ufthak growled as another ork was blown apart. He reached behind his back and pulled out what he'd decided he'd call a bombstikk. It was basically half the mob's stikkbombs all taped together courtesy of Da

Boffin's toolbox, and by 'basically' he meant 'exactly'. He took a quick two-step run-up and hurled it overarm.

When *that* hit the tinboy's force field it was like Gork himself had stamped on them all.

Ufthak's vision cleared a moment or so before his ears stopped ringing, and he picked himself up and peered down the corridor.

The Mork-damned thing was only still standing, wasn't it?

'Dat woz s'posed ta blow its bloody arms off!' Mogrot yelled.

'Nevamind!' Ufthak shouted. 'It's stunned, innit? Scrag da zoggin' fing!'

He ran forwards, snatching up the Snazzhammer as he passed it. Sure enough, the tinboy was standing wonky, and making confused buzzing noises. Shots began to fly past him from behind, and this time one or two of them raised sparks as they struck home: the force field had been overloaded.

Lenses in the tinboy's face whirred as the machine suddenly seemed to recover itself, and the 'eavy shoota lowered to target him.

Ufthak threw himself into a slide as the big weapon began kicking out shots again, and he felt the shiver of impacts as they chewed up the floor behind him. The tinboy's power klaws crackled into life as whatever tek powered it realised that he was getting close, but it was a shade too slow: it lunged for him, looking to crush him, but he was already sliding between its legs and lashing out with the Snazzhammer.

Which bounced clean off with barely a scratch caused, since he hadn't activated the power field.

'Mork's teef!'

The tinboy lurched around to follow him, alarmingly fast for such a big thing. The 'eavy shoota remained steady somehow, pouring shots into the boyz that'd been follow-ing him, but the two power klaws were all for Ufthak. It swung at him again, and he barely dodged back from it, then ducked under the counterswing from the other arm. When the tinboy tried to clobber him on the backswing, he set his feet and swung the Snazzhammer to meet it.

He'd activated the power field this time, and it took the tinboy's arm off at the elbow.

Laughter erupted out of him as the huge thing staggered, its balance thrown off by the sudden lack of weight on one side. The sound of its detached power klaw skittering away across the deck was the sound of his triumph.

Then it punched him in the chest with the other one.

Ufthak had never known such pain, and he'd taken shots from a beakie gun before that had left half his insides hang-ing out, until Dok Drozfang had stuck them back in and stitched him up once the fighting had calmed down a bit. It was like someone had let buzzer squigs the size of grots loose on his chest, and that was before he flew backwards and hit the wall behind him hard enough to dent it.

He lay there for a moment, vision foggy, as the tinboy turned its attention back to the rest of the boyz. They'd now reached it and were hacking away at it with choppas, blast-ing it point-blank with their shootas, and were surely going to bring it down any moment now. They didn't need him to help, he could catch his breath.

Any moment now.

'Zog it,' Ufthak muttered, as another boy got pulped by the tinboy's remaining power klaw. 'If you want somefing dun right...' He levered himself back to his feet, ignoring the sen-sation and indeed the smell of scorched flesh coming from his front, and took up the Snazzhammer again.

'Oi! I ain't finished wiv you yet!'

The tinboy didn't turn around, which was its second mistake, the first having been to not make sure he was properly dead. He ran at its back, crackling Snazzhammer held high, and smashed the axe side into its armour plating.

KRAKKA-BOOM!

The tinboy spasmed and fell forwards, circuits overloading and sparks shooting in all directions. Ufthak forced his own battered body to climb atop it, then raised the Snazzhammer for the killing blow, laughing as he did so. Let Mogrot try to lead the mob after *this*!

He saw Da Boffin raising one hand in apparent warning just as he brought the weapon down for the final time.

Everything went red.

He was on his back when his brain was actually working well enough again to figure out what was going on. He stared up at the ceiling, which looked to be blackened and scorched as though a massive explosion had washed across it. He could hear the sound of ork boots tramping past him, but no one seemed to be stopping to congratulate him on his kill.

A face appeared in his line of sight. It was Dok Drozfang, who was wearing what Ufthak thought of as his considerin' face, which was never a sight an ork wanted to see.

'Dok,' Ufthak managed, although it was surprisingly hard to speak. 'I can't feel me legs.'

'Well, dere's a reason for dat,' the dok shrugged. 'Look down.'

Ufthak managed to do as Drozfang suggested. For a moment, he couldn't work out what he was seeing. Then he realised that it was what he *wasn't* seeing that was the issue.

'Where's me legs?'

'One's over dere,' Drozfang said, pointing out of Ufthak's

view. 'Not too sure about da uvver one. Or yer arms, ta be honest.'

'Dat'd explain why dey ain't hurtin',' Ufthak muttered. He frowned. 'Wot about da hammer?'

'Mogrot's got it,' Drozfang replied. 'Said 'e's da boss now, an' no one argued wiv 'im.'

'Ungrateful grots,' Ufthak managed. Air was definitely becoming a problem, which was only to be expected when you looked to be missing the bottom part of your lungs. 'Well, see us off den, dok. No point waitin' – may'z we'll get back ta Gork 'n' Mork so dey can put me in anuvver body an' I can get back ta fightin' again.'

Drozfang frowned. 'Yeah, about dat… Wot if I'z got a better idea?'

Ufthak tried not to let his trepidation show. Painboyz were useful to have about if you needed stapling back up, or a new arm sewing on, but some of them could get a bit 'creative' at times, especially when the patient wasn't in a condition to have much say in the matter.

'Nah, yer all right, dok,' he said, managing a grin. 'Nuffin' ta worry about, is it?'

'Yeah, well, I ain't finkin' Mogrot is da best boss da mob could 'ave,' Drozfang replied, lowering his voice. 'I reckon dey could do wiv da sort of ork wot has da smartz ta plan for a tinboy, an' da gutz ta bring it down. An' if I could fix dat ork up, he might remember da painboy wot fixed 'im, coz I reckon dat ork might be goin' places. Know wot I mean?'

'Wotever you'z finkin', yer gonna 'ave to do it quick,' Ufthak told him flatly, as darkness began to encroach on his vision.

'Fankfully, da raw materials are at 'and,' Drozfang grinned, and pursed his leathery lips to emit a piercing whistle. High-pitched grunts and swearing heralded the arrival of the dok's grot 'disorderlies', apparently towing something heavy. They stopped next to Ufthak, and he turned his head to look at it.

It was Badgit Snazzhammer's body. Huge, battle-scarred and untouched apart from the small point of completely lacking a head, thanks to the tinboy.

'Now,' Drozfang said, producing an intimidatingly large cleaver and placing it at the base of Ufthak's neck. 'Dis may 'urt a bit...'

Ufthak hadn't really registered the blow given that, percentage-wise, he wasn't losing much more than he had already. The staples that the dok used to fix his head onto Snazzhammer's neck – which had been 'tidied up' with the same cleaver – only registered as minor pricks of discomfort.

What *really* hurt was the injection.

'You'd be lookin' at a day or so before you'd be up an' about, normally,' Drozfang told him matter-of-factly, as burning agony began to spread downwards from what remained of his neck into what had until recently been Snazzhammer's. The dok tucked his syringe back into his belt. 'But fanks to Dok Drozfang's Healin' Juice, da nerve endin's will connect right up an' you'll 'ave full control in a matter of minutes. Course, dere's always da side effects,' he added.

Ufthak tried to swear at him, but he was too busy convulsing.

The tinboy looked to have been the humie's last real line of defence of their 'fancy worky bitz', as Snazzhammer had called them. There were a few bodies scattered here and there on the route to the massive double doors from which an eldritch glow was emerging, but little sign of an organised resistance. The alarms going off suggested that perhaps

Da Meklord's 'destruction' techniques had been extremely effective. All Ufthak knew was that they weren't helping his headache much.

''Ere we are, boss,' Drozfang said with a grin, gesturing at the one open door. 'Da rest of da ladz should be in dere. Time ta make yer grand entrance.'

Ufthak bared his fangs, squared his – or possibly Snazzhammer's – shoulders, and strode in as though his neck weren't still leaking a bit, and his left leg weren't dragging slightly.

It was a vast space, as big as one of the humie's buildings which they seemed to put up simply to sit in and have a proper good think about their Emprah. However, whereas those had lots of empty space in, perhaps in order for the thoughts to fly around properly, this one was jam-packed full of… stuff, was the only term Ufthak could come up with. Huge metal pillars which gave off a glow that only partially obscured the runes carved into them. Enormous pistons, crackling with energy. Giant wheels larger than his outstretched arms. And yet, despite how impressive it all looked, there was the distinct impression that this place wasn't fulfilling its function. It was heavy with potential, an almost palpable heaviness in the air. It was as though the room itself were yearning for something.

Which probably wasn't Da Boffin and Mogrot Redtoof having a scuffle, but that was what it currently had.

'Gerroff it!'

'I'm da boss, I get ta push da button!'

'Yooz gonna break it, you stoopid–'

'Gonna break yer face in a minute–'

Mogrot, facing away from Ufthak, reared back with the Snazzhammer in his grip, ready to knock Da Boffin's lights out with it.

Ufthak grabbed it just under the head and yanked it out of his grip. Mogrot whirled around, fumbling at his belt for his chain-choppa, but pulled up short when he came face-to-chest with Ufthak. His brow creased in uncommon cogitation.

'Wot da zog...?'

'Sumfin' like dat,' Ufthak agreed, and nutted him.

Mogrot went down. Ufthak winced, and reflected that possibly hadn't been the smartest thing to do with a stapled-up neck, but what was done was done. He brandished the Snazz-hammer over his head.

'Anyone else wanna be boss?'

There was a distinct lack of volunteers, as the rest of the ladz took a sudden interest in their boots. They weren't sure if Badgit had got a new head or Ufthak had got a new body, but they weren't planning to argue with either eventuality.

'Dat's settled, den,' Ufthak said with satisfaction. He could almost feel Dok Drozfang grinning behind him, but that was fine. Fair was fair, and he'd see that the dok got his due. A few extra teef passed his way, the occasional 'volunteer' for surjury, that sort of thing.

'You done ya mek fing yet?' he asked Da Boffin, who shook his head.

'Mogrot wanted ta press da button.'

'Well, get on wiv it,' Ufthak commanded him. He wasn't interested in pressing buttons: that sounded like a mek job.

Da Boffin's device was surprisingly small, and was clamped to what looked like some sort of humie control panel. It had three buttons on it: 'STOP', 'GO' and 'MEGA-GO'.

'Wot is dat, anyway?' Ufthak asked.

'Dis,' Da Boffin said gleefully, 'is da Warp Dekapitator. You know how humies choose where dey're gonna fly through da warp?'

'Yeah?' said Ufthak, who didn't.

'Well, dey leave tracks behind in da warp. Sorta like squig trails, only nuffin' like dat,' Da Boffin explained. 'Dese are humie mekboyz, so dey prob'ly came from a humie mekboy planet, where dere's loadsa shiny tek Da Meklord can nab.'

'Right,' Ufthak nodded. Shiny tek sounded good. Da Meklord would get the best, obviously, but that didn't mean there wouldn't be some left over.

'So when I turn dis on, it uses da energy of dese warp engines to cause a katastroffic warp implosion!'

Ufthak frowned. 'Is dat good?'

'Course it's good!' Da Boffin scoffed. 'S'got a lot of fingies, syllables, innit? Like, "grot" is bad, but "Wazbom Blastajet" is good.'

Ufthak nodded. It was a powerful argument.

'Dis ship gets sucked into da warp, right back to da startin' point of da last warp jump it made, and den pops back out again,' Da Boffin continued. 'An' it sucks all da rest of da ships around in wiv it too, includin' Da Meklord's fleet. Job's a good'un!'

He reached out, and pressed the button labelled 'MEGA-GO'.

The control panel sparked. More alarms started sounding, but these weren't the high-pitched whiny klaxons that denoted a relatively minor problem like rampaging, murderous orks aboard the ship. These were bone-deep and throbbing, and bore an inherent sense of panic. If a star could have screamed a warning, it would have sounded like that.

All around Ufthak and his mob, the glowing, crackling parts of the room began to move: slowly at first, then faster and faster. Ufthak frowned. He could have sworn that something apparently solid just passed through something else equally apparently solid.

'Is dat s'posed to 'ap–'

There was a stomach-churning, resonant *bloorp!* and everything turned inside out.

It took Ufthak a few moments to check that his arms weren't now five miles long, or that his stomach hadn't swelled to the size of a planet, both of which felt like they could be viable options. He definitely had an annoying tic in his left eye, but that was less unusual, and he glowered at Da Boffin with it.

'If dat's your definition of "good"...'

Da Boffin held his hand up for quiet. Ufthak was about to clobber him for disrespect when he heard it too.

It was the screaming of tortured metal. And that, Ufthak realised, was not fancy words. It was the voice of actual metal, and it was actually screaming, and the whole thing was overlaid with a bubbling, wet giggle. From outside in the corridor came the slithering thump of something malformed dragging its huge bulk along with nothing more than brute strength and an endless malice directed at all living things.

'Course,' Da Boffin commented, 'dere's always da side effects.'

'All right, ladz!' Ufthak barked, laying about him. The boyz hadn't coped well with the katakrumpic warm diffusion, or whatever it was Da Boffin had said, and most of them were still on their backs or counting their fingers to see if they still had the same amount – which was causing some problems in Deffrow's case, as he couldn't now remember how many he'd started with. A few knocks with the haft end of the hammer got them back into it, however. 'Da entertainment's comin'! Up ya get!'

The other massive door slammed back, and something made of blood and steel and endless hunger squirmed in, all sharp teeth and barbed tongues, and glistening black talons that reached out hungrily for flesh.

Ufthak grinned at it. Time to see what his new body could do.

'On me, ladz! One, two, free...'

'WAAAAAAAAGGGGHHHHHHH!'

THE MANSE OF MIRRORS

Nick Horth

In Nick Horth's Inferno! *debut, we follow the intrepid aelven treasure hunter Shevanya Arclis, a fascinating character whom the reader may recognise from Nick's Callis and Toll novel* The Silver Shard. *Unable to resist a challenge, Shevanya is hired to investigate the mansion of Phylebius Crade, a famed wizard who has not been heard from in years.*

She and her accomplices discover a manse filled with wonders befitting such a renowned master of magic, but they get more than they bargained for – as with all places in the Age of Sigmar, there is danger around every corner.

I don't do break-in jobs, as a rule. The crucial thing about my line of work is that it involves searching for items of incalculable value and historical significance. Relics of a lost age, the sole remaining cultural evidence of civilisations ground down by time and damned by the gods. It is one of the immutable laws of existence that such precious things tend to fall into the hands of the realms' very worst people.

So I remain unsure as to the exact reason I agreed to break into the manse of Phylebius Crade, noted master of amethyst magic, former high thaumaturge of the free city of Lethis, and by all accounts one of the most dangerous men you could ever wish to meet. Fortunately, he'd been dead for something approaching fifty years, so running into him seemed an unlikely prospect.

As usual, Rhodus gave me the hard sell. Over a glass of overpriced Cyphian amber in an overpriced private room of the Silvermoon tavern, he massaged my ego and played upon my desires as only a merchant of the Ivory Circle could. Our meeting place was a fine, if rather gloomy establishment, its walls and chairs fashioned from polished black wood and decorated with all manner of gewgaws: dreamcatchers, rope-charms and brass tintinnabula that tinkled unsettlingly in the breeze. A lamp filled with whale tallow burned softly above our private table, releasing a strange, blue-white glow. The Lethisian aesthetic was not one I particularly admired. It felt as though I were drinking in a gigantic coffin.

Rhodus signalled a cadaverous member of the serving staff to refill my glass, and I made no objection. I never pass up an opportunity for free food or drink. The life of a roaming treasure seeker is one of dramatic highs and frequent, penurious lows, and currently my resources were worryingly meagre. It had not been easy to gain passage to Shyish; at great cost I had booked a berth upon a trade fleet out of Excelsis that had passed through the Lixian Realmgate, carrying vast quantities of augur-stones for the Raven City's markets. That journey had taken a season and more, and had drained the last of my coin. I was weary and broke. The perfect mark for a rogue like Rhodus.

'No one's heard a whisper from the place since the old wretch passed,' Rhodus was saying. 'And you must have heard the rumours. By the time Crade died he had gathered himself a hoard of Stygxxian relics, the sort of treasures that would bring in a cog-fort's worth of Azyrite coin on the shadow market. Now don't tell me that doesn't strike your fancy, because I know you better than that, Shevanya Arclis.'

He leaned back on his chair, his legs swinging ridiculously like those of an overeager child.

I took a long, slow drink, trying to mask my interest. It never pays to let someone like Rhodus know he's got his hooks in you. I had an inexplicable fondness for the odd little man with his gaudy robes and silly little pince-nez, but he was a business associate first and friend a distant second. You don't get to be a member of the Ivory Circle unless you have the predatory instincts of a wraith-spider. I liked Rhodus Blithe, but I sure as sigmarite didn't trust him.

'If that's true,' I said at last, 'I'm sure someone's already broken in and looted everything of value. It's been decades, Rhodus.'

'No!' the merchant squeaked, shaking his head excitedly. 'That's the genius of it! You know what these Lethisians are like, Shevanya, they can't empty their bowels without reciting half a dozen canticles of obeisance to Morrda. Besides, as far as the common folk are concerned, Crade may as well be Nagash himself. The entire city trembles at the mention of his name. No one goes near his manse, and those who've tried...'

I flashed him a look. 'Go on.'

He twitched a little, and flashed me a slightly sickly smile. 'Well, there's no profit without a little risk, is there, my dear? I have it all in hand. I have obtained the services of three most accomplished... ah, retrieval experts. But I require your discerning eye, Shevanya. In return I can promise an equal share of any items that we extricate, as well as fitting compensation for your efforts.'

The offer of coin was welcome, of course – show me a freelancer who doesn't appreciate a decent payday – but it was the chance to root through Crade's belongings that really piqued my interest. Of course I'd heard the tales. No one had explored as many of the dangerous wilds of the Land of Forgotten Gods as the former high thaumaturge. Stygxx is a land of mystery, home to the remnants of a thousand lost cultures. A graveyard of history. To someone like yours truly, an archaeologist who specialises in unearthing the bygone secrets of the Age of Myth, it's unendingly fascinating.

'I'll need to meet your crew before we continue,' I said, before draining my glass. The amber burned pleasantly as it slipped down. 'We need the best for a job like this. You know how protective wizards get about the things they've stolen. And by all accounts Master Crade was something of a prodigy amongst his kind.'

Rhodus couldn't keep the smirk off his face. He knew he had me, despite my attempts to feign professional disinterest.

'Of course,' he said, fairly rubbing his hands together in glee. 'Believe me, Shevanya, this is the best decision you've ever made. We'll be in, out and away with a fortune in priceless treasures before the week is out!'

As it turned out, Rhodus was wrong about all of that.

Phylebius Crade's mansion was not exactly what I expected. I'd pictured your typical wizard's abode, a monument to its owner's towering ego, some form of ludicrously extravagant tower looming over the city in a display of gaudy excess. In fact, the manse was an attractive yet rather nondescript building constructed in the Azyrite fashion, with a columned portico and a great domed roof. It stood amidst a tangled forest of hedgerows, which had been left to grow unchecked for many years. Spidery vines wrapped the mansion in a tight embrace, and patches of luminescent moss gave it a strange, silvery sheen, like meat gone bad.

I couldn't help but feel a tinge of unease as I gazed upon the house, not solely due to the typically Lethisian weather. An early morning mist had settled over the free city. Above, a baleful moon peered out of the clouds, bathing everything in a sickly green light. A gathering of black birds sat atop the dome, silently observing the grounds. These were the creatures that had earned Lethis its epithet – the Raven City. The locals worshipped them as living agents of their silent god, Morrda, an ancient deity of death whom they believed had escaped the clutches of the Great Necromancer. I found the cold and calculating stares of the carrion birds profoundly unsettling.

My companions joined me by the iron gate at the front of the property.

'Not much to look at, is it, aelf?' said Dhowmer, leaning against his ivory staff, smirking at me through bloodless lips. I had taken against the mage at first glance. He was a young, sallow human with an air of practised insouciance, dressed in richly embroidered robes with a high, sweeping collar, and sporting a painstakingly fashioned moustache. A prodigy of the Collegiate Arcane, according to Rhodus. That didn't explain why he had joined our little expedition. I had an inkling that if any of Dhowmer's masters caught wind of his business tonight, the punishment would be severe. Probably fatal. Not an unpleasant thought, as far as I was concerned.

'Certainly his groundsman's work leaves a lot to be desired,' I said.

'Crade weren't ever a flashy one,' said Goolan, scratching at a week-old tangle of grey stubble. This one was a master amongst thieves, allegedly, though at first glance he looked like any random drunk one might stumble upon in a seedy drinking pit in the early hours of morning: overweight, foul-smelling and with teeth like broken nails. Only his eyes gave his true nature away; they sparkled with the vigour of a man half his age, flicking to and fro restlessly without missing a trick.

'The old vulture Crade didn't need no flashy tower or a

set of gaudy robes like yourself, boy. All he needed was his name. People whispered it in fear. Still do, and he's been dead a long while.'

El-malia sighed theatrically. 'If we're going to do this, shall we press on? Lord Zainton hosts the Evenmoon Ball tomorrow eve, and I should like to attend if it's all the same to you three.'

Tall, statuesque and with enough knives strapped about her person to equip a butcher's shop, Lady Nazira El-malia was of Azyrite stock, or so she said. She certainly had the coin and self-assurance to back that up. I marked her as a noble-born thrill-seeker, and was not overly impressed. I'd seen plenty of her kind in my time.

'She's right,' I said. 'The longer we linger here, the sooner the Blackshore Guard or the Raven priests show up. I'd rather not see the inside of a Lethisian gaol. Your taverns are bad enough.'

Goolan worked his skills upon the gate and had it open in short order. It creaked ominously as it swung open to allow us passage. We advanced along the overgrown path towards the front door, the only sound the distant howling of the wind. All else was eerily still and silent, and the ravens perched atop the domed roof watched our progress with judgemental stares.

The mansion's main door was a great wedge of black iron, inlaid with a spiralling pattern of symbols that I could not decipher. In its centre was a huge brass ring, and beneath that a circular panel etched with more odd, angular runes. The disc glowed with a faint silvery light.

'Hmm,' said Goolan. 'Clever little enchantment. You got to press the right combination of the symbols, else it knows you're an intruder and boom... you're coiler-meat.'

'How do you know that?' I asked, impressed.

'I've been doing this a long time, girl,' he said. 'I've seen every type of lock, trap and enchantment you can imagine. These wizardly types, they always figure an ignorant thief's got no chance against their unmatched genius. I like to prove 'em wrong.'

'Can you break it?' asked El-malia.

'Course. You just keep your eyes open and your mouths shut, and let me work.'

The thiefmaster set down his backpack, and began to rummage through it. After a moment, he withdrew a conical brass instrument inlaid with purple gems, and a leather belt containing a selection of odd-looking implements whose function escaped me.

'Magic leaves a trace, same as anything else,' Goolan said. 'Just got to learn... to read it.'

He held the cone-shaped object near to the panel, and moved it slowly over the surface. The gems inlaid upon the device began to pulse gently. Goolan passed the cone over the area several times, and after each circuit he scribbled down something in a little leatherbound notebook.

Meanwhile, the rest of us shivered and shuffled about nervously, expecting a patrol of black-clad Freeguild to appear at any moment. A sudden gale picked up, scattering dead leaves as it whipped across the gardens. I frowned. For a moment the rush of wind seemed to take on an almost human sound, like a susurrus of hushed whispers. It passed in a moment, and I told myself it was just my ears playing tricks on me.

'Right then,' said Goolan at last. 'Think I've got it.'

'And if you don't?' I said, knowing the answer.

'Then I'll likely be splattered about these flagstones, along with the rest of you. Here goes nothing.'

El-malia, Dhowmer and I all took a discreet step backwards.

The thiefmaster's slender fingers danced across the panel, and the silvery glow intensified. There was a deep, low *clunk*.

With a groan, the door yawned open. Beyond, I could see a narrow corridor, shrouded in darkness.

Goolan got to his feet with a nod of satisfaction, and regathered his tools.

'After you,' gestured Dhowmer with a bow and a smile, clearly expecting me to defer.

I managed to refrain from rolling my eyes. My golden rule of exploration has ever been this: always take the lead, and trust your own eyes over anyone else's. Not being the one to trigger a trap yourself won't make you any less dead if one goes off in close proximity. No matter where in the realms they hail from, trap designers tend to operate on the same basic principles as Ironweld cannoneers – the more destruction and death you can leverage at a single location, the less likely there are to be any survivors.

I fetched a raystone from my belt, thumbing the central depression in the oval rock. Then I tucked the object into a pocket on the lapel of my coat, where it began to glow softly, illuminating the path ahead. These imports from Hysh aren't cheap or easy to get hold of, but unlike a flaming torch they don't go out, and they have the advantage of leaving one's hands free. I proceeded slowly along the hallway, scanning the walls and floor for any telltale signs of imperfection, any sudden gusts of air or strange smells that might signify something untoward. The stonework was flawlessly smooth obsidian, the floor richly carpeted with a length of crimson fabric upon which were embroidered skeletal pipers, cavorting madly across a corpse-strewn battlefield. Cheerful, I thought.

Eventually the passage opened into a large central chamber, dominated by a great spiral stair that ascended into the darkness of a domed ceiling. Lining the chamber on all sides were great oil paintings and embossed murals, arranged so tightly upon the walls that I could barely see the masonry beneath. I don't profess to be an expert on Lethisian art, but judging by the quality of the pieces, Crade was something of an aesthete.

'Oh my,' said Lady El-malia. 'Is that an original Ruthean? Throne of Azyr, that can't have come cheap.'

'A master of the Collegiate Arcane does not want for resources,' said Dhowmer. 'And Crade was one of the most powerful men to ever hold office in Lethis.'

There was a scattering of imposing landscapes. An immense mural depicted the towering presence of Deific Mons, the Mountain of the Silent Gods, rays of heavenly light bathing its highest peaks in a golden glow. I believe I recognised the darksome forests of Tzlid, and a tremendously unsettling image of a sea vessel caught in the crushing embrace of a great skullcoiler eel. Yet the majority of the gallery was comprised of portraits. Pale, austere men and women glared down at us disapprovingly. The majority wore fine robes and collars of fur, and were bedecked with golden jewellery and Azyrite sigils. Several possessed a more military bearing, clad in ornate armour and accompanied by similarly proud-looking animals: star-eagles, astral lions and hook-beaked gryphons. The gloom rendered these strangers ghostly and foreboding, and gave their hawkish stares an uncomfortably lifelike appearance.

Upon a landing at the top of the first flight of stairs was the largest painting of all. It depicted a stern-looking man in a white skullcap, standing beneath a full moon. In one hand he held aloft a cracked timepiece that trickled black sand. In the other, a staff of bone and gold, topped with the symbol of the comet. I recognised the staff of office. It resembled those carried by the masters of the Collegiate Arcane.

'So that's our host,' I said.

'High Thaumaturge Phylebius Crade himself,' nodded Dhowmer. 'Before my time of course, but the masters of the Centrellum can't talk for more than a minute without invoking his name. Most tiresome.'

I shivered, despite my warm rhinox-hide coat. Somehow it was colder in the empty hall than it had been outside. Each breath unleashed a curling wisp of fog, and the tips of my fingers ached painfully. There was an unnatural stillness to the house, as though we were frozen in time. Looking around I saw no dust upon the carpet, and no signs of life. The curtains and drapes framing each of the great murals were not moth-eaten and ragged, but richly coloured, as if they had only just been installed.

'This hardly resembles a house that's been abandoned for fifty years,' said Dhowmer, echoing my thoughts. 'Someone's here, or has been until recently.'

'That arcane ward on the front door's not been breached in at least a decade,' said Goolan. 'I'd bet my teeth upon it.'

'Perhaps our host is not, in fact, deceased,' said Lady Elmalia, nervously clutching a thin-bladed throwing knife.

'Come on,' I said, starting for the great stairway. The cold eyes of Crade's painting followed me across the chamber. I could tell the others were as unnerved as I. The look of self-satisfaction had temporarily disappeared from Dhowmer's face, and Goolan's eyes darted to and fro like those of a cornered alley rat.

The stairs curved around and led us to a circular landing.

Directly ahead lay a pair of doors, their surface panelled with amethyst glass. Cautiously I approached, the sensation of being watched growing ever more potent. My scarred visage stared back at me from the frosted surface – the ragged marks were the legacy of an old injury, an ever-present reminder of a time I'd rather forget. I stopped, my heart hammering. Reflected in the glass I saw a ghostly, withered hand reaching over my shoulder, taloned fingers stretching out to caress my neck. At the same time I felt something brush lightly across my skin.

I whirled about, panic seizing control of my limbs, and struck at the figure looming behind me, which recoiled with a shriek of its own. It was Goolan. He cursed as he clutched his face.

'What in Sigmar's name is wrong with you?' he growled.

'I saw...' I began, turning back to the glass door. No longer was there any sign of the gruesome apparition, only a deeply irritated thief nursing a bruised jaw.

Embarrassment battled fear for control of my emotions, and emerged triumphant. I muttered an apology, but I could not shake the image of that cadaverous hand coiling around my neck. I had the same feeling an arachnophobe experiences when they know that a spider is crawling and scuttling somewhere close by, but they can't lay their eyes upon it. It's somehow worse than being confronted with the creature itself. My gut was telling me that we should abandon this fool's errand right there and then, but foolish pride and a desire to lay my hands upon Crade's collection refused to allow good sense to prevail.

'Can we get a move on?' asked Dhowmer looking even paler than usual, trickles of sweat running down his face despite the cold air.

Cursing my overactive mind, I pushed open the double doors. A long corridor of dark, panelled wood stretched off into the distance. Lining the walls on each side were handsome dress mirrors set into oval frames of silver and gold. The raystone tucked into my coat illuminated the passage, causing the looking glasses to flicker unnervingly and sending a cascade of rippling light across the ceiling.

Cautiously, I proceeded down the corridor. Reaching the first mirror to my left, I glanced into its depths, half expecting to see that same withered hand wrapped around my neck. My reflection stared back, but to my disquiet it stood not in the halls of Crade's mansion, but upon the crystal steps of a teetering spire, a city of glass and shadow stretched out far beneath me, nothing but utter blackness above my head. As I watched, my mirror image raised a trembling hand, my mouth open in astonishment.

'Throne of Azyr,' whispered Goolan. He too was staring into the depths of the mirror as if hypnotised. To my disquiet I could not see his reflection in the glass, even though he stood no more than a few inches from my side.

'Beautiful,' said Dhowmer. 'It reminds me of a tale my mother used to tell. Of the City of Mirrors, where the damned are trapped for all eternity to suffer and rot, never granted the peace of death.'

'You Lethisians really are a cheerful lot, aren't you?' I said.

'All of these show the same location,' said El-malia, studying each mirror in turn.

She was right. The landscapes displayed were bizarre and incongruous, their physical dimensions impossible, but there was a uniformity in the architecture: grand, gothic spires and soaring arches; cramped, switchbacked streets; and above all, the ornamental use of dark, green glass. Entire walls and towers were shaped from the substance. In the midst of this dark grandeur there at first appeared to be no life at all. Yet as I looked closer, I saw hunched, crook-backed shapes lurking in doorways, slumped and hopeless. In the shadows of oubliettes and catacombs half-seen figures shuffled, avoiding the light like vermin.

More than anything I felt a sense of sorrow and anguish radiating from the city beyond the glass. The sensation was palpable, yet it was tremendously difficult to tear one's eyes from the strange sights. I dragged myself away, and continued on down the hall.

I shivered and clutched my coat around my chest. Across the walls and ceiling I could see a patina of hoar frost glittering in the half-light. As I watched, it began to spread, trickling down the walls in spidery patterns.

'This place is wrong,' El-malia said, and I could not disagree. Yet I set my jaw and tried to banish my unease. I've faced down slavering monsters and deranged sorcerers alike, visited cursed temple-cities and conversed with ancient beings whose sheer, alien otherness made me question my own sanity. I was not about to abandon our prize just yet.

'We press on,' I said. 'We're close, I'm sure. Just keep your eyes peeled.'

The next mirror showed a tower of emerald glass, its spires twisted into the image of a gargantuan, skeletal face. Hooded figures knelt before the tower. They bent and rose in supplication. As I looked in fearful fascination, the figure at the centre of the gathering rose and turned to face me. A gaunt, thin-limbed creature, its flesh pale as a corpseworm. It began to stride towards me, reaching up with spider-like fingers to pull back the hood of its robe. Beneath was a face from my darkest nightmares, a sunken horror with blackened teeth and a snakish slit of a nose. Yet far worse were the cadaver's eyes. Shards of green glass had been thrust through its eyeballs, and dried blood caked its cheeks. The robed corpse opened its arms, as if to welcome me home. A withered hand reached out, and with a crackle of splintering glass, black fingernails pierced the mirror and thrust into reality, reaching for my face.

Lady El-malia's gasp of horror stirred me from my trance. I tumbled backwards as the disembodied hand brushed past my face, its grasping claws missing me by mere inches. I fell on my backside and scrambled away across the floor. El-malia thrust out with her dagger, and the thing in the mirror withdrew its hand with a hiss of pain, falling to its knees. It began to sob and wail, pressing bleeding palms against the glass surface. As it turned its eyeless face towards me once more I registered not fury, but boundless sorrow. To my surprise I felt a stab of pity along with my revulsion.

Inhuman shrieks filled the air. All around us the glass portals stirred, as the skies above the strange city flared with emerald light. Soaring above the spires and glass-towers came shrouded horrors wreathed in ragged cloaks of black, their skull-like faces gleaming in the twilight. They wheeled and turned in the air, unleashing piercing cries filled with bitter hatred. In the presence of these apparitions the distant, praying figures fell to the floor and prostrated themselves in terror. Then, as one, the wraiths turned and fixed their soulless gaze upon my companions and me. I felt my heart stutter as dozens of pairs of baleful eyes bored into my own. I could keenly feel their predatory hunger. With another awful cry the spectral nightmares swept down towards us.

Behind us, glass shattered, and a ghostly form swept into reality. Then another mirror burst into pieces, and another,

THE MANSE OF MIRRORS

and suddenly the hall was filled with swirling, aethereal forms and flying shards of glass. Gaunt faces leered down at us, and clawed hands clutched rusted blades and verdigrised chains.

'God-King preserve us!' cried Goolan.

'Run,' I hissed, tearing my eyes from the awful sight. 'Run!'

Scrambling to my feet, I raced for the door at the far end of the chamber, icy rime spreading across the wooden floor ahead of me with a terrible crackling sound. Goolan was faster. His boots clattered across the floor, and I could hear Dhowmer and El-malia rushing close behind us, their breathing ragged. As we ran, I could see shapes stirring within the mirrors on either side, stretching out their hands to pierce the veil between worlds. The far door was barely a dozen feet away when a spider-limbed horror wrapped in pale rags burst from the mirror to the left of Goolan in an explosion of shattering glass, wrapping its spectral arms around the thief-master. Goolan was torn from his feet, and with a scream the gheist dragged the poor man through the glass portal.

As I raced past, I saw from the corner of my eye the thief-master struggling helplessly, borne away into the shadows of the mirrored city.

Again came the sound of shattering glass, and a high-pitched, terrified scream that I was almost certain was not my own. Ghostly hands swiped at me, but I threw myself into a headlong dive, tucking my shoulder and coming to my feet just a few feet from the door and, I hoped, sanctuary.

My shaking hands grasped the handle, and I tore it open. I would like to say that I stopped then for the sake of my companions, but in fact it was only the shattered remains of a broken table that halted my escape. I stumbled and nearly fell, one hand slamming down upon a carpeted floor to steady myself. Turning, I saw Dhowmer in full flight, his robes billowing behind him. He rushed into the room.

Lady El-malia was on his heels. She had made the threshold of the chamber when she froze in place, her body stiffening. A spectral claw tore through her chest, its long, curved fingernails protruding from her heart. The noblewoman collapsed to her knees, eyes glazing over, her face locked in an expression of purest horror. Then she too was dragged away.

I kicked the door shut, even though some distant corner of my mind registered that against the spectral dead such physical barriers were all but pointless. For a few, terrible moments I expected our hideous pursuers to come flooding through the thick oak of the door and into our chamber.

But silence fell once more.

Dhowmer began to chant urgently, weaving his staff in a figure-of-eight pattern. There was a burst of white light, and the mage fetched a leatherbound bag from his belt and began to sprinkle a fine, white powder across the floor beneath the door.

'Saint's Wort,' he explained. 'Mixed with Azyrite starwater and ground with the bones of a Devoted battle-priest. A ward against the dead.'

'Will it hold?'

He shook his head helplessly. 'If it doesn't, we'll be joining our late companions in whatever cursed place lies beyond.'

The thought stirred me into motion. I clambered to my feet and took in the chamber for the first time. It was a high, square room, almost every inch of it piled with workbenches and stacks of yellowed tomes. Around the edge of the chamber were a number of towering glass cabinets, filled to the brim with one of the most eclectic collections of magical and historical ephemera I have ever seen. Rhodus had been right about one thing: Crade's collection could have rivalled that of any Azyrite antiquarian. I saw Thraxian gunshields crafted from blue invictunite, sun carvings from the Hyshan sky-plains, a suit of ensorcelled plate bearing the sun and eagle of Lantea. My fear ebbed away somewhat, replaced by astonishment and wonder.

For all the splendour of the wizard's hoard, Crade had clearly had greater things on his mind than mere appreciation of his treasures. Several of the great cabinets had been shunted aside, stacked together about the edge of the chamber. The doors of some were hanging open, their contents lying scattered about the floor or piled up absent-mindedly upon stacks of unwashed plates and notebooks scrawled upon in an untidy hand.

Crade had been clearing space for a bizarre tangle of arcane machinery that occupied the centre of the room. Three pillars of gold were arranged around yet another looking glass. This one was far larger and more ornate than the others, almost reaching to the ceiling. It was wrought of gleaming obsidian and fashioned with the skill of a master craftsman, filigreed patterns of silver worked into every inch of the metalwork. The stone pillars were marked with runes and scrawled notes and arcane formulae written in what looked like glowing chalk. Each was capped by a disc of blue metal, upon which rested a geometric fist of violet crystal. I am no student of the arcane, but I could feel the power surging from these objects, sending an aetheric charge fizzing across my flesh. Looping trails of metal spilled from the base of the pillars like iron intestines, coiling across the floor.

Feeling a trickle of dread creep along my spine, I edged around the front of the mirror, peering into its calm surface. There was the faint outline of my reflection, but beneath it I once again saw an image of the strange city. This time I saw no eyeless ghouls or malevolent spirits. Instead I looked upon the interior of an emerald cathedral, a great, vaulted hall that possessed a cold and terrible beauty. The floor was polished obsidian, the walls lined with statues of tall and foreboding figures. Rising from the floor in the centre of the cathedral was a frozen river of glass that disappeared into the domed roof above. Swirling patterns of light rippled along the length of this strangely organic structure, and though the distance was too great to be sure, I thought that I could make out vaguely human shapes drifting within its crystalline depths, floating as if carried along by a swift current.

'This one feels different,' said Dhowmer, shaking his head. 'These pillars. The magic is beyond me, but I can sense their power.'

He frowned, then closed his eyes and fell silent.

'I don't want to distract you from your meditation,' I said with no small amount of frustration, 'but any minute now a horde of vengeful spirits is going to come flooding through that door.'

The mage's eyes snapped open.

'It's not my magic holding them at bay,' he said. 'There's an arcane barrier surrounding this chamber, radiating from the pillars. But it's more than that. There's an echo of something else, the lingering residue of a very powerful enchantment.'

Deciding that I was not going to be much help deciphering the mysteries of Crade's magic, I began rummaging through piles of scrollwork and scattered trinkets, searching for something we could use to escape. Crade had apparently kept nothing so organised as a journal. Instead, his writings and observations were scrawled across scattered scraps of parchment in an untidy hand. I found several mentions of ancient ruins and subterranean chambers that the wizard had excavated across Stygxx – several of these I pocketed for my own use. Crade did not appear to be particularly interested in uncovering the anthropological history of the region, rather he appeared to be searching for something he referred to in rather unembellished terms as the 'catalyst'.

'I see you find my studies intriguing,' came a thin, frail voice from behind me, almost causing me to jump out of my skin. Dhowmer started violently too, spinning around and knocking over a teetering pile of scrolls that collapsed in a cloud of choking dust.

In the surface of the mirror a small man had appeared. He was old and stooped, dressed in flowing white robes and wearing a grey skullcap, yet despite his frailty there was still immense power in his piercing grey eyes. I recognised him at once from the picture hanging in the manse's great hall.

'Phylebius Crade,' Dhowmer whispered.

'My wards still hold,' said the wizard. 'Good. You are the first in many decades to make it into this chamber. I have been waiting for you for a very long time.'

'What curse has taken hold of this place?' I said.

'A malediction brought about by my own arrogance,' Crade sighed. 'This prison in which you find me trapped, it is a vector for an ancient and terrible curse. In my folly I thought to break this dark enchantment, or even harness its power for my own ends. But as you can see, I failed.'

'The Mirrored City,' whispered Dhowmer. 'Shadespire.'

'Aye,' said Crade. 'Not a myth. Not just a story told by mothers to frighten unruly children. No, Shadespire exists. An entire city cursed by the Tyrant of Bones to an eternity of deathless torment. And just as Nagash's power swells with every passing year, so has the curse of the Mirrored City grown more powerful and deadly.'

'It's spreading,' I said, and Crade nodded gravely. It made a horrible kind of sense.

'So it is. This mirror you see here belonged to the Katophrane Demius Mavos, one of the masters of Shadespire-That-Was. It has a potent connection to the Mirrored City, and it left in its wake a trail of death and misery as it passed from noble house to merchant's hoard, from one collection to another, eventually finding its way to the Raven City. I believed that I could use my own magic to study this relic, and gain insight into the nature of the curse of Shadespire. Perhaps even curtail it.'

He laughed. It was an empty, mirthless sound.

'For my troubles, I was claimed by the very curse I sought to understand. Yet the power of my magic still lingers. I formed a chain between two places in time – my own manse, and the Mirrored City. That is all that anchors me to reality.'

'How can we stop this?' Dhowmer asked. 'Can we destroy this mirror somehow?'

'The device you see before you is a soul-circuit,' Crade said, gesturing at the three pillars and the crystals mounted atop them. 'Powered by Chamonic echostones and charged with the wind of Shyish. For decades I have held the curse at bay, but my power wanes. With every passing day a portion of my spirit is claimed by the Mirrored City. I am weak, and when I can no longer hold open this connection, the curse will spread like wildfire throughout Lethis. But you...'

He lowered his staff at Dhowmer.

'I sense power enough in you. Nothing to match my own, but perhaps enough to overload these echostones. Doing so may cause a cascade of arcane magic strong enough to shatter the Mirror of Mavos.'

Dhowmer flashed me a nervous glance, and I gave him a shrug in return.

'Don't look at me,' I said. 'You're the master magician, or so you keep telling me.

'And what happens to you if the mirror shatters?' I asked Crade. The archmage shot me a strange, narrow-eyed look. Either suspicion or frustration, I could not tell which.

'I will be lost of course,' he said. 'Trapped in this cursed place forever. It is not a prospect I relish, but it serves a greater good.'

'It's not like we have a choice,' said Dhowmer. 'We can't let the curse spread beyond this place.'

'I will join my power to yours from this side,' Crade continued. 'Begin now.'

Dhowmer nodded, and closed his eyes. The air sizzled with actinic energy as he began to mutter words in a tongue I did not understand.

'You, aelf,' said Crade. 'As soon as the process begins, it will disrupt the wards I have placed around this chamber. The dead will be granted entry.'

'And what exactly am I meant to do about that?' I said, helplessly. 'Throw books at them?'

Crade stiffened, and shot me a sour look. Clearly he was not a man used to dissension.

'The cabinet to your left,' he said, in curt voice.

Within was contained an array of polished weapons and unpleasant-looking instruments: hooked chains, iron masks with vicious spikes that would put out the wearer's eyes, and ritualistic daggers. I swung open the doors and made a quick inventory of the contents. Hanging from a chain above this collection was a broadsword with a golden, fluted blade. The ridges pulsed with blue light, and engraved upon the hilt in duardin runes was the epithet *Grum Damaz*. Grudge-settler. The weapon thrummed with barely contained power.

'Crafted by the forge-kings of the Dhammask Mountains, as a gift for their Lantean allies,' said Crade. 'A blade made for a king's hand, imbued–'

'What about this one?' I said, pointing to a blade that looked entirely incongruous amidst Crade's otherwise impressive collection. It was a dull-looking dagger of rough, black crystal. Runes were crudely etched across the flat of the blade.

'An unremarkable object,' said Crade, clearly irritated at being interrupted in mid-flow. 'One of many items found within the tomb of an Amethyst princeling. Loosely translated from ancient Fleizchan, those runes upon the blade denote the phrase "From the end."'

'No,' I said. 'They don't.'

Crade's voice grew even icier, if that were possible. 'I have spent a great deal of time exploring the ruins of the Amethyst Princedoms. My grasp of Fleizchan runeography is unrivalled, I assure–'

'It can be a difficult language to grasp,' I said. 'The subtleties can fool even the most learned scholars. My father had something of a professional interest in the history of the region, and it took him many years to master the language. The placement of the rune "ucht" changes the entire meaning of the words. Really, it's closer to "Death's ending."'

'Fascinating,' said Dhowmer, with potent sarcasm. 'But is this really the time for a linguistics lesson?'

I took up the dagger and flipped it in my hand, then balanced it across one finger. Despite its crude craftsmanship, it was beautifully weighted. As I clutched the weapon, the chill air of the chamber seemed to bite into my flesh with less intensity. Though the etched runes were in Fleizchan, the dagger itself was clearly not crafted in the elaborate manner of the Princedoms' weaponsmiths. It barely looked shaped by mortal hands at all, more like a shard from a broken rock. I didn't quite understand why, but merely holding it steadied my heartbeat and filled me with a strange calm.

'King Rhanuld Fireheart slew the Drake of the Void with Grudgesettler after a duel that lasted three days,' said Crade. 'I used that worthless relic you're clutching to break open wax seals.'

'I'm not much of a duellist,' I said. 'Think I'll keep this, if it's all the same to you.'

'I have no time to argue,' said Crade, waving his hand in disgust. 'Are you ready, boy?'

Dhowmer gave a determined nod. 'If those things try to take me, you use that dagger,' he said. 'I'll not be dragged away to some lightless prison for all eternity.'

'Oh, don't worry,' I said. 'When the opportunity arises I will be all too happy to stab you.'

He snorted with laughter.

'Enough!' barked Crade. 'Begin!'

Dhowmer took a deep breath and stepped to the nearest golden pillar. He levelled his staff, and purple lightning spat from its bone headpiece, dancing across the echostone. At the same time, Crade began to chant arcane phrases, weaving his own staff in an intricate pattern.

The room was bathed in purple light, and the floor began to shake beneath my feet. The pillars surrounding Crade's mirror began to slowly rotate, creaking and groaning as they moved. A piercing whine filled the chamber, sending a wave of agony pulsing through my skull. There was a sudden and violent pulse of white light.

And then the howling began.

With screeches of blood-chilling hatred the dead swept into the chamber. Five spectral, shrouded figures, clutching cruel weapons stained with verdigris and glittering with hoar frost. They swooped down over our heads, empty eye sockets blazing with deathly light.

I threw myself to the floor, seized by panic, all thoughts of defending myself or my companions instantly obliterated by a desperate desire to flee. As my palms struck the wooden floor, I turned into a half-roll, scrabbling across the surface on my elbows as the gheists soared above me, circling the ceiling. One of the dread things rushed towards me, one clawed hand outstretched to pierce my heart. I twisted aside, but ice-cold talons tore across my arm. Immediately I felt a terrible numbness creeping across my flesh, accompanied by a surge of revulsion and horror. The spirit whirled about and came on again, raising a rotting club to strike me down.

Unthinking, delirious with fear and pain, I slashed out with my crude dagger.

There was a keening note, and a quivering tremor ran up my arm. The dagger swept through the spirit's arm, parting aethereal matter like smoke. The gheist-thing howled, not in triumph this time but in an agony I had not imagined it was capable of feeling. It careened away from the blade, its translucent form coming apart in a cloud of spectral motes.

The remaining gheists recoiled. I brandished the dagger like a drunk with a broken glass, swiping it back and forth madly. They feared this weapon, I realised, and the thought granted me a measure of hope.

'Yes!' came Crade's voice, sounding fuller and more insistent than ever. I looked to the mirror and saw the wizard pressing his hand against the glass, a look of wild-eyed triumph upon his skull-like face. 'I am so close!'

Dhowmer did not look so jubilant.

The mage's normally pale face was puce with strain. Trails of amethyst light coalesced around his body, and his staff spat purple sparks of fire that scorched his flesh and the sleeves of his robes. He trembled as he tried vainly to control the potent magic coursing through his body. The coils of twisted metal spilled across the floor were pulsing with blinding light, and the air shimmered like a heat haze.

More spectres drifted through the walls, and glowing skulls rose through the very floor, spectral chains rattling as they turned their baleful gaze in my direction. Another gheist swept down upon me, and I stabbed out again. The rough stone blade sank into its eye and the thing came apart in another eruption of spectral matter.

Dhowmer began to scream. Beneath his skin I could see something straining, yearning to break free. Crade's eyes were fixed upon the young mage, filled with a terrible intensity. The old archmage's face was strained with concentration. His fingers pushed through the glass of the mirror, unleashing a spider's web of cracks.

Crade was laughing, the effort turning his face into a rictus grin.

'At last,' he was muttering to himself. 'At last!'

'Dhowmer!' I shouted. Something began to seep from beneath the mage's skin, a translucent shadow of purple light. He was convulsing madly now, yet the purple flames still poured from the end of his staff.

Glass shattered. I turned to see Phylebius Crade almost free of the mirror, his face as twisted and filled with bitter madness as the gheists that circled above. His hand was outstretched like a claw, and he was reaching for Dhowmer's face like some ravenous ghoul, his eyes full of hunger.

I was certain at that moment that Crade had lied to us. This was no noble act of self-sacrifice. The mage was siphoning Dhowmer's very soul solely to enable his escape from the City of Mirrors.

I made the decision in a split second. Trusting to my instincts – a strategy that has proved varyingly successful in the past – I raced to the nearest pillar and leapt atop it. The device continued to spin madly, and I felt a surge of nausea as it whipped me about. My hands burned where they touched the golden metal, but I held on tight. Flipping my dagger into a backward grip, I thrust it into the centre of the glowing echostone at the top of the pillar. I felt the crystal splinter under my strike.

There was an explosion of white light that lifted me into the air and sent me crashing into a glass-panelled armoire, in the process earning me several new scars to supplement the ones upon my face.

Crade screamed, a wordless cry of outrage.

The room was filled with snaking chains of purple lightning that licked the roof and swept across the floor, leaving smouldering, black flames in their path. Dhowmer was slumped on the ground, unmoving, his staff lying broken and smouldering at his side. Yet I could see that the man's chest rose and fell with shallow breaths.

'Curse you!' Crade was screaming. He was poised halfway through the mirror, struggling vainly to push into reality. 'You have damned us all, fool!'

Shards of the sundered crystal were embedded in the ceiling and floor. I felt a burning scorch mark across my neck where one had narrowly missed decapitating me. The pillar it had rested on was toppled and melted, gold bubbling across the floor and setting fire to scraps of scattered parchment.

THE MANSE OF MIRRORS

The remaining two pillars shuddered, and the echostones mounted atop them began to glow fiercely. I saw cracks of light ripple across their surface. A lash of purple fire spat from the nearest stone and whipped straight past me, slamming into the wall of the chamber and blasting apart masonry and woodwork. Lurid moonlight spilled into the breach, and with a rush of relief I saw the open air and the looming spires of the Lethis skyline. Freedom, if I could just summon some strength to my aching limbs.

Dhowmer groaned. The gheists, driven back by the sudden explosion of magic, swept back towards the prone figure, hands outstretched.

I could have run. I didn't particularly like the man, and charging a pack of ravening gheists is not the sort of thing I would normally consider my area of expertise. Yet for some ridiculous reason, I clambered to my feet and charged towards Dhowmer, swinging my new-found dagger madly.

What can I say? It was one of my nobler moments.

My first strike slashed another spirit to pieces, my second drove its fellows back with shrieks of hatred. I bent and grasped Dhowmer by the collar and began dragging him away from the rapidly disintegrating machinery. Crade was screaming threats and curses, promising a cruel and bloody vengeance upon me and everyone that I cared for. Dhowmer stirred at last, muttering insensibly.

'Get up!' I bellowed directly into his confused face. 'Get up or I swear to Sigmar I'll leave your useless backside in this cursed place.'

He stumbled to his feet, leaning on me for support.

'I will find you!' Crade was screaming, his formerly serene face twisted in rage. 'If it takes me a thousand years I will free myself from this place and find you! I swear it.'

The hooded gheists descended upon Crade, locking spectral hands around his throat and his arms. His eyes were wide with terror and rage, and he struggled helplessly against their freezing grasp. They dragged him screaming into the depths of Mavos' mirror, which no sooner than he had disappeared exploded in a shower of glass and torn metal.

Ignoring the stabbing pain of a twisted ankle, I hobbled towards the blasted opening in the wall, Dhowmer groaning as I dragged him along. Behind us the echostones were glowing with the fury of a purple sun. Cracks began to open in the walls and floor. With a deafening roar the crystals shattered, unleashing a shock wave of magical power that swept across the room, shattering glass and stone and sending priceless relics flying across the chamber. The force of the blast caught me and my injured companion and lifted us into the air, hurling us bodily through the breached wall and into the cool Lethis air. The world was a blur of sickening motion. I waved my arms helplessly as I tumbled towards the earth.

Thank the God-King for Crade's poorly maintained grounds. I struck an overgrown tangle of hedges, feeling stabbing pains across my body as thorns sank into my flesh. Yet mercifully the vegetation prevented me from dashing myself to pieces upon the flagstones of the entranceway to the manse. I rolled, tumbled and fell free, smacking my jaw painfully upon rough gravel. Just as I was staggering to my feet, Dhowmer landed atop me and drove me to the ground once more. Cursing and groaning, we clambered to our feet. Above us the sky was limned with fire. Stones and masonry rained from the ruin of the domed roof, and cracks spread across the front of the building like splintering glass. Spectral forms burst from the breaches, rising into the night sky with terrible cries. The ravens of Morrda screeched in warning, flocks of the black-feathered birds swarming about the swirling spirits.

Hobbling like the newly risen dead, Dhowmer and I made our escape along the tangled pathway, the screams of restless spirits echoing in our ears.

Just as we reached the front gate, still hanging open, there was a tremendous explosion that momentarily turned night to day. The entire front of the domed manse was hurled into the air on a sheet of purple flame, smouldering debris thrown a hundred feet into the sky to shower across the grounds. I threw myself down and tucked my arms over my head as the cacophonous explosion went on. Heavy chunks of stone and metal struck the stone around me. The thunder rolled on for several terrifying moments, and then there was abrupt and blissful silence. Warily, I rolled onto my back and looked up at the night sky. Where the manse once stood was little more than a smoking pile of stone and rubble.

'Well,' said Dhowmer, nursing a bloodied scalp and observing the devastation. 'Hell of an evening.'

I grunted in acknowledgment, temporarily unable to form a coherent sentence.

'How did you know?' he said. 'That Crade meant to seal me in his place?'

'There was just something about him that I misliked. It may have been the way he cackled in triumph as he crawled through a haunted mirror.'

'Mmm. In retrospect I was perhaps a little too eager to heed his word. In any case, you have my thanks. I thought for certain that was the end of us.'

'Fortune smiled upon us this night. And I did not leave entirely empty-handed.'

I raised the strange dagger, which gleamed in the moonlight.

There was a mystery to unlock there all right. And safely tucked into my coat pocket were the notes I had purloined from Crade's chambers. Not exactly what I had been hoping for, but perhaps the old wretch had stumbled upon some worthwhile secrets during his exploration of the Stygxxian wilds.

'All in all, it could have gone a lot worse,' I said.

Something cold and metallic pressed against the back of my head. Slowly, I raised my arms and turned around. There stood four burly men, clad in black and white jackets with gleaming breastplates of silver. Each clutched a blackwood musket, hung with trophies of polished bone and pouches of sacred herbs.

'You,' said the leader, his expression grim, 'are under arrest.'

And so, in the end, I found myself visiting the dungeons of Lethis after all.

BLACKOUT

J C Stearns

Midwest-based author J C Stearns makes his second Inferno! appearance with this heart-pounding story which focuses not on the drukhari this time, but instead the lives of hive world gangers.

Life is hard for Chib and the rest of the Seventy-Sevens. But as Seidon Hive goes dark, and the gang faces an unfamiliar enemy, it's about to get a lot harder.

'It's definitely not a blackout.'

Chib and Zaylin rolled their eyes. It was most definitely a blackout. Anyone could tell that. Even if the dozen gangers huddled around their lume-sticks wasn't evidence enough, all they had to do was look out of a window. Seidon City was dark from root to tip. Seventeen thousand square miles of hive, plunged into obsidian blackness lit only by the occasional waste-bin fire. Chib and Zaylin knew what Bugeye meant, of course: it wasn't *just* a blackout. The uphivers still had light, but no one in Chib's neighbourhood could afford a private power source strong enough to illuminate an entire home.

'Mama said there was an accident at the generatoria last month,' said Zaylin. She shook her head, jangling the coins threaded through her braids on the right side. The left side had been shaved clean. 'Maybe that's why?'

'Maybe,' said Chib. He tapped one finger on the slide of his springbow. The lume-stick on the table gave him just enough light to adjust the tension on his weapon. In a hive where rolling blackouts were common, portable light sources were a high-value commodity. Buried in Zone 77 of Silverside, Seidon City's hydro district, where artificial illumination was the only kind most hivers ever saw, they were even more valuable.

The sign on the door said *Mama Jula's,* and advertised a daily special of fresh grox steak, but it had been years since any kind of fresh food had found its way into the building. For as long as Chib could remember, Jula's had been a gang hideout for the Seventy-Sevens. The kitchen had long ago given way to a storeroom for the gang's mediocre cache of weapons, the tables and booths eroded by years of intricate graffiti or casual mindless property destruction. The gang lounged around the dining area most days, occupying their time drinking, throwing flipknives into the furniture, or defacing the walls and flakboard barricades over the windows.

'You think this is just a cogboy frak-up?' Rekker slid onto the torn bench seat. The three juves regarded the older ganger with calculated disinterest. The direct attention of a veteran might mean an opportunity to prove themselves and move up in the world, but the foul-mouthed Rekker was more likely to corner youths like themselves just to taunt them or send them on some degrading task he couldn't be bothered with.

'My ma–' started Zaylin.

'Zaylin's mom can say whatever she likes,' Bugeye interrupted. 'That don't mean we think it's so.'

Rekker laughed. His teeth were covered in black streaks, and were so pervaded with rot that you could smell them if you got too close.

'What is it, then?' Zaylin asked. The other two crossed their arms but didn't turn away. There was always a possibility Rekker knew what he was talking about.

The older ganger leaned in over the table, the light from the lume-stick below casting ghoulish shadows across his face.

'You been up to the Carridian Arch, yeah?' The juves nodded. The Carridian Arch was a monument to the world's Astra Militarum regiments. Buskers and peddlers hawked and wheedled beneath the rows of statuary depicting fallen heroes of the Imperium. It was a great place to lift a few coins or lose a marshal in a crowd.

'You ever know anyone who actually volunteered for the rifles?' As Bugeye shook his head, Rekker leaned in closer. 'That's cuz no one does. No, every so often, they come to a hive with too many people and not enough food…' Rekker paused, allowing the juves a moment to remember a night or two when they'd gone to sleep hungry, or had a desperate adult tear a nutribrick from their hands: the exact sort of experiences that had driven them to join a gang. 'And they cut the power. Then they move, level by level. They find the people who ain't got a home to go to, who ain't got a job to work, who got convictions. The poor bastards get a black bag on their heads, zips on their arms, and shoved into the back of a grav-truck. Next time anyone hears their name, it's on a Roster of the Fallen, if you ever hear about them at all.'

Chib hadn't listened to the Roster of the Fallen announcement, rolled forth from the megaspeakers in the cathedral district in years, not since he'd heard Madge and Farlon Bannisarios' death announcements. After his parents, none of the other names had meant anything to him.

'I wouldn't listen to that scummer if I were you.'

The juves turned to face the speaker. Little T rarely engaged with the youngest members of the gang, but when he did it was almost always to impart something important. Sometimes that lesson came with a cuff upside the head, if the juve had erred badly, but none of the three of them had done anything to invoke the huge ganger's wrath.

Little T still carried the diminutive nickname of his own days as a juve, although he had gone on to outclass Big T by a full head's height and over ninety pounds of raw muscle. Chib had heard that the last time the marshals arrested Little T, they'd been forced to use shackles to restrain his arms, since handcuffs and zips were too small to encircle his massive wrists.

'What you know about it, cogboy?' Rekker half spun, sneering at his larger peer. Little T had never been in service to the tech-priests, but Rekker enjoyed mocking him for his mechanical skills.

Little T pulled his chem-shades down to the end of his nose. Unlike the majority of the gangers, he didn't sport the acid-burned killtats advertising his victories. He usually went around with only a loose vest to cover his barrel chest, his dark complexion devoid of any visible scars, a subtle reminder that he didn't start fights he was going to lose. He didn't say anything, just stared until Rekker broke and turned away, muttering under his breath.

'The Stratigardian Rifles aren't conscripting from Seidon Hive this year,' Little T said.

Some of the other gangers began nodding.

'Groxshit,' said Trexx. Several of the gangers turned to look at her. Rekker's eyes lit up. Chib and the other juves kept themselves as still as possible. Arguments between gangers had a habit of turning violent, and none of them wanted to be mistaken for having taken sides if the knives came out.

Rather than flex and puff up at being contradicted, Little T leaned back against the table he was sitting at and gestured for her to explain. The tension drained from the room. Trexx sat on top of a table across from Little T, rolling a flipknife over in her fingers. She was his polar opposite: small and skinny, with skin as pale as a sub-hive mutant that had lived in darkness its whole life. Where Little T was muted and understated, Trexx wore a tall, violet mohawk, and had covered the left half of her body in a sheath of winding killtats.

'What if the greenies are attacking Two Heads again?' she asked. Chib was vaguely aware that the Two Heads penal colony on Stratigardin's neighbouring planet had been attacked by orks at some time in the past. 'If there's aliens rampaging through the system, you think they're going to keep to their little schedule? Or you think they're just going to snatch up any soldier they can find with enough fingers to work a lasgun?'

Little T shrugged. 'Administratum don't move that fast. When the nitro-pipes started leaking in Zone 40, the Administratum kept to the blackout schedule for two years. A thousand hivers froze to death. If there was a battlefront that was bad enough for them to jump the schedule, we'd have heard about it months before the black baggers showed up.'

Trexx slid to her feet, her face contorted into a sneer. Chib gripped his springbow a little tighter, easing his finger towards the safety. Little T didn't move.

'That true, meatslab?' Trexx hissed. She was holding her flipknife back, blade away from the veteran ganger she was facing, but Chib wasn't fooled. She could draw and throw the blade in the time it took most men to blink. 'You hear the sec briefings now? Sit in the governor's palace of a morning? Having solian tea and nafar biscuits, talking about which hives are getting uppity and need a good cull?'

Little T rose to his feet, slowly. 'You ain't need to sit in with the governor to know which way the wind's blowing, Trexx. Something as big as a war next door is going to be obvious to anyone who ain't soaked their brains in tat-acid.'

Trexx kicked a chair and started storming across the floor. Chib flipped the safety on his springbow, but a harsh look from Rekker brought him up short. The rotten-toothed ganger shook his head at the juves; he was too eager to see bloodshed to let any sort of loyalty enter the equation.

A couple of gangers tried to intervene, and Trexx might have pushed past them and brought the confrontation to a head if the side door hadn't burst open.

Soter and Jerrick lurched inside. The first thing Chib saw was the blood: so much blood. Jerrick's entire right side was soaked with it. Red streaks covered Soter's arm and chest where she'd supported Jerrick's weight. With a heave, she managed to get Jerrick onto a torn bench. Two gangers hurried to close the door behind her.

'What the frak happened?' Trexx yelled. The adult gangers crowded around the two new wounded arrivals. Chib and his friends hovered at the back of the circle, trying to see what was going on. Little T was leaning over Jerrick, doing what he could to staunch the bleeding. Soter leaned back, grabbing the nearest bottle of rakia and taking a shallow swig.

'I had us posted up in the alley outside the distill,' said Soter, 'looking to do the Hyd-Rats dirty.' This wasn't a surprise to Chib. Everyone knew the Hyd-Rats hid out at the abandoned distillery in Zone 21. The two gangs had a long and bloody history, and a blackout was the perfect time to settle old scores.

'Hyd-Rats did this?' said Rekker.

'Frak, no!' said Soter. Chib felt a flutter of fear in his gut.

Soter was pale, her hands shaking. He'd once seen her stare down the barrel of a marshal's shotgun and quip that the scummer didn't have the balls to pull the trigger; Chib had never seen her afraid before. 'Someone else got to 'em first. We heard gunfire from the other side of the distill, but before we could move around to get a better look, something inside exploded.'

Little T looked up at her, pointing one bloody finger down at Jerrick. 'Did he catch shrapnel?'

Soter shook her head. 'No. The Rats came running out, scattering every which way. We were too far from the action to see what they were fighting, but they were getting cut to street meat.'

Little T pulled Jerrick's nauga leather jacket away from his back, and several gangers winced. Rekker looked as though he were going to be sick. Chib craned his neck, but all he caught was a brief glimpse of Jerrick's shoulder in bloody ruins. A huge gory crater marked where the ganger's arm had joined to his torso, now held on by some strands of red meat, jagged shards of bones jabbing out accusingly.

'Throne's pisswater,' swore Trexx. 'Did he catch a grenade?'

Soter downed another shot of rakia. 'Hell no. This was just a stray bullet,' she said. 'One shot from whatever they were firing. I saw some of the Hyd-Rat juvies jumping into the storm drains, but none of the true gangers got away. Some of 'em tried running, others tried to make a stand, but they died just the same, blown apart like they got hit by a cannon.' She shook her head, and licked her lips. 'Then one of them came out of the distill. He had armour like an arbitrator, but bigger than any street pounder I've ever seen. Goddy Sten and Eritz were closer than us, and I guess they figured they had the drop on 'im, because they opened up with those autoguns like they was gonna be downhive heroes.'

The gang murmured. Goddy Sten and Eritz had paid top coin for their Quillion Arms '76s. The bullpup autoguns were the slickest, most brutal professional firearms Chib had ever seen. Even arbitrators took cover if they saw them. Only Little T's custom-made rattlegun could compare.

'The scummer didn't even react. Not a flinch. He just turned and put that gun on 'em, blew them to pieces.'

Little T stood up and made the sign of the aquila over Jerrick.

'He's gone,' he said. A murmur started rippling through the ganghouse. Trexx screamed in anger. Soter threw the glass bottle in her hand against the wall and dropped her head into her hands.

'Where are they?' yelled Rekker. He pounded a fist on a table. 'Let's load up and show these uphive pounders what happens when you mess with Silverside!' The gangers started shouting, filling Jula's with howls of rage. Chib scowled and nodded. His blood brothers and sisters snarled and spat oaths, hissing threats and vowing their devotion to Jerrick's memory.

This was what it meant to be an underhiver: this was the rage born of pure desperation. All of them, from Bugeye right up to Little T and Soter, had seen mothers and sons and friends killed in the streets for a pocketful of coins or a new pair of shoes. They had all seen fathers and daughters and cousins worked to death in the desalination banks, their skin parched and withered from salt exposure, hanging loose on their bones from dehydration, making wages barely enough to cover their own lodging, all so a handful of uphive families could sell fresh water off-world, sleeping

on trisilk sheets and eating stuffed vorder leaves. This howling frenzy, this was what happened when the pressure got to
be too great, when the people with the boot on their throats
pushed them too far. It would only end in blood, now. Chib
found himself screaming along with Zaylin and Bugeye.

'That doesn't sound like Arbites,' said Little T. The chaos
dimmed, at least a little. Several voices cried out in opposition, but the veteran ganger held up his hands to stave
them off. 'Listen. The Hyd-Rats didn't do anything to justify
a kill order. Any of y'all ever hear about a squad of Arbites
pulling something like this?' He pointed down to Jerrick's
corpse. 'Wasn't no arbitrator shotgun did this, neither. We
don't know the first thing about who's out there, and running
half-assed into the dark ain't gonna do Jerrick or anybody
else any good.'

'Who gives a damn?' Trexx leapt atop a table near the
boarded-up windows at the front of Jula's, bellowing to
address the entire assembly. They fell silent for her in a way
they hadn't for Little T. Chib nodded. Little T had been trying to mute the fire inside of them, but Trexx was stoking
it. And tonight, every one of them was in a mood to burn.

'Trexx,' said Little T, 'listen–'

'No!' she shouted. She pointed her flipknife at Little T,
then swung it wide to gesture at the city behind her. 'We're
dyin' out there, Tee! I don't give a frak if it was the marshals, the Arbites or the damned Guard! Someone killed
three of our people tonight!' She held up a hand as if offering up a poisoned fruit to the gang before her. 'Did you all
join a gang to just sit around and take beatings from these
scummers? I don't know about you, but I crewed up with
the Seventy-Sevens so I could be the one doing the kickin'
for once!'

'Yeah!' screamed Rekker. Chib and Zaylin did the same, along with several other gangers.

'Let's get out into the streets,' she yelled. The gang cheered. 'We're gonna find these back-shooting pounder scum, saw them into pieces and mail each little chunk to a different pounder precinct to show them what happens to stum-heads that frak around with the Seventy-Sevens!' She raised a fist above her head. The gang roared with collective bloodlust.

There was no warning. The first shot hit Trexx in the hip and exploded, blasting a fine mist of meat and bone over the faces of the screaming gangers and pitching the violet-haired ganger to the floor like a discarded rag. The wall of boarded windows behind her disintegrated as gunfire poured into Jula's.

Chib hit the ground the moment the gunfire started. Zaylin had thrown herself down almost at the same time he had. Bugeye stood staring, shocked at the chaos around him. Gunfire poured into the restaurant. Explosive rounds detonated against the walls like grenades. Chib grabbed Bugeye's arm and yanked him to the ground. He wrenched a fallen chair between the three of them and the weapons fire, knowing it would offer little protection.

All around them, the air was filled with the stench of burnt fyceline and spilled blood. Trexx's left leg still lay on the table she'd been standing on. Someone's stray round had hit a halon-pipe, and the air had begun slowly filling with tendrils of thin, cold, white smoke. The least experienced gangers were cut down in moments, too confused and terrified to commit to a course of action before the flood of gunfire tore them to pieces. The rest of the gang reacted in the manner of cornered rats, baring their teeth and lashing out at the hand that would crush them. A few of them took cover behind the bar, leaning over the top of it to shoot blindly out into the darkness. The bravest and most foolish pressed themselves against the wall the attack was coming through, clinging to the low brick base, exposing only enough of themselves to fire out at their attackers. If they were able to see anything in the blackness, they didn't call it back.

Chib's head snapped around at the sound of the storeroom door bursting open. He had a vision of the Arbites attacking them from the inside of their own hideout, having breached the wall while the gang was distracted by the attack from outside. Instead, Little T came striding through the smoke, a Guard-issue lasrifle slung over one shoulder, cradling his custom-built heavy stubber in his arms. The cyclic, multi-barrel weapon was a marvel of hive engineering, capable of laying down as many shots as an entire gang's worth of small-arms fire.

Little T braced himself and levelled the heavy stubber at the bank of windows. With a short whine, the barrels spun up and spat hot death back through the breach. The feed belt rattled at Little T's side, shell casings sprayed out onto the floor. The dark-skinned ganger roared, standing tall as explosive bolts tore the room around him to pieces. Gangers at the wall echoed his rage, bracing themselves and adding to his avalanche of gunfire.

The enemy fire paused, and Little T tossed the lasrifle to Soter. The savage gang leader caught the gun and slid behind a table, taking aim at the windows. Little T knelt by Chib and the other juves.

'Get out of here,' he said. Chib looked around in confusion. 'Use the storeroom.'

Chib shook his head. A round from the darkness beyond the window hit one of the gangers, who flew backwards with the impact of the explosion.

'I ain't afraid of pounders,' he said. 'Gimme a piece, Tee. We can help.' Chib's friends echoed his bravado, but their bluster was a lie: the truth was that they were more afraid of facing the horrors of the street without the strength of a gang beside them.

Little T rose to his feet.

'We're already done up, li'l bit. Get you gone before they get inside.'

'Stand tall!' Little T yelled to the rest of the Seventy-Sevens, even as the juves scrambled for safety. 'Stand tall for Jerrick and Goddy Sten!' Then he was gone, pushing through the thickening smoke, the muscle-bound ganger's bellows all they could tell of him. 'Arbites and marshals alike are afraid to step foot in Zone 77! Spell it out for these bastards! Spell it in blood!' Chib started looking around the floor, trying to find a pistol on one of the dead gangers. He was a Seventy-Seven, and he wasn't going to cut and run now.

Chib heard the crunch of wood and the dull thunking sound of something hitting the floor, and he didn't need to see the thrown object to know what it was. He slammed into Zaylin and Bugeye, knocking them to the ground before the frag grenade went off. A renewed salvo of enemy gunfire accompanied the explosion.

Chib slung his springbow over his shoulder and rose, rushing towards the storeroom in a hunched half-run. The smoke was too thick to see anything, but he could hear the gangers by the window screaming. Chib and the other juves dashed into the storeroom, slamming the door behind them.

'Come and get it!' Little T's roaring battle cry rose even over the other mayhem, still rallying the gangers outside. 'Come in and get some! Welcome to Silverside, you mother–' His screams and those of the other gangers rose in pitch and became incoherent, undercut by the horrible sound of revving chainblades.

'What the frak is going on?' Zaylin yelled. Chib shook his head. The street pounders always marched under a semblance of law and order. They suppressed rebellion and crime with shocking brutality, true, but this wasn't a crackdown. This was a slaughter.

Chib looked around the storeroom. Little T's workbench stood, cluttered, covered with various weapons in states of disrepair. All the serviceable guns were already in the hands of the Seventy-Sevens being murdered outside their door.

'Bar the door,' said Bugeye. His voice was cracked, laden with terror. 'Maybe there're some grenades.' He started rifling through dust-covered boxes that hadn't been disturbed since Jula's had been an actual eatery.

'The loading hatch!' Chib yelled. The other two juves looked where he was pointing. There was a single steel hatch set midway up the exterior wall. Once upon a time it had been used to offload crates of foodstuffs from trucks in the street, the loaders simply extending a roller-ramp through the portal and then hurling boxes into the storeroom. Now it was their best chance at survival.

Chib wrenched the locking pin back, and it gave way with a rusty squeal. He grabbed the ring in the centre of the hatch and tried to yank it open, but the corroded metal refused to budge. Outside, a deafening crash announced the arrival of something huge tearing its way through the front door of the hideout. Desperate, Chib pointed to a pry bar on Little T's workbench. Zaylin grabbed the tool and slammed it under the lip of the hatch. Bugeye threw his weight on the end of the bar, and the hatch popped open, showering flakes of rust onto the three of them.

Chib laced his fingers together, boosting his friends through the hole. Bugeye dropped to the street below, but Zaylin clung to the wall, offering a hand to pull Chib up through their escape portal. Chib grabbed her outstretched hand, but without help she lacked the strength to pull him up. They both fell backwards, Zaylin to the street outside, and Chib back into the storeroom. Behind him, Chib could hear heavy footsteps and the sound of protesting wood as something massive forced its way past the counter to the storeroom door. Terror gave him strength, and he jumped for the lip of the hatchway, pulling himself out into the darkness, away from the monster behind him.

The side street was dark, just like the rest of the hive. The sound of gunfire had killed what little light there was in Seidon City. Wary citizens had covered their glow-globes and lume-sticks, ducking under their furniture and praying that the shots weren't intended for them. Fires burning in the front of the ganghouse provided the only light, casting the street in yellow and orange. None of the scummers had dared set up a waste-bin fire outside of the Seventy-Sevens' ganghouse, and the streets were almost completely hidden by the darkness.

'Where do we go?' Bugeye looked back and forth, panic rising in his eyes.

Chib was already prying at the edge of a service hatch. Zaylin and Bugeye joined him, levering the rusted metal lid up with their fingers. One by one they dropped into the maintenance crawl beneath.

The serviceways that ran between Seidon City's zones were a juve's best friend: too small and cramped for an adult, or heavily armoured marshal, to navigate, and riddled with side passages, ductwork and maintenance hatches, allowing an athletic youth easy shortcuts throughout the city. The power conduits were cool and silent, but the tox and hydro pipes that provided Seidon City's lifeblood continued to thrum, pumping liquids both pure and foul from one destination to another.

'What now?' whispered Zaylin. The three of them were hunched over; even a juve had to navigate the serviceways on all fours.

'We head to the K-street habs,' said Chib. 'They're all abandoned, so whoever's killing everyone won't be going there, and the K-habs don't drop into 78, so we can just crawl right under them.' His friends nodded, but he continued anyway, just to reassure himself by saying it out loud. 'Then we sit pretty with a few tons of hab-block over our heads, and wait for the lights to come back.'

The thud of footsteps on the street above brought the nodding, satisfied juves up short. All three of them stared at one another in horror. Chib covered his lume-stick, wondering with rising panic if the things that had destroyed Jula's could somehow see through the street.

In the sudden silence of the serviceway, they could hear the creaking metal grates as something heavy strode overhead. Chib tapped Zaylin and Bugeye on their legs, prodding them down the serviceway towards K-street. The three of them began picking their way blindly over the twisting pipes and conduits, afraid even to breathe too loudly. Chib allowed himself the luxury of hope: they were small, they were escaping. They only had to make it a few streets away to lose themselves, and let the monsters pursue more entertaining prey.

The service hatch the three of them had struggled to even lift was torn away into the darkness with a shriek of abused metal. Chib and his friends scrambled down the service-way, all thoughts of stealth gone. The booming report of an explosive round filled the tunnel, briefly illuminating the trio in the flash of its impact on the wall behind them. Zaylin shrieked as the rancid stench of sewage sprayed into the crawl space, pouring forth from a ruptured pipe.

'Turn left!' Chib yelled as they came to a branch in their path, 'towards K-street!' He pointed to the right, however, and led his friends in the opposite direction his panicked cry had indicated to their pursuers. Crawling through the darkness, he put his hands along the wall, searching for the slatted fins of a wall duct. When he finally found one, he smashed it with his shoulder. The thin metal buckled, the retaining screws popping loose. Chib wrenched the flimsy duct cover free, and wiggled backwards into the space beyond.

A heavier person would have plummeted straight to the bottom, but the three juves were as skilled at duct-crawling as any of Seidon City's youth. They climbed down the shaft, arms and legs pressed into the walls to keep them from falling, until they found a ground-level vent they could kick out.

Zone 78 was no less dark than 77 had been. The street they found themselves on was lit by a small scattering of waste-bin fires, but their tenders had abandoned them at the sound of approaching violence, and the weak, flickering light they provided only served to deepen and exaggerate the shadows around them. Chib pulled his lume-stick out briefly to get his bearings. Spiralling graffiti on a nearby wall advertised the area as Augurs territory, which told Chib all he needed to know. The Augurs had been wiped out in a clash with the F-Street Wardens when he was about nine, but they had only ever held a small territory to begin with.

'What do we do?' Bugeye hissed. Chib shook his head, his

mind reeling too much to realise Bugeye couldn't see him. The things hunting them weren't even content to let a juve escape their wrath, it appeared.

'A serviceway down here,' said Zaylin. 'We can still find a place to hide.'

'No,' said Chib. 'They can still get us in a serviceway. If they're tracking us, they'll just blow us out with a grenade, or tear their way in.' He snapped his fingers as an idea occurred to him. 'The Falls.'

The other two said nothing. Chib read the fear in their silence, and he didn't blame them. The Falls were in the lowest levels of Seidon City's hydro district, the sumps that ran beneath the entire city. Down there the auto-desalinators ran constantly, filling the air with a mechanical racket at all hours. Even with the power off, the desalinators kept running: the water of Seidon City was too precious to let go to waste. More than just water pipes ran down into the Falls, however. The tox pipes from the chem-plants, the waste sluices, fuel conduits for the generatoria: everything that needed to be piped a great distance through the hive dropped into the Falls to run underneath the city.

Down in the darkness of the Falls, a person could lose even the most determined of trails. Auspex and therm-scan were useless, the constant cacophony of chugging pipes and hissing pressure valves drowned ambient noise. The stench of industrial lubricant and leaking chemicals obscured even the heightened senses of the cyber-mastiffs.

A burst of gunfire drew their attention down the abandoned street.

'That's coming from the grav-ramp,' said Bugeye. He turned back to Chib and Zaylin with a face paled in renewed horror.

'They're coming for us.' Chib scowled, a suspicion he

couldn't quite give voice to weighing at the back of his mind. So far, the enemy had torn through every defence without effort, seen through every downhive trick. It was a miracle they'd even got enough respite to catch their breaths.

The rattling explosions were punctuated by the sharp, high whine of a chainblade. Far down the street, only barely visible in the thin light of the street fires, a huge shape stomped into the street.

Chib ducked down, scuttling back into the duct. The hunters coming after them were too large to manoeuvre the serviceways, but it seemed they were determined to continue their hunt nonetheless. Behind him, he could hear Zaylin and Bugeye following.

The truth was, their fears weren't unfounded. The only life forms that called the Falls home were those people desperate enough to live in such a hellish landscape. Mutants, heretics and the worst criminals in the city all went to places like the Falls to avoid the eye of the Imperium, and were loath to share their living space with intrusive hivers. Chib was less concerned with anyone in the Falls than he was the monstrous thing hunting him and his friends. Indeed, he hoped that the inhabitants of the Falls might provide alternative targets for their pursuers.

The duct rattled with a titanic impact. Chib had to press his full weight into the sides of the metal chute to keep from falling. Above him, he could hear a squeal of tearing metal, and a panicked shrieking that was so high and terrified he couldn't tell if it was Zaylin or Bugeye.

Chib felt a weight pressing on his shoulders, and let loose from the sides of the chute, slowing himself as little as possible. He rocketed down the duct, fear of being crushed compelling all the speed he dared.

The impact with the bottom of the duct came without warning, and forced his knees up to crack the bottom of his chin. A moment later, smothering, crushing weight descended on him, driving his jaw into his knees all over again.

Then the weight was gone, and Chib felt a small hand pulling him up and back. He stood, shaking slightly, but managed to wiggle out of the vent behind him. Bugeye crouched against the wall, just outside of the opening, tears on his face.

'What was that?' Chib snapped, looking back into the duct. 'Where's Zaylin?'

'Thing got Zaylin,' Bugeye said. 'We were coming down, and it just reached straight *through* the duct. It was a huge hand, and it was all metal, and it grabbed her by the hair and then she was gone.' Bugeye rocked himself back and forth, his breath coming fast and shallow.

'Take deep breaths,' said Chib, 'or you're gonna pass out.' He needed Bugeye if he was going to survive, and shock was one of the surest ways a young ganger could get themselves killed. The first time he'd got caught in a crossfire, the strain had been too much for him. He could still only recall the ambush in flashes. Rekker standing on a garbage bin, screaming and firing pistols into a storefront; a body of a Hyd-Rat lying in the street, a springbow bolt in its throat; rolling beneath a grav-car, hyperventilating as he frantically tried to reload his bow, not yet aware that he'd pissed himself: only snapshots of what had happened. That had just been a street market shoot-out. This was so much worse.

'You're going to be okay,' he told Bugeye. 'You get through this, it gets easier. Promise.' Chib knew he was lying, but it was for the best. There would be nightmares, yes, and Bugeye would probably never be able to crawl inside a serviceway after tonight without fighting down unreasonable panic, but at least he would be alive.

Chib took the opportunity to scan their surroundings. Down here, in the Falls, there was light. Not much, but the soft glow of maintenance panels and the warning lights near overpressure vents gave enough illumination for a savvy juve to pick their way through the darkness. He reminded himself to take his own advice and breathe.

The booming explosion made them both jump.

'That had to have come from above,' said Bugeye, but both of them knew he was lying to himself. Like most hivers, their ability to pinpoint the origin of echoing noises was excellent. Even through the din of the machinery, there could be no mistaking that the noise had come from deeper in the maze of pipework.

'Maybe it's just a pipe giving way,' whispered Bugeye. 'It can't have got down here that fast.'

'That was the same sound as before,' said Chib. The double beat of impact and explosion was unmistakeable. 'They're in the Falls.' Chib slung his springbow over his back and headed into the forest of tubes and conduits.

His instinct had been correct. The pipes were spaced so closely that even he and Bugeye had to squeeze between them, wiggling over some and under others where they ran parallel to the floor, ducking the hissing steam from leaky joints. Occasionally he heard another bolt-round firing in the darkness, a pointed reminder that the predators were still out there, but Chib reasoned they had to be sticking to the largest passages through the field of pipes. Still, the two juves kept to the smallest passages they could find, travelling in as much silence as they could manage.

Over the sound of clanking machinery and pumping

chemicals, Chib almost didn't hear the soft mechanical purr until it was too late. Eyes widening in realisation, he spun around and clamped a hand over Bugeye's mouth, pointing frantically ahead of them with the other. Bugeye looked dutifully where his friend was pointing. The passage they were following branched around a large hydro pipe, but it appeared clear. There didn't appear to be any hiding places or tripwires. He looked back and shook his head.

Chib pursed his lips in exasperation and pointed to his ear, then pointed back the way they were headed. Bugeye listened closely. His face paled when he finally detected it too: a soft mechanical chugging sound, almost completely inaudible under the noise of the Falls. He looked back to Chib.

What is it? he mouthed, holding his hands up in confusion. Chib pantomimed holding up a knife, then rotated his free hand over the imaginary blade. A chainblade. Bugeye's mouth went slack, his eyes desperately looking back and forth for an escape route.

Chib thought for a moment, then licked his lips. This was the first opportunity they had to get the drop on their enemy and maybe get a good look at them. He pointed to Bugeye and then down at the spot he was standing on: *stay here.* Then he crouched low, squirming his way under a bank of pipes, and edged forwards.

He didn't know what would be lurking behind the huge hydro pipe, but as he inched his way along, he could imagine. A runaway, berserk servitor? A mutant with a stolen suit of power armour? The possibilities were as varied as they were grim, and the thought that such a creature was stalking him specifically made it even worse. What if they were waiting specifically for this? The thought that he might work his way around the pipe to find the thing hunting him laid down on the ground, bolter aimed directly into Chib's face, nearly caused him to back out.

He crept forwards a finger's length at a time, ready to squirm backwards the moment he saw something. No shape manifested, however, and eventually he had crawled far enough forwards to see the back of the pipe entirely. There was nothing there. Chib sighed, the paranoid tension draining away.

As if it could hear his relief, the chainsword roared to life behind him. A scream cut through the tunnel, but it was lost beneath the roar of the blade and the shriek of metal on metal. Chib looked back, but he had worked his way around the pipe, and could no longer see Bugeye. He wormed his way to the side, kicked to his feet and pulled his bootknife. He raced around the pipe, his concern for his friend outweighing the survival instinct that told him to flee instead.

There was no giant thing menacing his friend. In fact, there was nothing at all where he had left Bugeye. He looked around, confused. There was no blood, no bullet casings, no footprints leading away, not even any sign of what the chainsword had cut through. There was no evidence that anyone had ever been in the pipes with Chib at all. Chib frowned, held his breath and listened carefully.

At first, nothing. Then, there, to his right: the soft chug of an idling chainblade. Realising the danger he was in, Chib lurched to his left, pounding his way down the passage. The chainblade growled over his shoulder, squealing as it slashed through pipes, spraying containment fluids over Chib's fleeing back. He could hear the whir of the blade's teeth mere inches from his ear. Chib lowered his head and pumped his arms, powering his way forwards as fast as his legs would take him. Behind him, he heard an enraged bellow and the crash of pipes being torn away.

Chib squirmed his way through a pair of pipes, the sound of pounding footsteps so close behind him he could feel the vibrations in his feet. He ducked under a string of electrical conduits, bundled together as thick as a tyre. The obstacles between himself and the pursuing enemy bought him precious seconds, and he used them to climb. Using the thick union of pipe elbows as hand and footholds, he scrambled up, scampering along a long length of pipe on hands and knees.

A round exploded in the ceiling above Chib's head, and he nearly fell. Heart hammering, he dropped onto the flat top of a coolant tank. A second shot rang out, and the pipe Chib had been crawling on burst open, sagging underneath the weight of the sewage flowing out of it.

Chib scowled. He was never going to outrun his pursuer. He didn't know how the thing tracked him, how it moved so fast, or even why it was pursuing him in the first place. What he did know was that he was tired of running. He slid himself off the side of the coolant tank and lowered himself to the ground, then set off through the pipes again. He was scared still, but he controlled his fear: he could move quickly without making a racket and advertising his location. Chib knew that staying quiet wouldn't keep his pursuer from finding him, but it would at least slow them down.

He clambered over a huge steam vent, and froze at a metallic clanging sound. Chib unslung his springbow, his eyes searching for a target. After a moment, he saw a cloud of billowing steam issue out of a nearby pipe, and recognised the clang as a pressure relief outlet. Chib crept closer, the beginnings of a plan forming in his mind.

The pipe ran at chest height for a grown-up, easily large enough for an adult to hide in. A corpse was sprawled underneath it, and Chib looked over his shoulder, wondering if this was another ambush. He couldn't hear his pursuer crashing through the pipes, but neither did he detect the low growl of the chainsword. Chib poked the body, but it didn't respond. Instead, a gout of chem-steam burst from the pressure outlet with a metallic clang.

Chib looked at the pressure valve: a large clapper on the side of the pipe which swung on its hinge when enough pressure built up behind it to raise its weight. Most likely the release was a secondary system, and the pipe was damaged further along its length, unable to vent the pressure normally. The corpse was covered in hideous burns on the face and hands, but the clothing wasn't the rags and rat-leather of one of the dregs that called the Falls home. The body belonged to a downhiver like Chib, someone who'd come to the Falls to hide from the murderers on the streets. Chib patted the corpse down, looking for a weapon, but the only thing he found on the man was a flipknife with the blade snapped off. The corpse's skin was still warm from where the chem-steam had cooked it. It couldn't have been dead more than an hour.

Chib threw one of the corpse's arms over his shoulder. The body weighed more than he thought it would, but he had a plan, and he wasn't going to lose out on his one opportunity because his back wasn't strong enough for the task. He managed to heave the top half of the corpse onto the pipe, and with the steam conduit supporting part of the weight, he slid the body down like a sealing clamp, covering the pressure release. With the body balanced, Chib pulled his jacket off and used it to tie the corpse's arms over the steam pipe, lashing it in place.

He stepped back to inspect his handiwork. Unless he was standing right next to the body, it looked just like a hiver trying to climb up the pipe to safety. His pursuer might see through the ruse, but it was worth a shot, and he was running out of time.

About ten yards from the trap he found it: a bank of sewage overflow pipes badly in need of repair. Chib climbed on top of them, ignoring the foul stench and the grime which dribbled out from an identical bank of pipes overhead. With any luck, the odour would obscure him even further. A high-pitched squeal emanated from beneath the corpse he had positioned, and Chib dropped to his stomach.

He grinned in the darkness. The squeal rose to a piercing scream of pressure struggling to escape from the pipe. Whoever this thing was, hunting gangers through the hive, they were about to learn you didn't frak with the Seventy-Sevens.

The pursuer came around a corner, silent as a shadow. A curtain of steam shielded it from view, but after a moment of listening to the scream from the pipe, the thing approached closer, the huge silhouette breaching the mist like a performer emerging through a stage curtain. All of Chib's optimism evaporated at that moment.

Chib could have stood on Trexx's shoulders and still not been eye to eye with it. Arms the size of lightpoles gripped a combination of weapons: a three-foot-long purring chainsword, and a bolt pistol that even Little T would have struggled to hold. The riot suits of the arbitrators were like pauper's rags compared to the smooth ceramite power armour he was looking at, coloured a deep crimson save for the pearly white of the arms, helmet and massive pauldrons. The armoured barrel chest, with its glittering onyx aquila spread across it, was an image Chib had only ever seen in the baroque statuary and bas-reliefs decorating the Administratum buildings. An Imperial Space Marine.

The titanic warrior leaned around a corner, examining the bait Chib had laid out. Chib's mind raced. Why was a Space Marine hunting them? What could he possibly have done? And how could he even begin to think he could fight one?

'Because if you don't, you're going to die,' Chib said to himself. Little T, Soter, Trexx, even Rekker: at the end of the day a Seventy-Seven didn't lay down and die for anyone. Not for a marshal, not for an arbitrator, and not even for a Space Marine.

The Space Marine leaned over the body, reaching out its chainsword to prod the corpse. It shifted slightly, a thin ribbon of chem-steam wafting out. Chib exhaled slowly, just like Little T had taught him the day he first put the spring-bow in Chib's hands. He pulled the trigger.

The bolt struck the pipe just to the side of the corpse. The tip of the bolt hitting the steel pipe created a tiny spark, but it was enough. The Space Marine barely had time to throw an arm over its face before the vapour escaping the pipe ignited. It burned for a split second, a halo of green fire ringing the dead hiver, before the pipe exploded.

Green fire roared out, enveloping the Space Marine. Shards of steel blew across the forest of pipes, shredding dozens of them. A piece of shrapnel the size of Chib's hand lodged in the conduits he was lying on, nearly decapitating him. He was already reflexively reloading his springbow.

Automated shut-offs kicked in, clamping the flow of waste steam, and prevented the explosion from travelling more than a few yards down the pipe. Fire suppression systems ejected billowing white smoke into the area, extinguishing the flames almost immediately. Chib watched the dispens-ers venting the white gas carefully; if the perlex reached his hiding place, he would need to move before it suffocated him. He grinned wildly, scarcely able to believe his luck. He hoped a few of the gang had survived the attack – he needed someone to brag to.

His grin disappeared as the smoke billowed, a huge form moving within the cloud. Chib felt an icy stab of fear in his gut, insisting to himself that it was impossible. Despite his internal protest, the white and crimson form of the Space Marine strode through the smoke, bolt pistol aimed directly ahead. The Space Marine's head swivelled slowly from side to side, and then fixed directly at Chib's hiding place. The figure locked eyes with Chib, raised the bolt pistol and took a step forwards.

Chib's reflexes kicked in. No matter what Trexx or Goddy Sten said about juves, or what Rekker had said about him in particular, Chib was a true Seventy-Seven to the very end. If he was going to die, he would die fighting, grasping any chance at survival, no matter how small. Still prone, he lowered his eye to the springbow, picked the only vulnerable spot he could see, and fired.

The springbow bolt hit the Space Marine in the armpit of the arm holding the pistol, in the black joint between the ceramite plates. The warrior stopped, staring at Chib for a brief moment before turning his head to look at the bolt protruding from his armpit. The joints looked rubberised; Chib hadn't realised they were somehow both armoured *and* flexible. He couldn't even tell if his shot had penetrated the seal of the joint, or just lodged between the two armour plates. The Space Marine pulled the bolt free. In his massive hand, it seemed so tiny and insignificant. The gargantuan warrior's head turned, with glacial slowness, to lock eyes with Chib once more.

The Space Marine rushed forwards with a speed beyond

anything his size would indicate. The warrior smashed his left arm through the pipes, grabbed Chib by the chest and pinned him into the ground with one hand. Chib screamed defiant curses, spat every profanity he could bring to his lips. He thrashed his body, but there was no point. His arms were pinned to his sides, his springbow lost in the darkness. He muttered a defiant curse and waited for the gauntlet to crush his bones.

The end never came. Instead, the Space Marine's enormous ceramite-clad hand curled around Chib's chest, and hauled him up and over one shoulder. The Space Marine set off through the Falls, carrying his prisoner with him. Chib's captor was none too gentle, and any thought of escape was buried beneath a curtain of agony emanating from his knee, ribs and shoulder.

Exhaustion was beginning to set in. His limbs and joints ached from a score of injuries suffered throughout the evening. Adrenaline-flooded muscles, finally at rest, seized and cramped. Chib's head, banging occasionally against the rim of the Space Marine's pauldron, began to swim. He wasn't sure how long the Space Marine walked, only that his captor navigated the twists and turns of the underhive as if he had been born to them.

Finally, the Space Marine exited the Falls, returning to the streets, and Chib found he could barely focus enough to wonder why he was being spared. Execution? Experimentation? He was in too much pain to give any possibility much thought. He closed his eyes and prayed silently for his torment to end swiftly.

Finally, the Space Marine dropped him, sending a fresh wave of agony through Chib's bruised body. Chib's captor had taken him to a vacant warehouse, somewhere within

Hyd-Rat territory if the gang tags were any indication. Eyes open again, Chib was unsurprised to see several other Space Marines, all clad in the same armour. He was more surprised to see several other juves lying on the warehouse floor with him. Most of them were wearing ganger colours. He recognised Mathy Nittle, who had once lived on his hab-block but had gone on to join the F-Street Wardens.

Before he could study the other children too closely, one of the Space Marines approached them. All of those who were still conscious raised their hands to defend themselves, despite the futility of continued resistance. The Space Marine lifted an arm encased in a horrific-looking weapon: a swollen metal fist with a variety of gruesome implements projecting from it, including a wicked drill and a gleaming chainblade. Several of the juves made growls or gasps as they saw the menacing device, but the warrior merely unlocked his helmet with a hiss of escaping air, removing it to expose the brutal face beneath. Several grisly scars crossed the warrior's craggy features, from the square jaw to the high forehead studded with metal bolts driven into the skull.

'I am Brother Herodytes, Apothecary of the Crimson Shades,' said the Space Marine. His voice was deep and loud, like the tolling of a cathedral bell. 'We have received the blessing of Governor Galliarnos to select new recruits from the population of this world.'

The Space Marine regarded the score of youths in front of him. One or two of the juves were weeping silently. Several had soiled themselves. Chib heard one of them moaning *no, no, no* over and over again, and realised that the droning plea was coming from his own lips.

'We have made our selection.'

ABOUT THE AUTHORS

George Mann is an author and editor based in the East Midlands. For Black Library, he is best known for his stories featuring the Raven Guard, which include the audio dramas *Helion Rain* and *Labyrinth of Sorrows*, the novella *The Unkindness of Ravens*, plus a number of short stories.

Guy Haley is the author of the Siege of Terra novel *The Lost and the Damned*, as well as the Horus Heresy novels *Titandeath, Wolfsbane* and *Pharos*, and the Primarchs novels *Konrad Curze: The Night Haunter, Corax: Lord of Shadows* and *Perturabo: The Hammer of Olympia*. He has also written many Warhammer 40,000 novels, including *Belisarius Cawl: The Great Work, Dark Imperium, Dark Imperium: Plague War, The Devastation of Baal, Dante, Baneblade* and *Shadowsword*. His enthusiasm for all things greenskin has also led him to pen the eponymous Warhammer novel *Skarsnik*, as well as the End Times novel *The Rise of the Horned Rat*. He has also written stories set in the Age of Sigmar, included in *War Storm, Ghal Maraz* and *Call of Archaon*. He lives in Yorkshire with his wife and son.

Denny Flowers is the author of the Necromunda short story 'The Hand of Harrow' and novella *Low Lives*, featuring the characters of Caleb and Iktomi. He lives in Kent with his wife and son.

By day, **Filip Wiltgren** is a mild-mannered communication officer at Linköping University, where he also teaches communication and presentation skills at a post-graduate level. But by night, he turns into a frenzied ten-fingered typist, clawing out jagged stories of fantasy and science fiction, which have found lairs in places such as *Analog*, *IGMS*, *Grimdark*, *Daily SF*, and *Nature Futures*. Filip roams the Swedish highlands, kept in check by his wife and kids.

Jonathan Green's contributions to the Warhammer 40,000 universe include the Black Templars books *Crusade for Armageddon* and *Conquest of Armageddon* and the novel *Iron Hands*. In the Warhammer World, he wrote *Necromancer*, *Magestorm* and *The Dead and the Damned*. He is also the author of numerous short stories and the Path to Victory gamebooks *Herald of Oblivion*, featuring Imperial Fists Space Marines, and *Shadows over Sylvania*. He lives and works in London.

Eric Gregory's fiction has appeared in magazines and anthologies including *Lightspeed*, *Interzone*, *Strange Horizons*, *Nowa Fantastyka*, and others. 'The Fourfold Wound' is his first story for Black Library. He lives and works in Carrboro, North Carolina.

Jamie Crisalli writes gritty melodrama and bloody combat. Fascinated with skulls, rivets and general gloominess, when she was introduced to the Warhammer universes, it was a natural fit. Her work for Black Library includes the short stories 'Ties of Blood' and 'The Serpent's Bargain', and the forthcoming Age of Sigmar novella *The Measure of Iron*. She has accumulated a frightful amount of monsters, ordnance and tiny soldiery over the years, not to mention books and role-playing games. Currently, she lives with her husband in a land of endless grey drizzle.

Thomas Parrott is the kind of person who reads RPG rule books for fun. He fell in love with Warhammer 40,000 when he was fifteen and read the short story 'Apothecary's Honour' in the *Dark Imperium anthology*, and has never looked back. 'Spiritus In Machina' was his first story for Black Library, and he has since written 'Salvage Rites' and the novella *Isha's Lament*.

Edoardo Albert is a writer and historian specialising in the Dark Ages and the Imperium of Man. He finds that the wars and cultures of the early Medieval period map very well on to the events of the 40th and 41st millenniums. His Black Library fiction includes 'Green and Grey' and the novella *Lords of the Storm*.

Mike Brooks is a speculative fiction author who lives in Nottingham, UK. His work for Black Library includes the Warhammer 40,000 novel *Rites of Passage*, the Necromunda novella *Wanted: Dead*, and the short stories 'The Path Unclear', 'A Common Ground' and 'Choke Point'. When not writing, he works for a homelessness charity, plays guitar and sings in a punk band, and DJs wherever anyone will tolerate him.

Nick Horth is the author of the novels *City of Secrets* and *Callis and Toll: The Silver Shard*, the novellas *Heart of Winter* and *Thieves' Paradise*, and several short stories for Age of Sigmar. Nick works as a background writer for Games Workshop, crafting the worlds of Warhammer Age of Sigmar and Warhammer 40,000. He lives in Nottingham, UK.

J C Stearns is a writer who lives in a swamp in Illinois with his wife and son, as well as more animals than is reasonable. He started writing for Black Library in 2016 and is the author of the short story 'Wraithbound', as well as 'Turn of the Adder', included in the anthology *Inferno! Volume 2* and 'The Marauder Lives', in the Horror anthology *Maledictions*. He plays Salamanders, Dark Eldar, Sylvaneth, and as soon as he figures out how to paint lightning bolts, Night Lords.